MW00535497

DEATH
COMES
AT
Christmas

ALSO AVAILABLE FROM TITAN BOOKS

A Universe Of Wishes: A We Need Diverse Books Anthology
Black Is The Night: Stories Inspired By Cornell Woolrich
Bound In Blood
Christmas And Other Horrors
Cursed: An Anthology
Dark Cities: All-New Masterpieces Of Urban Terror
Dark Detectives: An Anthology Of Supernatural Mysteries
Daggers Drawn
Dead Letters: An Anthology Of The Undelivered,
The Missing And The Returned...
Dead Man's Hand: An Anthology Of The Weird West
Escape Pod: The Science Fiction Anthology
Exit Wounds
Ink And Daggers: The Best Of The Crime Writers' Association
Short Story Awards
In These Hallowed Halls: A Dark Academia Anthology
Invisible Blood
Isolation: The Horror Anthology
Multiverses: An Anthology Of Alternate Realities
New Fears
New Fears 2
Out Of The Ruins: The Apocalyptic Anthology
Phantoms: Haunting Tales From The Masters Of The Genre
Reports From The Deep End: Stories Inspired By J. G. Ballard
The Madness Of Cthulhu Anthology (Volume One)
The Madness Of Cthulhu Anthology (Volume Two)
Vampires Never Get Old
Wastelands: Stories Of The Apocalypse
Wastelands 2: More Stories Of The Apocalypse
Wastelands: The New Apocalypse
When Things Get Dark: Stories Inspired By Shirley Jackson
Wonderland: An Anthology

DEATH COMES AT *Christmas*

Edited by
MARIE O'REGAN
and **PAUL KANE**

TITAN BOOKS

Death Comes at Christmas
Hardback edition ISBN: 9781803369419
E-book edition ISBN: 9781803369433

Published by Titan Books
A division of Titan Publishing Group Ltd
144 Southwark Street, London SE1 0UP
www.titanbooks.com

First edition: October 2024
10 9 8 7 6 5 4 3 2 1

This is a work of fiction. All of the characters, organizations, and events portrayed in this novel are either products of the author's imagination or are used fictitiously. Any resemblance to actual persons, living or dead (except for satirical purposes), is entirely coincidental.

INTRODUCTION copyright © Marie O'Regan & Paul Kane 2024.
HOW TO COMMIT MURDER IN A BOOKSHOP copyright © C. L. Taylor 2024.
CHRISTMAS YET TO COME copyright © Helen Fields 2024.
WHAT SHE LEFT ME copyright © Tina Baker 2024.
THE RED ANGEL copyright © Russ Thomas 2024.
O MURDER NIGHT copyright © J. T. Ellison 2024.
CHRISTMAS LIGHTS copyright © David Bell 2024.
THE MIDNIGHT MASS MURDERER copyright © Alexandra Benedict 2024.
THE WRONG PARTY copyright © Claire McGowan 2024.
UPON A MIDNIGHT CLEAR copyright © Tom Mead 2024.
LAST CHRISTMAS copyright © Fiona Cummins 2024.
THE NAUGHTY LIST copyright © Sam Carrington 2024.
INDIAN WINTER copyright © Vaseem Khan 2024. Characters used with permission of Hodder & Stoughton.
POSTMARKED MURDER copyright © Susi Holliday 2024.
FROSTBITE copyright © Samantha Hayes 2024.
A DEADLY GIFT copyright © Angela Clarke 2024.
SECRET SANTA copyright © Liz Mistry 2024.
MARLEY'S GHOST copyright © Sarah Hilary 2024.
ICARUS copyright © Belinda Bauer 2011. Originally published in *The Mirror* newspaper. Reprinted by permission of the author.

The authors assert the moral right to be identified as the author of this work.

No part of this publication may be reproduced, stored in a retrieval system, or transmitted, in any form or by any means without the prior written permission of the publisher, nor be otherwise circulated in any form of binding or cover other than that in which it is published and without a similar condition being imposed on the subsequent purchaser.

A CIP catalogue record for this title is available from the British Library.

Printed and bound by CPI Group (UK) Ltd, Croydon, CR0 4YY.

CONTENTS

For our dear friend Christopher Fowler,
with much love.

INTRODUCTION

Marie O'Regan and Paul Kane

CHRISTMAS.

A time of loving and giving, of peace and harmony. Of goodwill towards all people... Or is it? There's a very long tradition of crime stories being set during the festive period, highlighting the much darker side of this very special time of year.

Think back to that famous tale involving the world's greatest consulting detective, Sir Arthur Conan Doyle's Sherlock Holmes: 'The Adventure of the Blue Carbuncle' from 1892. A mystery involving a priceless jewel falling into the wrong hands that, whilst it doesn't contain a murder as such, definitely involves a death – that of a Christmas goose! Then there's Agatha Christie's protagonist Hercule Poirot, set up to test his detective skills with a staged murder in 'The Adventure of the Christmas Pudding'.

Everyone from Margery Allingham ('The Case of the Man with the Sack') to P. D. James ('The Mistletoe Murder'), from Ian Rankin ('Cinders') and Val McDermid ('A Traditional Christmas') to Michael

Connelly ('Christmas Even') and Mark Billingham ('Underneath the Mistletoe Last Night'), has tried their hand at a seasonal crime scenario. Even the author who this book is dedicated to, Christopher Fowler, our dear friend who passed away in 2023, set tales involving his elderly detectives Bryant and May around this holiday period. And no wonder: it's hugely popular!

So, when the idea for a Christmas crime anthology was first talked about, even though it was springtime and we were feeling anything but Christmassy, we jumped at the opportunity. The chance to put together a brand-new collection of mysteries under the banner of *Death Comes at Christmas*. Because, let's face it, most crime fiction deals with death of some kind at some point or another, doesn't it?

In the following pages you'll find a raft of stories which tackle that topic head-on in various ways, written by the cream of crime fiction authors. C. L. Taylor (*Every Move You Make*) ponders how best to commit such a deed during a Christmas bookshop party, while Fiona Cummins (*All of Us Are Broken*) looks back at her titular 'Last Christmas' for clues as to how such a thing could happen. Authors who have a wealth of experience with Christmas crime fiction, Alexandra Benedict (*The Christmas Jigsaw Murders*) and Susi Holliday (*The Party Season*) offer us a unique Mass murderer and some deadly memories.

Creator of Joseph Spector Tom Mead (*Cabaret Macabre*), Helen Fields (*Profile K*) and J. T. Ellison (*It's One of Us*) take us on a trip back in time for their own period Christmas tales. Tina Baker (*What We Did in the Storm*) and Liz Mistry (*The Blood Promise*) bring us back to the present with a jolt in their nail-biting entries, while Angela Clarke (*Seven*), Vaseem Khan (the Malabar House novels) and Sarah Hilary

(*Sharp Glass*) focus on horrendous family gatherings to deliver their head-scratching puzzlers, and Claire McGowan (*Let Me In*) writes about the dangers of attending the annual office party. David Bell (*Try Not to Breathe*) gives us a poignant story about lost people and lost Christmases, Samantha Hayes (*Mother of the Bride*) raises the hairs on the back of your neck with a touch of 'Frostbite', Russ Thomas (*Sleeping Dogs*) draws on the culture of true crime podcasts for inspiration and Sam Carrington (*The Girl in the Photo*) tells us why you really don't want to be on Santa's Naughty List. Rounding off our assortment of tasty treats, Belinda Bauer (*Exit*) proves that you can pack an emotional punch with a short character study that will definitely stay with you *long* after Christmas.

Gather round your tree, sing your carols, hang your stockings, enjoy your mulled wine and turkey. But take our advice, whatever you do – watch your back this Christmas!

MARIE O'REGAN & PAUL KANE
MARCH 2024

HOW TO COMMIT MURDER IN A BOOKSHOP

C. L. Taylor

"AT LEAST one of you will die tonight!" Amy, dressed as an elf, complete with hat and bells attached to the laces of her Doc Martens, is standing on a stool in the centre of the bookshop. For the last five minutes she's valiantly tried, and largely failed, to explain the rules of the murder mystery game to the attendant readers, authors, literary agents and publishing professionals who have gathered in Paper Palace – London's largest, oldest and most established bookshop – for their annual Christmas party.

Eleanor, Amy's colleague and lead bookseller, looks on sympathetically. Normally their Christmas parties are more of a drink-and-mingle affair, but this year Amy suggested that they play a game instead. Her thinking was, because no one ever really mingles outside of their groups, that it might be a good way of getting their guests to interact. Eleanor couldn't help but agree.

In her experience the lesser-known writers huddle together in corners, and the well-known authors attract readers like bees to honey – well, the confident ones anyway. Most readers are of a more nervous disposition and tend to avoid interaction completely, preferring the company and safety of the books. They're Eleanor's favourite kind of human and she loves watching the way they reverentially drift from bookshelf to bookshelf, occasionally pausing to softly stroke a spine or carefully remove a novel from its resting place before they lovingly turn it over in their hands.

Publishing professionals are a different species. To Eleanor, who's in her early fifties, they all look so impossibly young, thin and fresh-faced. They're the newest recruits of course – overworked and underpaid but huge fans of literature, still so excited to acquire, market or publicise novels they love and launch them, with fanfare, out into the world. There aren't many publishing employees that are the same age as Eleanor but those she can see have the same weary air of cynicism. They have survived the industry, possibly brought up children too, carried the weight of household tasks, and now they're too exhausted to do anything else. There are a lot of agents in this group too. In contrast, the sales guys (both male and female) exude a confidence and bonhomie that she only wishes she had. Their laughter rings throughout the bookshop like chiming (sales) bells as they knock back the wine that the bookshop provided. Unlike their colleagues, they've dressed for the season in Christmas jumpers, headbands and ties.

The reaction to Amy's murder mystery game is, understandably, mixed. The readers look horrified, the authors apprehensive and the publishing professionals and agents simply look resigned. Only

Amy, the two well-known authors and the sales guys are excited about donning different personas and playing the game.

"Hello, Eleanor." A tall grey-haired man with a ruddy complexion, generous nose and an air of dishevelment touches her on the elbow, making her jump.

"Martin, hi!" There's genuine delight in her voice, tinged with a hint of apprehension. Back in the day – the mid-eighties to mid-nineties to be precise – Martin Rothschild was a huge name in crime fiction, up there with Elmore Leonard, Tom Clancy and Jeffrey Archer. He's fallen out of favour since then – his blend of cynical private investigators, femmes fatales and hard-boiled storylines are no longer fashionable. While the supermarkets and Waterstones no longer stock his book, Paper Palace and a handful of other independent bookshops still place small but regular orders to cater to his diminishing band of loyal but ageing fans. Three of them were supposed to attend the party but cancelled at the last minute, citing illness, family emergencies and, in Cecile Hampton's case, "an unfortunate reaction to an overly ripe Camembert cheese". Eleanor didn't ask for details.

"Christmas present for you." Martin thrusts a beautifully wrapped parcel into her hands. She can tell immediately by its shape and weight that it's a book.

"My latest hardback," he says. "My last one."

Before Eleanor can express her dismay, he adds, "It's my own creation, in every way. I had it printed myself, commissioned a small run. I ensured it's made of the very best quality paper with vibrant endpapers, sprayed edges, a ribbon – the works. I think that, if you're going to bow out of publishing, you should do it in style. It's a Yuletide tale, by the way."

She turns the parcel over in her hands, touched by the gesture. "Thank you, Martin, this means a lot."

Rather than respond, he gives a pursed-lipped nod then heads back into the fray, a weighty-looking plastic bag hanging from the crook of his arm.

"So those are the rules to the game!" Amy announces from across the room. Her elf hat has slipped so far back on her head that it looks like it's trying to make its escape. "If everyone could please take a card from the table – don't show them to each other please! – they'll tell you all you need to know about your character, and whether you're the murderer or not. To the victim, make sure you die in style!"

There's a chorus of laughter, then the assembled guests drift towards the table, some more keen than others. Eleanor searches the crowd for Martin, but he appears to have disappeared, or else he's hiding out of sight. She can't help but feel sorry for him. After such a long career it feels wrong that he should have to self-publish his last book. Not that there's anything wrong with self-publishing – she stocks several local self-published authors – but Martin Rothschild should have bowed out with aplomb during a celebration thrown by his publisher, given some kind of award, and maybe a re-jacketed anniversary edition of his most famous book. To end his career in such a quiet way makes her feel sad.

Forty-five minutes have passed since Amy invited the guests to select their characters, and the murder mystery game has descended into chaos. Almost everyone's drunk, someone switched the festive tunes for Rage Against the Machine (which meant she had to run to turn it off before the lead singer reached the sweary chorus), and one of the literary agents, who was walking backwards to try and widen the gap between her and an aspiring author, tripped over the game's 'victim', who had just that moment decided to lie on the floor and act dead. The glass of red wine the agent had been holding went flying and soaked an editorial assistant's white dress. For the next fifteen minutes, everyone who hadn't witnessed the incident approached the poor woman and questioned why she was walking around if she was a victim who'd been stabbed to death.

A handful of readers are still playing the game, tentatively approaching people with a notebook and pen in their hands. In contrast, the sales team are charging around the room demanding that a certain character 'fess up', promising books and freebies if they tell them the truth. Of the other publishing professionals, the senior editors are surreptitiously checking their watches, the agents are mingling, and the marketing and publicity girls are chatting about how much their contemporaries earn and how long they have to sit it out in their current roles before they can move on. Meanwhile, the authors are either wandering around aimlessly, talking to their agents or gossiping in small groups. The two high-profile authors, who've resolutely ignored each other all evening, have somehow been drawn together and are arguing loudly about the latest divisive scandal that's hit the publishing world. As for the readers and book club members, all but a handful have slipped out of the front door and disappeared into the night. Eleanor's been scurrying around all evening, mopping up wine spillages, rescuing book tables from being knocked over, and trying to stop random passers-by from wandering inside whenever one of her guests leaves or goes outside for a smoke.

"If everyone could gather round please!" Amy's back on her stool, her hat abandoned, her cheeks flushed with stress. "That's the end of the interrogation part of the game. If you could all please take a slip of paper from the table and write down who you think the murderer was, and what their motive might have been. When you've written it down, please fold the piece of paper in half and drop it into the Santa hat. There's a bottle of champagne for the winner!" She waves it desperately above her head. "You've got five minutes to submit your answers. Just five minutes please!" From her raised vantage point she searches the crowd until her gaze falls on Eleanor. Her expression is pure *Please God, let this end!*

Eleanor shoots her a sympathetic glance then continues ringing in the last few alcohol-fuelled purchases through the till. When she looks up again, five minutes later, she spots guests pulling on their coats as Amy sorts through the guesses in the hat. She exhales softly. It's nearly over, the party's winding down. Movement in the corner of her eye makes her turn her head. Bill, one of only a handful of remaining book club members, is weaving his way through the shop carrying a tin of *something* in his hands. It's mince pies, she realises, as he offers one to an author, then an agent, then a sales guy. Unusual, she's never had him down as a *Great British Bake Off* type of man. Whatever his baking skills, he definitely seems to be avoiding his fellow readers. Each time they reach for the tin he swerves away. That's not very Christian of the Reverend Bill Brown.

"Okay, everyone! It's results time!" With the party now half-empty Amy doesn't even bother to clamber up on her stool. The readers draw closer but authors, sales guys, editors and agents all continue on with their chats. Eleanor's heart goes out to Amy. She's been trying her best to make sure everyone has a good time and this is how she's repaid? Irritated, Eleanor turns off the Christmas music, cups her hands to her mouth and bellows:

"Amy has the winner!"

The reaction is immediate. Conversations cease, apologetic faces are pulled and suddenly everyone's feigning interest in the exhausted elf with a piece of paper in her hand. There's a good reason why so many authors, agents and publishing staff have turned up to the Paper Palace Christmas party. With a subscription box boasting five thousand subscribers it's enough to ensure that a hardback shoots straight into the *Sunday Times* Top Five on release. None of these people want a black mark against their book, client or publishing house – not when it's Eleanor who chooses the novel for the box.

Amy flashes her a grateful smile then continues, "I'm pleased to say that a lot of you correctly guessed the murderer." There's a ripple of excitement (possibly faked) from the small crowd. "But only one of you guessed the motive correctly. The gardener, Ned Chambers, was indeed the murderer of Lady Elizabeth Arnold!" Several people cheer, one person claps, and one of the readers – a man called Arthur – takes a bow. "But," Amy shouts, "it wasn't anything to do with his prize-winning turnips." She pauses as one of the sales guys boos. "It was because…" she leaves them hanging for a couple of seconds "…Lady Elizabeth walked in on him while he was making love to the cook, and she'd threatened to tell his wife.

"That's right!" she adds as an excited squeak erupts from Rosie Bradford who, at eighteen, is the youngest member of the book club. "You're the winner and this bottle of champagne is yours." She hands it over to the blushing young girl. "Happy Christmas. Don't drink it all at once!"

Eleanor slips from behind the counter and opens her arms wide. "On behalf of Paper Palace, I'd like to thank you all for coming along to our Christmas party. It certainly has been quite the night! I'd like to wish you all a very Merry Christmas and I hope Father Christmas brings you lots of books."

Her speech generates nods, smiles, *thank yous* and a lot of Christmas greetings as the guests do up their coats and slowly file out of the shop until only Eleanor, Amy and Reverend Brown remain. Suddenly famished, she reaches inside his tin for the last remaining mince pie. Before her fingers so much as graze the soft, crumbly pastry, he whisks the tin out of reach.

"Not for you I'm afraid. I was given strict instructions."

"By whom?" Eleanor stares at him. "I don't think Mrs Brown would be that cruel, would she? I'm assuming it's your wife who made them, rather than you?"

"Oh no, no, no." The Reverend shakes his bald head briskly. "They were handed to me earlier, by a departing guest. I was told that, under no circumstances, should I give them to book club members, readers or booksellers. I did ask why but no answer was forthcoming. They were very clear – under no circumstance was I to give them to anyone who doesn't work in—"

"Which guest?" Eleanor asks.

"Absolutely, yes. You'll want to thank them of course. It was… um…" The Reverend frowns and touches his thumb to his chin. "It'll come to me in a second."

"Could you describe them? It's important."

"Eleanor." Before he can answer, Amy approaches in a thin Christmas jumper and leggings, her elf costume discarded. "I'm confused."

"About what?" Her gaze still fixed on the Reverend, Eleanor doesn't immediately notice the card her colleague is holding out to her.

"Why did you change the rules to the game?" Amy asks.

"I'm sorry?"

"On the card. The printed instructions said *one of you will die tonight* but you added *at least* so it read *at least one of you will die tonight.* That's why the game went on for as long as it did. I was waiting for someone else to drop dead."

Eleanor peers at the card. Sure enough, someone's added a handwritten *at least* to the top of the card. "That wasn't me." She glances at the Reverend, who shrugs.

"Nothing to do with me."

"I thought the game was new," Amy continues, "when it arrived in the post, but it's obviously second-hand. If I'd known you hadn't altered the instructions, I wouldn't have read out the amendment. Whoever sent it to me obviously plays it differently. Maybe the second victim adds a bit of a twist?"

Eleanor's brain is whirring, and she's got a sick feeling in her stomach, and not because she's hungry. "I thought the game was your idea, that you'd bought it specifically."

Amy shakes her head. "God no, I haven't even got my tree up yet, I'm not that organised. There was a card that came with it. It said, *The Paper Palace Christmas party is nearly upon us, and I thought this might help set the mood.* I thought that was a bit odd. I mean... how does a murder mystery game set the mood for a Christmas party? But then I—"

"Thought it might get our guests to mingle and interact." Eleanor turns sharply towards the Reverend. "Have you remembered who gave them to you?"

"Yes!" The older man's expression brightens, he's very keen to help. "I've got it. It was that wonderful author. Big hit in the eighties and nineties. What's his name? Martin… Martin something. Oh gosh. It was on the tip of my tongue a second ago, and now it's… wait, I've got it! Martin Rothschild!"

My own creation, in every way…

Heart pounding, Eleanor rushes back to the counter. *You're overreacting*, says the logical part of her brain as she searches for the present Martin gave her earlier. *It's the murder mystery, it's got you thinking about crime.* But there's no reasoning with the rush of fear that just passed through her body.

"What's going on?" Amy joins her as Eleanor plucks at the tape on the parcel with trembling fingers.

She doesn't reply, she can't. She's too focused on getting the paper off the book and—

A strangled gasp catches in her throat as she reveals the title.

"How to Commit Murder in a Bookshop," says the Reverend, leaning over the counter, his head tilted to get a better look. "That's prescient, given the game we just played."

Trembling, Eleanor flips through the pages until she reaches the dedication:

To all the agents and editors who gave the thumbs down to my ideas, the sales teams who failed to get my novels into supermarkets, the marketing and publicity teams who paid my books lip service, and the authors who refused to give me a quote. This book is for you.

Too scared to read on, it takes all of Eleanor's courage to turn the page. Voice trembling, she reads aloud:

"Chapter One.

"The perfect place to commit murder is at a party. A bookshop Christmas

party, *filled with all the people who have wronged you, is even better than that. All you need is a motive, an escape plan (ideally a flight abroad, the same day), a warning delivered via a game, an unsuspecting but helpful reader, a slow-acting and untraceable poison, and some home-cooked mince pies in a tin…"*

CHRISTMAS YET TO COME

Helen Fields

MARLEY WAS alive, to begin with.

He would remain that way until his body was found on New Year's Day of the freshly birthed century. He was red-cheeked and jolly on Christmas Eve 1899, ready for the afternoon's visitors, and dressed in a charcoal grey frock coat, a plum-coloured waistcoat, finished off with a champagne silk cravat. And if the buttons on his waistcoat were straining somewhat, then that would simply signal to his visitors how well he was doing.

"Money begets money," he told his mirror image, tucking a few strands of hair behind his ears. He really should have visited the barber, but there was so little time and too much to do. Such were the burdens of being a successful businessman.

A mousey knock at the door irritated him, mainly because it reminded Marley of his wife, who had died the previous December. Malnutrition, the physician had claimed, which was ridiculous. She'd had access to plenty of food. The woman must have taken leave of her senses to have deliberately stopped eating. Her family hadn't ceased hounding him since.

"In!" he commanded. It opened a crack and a young man put his face to the gap. "What is it?"

"They're gathering in the great hall, sir. Cook is mulling the wine, and it will be ready to serve as soon as you come down."

"Good. And tell Cook to use the smaller ladle so the wine goes further. Better that they see us offering a second cup rather than one large one."

"Yes, Mr Marley." His Adam's apple was bobbing in his throat and Jonathan Marley was tempted to grab ahold of it to keep it still. The door closed softly and Marley checked his image one last time.

Sixty-five years had barely marked his face. His skin was smooth, his lips generous, the thickness of his hair undiminished by age, resembling the pictures of his father as a young man. But it was his own natural intelligence that had allowed him to take his uncle Jacob's riches and put them to even more astute use than the old man. Jacob Marley had passed in 1836 when Jonathan was taking his first steps. His own father's earlier death meant that the family inheritance had passed to him upon his majority. And hadn't he done his uncle proud?

Exiting his personal chambers, making sure to close the door to keep in the warmth from the fires – one in every room, because cold was the enemy of health – Marley walked slowly down the stairs, past the entrance to the kitchens below and into the rear hallways of the Marley Memorial Workhouse.

Two small boys stood in front of the doors to the great hall, wearing matching woollen jackets and smart new trousers, faces gleaming from a recent scrubbing. As Marley approached, they lowered their heads and pushed open the doors.

Those who had been sitting stood, and those already standing put down their drinks to issue a polite round of applause as Marley meandered across the room in the direction of the enormous fireplace at the far end, surrounded by a huge wreath of winter greenery and white-berried mistletoe. Spices heated in candle wax created a fragrant cloud, and the fire's glow enhanced the sheen of glistening carved meats and candied fruits laid out on a long table. Several of the platters were already half empty, Marley noted. His guests would strip the place clean if he let them. Still, if a little expenditure was what it took to do business then he knew better than to skimp. His uncle had been frugal, making his fortune from money lending and foreclosure, and he'd done well at it. But the younger Marley, as he thought of himself, had embraced the new age. Production was where the money might be found now, in large-scale operations needing an endless supply of cheap labour. Greenwich, where the workhouse was situated – with its docks, factories and sugar refineries – was a veritable goldmine. With financial success came greater social standing, and with that came even more business. So much so that he was contemplating opening another workhouse in south London as industry expanded in that direction.

A servant offered Marley a large cup of Smoking Bishop and he took a sip of the steaming wine before raising his hand for quiet.

"My dear guests, I thank you for joining me this afternoon for our humble Yuletide celebrations." There were around one hundred people in the hall and it wasn't even a fraction full, used as it was to seating five times that number for meals. "Join me in a toast if you will, to the year behind us and the year ahead. May it be even more profitable!" A cheer went up and he raised his cup high. "Now, you are invited to join me on a tour of our home for the destitute, to whom you so kindly provide employment and the benefits it brings – food, clothing, medicine and education. The Marley Memorial Workhouse is proud of the services we offer you, and grateful that we give so much to the needy." It was, give or take a phrase, the same speech he offered every year.

Tim Cratchit stood close to the fire and let the heat soothe his aching leg. The rickets he'd suffered in early childhood had taken its toll, not that he wasn't grateful for the long life he'd enjoyed since then, but the winter made him feel every one of his sixty-eight years. The inheritance he'd received from a benefactor – his deceased father's employer – gave his family sufficient to live on, although they eschewed excess and luxury, preferring to keep a simple home. Instead, with a wife he adored and a daughter who was the light of his life, Cratchit could cope with anything except cruelty. Cruelty was the thorn beneath his skin that no needle could extract, and it was the reason for his visit to the workhouse that Christmas Eve.

The Cratchit family had heard tales of the Marley workhouse: how it was one of the few workhouses that allowed families to remain together and that school mistresses taught letters and numbers to the children. It was said that food bowls could be filled more than once, and that cheese was served on a Saturday and meat on a Sunday. Fresh milk was given to the children so that their bones might grow strong. A far cry from so many similar places that the Poor Laws controlled, where silence was mandated at all times.

Tim Cratchit wanted to believe it. He needed, perhaps desperately, to see an improvement in the behaviour of the wealthy and privileged in London after his many years of peaceful campaigning and purposeful persuasion. And yet his spirit was waning, and his daughter Adelaide was worried about him. Not that she'd ever said it out loud, but he knew.

"Father, Mr Marley is starting the tour." They moved towards a small door at the side of the great hall. Cratchit prepared for the chill of the hallway, yet when the door opened, there was no river of cold air. The diminutive windows were covered with thick curtains to keep the winter at bay, and lanterns spilled golden light onto the stairs before them. A bottleneck formed as they went one by one to the upper floor, and Adelaide dropped back to allow him to go ahead.

"Doesn't seem so bad," the man behind Cratchit boomed as he hauled himself up the steps. "Don't know what all the fuss is about from the do-gooders. Place is as warm as my home, and Marley's not afraid to burn the candles, is he?"

"Indeed," Cratchit replied pleasantly. "I'm pleased to see so much light. The eyes of those who inhabit these places are often the worse for such dark conditions."

"Quite right," came the reply amid the huffs of one who climbed fewer stairs each day than was healthy. "Poor eyesight leads to shoddy workmanship. Marley has calculated what's in his best interests. A healthier workforce means he can charge more for their labour."

Their first stop was a schoolroom with a teacher pointing at a slate in front of a row of boys who were dutifully repeating the letters she said aloud. They wore felt jackets over woollen shorts. It was only the second time he'd seen a workhouse providing education, and it gladdened his heart. Without teaching, those housed under the Poor Laws had no hope of anything better. Education was everything. He and his wife had begun teaching Adelaide to read as soon as she could hold a book. Perhaps, his wife said now, they had focused a little too hard on her education at the expense of her private life. Adelaide was in her mid-thirties and unmarried, and it was not for want of a pretty face or a pleasant character. She was skilled, too: accomplished at calligraphy, drawing and painting, able to reproduce the works of botanical illustrators Margaret Flockton and Arthur Church so finely that none but the original artists themselves might tell the difference between their own work and Adelaide's reproduction, in either the artwork or the scientific notes below. Adelaide's work brought the world's flora and fauna inside their house so that every room resembled Adelaide's beloved orangery at Kew Gardens.

Tim Cratchit moved along and rounded a corner just as Adelaide stopped to watch the lesson in progress. She leaned against the doorframe, listening to the rote learning of As, Bs and Cs as the remaining onlookers filed past her. Jonathan Marley could still be heard in the distance, instructing his crowd of well-fed followers on the comings and goings of his residents. He was something of an enigma in London society, not dissimilar to Adelaide herself.

She knew perfectly well that people regarded her as an oddity. What sort of woman did not crave the security of matrimony? She'd had enough offers, after all. Worse than that, she was a woman who appeared unconcerned by the prospect of never having children. People asked, from time to time, why she had not fulfilled her duty to marry and become a mother. Her answer was because she'd never found a place where her skills were in demand.

One of the boys glanced over at her. Adelaide offered a sweet smile and a nod of encouragement for the lesson. His eyes widened, his head whipped back to focus on the teacher, and he rubbed the back of his right leg with one hand as his lips caught up with sounds they were supposed to be making.

"We should move along, Miss," a voice cautioned from behind Adelaide. "Mr Marley said everyone should stay together."

Adelaide looked at the serving girl, who was wringing her hands and biting her bottom lip.

"Of course. It's just so nice to see children learning. Are the girls taught in the same way?"

"The girls are taught sewing, laundry and housekeeping."

"I see. May I ask your name?"

"Saddler, Miss."

"No, your first name. I couldn't possibly call you by your surname."

The young woman's cheeks reddened. "Clara."

"Well, Clara," she said. "Could I request a glass of water, please? A little of the salt beef seems to have caught in my throat. I'll catch up with the group, if you could bring it to me?"

The girl shifted her weight from one foot to the other. "I'll bring some water from the kitchen." She dashed back towards the great hall.

Some way ahead, Adelaide's father was inspecting dormitories. Each bed had a pillow and blanket, and at the end of every room was a fireplace stacked high with wood. Better than all that though – a revelation, actually – was the fact that some of the rooms featured a full-size bed for a mother and smaller pallets or cots for children. Family rooms, unheard of in the workhouse system, had finally arrived. Cratchit put a hand to his chest. The thing he'd been advocating for many decades, preventing mothers from being separated from babies and young children, was a reality. It would help, he believed, in reducing infant mortality rates and maternal suicides. Time and again, doctors diagnosed hysteria in women whose children were taken from them, and after that they were fit only for Bedlam.

"Adult residents work only ten hours per day," Marley was announcing from the head of the line, "and children below the age of fourteen work only eight. Those younger than that work only as many hours as their supervisors assess them fit to safely undertake."

"You're going soft, Marley!" someone called. "And asking us to put our hands in our pockets to support this? These people are lucky to have a roof over their head at all!"

Cratchit sighed. It was the same old refrain. Why help the poor? *Because we are brothers*, he always replied. Some more fortunate than others, granted. Some born onto straw and others onto silk, but all their blood ran red.

"Nothing more than good business," Marley retorted. "Employ the workers I house, and you will get the finest low-cost labour on the market."

A maid appeared at the back of the hallway carrying a glass of water and looking frantically around, which made Cratchit wonder where his daughter had got to. It was ever her way, wandering off.

Adelaide was more than most men wanted to take on – too intelligent, too enquiring, too irrepressible. From the moment she could walk, she'd run them ragged with her curiosity, and they had encouraged it, little thinking of a future where she might end up alone. He felt the familiar flush of pride and sting of sadness as he imagined it.

As if he'd summoned her with his mind, Adelaide appeared behind the maid, tapped her on the shoulder, and took the glass of water with cheerful thanks. Cratchit made his way to her as Marley led them down a final set of steps and back into the great hall, stepping to the side of the doorway to shake the hand of each of his guests as they filed past him. Cratchit and Adelaide were last.

"Pleased to make your acquaintance." Marley extended his hand. "I do hope you and your wife found the visit informative."

Cratchit almost managed to keep the frown off his forehead. "This is my daughter," he corrected.

"Ah," Marley said, extending the vowel as he turned to Adelaide and bowed. "Forgive me, Miss. Then you are unmarried?"

"Indeed," Adelaide said, smiling pleasantly and causing Cratchit to wonder if she was feeling quite herself. "I've been astounded tonight, sir. You're quite the forward thinker."

"A rare compliment coming from a member of the fairer sex," Marley said. "May I ask your name?"

"Adelaide, and this is my father, Timothy Cratchit."

Marley's smile faltered only for the briefest of moments.

"Cratchit. Of course. I hadn't been made aware that you were visiting. Your reputation for campaigning on behalf of the less fortunate in society precedes you."

"And we are greatly relieved and impressed that much of that work has been reflected in the changes you've made here, Mr Marley,"

Adelaide murmured. "I've waited so long to visit an establishment with a classroom and proper heating, not to mention the family rooms. Whilst I would be happier if such institutions did not exist at all, I recognise that we would need to rid the world of poverty for that to become a reality."

Marley drew himself up, chin out, a smile playing at the corners of his mouth.

"Miss Cratchit, you do your father proud. So few women are able to understand the wider world. Allow me to escort you to find a proper drink. Our cook has expertly mulled the wine this year." He held out his arm, and Cratchit watched his daughter slip hers through. Whatever Adelaide had seen that night must have impressed her. She was no more easily charmed than a viper.

One full hour later, as the unburdened platters meant that the hall was also emptying, Cratchit made his way back to Adelaide, who was laughing at whatever story Marley was telling. She looked sheepishly at him as he approached.

"Father," she said sweetly, "tell me it is not time for us to leave already."

"I'm afraid it is, my dear. Your mother will be waiting. And it is Christmas Eve. There are gifts to be exchanged. I'm surprised you had forgotten."

Adelaide looked at Marley and beamed. "I do so love Christmas. It's my favourite time of the year."

"The servant will find your coat and gloves, Miss Adelaide, but I wonder if I might have a private word with your father before you depart."

"No need for that," Cratchit said, many years past thinking Adelaide would walk away and leave men to converse behind her back. "Whatever you wish to say, Mr Marley, my daughter is equipped to hear."

Marley moved his shoulders one at a time, and raised his chin. "Very well then. I understand that this may be forward, but I am well acquainted with your reputation and I'm sure you're fully familiar with my status. What you may not know is that my wife sadly left this Earth after a brief illness one year ago, and we were never blessed with offspring. I have since hoped that I might meet another who could fill her shoes, and I would very much like to discuss the possibility of taking your daughter's hand in—"

"Out of the question," Cratchit snapped.

"I appreciate that this is unexpected, but I have been impressed by Miss Cratchit's bearing and self-possession."

Cratchit took a deep breath and folded his arms. Adelaide put a gentle hand out between the two men.

"Father, you've been taken by surprise, as have I, but I am not averse to the suggestion. I've waited beyond what is considered reasonable for a marriage proposal, and I believe that our campaign might be bolstered by showing others that we respect the example Mr Marley has set here."

Cratchit stared at his daughter, lips slightly apart. "I don't understand," he said softly.

"It's time for me to leave home. A decade past time, if we're honest. Here I will have the opportunity to continue your good work."

"I would take a house in due course," Marley cut in. "My accommodations upstairs are comfortable, but I would not expect a new wife to live for long in such a place."

"We should discuss this at home. It is not a matter to decide in haste—"

"I am lonely, Father. And a man who has been married before is likely to be kinder. Mr Marley can take care of me, much as you have done, and I'm grateful for his offer. More than grateful. I'm minded to accept."

Marley took Adelaide's hand and gripped it. Cratchit knew his tight smile would not fool his daughter, but he knew, too, that once her mind was set on something there would be no changing it.

Cratchit nodded at his offspring. "So be it. I will not withhold my consent if this is what you truly wish, Adelaide, not that my consent should be relevant at your age. You know your own mind. I would prefer only that you did not rush matters."

"But too long a wait might be foolhardy. We none of us are guaranteed tomorrow," Marley said, raising his eyebrows sagely.

Adelaide pressed her lips together, holding back a smile.

"Quite so, sir," she said. "But I believe we have some terms to agree before our engagement can be formalised."

Across the hall, the maid was coughing quietly into the crook of her arm while she gathered used cups with her free hand, her skin a slick, waxy grey. At the far end, a manservant was staring across at her, his brows drawn into a deep frown. He handed hats and scarves to a group of three men who were standing in a corner, whispering fiercely to one another and watching Marley.

"Mr Marley," one of the men called over. "A word?"

Marley pulled a face. "Now is not the time. I can offer you an audience in the New Year."

"Unacceptable," another of the men said. They approached briskly. Marley stepped forward to intercept.

"Gentlemen, allow me to introduce my wife-to-be, Adelaide,

and her father Timothy Cratchit. I'm sure you've heard of his charitable and reform works."

The men glared at Cratchit. Adelaide broke the thick silence.

"Are these friends of yours, Mr Marley?"

"Partners, of a sort," one of them answered before Marley could speak.

"Then I would not keep you much longer. I understand that in business, even Christmas sometimes must wait. Gentlemen, may I request an hour with Mr Marley before you speak with him? Perhaps, sir, you could meet your associates thereafter?" She touched Marley's arm gently as she put the question to him. "Is there not an inn close by that would provide a suitable venue?"

"Indeed," Marley said, nodding. "The Sea Witch Pub is but a few minutes' walk from here."

The men mumbled and rolled their eyes, but did not argue and soon disappeared. Cratchit agreed to depart for home, provided the maid remained with his daughter for propriety's sake while she and Marley finished their conversation.

"You are sure, dear one?" he whispered as he hugged her goodbye.

"Never more sure of anything, Father. It was fate that brought me here tonight. Do not worry. I will see myself home. And do not wait up! We will celebrate tomorrow."

Once her father had gone, Marley took Adelaide's hand and they stood talking before the dwindling fire.

"I have an engagement ring, Miss Adelaide, in my rooms. It was my mother's, although I appreciate that you might wish for a newer one to be purchased."

"Not so," Adelaide replied. "I'm all for traditions, Mr Marley, and not a vain woman. A ring is a mark of commitment. It should remind us of family and values. I would be pleased to accept your mother's. I can ask the maid for wine to toast with while you fetch it."

Marley exited, and Adelaide called for more cups of mulled wine, as hot as they could come. The maid disappeared and Adelaide considered everything she'd seen that evening. Outside on the street, carol singers sang 'God Rest Ye Merry Gentlemen' and her heart soared. There was so much beauty in the world, so much potential for good. She was right where she was needed at that moment, heralding in change.

Clara brought the steaming cups and, regardless of what her father had said, Adelaide dismissed her – the girl looked fit to collapse. She stumbled on her way towards the door and was helped up by a manservant who escorted her out. Adelaide busied herself adjusting the flora of the Christmas wreath as she awaited Marley's return.

He took the cups from her and set them on the hearth, before drawing a red velvet box from his waistcoat pocket and opening it to reveal a small but perfect pear-shaped diamond set on a gold band.

"Adelaide Cratchit, would you do me the honour – as unexpected as the evening has been – of becoming my wife?"

"I will," she said. She allowed Marley to slip the ring on her finger. It was a little large but it flickered merrily in the firelight. She picked up the cups of wine and handed Marley his. "Let's toast to our nuptials, and set the wedding date for a month to the day."

"A month to the day." He knocked the rim of his cup against hers. "I should call on your family to meet your mother. Would Boxing Day be an appropriate time?"

"Oh, we are rather overrun with charitable and church commitments this season. On Boxing Day we deliver food and coal to those who are most in need. Would you care to join us?"

"I think perhaps, then, that I should wait. It hardly seems a fitting way to spend my first hour with your family. Perhaps a day or two after New Year, once your commitments are done?"

"Perfect! And you will allow me to assist you here when we are married? I should like to be involved in the good you are doing."

"I have a better role for you. You are so warm and welcoming, I would appreciate it if you would spread word of the changes you have seen here. I would like people to know that I keep my residents fit, healthy and fed. To encourage others to bring change, you understand."

"I do," Adelaide said, raising her cup once more. "To you, my husband-to-be, and to change. And to the poor who have not the power to help themselves." She finished her wine and Marley did the same, putting his cup down and looking up at the wreath above them.

"May I kiss you beneath the mistletoe, Miss Adelaide? It seems the most fitting way to seal our happy agreement."

She leant forward and offered him her cheek. He kissed it with lips still wet from the wine; she paused before wiping it daintily away.

"I should go. My mother will have questions about dresses and wedding feasts. And you have a meeting to attend."

"I do," he said with a sigh. "It will be a blessing to have a wife to take care of me."

Marley called for a servant, and the young man appeared who had stopped the maid from stumbling, bringing both Marley's cloak and Adelaide's coat with him. They wrapped up against the cold and departed together. Marley heading for the Sea Witch Pub and Adelaide looking for a coach to hail. She looked over at Marley as he disappeared around a corner, then made her way back to the workhouse, knocking loudly. The same man answered, himself in a coat and ready to exit.

"I'm sorry to bother you. You'll be aware by now that Mr Marley and I are engaged to be married. I had planned to ask him to show me his rooms, but we were carried away making arrangements. Do you think you could accompany me to them briefly? I have a gift I wish to leave there."

"I'm not sure, Miss," he said.

"I would not ask, but if I'm to live here until a house is purchased then I should like to see my new home. I confess, I am a little nervous."

He bowed his head, and showed Adelaide to the back stairs and Marley's chambers.

"If you don't mind, I'd like to check on my sister. She's been taken proper bad."

"Not Clara?"

"The same," he replied, his voice cracking.

"Poor girl," Adelaide said. "Is there anything I can do to help?"

He hesitated. "You could show yourself out when you've taken a look? I need to tell her boys that their ma is unwell. I wouldn't normally ask but—"

"Absolutely. It will be our secret that I was ever here. I know my way back to the door. May I ask your name before you go?"

"My given name's Perry, 'though we go mostly by surnames here."

"Well, that's not how I do things. Thank you, Perry. You may go."

He left, wringing his hands, his face gloomy.

Adelaide looked around Marley's sitting room and study, with its comfortable velvet armchairs and walnut desk. The curtains were luxurious, and the fireplace generous for the space that required heating. She didn't bother looking into the bedroom or the bathroom. Instead, she sat at the desk. It was covered in business agreements and personal letters ready to send with Marley's grand, swirling signature. She imagined drawing there in the light of the bay window. Adelaide lit a candle, then picked up a pen and a clean sheet of Marley's headed paper, looked around the desk for inspiration and began to work, intent on leaving a picture of mistletoe on her fiancé's desk to mark their first kiss.

Jonathan Marley's body was discovered on New Year's Day in the fresh century. His remains had washed ashore near the Broadness Lighthouse – swollen, battered and blackened to such an extent that he would have been unrecognisable but for the gold pocket watch, inscribed with his name, that was still fastened to his waistcoat by its chain. He was first spotted by a ragtag group of children throwing stones into the Thames and hunting the river's edge for lost treasures. The body was more than they had bargained for, though the tale would earn them pennies at the local ale houses, enough to make up for the shock.

The police hooked the body out of the water by boat, the bank too treacherous with ice for anyone to get close. From there, Marley was rowed up the river to the dead house and inspected by the County Coroner.

The police knocked at Cratchit's door before the London papers could put the details to press, and found Adelaide and her mother baking brown bread pudding.

"Miss Cratchit. Sorry to bother you."

"It's no bother," Adelaide said brightly. "Happy New Year! Can I offer you a drink? We still have a little wine from Christmas." The constables shifted uncomfortably on their feet until Adelaide's face dropped. "What's happened? Is it Father?"

Mrs Cratchit's hand flew to her chest.

"Not Mr Cratchit, no, but I'm afraid there *has* been a tragedy. Mr Jonathan Marley, to whom I understand you had recently become engaged, has been found dead."

"But… how? I don't understand. He was due to come here and meet my mother. Surely there's been some mistake. He was in good health when last I saw him."

"The coroner has determined that it was not a drowning. It's hard to say if there was an attack, forgive me for speaking so in front of you ladies, but when a body has been in the water any length of time it no longer resembles the man. Mr Marley suffered no broken bones and had not been relieved of his pocket watch, so the motive seems not to have been robbery."

Adelaide sank into a chair and put her hands to her face. "We were to marry at the end of this month! I had begun sewing my dress." She pointed with shaking fingers to a simple cream dress that was hanging in the corner of the room, covered in paper to protect it from the fire soot.

"I'm sorry to ask, but did his behaviour seem odd to you the last time you saw him?"

"Not at all," she cried. "We toasted our agreement and made plans, then he went to meet some gentlemen at the Sea Witch Pub, near the glucose refinery."

"Indeed, one of Mr Marley's wardens said he'd set off for a meeting there, so we enquired with the landlord. It's not unknown for their customers to end up in the Thames after an excess of drinking, but apparently Mr Marley was somewhat pensive, and left quite soon after he'd arrived. He appeared to exit rather fast: 'like the Devil himself was chasing him', were the landlord's words. Perhaps his business meeting did not go so well…"

"May the poor man rest in peace," Mrs Cratchit muttered. "How terrible." Adelaide reached out and gripped her mother's hand.

"As Mr Marley had his own keys to his accommodations, we know little more about his movements thereafter."

Adelaide drew a handkerchief from her pocket. "He was my last chance. I am considered too old for matrimony already."

"Do not cry, my love," her mother said. "You will have other suitors. Gentlemen, unless you have any other questions, perhaps you would leave us in peace?" she asked gently.

One of them stepped forward to talk quietly to Mrs Cratchit. "It was, in fact, Mr Timothy Cratchit we were hoping to speak with."

The front door opened as if Cratchit had been waiting for his cue. He looked around the room, took off his hat, and stepped forward to put a protective arm around his wife.

"What's all this now? Constables, is something wrong?"

"Mr Cratchit, forgive the intrusion, but did you happen to communicate with Mr Marley between Christmas Eve night and the twenty-seventh of December?"

"Not at all. I've been with my family," he explained.

"What is the point of the question, may I ask?" Mrs Cratchit was suddenly bristling.

"Father, Jonathan Marley is dead and there are outstanding questions regarding his fate," Adelaide explained.

"Surely it is not true," Cratchit said. "Adelaide, my dear, this is such a shock. Tell me how I can assist."

"We thought you might have had some contact with him, sir, to do with your business dealings." Cratchit shrugged. "Mr Marley having died unexpectedly, we at once checked his accommodations and discovered what appears to have been his final correspondence, dated the twenty-fourth day of December, indicating that he must have returned home safely from the Sea Witch and perished some time after this. His solicitor, Nathaniel Coggleton, will be in contact in due course."

"I am at a loss as to the relevance," Cratchit muttered.

"Mr Marley left a letter of instruction to his lawyers, and with it a signed directive that made you a full equity partner in the Marley Memorial Workhouse, including access to the funds in the business bank account, in return for you giving your consent for your daughter's hand. Mr Marley's handwriting and signature have been verified by his lawyer. With no offspring or other partner, it appears that you are now the guardian of the workhouse."

"I don't—" Cratchit began.

"Oh, Father! Mr Marley told me it was his intention to immediately make you a partner in the workhouse when I accepted his proposal. We agreed that he would announce it to you when he visited. It can stand as a testament to the good work he'd begun. I feel blessed to have been engaged to such a good man, and we must arrange a fitting funeral."

"You are actively investigating his death, constables?" Cratchit asked.

"We are. There have been... rumours that he was not the most popular man in some circles, talk of business disputes, and his former wife's family were not enamoured of him. It is possible that someone wished him harm, perhaps because of his intended union and change in circumstances? That might be how he found his way into the Thames… In any event, we'll leave you now. Sorry to have come with such sad tidings."

They departed quickly and quietly, Adelaide clutching her father's hand as the door shut.

"Adelaide, I know I was not convinced it was a good union, but I am nonetheless sorry," Cratchit said. "What can I do for you?"

"Come with me to the workhouse," she said, fetching their coats. "There is no one in charge now, and the wardens will be cruel if they fear that their wages will not be paid. Mother, would you visit Marley's solicitor, Mr Coggleton, and tell him to send instructions to the wardens that we are to take charge immediately?"

"Of course, my love," her mother said, already picking up hat and gloves.

A carriage delivered them to the workhouse, where a purple-faced woman with a weighty keychain around her middle opened up.

"I need to talk with Clara," Adelaide said.

"Clara's sick. Her brother's with her. Doubt she'll see tomorrow, truth be told. We're about to lock down for the night. They've had their rations, so it's lights out."

Adelaide took a deep breath. "I will see Clara now, no delay. Everything else can wait. My father, your new employer, will come with me."

The woman huffed but attempted no further argument and escorted them along the corridor they'd walked on Christmas Eve.

"Where are the desks?" Cratchit asked, as they passed what had been the schoolroom.

Adelaide took her father's arm. "Not now, Father," she said. "There are more important matters than one schoolroom."

She hurried along until finally they reached a low door, behind which the sound of coughing could be heard.

"I won't go in with you. It might help to say a prayer before you enter," the woman commented, bustling away before she'd even finished the sentence.

"Prayers do not heal the sick, nor do they heat rooms or fill bellies," Adelaide replied quietly. She opened the door, covering her mouth with a handkerchief and warning her father to do the same.

They had known Clara would be in a bad way, but nothing prepared them for the rows of beds with ailing men, women and children, lying not on mattresses but on wooden pallets with no blankets, in a room with nothing but two tiny, closed windows and a hearth with no fire. The children's ribs stuck out against their taut, pale skin and the adults clutched their ragged clothes around themselves for what little warmth they gave.

"For God's sake, what is this? Marley said there were blankets and access to physicians," Cratchit exclaimed.

Adelaide was already striding down the room giving instructions. "Open those windows. The room requires ventilation. And bring all available bedding. Hot water and soap, too. You!" She pointed at a girl who was sweeping the floor. "To the kitchens, quick as you can. Bid the cooks make broth and bring bread with it, enough for everyone here. Father, Mr Marley has stables below. Would you ride into town and persuade every doctor you can to come? We have access to the accounts. They will be properly paid."

"I will," Cratchit said, wasting not a second in exiting.

"Clara!" Adelaide knelt at the young woman's bedside. "We will get you help. I'm sorry I could not come sooner."

"Miss," Clara's brother, Perry, whispered. "What happened to Mr Marley? The wardens were questioned by the police, and none of them will say what's to become of us."

"And have you spoken to the police yet, Perry?" she asked softly.

"They didn't bother with me, Miss. I'm not important enough, and I've mostly been by Clara's side in the sick room since Christmas Eve. The wardens are too scared to go in there for fear they'll catch their deaths."

A line of boys carried in wood, blankets and pails of hot water. Adelaide made sure the fire was laid and that everyone was washing their hands and faces, before asking Clara's brother to follow her to Marley's quarters.

"You are not to worry," Adelaide said. "It is true that there has been a tragedy, but you will be safe and cared for, I give you my word."

"Will the doctors really come, do you think?" Perry asked.

"I will make sure of it," Adelaide said. "You should know that Mr Marley was found in the Thames. My father will be guardian here from now on, and I am a widow before I was even married."

"Very sorry, Miss. Can I ask what happened?"

"My Marley had enemies, apparently. Perhaps they were people to whom Mr Marley promised a fit, healthy workforce for a higher labour price than is customary and who found his claims to be rather empty?" She raised her eyebrows with the question.

"Maybe so," Perry answered quietly.

"Well, my father has no such enemies because he is a fair man. A kind man. He has campaigned for years to reform the workhouse system. He is the sort of man who will ensure the attention of doctors for those who need it, and properly tend to the needs of the people in his care." Adelaide sat down at Marley's desk. "I understand from the police that Mr Marley left a deed making my father a partner following our engagement. Without a witness to that letter, however, I believe the transfer might be challenged by those who want this place for themselves." Perry stared at her. "I must ask you to think carefully. Did you by chance see Mr Marley return here Christmas Eve night? Did you see him writing the deed in question and signing it?"

Perry thought hard, then spoke slowly.

"Why yes, I believe I did." Perry took a few more seconds to ponder this. "He came back here Christmas Eve night, although it was late, and I brought coal for his fire and seen him signing a paper he'd written. He said he was planning on visiting friends out of the city for Christmas so he wouldn't be needing me for a few days."

"A tragedy, indeed. I'm grateful for your recollection and I will arrange for you to clarify that with Mr Marley's solicitor as soon as possible, not to mention the police. Now, go back to Clara and await the doctor. When all is well, you and I will talk about what improvements are needed here and how you can help. Would you do that?"

A smile lit up his face. "Yes, Miss."

"Thank you. And tell my father where he can find me. We should start getting things in order."

Tim Cratchit found his daughter at Marley's desk, taking an old picture of a horse and hound from a frame and inserting her sketch of mistletoe in its place.

"The doctors are helping those they can. You are moving fast, Adelaide. I'm not sure we should assume our place here is settled yet."

"Good news, in fact," she said. "Perry, Marley's manservant, remembers him writing the partnership deed and signing it."

Cratchit lit the fire and sat down to stoke it.

"And when did you become the expert on legal matters, daughter?"

"Father, when did you ever see me without a book in my hand?" She set her drawing on the picture hook, straightening it on the wall.

"This place is not as it was presented to us. I wandered through the dormitories. Not a one was heated. The so-called family rooms are crammed full of those being punished for misdemeanours. The school mistress is nowhere to be found. It is as foul and heartless a place as I have visited, and the tragedy is that you promised yourself to a man who lied to us both and fooled so many of his fellow men."

"But, Father, you have the opportunity to do great things here, and sufficient income from the workhouse contracts with which to make the necessary changes."

She was opening Marley's desk drawers and perusing papers.

"You do not seem surprised by our discoveries."

Adelaide put down the contract she was reading and went to sit opposite her father.

"Was it not you who taught me that when a thing seems too good to be believed, you should doubt even your own senses?" She gave him a warm smile. "The boys in the classroom were wearing clothes that made them itch. They were clearly unused to the material. On closer inspection, the backs of their little legs were red. They had been beaten, I assume, to ensure their compliance. I managed to slip away from the crowd by sending Clara to fetch me water. I walked where I should not have done, and I saw the truth."

"But, Adelaide, you agreed to marry Marley, knowing the man was a monster. How could you?" He leaned forward and grabbed his daughter's hands.

"Because history has shown us that change comes fastest from within. I believed I could do more good as his ally than his enemy. He thought so too, which was his motivation for our engagement. How better to stop you campaigning than by marrying your only child?"

"Such a risk. And now the man is dead." Cratchit grew still and quiet.

"Jonathan Marley was an astute businessman, Father, like his uncle before him. By making every factory owner in the district believe that the residents here were in good health and well cared for, he was able to engage in labour contracts at favourable rates whilst running the workhouse for a pittance and creaming the profits off the top. Those contracts, shameful and immoral as they were, are now yours to deal with as you see fit. You can change the way the residents are treated, feed, clothe and educate them. You can keep families together and give a portion of wages back to the residents to save for the day they can support themselves and leave. This was the dream, Father. Your dream."

"Adelaide, I must ask—"

"I do not accept that," she said, "respectfully. There is nothing you must do, save for making improvements here. Clara's brother, Perry, will help. The current wardens must be dismissed immediately."

"Daughter, the deed left on Marley's desk... was it—"

"Marley had enemies, and plenty of them. People unhappy with the work the residents did because they were sick and weak. Debts he could have paid but chose not to. His former wife's family, presumably for his treatment of that poor woman. The residents here. Whatever happened to Jonathan Marley, he brought it on himself, and I will lose not a minute's sleep over it. My conscience is clear."

There was a knock at the door and Perry entered.

"Sir, the wardens have questions and the doctors have finished in the sick room. I wasn't sure where to take them."

"To the great hall, please. I will speak with the doctors first, then the wardens. Thank you. How is your sister?" Cratchit asked.

"They say that with medicine, rest and food she might recover. I'm grateful, sir. It looked like her time was up."

He disappeared again and Cratchit watched his daughter as she began bringing bundles of thick bedding and piles of clothes out from Marley's bedroom.

"Do not wait for me, Father. There is much to do, beginning with taking these blankets to those who most need them. I will see you at home. Mother will be desperate to hear the news."

Tim Cratchit kissed his daughter's forehead and gazed around Marley's chambers. Adelaide was transforming the place already. His daughter was, truly, a force to be reckoned with. And if he was concerned at just how great a force that might be, then perhaps it was best not to think too hard on it.

Adelaide salvaged what she could from Marley's chambers and compiled a list of the contracts the workhouse had outstanding.

If nothing else, Marley had been well organised. After that, she put on her hat, coat and gloves, walked out past the stables and round the back of the workhouse, then took the lane down to the Sea Witch Pub, past the back of the glucose refinery, and onto the river path. She paused to gaze along the Thames to the distant lighthouse where Marley's body had been found.

She stepped carefully as she walked to the water's edge where Marley might well have stopped to empty his stomach into the water. She made sure to keep clear of the mudbank, slippery as it was, and perilous to anyone half-blinded by tears, clutching at their stomach for cramp, struggling to breathe and wondering why their heart was beating so irregularly. The slightest misstep would lead into the icy tidal flow and death would surely follow. Only the river, London's own toxic lifeblood, would dictate when that body might wash up, and where.

She tossed a small bouquet of greenery from the extravagant fireplace wreath into the water and prayed for Marley's soul.

Adelaide began the short walk back to the workhouse. There was work to be done, and plenty of it. Her father was not a young man. He would be relying on her to help. She would begin in the great hall, making it a comfortable place for the residents to eat, but also somewhere they could spend time with each other, a place to play games with their children. She would begin that night, she decided, just as soon as the mistletoe wreath had been removed. Carefully, though. It should never have been in a room where food and drink were consumed. The berries were terribly poisonous. Not enough to kill fast, perhaps, but certainly dangerous enough to make a man feel *like* he was dying. Certainly enough to make him vulnerable to even the most innocuous of predators on a darkened path at night.

After all, we none of us are guaranteed tomorrow, Adelaide thought to herself.

It was such a misleading plant – pretty, dainty, romantic, pure – that it hid perfectly all those other qualities it possessed. It was quite her favourite Christmas decoration.

WHAT SHE LEFT ME

Tina Baker

HER FAVOURITE scent was lavender. There are echoes of it in her bedroom, from little sachets I guess would have been layered between neatly folded clothes in the drawers; vaguely antiseptic – the smell of moths and wrinkles.

My sister-in-law has already cleared away the clothes and the bed linen, and stacked them in bin liners ready to be taken to the charity shop or the tip.

I hadn't expected to feel the absence so viscerally. I have to sit on the naked bed for a moment to gather myself.

I shouldn't have come. Not while I'm jet-lagged and queasy; not in the middle of the night. I should have gone straight to the hotel and lain there, unable to sleep perhaps, but at least resting until my brother picked me up and brought me over here in the morning. Then, fired by caffeine, bolstered by daylight and his resolutely pragmatic presence, I could perhaps face my old family home with equanimity and at least start to deal with the death of my mother.

Home. Mother. The words are ludicrous.

The taxi driver waited while I made sure my key still worked. Then he was gone. Now, for the first time in years, I am alone in my mother's house.

It feels too intimate to be sitting on her bed, so I go downstairs to make myself what laughably passes for coffee here – powdered milk and granules of a substance that at no time has borne any resemblance to a Java bean.

The Christmas tree seems a cruelty in the circumstances. Of course she'd have one. She always made an effort – the birth of the baby Jesus being the main event in her calendar. She would spend the day itself with my brother and his family after a Midnight Mass and lashings of sherry.

Not once have I returned from America to spend Christmas with my so-called family.

There are six or seven Christmas cards displayed on the mantel, all with religious themes, apart from mine, which shows a snowy Central Park with the greeting *Happy Holidays* – a mighty *Up Yours* from across the ocean.

I slump on the sofa to sip my vile drink. A heavy silence clogs the house and hangs over this entire cul-de-sac. It is not peaceful. This silent night, the total absence of noise, is disturbing after the comforting cacophony of New York City life. Creepy. I find myself listening hard – for what, I'm not sure.

There's a small stack of papers laid out on the table in the corner, involving the usual loose ends. A life reduced to a modest pile of documents. I need to go through these with my brother tomorrow. I'd told myself this is the reason why I've come. It's a lie. I could have done it all via electronic signature.

I'm not sure what has drawn me back. I couldn't even explain it to my husband when I told him I wanted to come by myself, that I need to face this part alone. He will bring the girls over for the funeral, whenever that might be – sometime in January; we haven't yet got a date.

I put the coffee mug down on the table, flinching because I've forgotten the coaster. Then I remember it no longer matters.

The thought makes me bold. I return to her bedroom and start snooping.

I'd rarely been invited into this room, even as a child, and I was too afraid of my mother's temper to ever look through her personal things when there was the faintest chance of her catching me. Now I feel like an intruder, a thief. I start rummaging around, furtively leafing through her books. Pressed flowers in a few, prayer cards in others, extolling the usual virtues. My knee-jerk reaction is eye-rolling exasperation.

I sometimes wonder how much of my personality has been forged rebelling against anything my mother championed.

There are several photos of my brother, his wife and their children – all in a line, in matching frames on a shelf. Not one of me anywhere. I didn't have the things to celebrate – the graduation, the acceptable marriage, the kids. I'd had the arguments.

She never came to my wedding. The excuse was *because he's Jewish*. Jack isn't at all religious and we had a humanist ceremony, but she could hardly voice the real reason – *because he's black*.

That tells you pretty much all you need to know about my mother.

The fact that I look so like her, inheriting her shock of hair and Amazonian physique, was a torment to me as a teenager, although the broad shoulders did come in handy for the swimming club.

We never *got on*. She had a much easier relationship with my brother.

I once asked him how he put up with it, with her, and he smiled vaguely and said, "I don't really listen. I let it all wash over me." Uncomplicated, my brother.

Things will feel easier when I see him tomorrow.

My last years in Britain were unbearable in this house. My brother had left by then and my father was working away most of the time, so it was only me here, chafing against almost everything she believed in, everything she did, everything she said. It became too painful. As soon as I could escape I did – I moved abroad, and we left it at that. A brief phone call every few months, saying little. Hollow pleasantries. A fragile connection across thousands of miles. A safe distance.

Yet, after all these years, this house feels familiar. Everything is where I expect it to be because she's not changed anything. Her room is exactly the same as when I'd slept down the hall, my walls splattered with posters, dreaming my own dreams, plotting my getaway. In my eyes her room is a small, sterile cell. Hers was a stilted life. Pitiful, really.

I open her plain wooden jewellery box. Inside is her booklet from the slimming group – not that she'd ever needed to go; she'd been at her *target weight* for years. There are also a couple of cuttings from the local paper about my brother's career and the cat's inoculation record, from the time when she'd once, improbably, had a cat. It never had much to do with us. There's an old rosary, a St Christopher...

She has touched each of these unremarkable items. Her atoms remain here, the dust of moth wings. I handle her things, these *relics*, with respect. This is the closest I've felt to her for such a long time.

She is still somehow present, yet there is no record that my father ever lived here.

I sometimes wonder if I'd moved to America to feel closer to my dad. He left for good when I was fifteen. My brother was already engaged by then, already about to start his own life in his own flat. He seemed unbothered by the disappearing act.

I was broken by it.

My father had *gone back home*, according to my mother. And that was that. No call, no letter, not a single communication after he abandoned us.

When he first left, I assumed he'd come home at some point. I was always listening for his key in the door. He'd done it before – storming off, then after a few silent weeks, slinking back. He tried to leave her several times, notably one Christmas Eve as things came to a head, like they tend to at such a stressful time of year. When he returned, we were instructed never to ask questions about where he'd been – more pertinently, who he'd been with. And he was only ever back sporadically. He worked away as often as he could. A couple of years of limbo ensued, characterised by accusations and rows, followed by glacial silences which were worse than the fights.

I started spending most school nights at my brother's flat, weekend sleepovers with my school friends. I became a part-time child.

I could see why he'd finally leave *her*, but I never understood why he'd severed all connection with me and my brother. I remember sobbing the day after my sixteenth birthday when there'd been no word.

Where had he gone? Why did he not stay in touch?

She claimed it was shame. She seemed to take some delight in reminding me that adultery is a *cardinal sin* – one of the worst, along with murder and pride and cheeking one's mother.

"He doesn't care about you, your brother, or me. He's upped and left to be with his fancy woman – some American tart." She spat out the accusation. Sherry had been taken.

She convinced me that he didn't get in touch because he felt too guilty. I didn't believe her. I felt sure he would contact me. But time proved her right.

I notice I'm breathing faster but deliberately quietly. These are difficult memories. I move slowly, turning over objects and opening drawers as I continue looking through her things, as if I'm searching, half-listening for something.

Could he have somehow heard that she'd died? Might he come back now the Wicked Witch is dead? Childish thoughts.

I find a batch of old Mother's Day cards in a fancy biscuit tin. I'm not sure why she kept these few and not others. Perhaps they were from significant times – like the year she became a grandmother to my brother's firstborn, fulfilling her life's ambition.

At the bottom of the pile there's the Easter card with the drawing of a wonky duckling – no, chick – that I'd made when I was at infant school. Corny sentiments from the time before cynicism.

Inside this card there is a passport.

My breath catches. I had no idea she had one. She'd never even left the country.

Odd that she kept it here – an official document not filed with the bank books and council tax bills where you'd expect. Inside, the photo of my mother, as inscrutable as ever, stares back at me. Unsmiling, as usual.

It makes no sense. This is the woman who had never left her hometown. Apart from a few day trips to Blackpool, she'd never been on holiday. In her entire life, had never spent more than two nights away from her own bed – and then only to give birth to my brother and, years later, me.

I stare at my mother's face. It's a recent picture. She looks older than I recall. Drawn. The shadows under her eyes are stark. Perhaps she already knew how ill she was.

A pain stabs my throat with the force of unsaid words, and I know, without a shadow of a doubt, what it means. She was coming to visit me.

Suddenly I'm no longer an adult, but a grieving child. I take giant breaths to stop myself from crying out, crying for my mummy. I hold her passport and lie on her bed, bringing my knees up to my chest, curling into a tight foetal position until I can breathe calmly again.

My brother and his wife had been planning to bring the kids over to see me, Jack and the girls in the spring, although my niece and nephew were not thrilled when they discovered that I live nowhere near Disneyland. I recall my brother mentioning that he might be able to persuade my mother to come with them, but I hadn't believed it for a second.

How strange it would have been to see her uprooted from Oldham, Greater Manchester, and plonked down in the middle of a city like New York. I couldn't imagine it. She'd only go to the town shopping centre first thing in the morning, before it got *too crowded*.

The last time I saw my mother in the flesh was when I was staying at my brother's, just before I left for my new life in the USA. She came round to say goodbye.

She stood on my brother's doorstep, grabbed my hand, and prophesised that I was *heading on my way to ruin*. "I know you can't help it," she whispered. "You have the devil in you, just like your father. I will pray for you."

The hiss of that goodbye, the memory of the kiss on my forehead brushing my skin like a spider's web, can still make me shiver.

I get up off the bed to escape the images, go back down to the living room and switch on the Christmas tree lights. The place is instantly more welcoming, although my coffee is already cold. I start to make myself another but think better of it. There is a bottle of sherry by the cake tin. I slosh some into a mug and help myself to an outrageous slab of the homemade Christmas log while I'm at it.

I bring my makeshift supper back to the sofa. As I take a bite of the cake, I notice there's a small package with my name on it laid next to a pile of neatly wrapped presents under the tree.

A gift for me? Here? It doesn't make sense. Did she expect my brother to send it on to me? Why would she think I might visit?

A wave of nausea hits me. The accident – could it have been something else?

Instead of falling into the path of the lorry – fainting due to the chemo, as we'd assumed – knowing what lay ahead of her with the progression of the disease, was it a deliberate act? Would she have risked her eternal soul for a swift end?

No. Of course not. She had a passport. She was coming to see me in a few months. Or at least she'd hoped to. But then, people's motives are messy. They are not neatly tied up with a shiny bow like a present.

My hands tremble as I open the wallet-shaped parcel, the festive paper mocking me.

Inside is a small pile of photos held together with an elastic band.

The first Polaroid makes no sense – a good-looking young man I've never seen before. Shirtless.

Bizarre. No idea who he is.

I turn over the next. My father! He sits with his arm draped around the same man's shoulders, both of them beaming at the camera. They seem to be in some bar I can't identify.

Another – the same night, I assume; a close-up of the man kissing my father's neck, a look of rapture on my dad's face, his head thrown back. I have never seen him look so happy.

It takes a moment to process.

I only have four photos of my father. In one, he's holding me aloft like a prize marrow – a chunky toddler, face scrunched up with giggles. Another is of him as a child himself – goofy grin, skinny legs, the Statue of Liberty in the background. The other two show him posing rigid and formal in a suit on his wedding day. In both of these my mother gazes at him with adoration. She leans her head towards his to minimise how she towers above him, even though she only wore a tiny heel. The early days of their romance – a fairy tale, a myth.

It was not a happy marriage. But she soon got pregnant with my brother, and she stayed, because that was what you did in those days. Perhaps they had fun for a time, although it is hard for any child to see their parents as sexual beings. Perhaps she'd fallen pregnant with me during a making-up session between the absences?

My own wedding pictures are not posed like those of my parents' generation. They are casual, joyful.

I met Jack after I went to America to work in a summer camp for a season: a ludicrous scheme whereby foreign teenagers, supercharged with hormones – many, like me, giddy with being away from home for the very first time – are put in charge of vulnerable youngsters, teaching them life-threatening pursuits such as archery and canoeing. My swimming medals and performances as part of the school's drama club stood me in good stead when it came to getting that job. I also had a slew of testimonials from the families around here – those I worked for as a babysitter. So many extracurricular activities, anyone would think I didn't want to come home.

Jack's girls adored me. Twins. I taught them to swim at that camp. They loved my accent and my hair, and when they went home they pestered their daddy to invite me to their birthday party. I turned up with books and sweeties and basically never left. We married within six months. Anyone might think he wanted a replacement mother for his little ones; that I was searching for a father figure.

But it works. My husband is kind and generous and he loves me. It is more than I was brought up to hope for. I have a ready-made family and a ready-made home. Why would I ever want to return to this?

The last photo in the mystery package is even weirder – a shot of the rockery in the back garden.

I've finished my sherry before I look closer and see there is a small mark on it – an X seems to have been scratched on one of the larger boulders, like you'd mark the spot of buried treasure.

I unlock the conservatory door and walk outside. The security light flashes on like an accusation and I panic about disturbing the neighbours this late at night. Then I remember my mother is dead and I don't have to worry about her displeasure any longer.

It is disgustingly cold in that damp English way that penetrates your soul.

I look down at the Polaroid of the rockery and back at the actual garden feature in front of me. It makes no sense.

I hurry back inside, feeling slightly sick.

I shuffle through the pictures again, looking for clues. It is only when I turn them over that I see there is a partial date on the back of the rockery photo.

I've poured myself another mug of sherry before I think, *Not a date, no*. A Bible reference.

She keeps – kept – her Bible in the top drawer of her bedside cabinet, as if she was staying in a motel. I brace myself for a long hunt, but there is a bookmark placed in at the actual page, Ezekiel 6:11, *Smite with thine hand and stamp with thy foot and say Alas for all the evil abominations…*

In tiny writing she has neatly printed the word *Sorry* in the margin.

The revelation takes my legs from under me, and I sit heavily on the mattress.

But—

She could not—

I have no idea how exactly, but I *know*. I know in my bones what lies beneath the boulders of the rockery.

Did I not notice the gardening project at the time? I was probably too involved in my own misery.

For the rest of the night, I sip the sherry and determine what to do next.

⌐

I am outside in the garden by the time my brother arrives early in the morning. It is already light – a dishwater grey which characterises Christmas holidays here in the North. The small fire I have made in the old barbecue grill is the only jolly thing.

We exchange greetings. We do not hug.

"I thought I'd get rid of some of the stuff we didn't need," I tell him by way of explanation.

He nods. We stand looking at the flames, not speaking. He is not a curious person, my brother.

The Polaroid of the rockery was the first thing I burned.

I have kept the picture of my father and the man I believe was his lover, hiding it in my luggage. Knowing he had some happiness in his life before it was over is a form of consolation. I have left out the wedding pictures and the one of me and my dad to show my brother.

I crumple a few more old bank statements from years gone by and throw them on the fire. My brother doesn't even look.

I say, "I've not got anything for the kids. I should have grabbed something at the airport."

"No worries," he replies. "They prefer cash anyway."

Eventually I ask, "What will you do with the house?"

"Sell up, I suppose." He rubs his hands over the flames as if toasting them.

"I wondered about renting it out," I suggest. "A regular income. Better for tax."

"Good idea."

An excellent idea if we want the garden undisturbed. I wonder if that is what she really wanted. Or did part of her hope it would all come out?

Whatever, it seems I am to be her judge and executioner.

I take brief furtive glances at my brother. His face looks like a benign potato. It is peaceful, untroubled. She would never have told him. And there's no way he was involved.

This knowledge is her final, bitter gift. She trusted me with it.

At least that's the conclusion I've come to, after raking it over for hours, wondering why she chose to reveal her secrets. Why so cryptic? Was it spite? Was it an apology? And why me?

Because I am my mother's daughter.

In the end, what does it really matter? I will never know for sure. There are no neat endings.

My gift to her will be my silence.

My brother mumbles, "It'll be a lowkey Christmas anyway, this year, because…" He might be talking to himself.

"Yes."

"Let's go in, I'm perished. Coffee?" he suggests.

"Let's go out for one," I reply.

"Nothing open at this time round here."

"Oh. Can we go back to yours?"

"Okay."

He stacks my case in the back of his car as I shut the conservatory door on the fading embers.

THE RED ANGEL

Russ Thomas

T HE ARGUMENT had been simmering gently for thirty miles now, but its origins were rooted in a distance much further away than that.

Gary stared out of the window at the snow-covered landscape whizzing past them. Sarah was driving too fast, and every turn was accompanied by a savage jolt of the steering wheel that effectively conveyed her continued anger. He refused to give Sarah the satisfaction of telling her to take it easy, though.

It had started back in June, when she'd first suggested they spend Christmas with her parents. They'd been coming back from a friend's birthday on that occasion, and Sarah had been driving because he was a bit tipsy.

"Do you think it's a good idea?" he'd asked, after what had seemed to him a long enough period of reflection that she would think he'd given the matter suitable consideration. "I mean, for the first time? At Christmas?"

"There's plenty of time between now and then for us to set something else up," was Sarah's predictable response, and he'd been annoyed with himself that he hadn't predicted it.

That was the opening salvo in a war that had stretched out for six months now.

Sarah drove on in silence through the snowstorm, windscreen wipers squeaking urgently back and forth in their own battle with the elements. The furious sound only punctuated the horrible silence that had swollen up between them.

Gary knew, deep down, this was his fault. He thought she had marriage on her mind. Something to do with turning thirty soon, he imagined, and wanting to have kids before it was too late. And it wasn't that he was wholly against the idea, any more than he didn't want to meet her parents. Not exactly. But it was true that every time she attempted to engineer an opportunity he found another way to thwart her, pleading work commitments or organising a paintball trip with the lads for someone's birthday. He'd deliberately arranged one visit to coincide with the weekend he knew Jess was going to invite Sarah on her hen do. "That's a shame, love, but it *is* their wedding. We can go to your parents' any time."

It was just that meeting the parents was such a big step, and in previous relationships it had always pre-empted the death of the romance. Gary didn't impress in-laws. They saw through him in some way. Mothers were revolted by his attempts to charm them, and fathers treated him as though he were some kind of weirdo sex pest, determined to steal their daughters away. Once the parents disapproved, it wasn't long before the spark in the girlfriend's eyes died as well.

Maybe he was overthinking it, but he thought he knew the exact moment when this happened.

"What do you do for work, Gary?" the prospective father-in-law would ask.

"Well, Jeff, I trained in broadcast journalism, but at the moment I direct and produce a rather interesting true crime podcast called *Dead Not Buried*. You might have heard of it."

"No, Gary, I'm not sure I have. There's money in that, is there?"

"Not as much as you'd think, Jeff." Cue high-pitched laugh, attempt at a charming wink and before he knew it, it was all over.

Things felt different with Sarah. They'd met when she'd joined an online discussion forum he'd been hosting after an episode aired, and offered up some pretty insightful comments about that week's specialist subject. The conversation had ultimately ended with just the two of them chatting with each other and Gary had struck up the courage to ask if Sarah would like to meet IRL. She'd agreed. They'd moved in together six months later.

Granted, no one wanted a boyfriend for their daughter who was obsessed with serial killers, but surely they couldn't complain when it was the very thing that had brought them together?

Still, he wanted to make sure he'd sealed the deal with Sarah before he gave anyone else a chance to ruin it. How was that a bad thing?

Another sharp turn and a screech of brakes. Gary grabbed the door handle to steady himself, but steadfastly refused to tell her to slow down. He glanced across, though, and saw red in her cheeks. Her foot eased off the accelerator slightly.

It wasn't as though Sarah had behaved impeccably either. "If you won't spend Christmas with my parents," she'd announced a week ago, "I don't see why I should have to spend it with yours."

His parents loved Christmas. He'd told his mother it was work but he didn't think she believed him. The compromise had been this truncated Christmas Eve visit. But throughout it, his father had been cold with them and his mother's face as they'd driven away had broken his heart. She looked as though she fully expected never to see him again.

Now, here they were battling their way through a blizzard to get home for no specific reason. Sarah was sulking and he wasn't exactly full of festive spirit himself. He didn't see what they could salvage of Christmas now.

Another tight bend and another jolt. It was as though she was using this drive as his punishment. He could have pointed out to her that he'd done an advanced driving course and she ought to listen to him when he gave advice. But he didn't. Instead, he made a point of turning away and not even watching the road ahead.

That's why he didn't see the fox that made her swerve. Neither did he notice the car had left the road until the airbag exploded in his face.

"Well?" Gary shouted. He had his hands rammed in his jacket pockets and was stamping his feet in a vain attempt to keep them warm. Snow was piling up around the car at an alarming rate.

"I think some water must have got in the air filter or something," she shouted up from the vehicle. Her words were distant over the noise of the wind whipping past his ears.

"Surely they design these things to stop that happening?"

Sarah squinted at him through the driving blizzard and shook her head as though to highlight his ignorance. It was a constant annoyance to him that, despite his advanced driving course, she knew more about cars than he did. She'd grown up on a farm, apparently; to hear her talk, her father had had her rewiring tractors at the age of five.

He pulled out his mobile and tried turning it on again, as though it might have magically found some charge from somewhere. He could have sworn he'd switched on the power when he'd plugged it in last night, but the fact that he hadn't prevented him from firing the same allegation at Sarah.

He began another round of accusations. "You were driving way too fast for these conditions!" But they'd been over this several times already, and were now firmly entrenched in their positions with her final, repeated justification being, "What was I supposed to do, just hit the bloody thing?"

Never mind, there would be time to apportion blame later and – Gary found himself cheering up at the thought – he'd be able to hold it over her for a good while. In the meantime, they were in this together and they needed to find a way out.

He rubbed at his aching nose to cover his irritation and her head disappeared again. He reckoned he was probably in for a black eye tomorrow. Maybe two. That would be a glorious first present for Christmas morning. Still, it was a minor miracle neither of them had been hurt worse. The car defences had done their job and they'd got away with only minor cuts and bruises. Unless the cold was numbing their senses to something worse.

"It's no good," Sarah said, disengaging the prop and letting the bonnet fall back into place with a click. "Even if I could fix it, we'd never dig it out now."

He wanted to argue but she was right. They'd ploughed off the road into a three-foot ditch that might have done them a lot more damage had it not already been filled with snow, and the back wheels had nothing to grip. They'd probably need a tow truck to lever them back onto the road even under normal conditions.

"What the hell are we going to do, then?" he asked as she clambered up the bank to join him. Despite his anger, he reached down to help pull her up, and didn't that only go to show he was the bigger man? "We can't just sit here and wait for someone to come past." They hadn't seen a single car in the half hour they'd been stuck there, and given the late hour, the conditions, and the day of the year, they might not see one until Boxing Day.

"You were the one who insisted we come this way."

This was too much, even for him. "*I* was the one who said we should use the motorway," he told her. "*You* were the one desperate to get home for no explicable reason." They could be drinking eggnog in front of the Christmas tree now and unwrapping one of the smaller presents. Mum always got him something Man U related for Christmas Eve – a pair of socks, some cufflinks. The thought made him sad all over again, and the fact their presents were in a bag just a few feet away didn't console him any.

Sarah sighed. "Oh, for pity's sake, can we not do this now?" It was such a grown-up, sensible thing to say he found he'd run out of arguments.

"Look, let's at least put some more gear on," he told her, trying to be equally as sensible, and she nodded at this.

They didn't have much in the way of heavy winter clothing – the storm had taken the whole country by surprise – but they did have a couple of thick woollen jumpers with them, because his dad often refused to put the heating on unless it dropped well below zero. They dug these out now and did their best to wriggle inside without getting blasted by the wind.

When they'd finished, she wrapped her arms around him and burrowed her face into his chest. It wasn't an unpleasant sensation, and something more than the snow covering their jumpers melted; it was hard to stay frosty with someone when you were pressed up against them.

"There must be a house," she whispered. "You were right. We can't stay here."

He resisted the urge to gloat, but his answer came out whinier than he meant. "We haven't passed anything for miles."

He felt her stiffen but all she said again was, "We can't stay here," and he could hardly argue with his own words thrown back at him.

He glanced at the car and said, "What about the presents?"

She pushed away from him and even through the dark and the weather he could tell she was rolling her eyes.

"Fine," he said. "Onward, then." He smiled to show they were on the same side now. "Walking will help keep us warm and at least we'll feel like we're making progress."

They trudged through the bitter wind and driving snow. Gary's hands were frozen solid, even tucked as they were under his armpits. Sarah seemed to be doing a bit better and it wasn't long before she was a fair distance ahead of him. He wanted to shout out to her to slow down but resisted the urge. It wasn't his fault she was less bulky than him; *of course* she found the going easier. As the snow settled deeper and each footstep grew harder, their chances of a car passing seemed to diminish, but there was bound to be a farm track or something sooner or later, wasn't there?

Gary's trainers were soaked and he'd lost the feeling in his toes. They were only a few miles from civilisation but were entirely at the mercy of the elements. This was potentially much more than just a ruined Christmas they were now facing. It could be their last. Was it even Christmas yet? He refused to unclamp his arms and look at his watch. What did it matter? He could feel the panic bubbling up inside him. It wouldn't help to lose his cool but… he just couldn't see a way out. He realised Sarah had disappeared into the distance ahead. A jolt of fear radiated up from his stomach and for a moment Gary thought he might be sick.

"Sarah!" he shouted. "Sarah!" Again and again he called out and, finally, a shape coalesced into a figure and then into Sarah, hurrying back towards him.

"Come on," she yelled over the noise of the wind. "There's a house!" She turned again and started running, but this time he wasn't going to lose her and caught up quick enough to see Sarah turn off the road down a track.

"Wait!"

"Come on, slow poke! Salvation is at hand." Her tone was light and breezy and he felt foolish for panicking. Of course there was a house, although he couldn't see any lights on. It was Christmas though, they had to be in. And whoever lived there would hardly turn them away in this weather. They'd be forced to make awkward small talk with some farmer for a couple of hours while they waited for the AA but… well, recovery vehicles were used to these sorts of conditions, right? They'd have special wheels or treads or something. It was late, and it was Christmas, but someone would come to their rescue. Wouldn't they?

The house was big and sprawling, and Gary could make out

the shadows of a number of outbuildings behind as well. A typical farmhouse for this area and, if it was in a bit of a state of disrepair, then weren't all farmhouses? It was probably quite beautiful and cosy on the inside. A smoking chimney above promised at least some warmth. There was something familiar about the place but then, there were hundreds of places like it in this part of the country. He'd probably seen the house a dozen times on his way to Mum and Dad's.

Sarah, ahead of him again, perhaps spurred on by the promise of heat and dryness, was already hammering on the door with an elaborate black knocker. It was a grand entrance with a gabled roof above the front door. He wished he'd had a chance to talk to her first, to work out exactly what they were going to say. Why did that seem important? It wasn't as if they had to come up with a story, they hadn't done anything wrong. But for some reason, all the fear and dread that had built up inside him on the hike here refused to evaporate at the promise of shelter.

It took a while, and several more knocks, but finally some small light bloomed in whatever room lay behind the door as, presumably, another, internal, door was opened. It was the first proper sign of life and Gary saw Sarah's shoulders relax a little. His own anxiety stubbornly refused to lift.

The front door still didn't open.

"Who is it?" came a tremulous voice from the other side and Gary realised that whoever was behind there was probably just as anxious as they were. Perhaps more so. No one appreciated a knock on the door at eleven o'clock at night.

"Hi," Sarah said, her voice lighter than normal. "We've had an accident. Our car's stuck. Could we… could we possibly use your phone or…?" She trailed off and he wondered what she had been planning on saying next.

There was a short hesitation and then the sound of various chains and locks being disengaged, and finally the door peeled open. The woman in front of them was short and fat, lit unflatteringly by the candle she carried in her hand. Dumpy was the word that sprang to mind. She was wearing pyjamas with a fluffy pink robe over the top that she clutched to her ample bosom against the cold night air. She had long, greasy hair held back by a band that was covered in plastic holly and berries. The ornament was cheap and nasty and wouldn't have looked out of place on a work's Christmas do, but here, on this dishevelled, pyjamaed woman it looked a tiny bit sad.

"Oh my goodness!" she exclaimed, and there really was no other word to describe how she said it. She exclaimed. "Oh my! Golly gosh! Look at you poor things!" Perhaps she only *ever* exclaimed. "Come in, come in!" She gestured for them to come inside and Sarah almost leapt across the doorstep into the house.

Gary was a bit slower, that strange anxious reticence still battling his subconscious. But in the end, what choice did they have? He glanced back once at the snow already obscuring their footprints to the house and stepped into the relative warmth.

"I'm Joni," she told them, and Gary felt he could almost hear an exclamation mark in that as well. "Come on in! Let's get you warmed up." She fussed over them in the hallway, encouraging them to take off their outer layers and shoes. "Let me grab you some towels. I'm sorry about all the candles. The electric went out hours ago."

No chance of charging their phones, then.

Whatever else she was or wasn't, Joni was incredibly efficient, and no more than ten minutes later they were sitting in front of the fire on two old-fashioned kitchen chairs padded with cushions, wrapped in blankets, towels piled on their heads and feet, and clutching warm mugs of cocoa in their hands.

"Now," Joni said, settling herself in an armchair she clearly hadn't long since left, and tucking her legs up under herself like a schoolgirl, "tell me everything! What on earth has happened to bring you here? Tonight, of all nights!" She sipped from her own mug.

Gary let Sarah explain their predicament while he examined the room. It was a fairly traditional-looking farmhouse kitchen, although it had been modernised a fair bit, and tastefully too, with matching kitchen cabinets and a huge oak table and chairs that were clearly old but had been restored or upcycled or whatever they called it these days. The windows were modern and double-glazed but still original in design; the tiled floor looked original and one or two of the terracotta tiles had cracks cutting across them.

In one corner there was the most enormous Christmas tree Gary had ever seen. It was real, too – he could smell the fresh scent of pine even over the smell of the logs crackling in the fire. The odd thing, though, was how it had been decorated – or 'hadn't been' might be more precise. There was only a single ornament on the whole thing – a dusty pink angel that sat on the topmost branch, bending it over with its weight. Again, he was struck by that peculiar sense of déjà vu. There was something nagging at him about all of this, but he couldn't pin it down.

"It's a bit sparse, isn't it?" Gary said, and didn't realise he'd spoken aloud until he looked up to see both of them staring at him. He felt himself blush as though he'd been caught doing something wrong. "No, it's… it's a very beautiful tree," he finished.

Joni smiled at him. It was an ugly smile and didn't do her any favours. He wasn't sure he'd ever seen a smile un-improve someone before. With her old-fashioned name and way of talking he'd taken her for middle-aged but now, even in the flickering firelight, he could see she was probably younger than that.

"There's a fella farms 'em on the other side of the valley. I shouldn't have bothered really, it being just me since I lost my folks… But you still have to make an effort at Christmas, don't you?"

He nodded, but glanced at the tree again. She hadn't made any effort. Or not much of one, anyway. Gary realised Sarah was frowning at him and he did his best to smile and reassure the woman her efforts had borne fruit.

"Lovely," he said.

Joni chuckled and the sound made the hair stand up on Gary's neck. "I found the stuff in the attic—" She gestured to a dust-shrouded cardboard box that had been unceremoniously shoved behind a chair next to the tree. "—but when it came down to it… Ah, it all seemed a bit of a waste of time once I realised it was just for me."

"Joni's on her own here," Sarah told him, and he realised he'd missed an important part of the conversation. "She's going to let us stay the night."

"What?" He couldn't help it, the word just came out before he could stop it. He saw the frown deepen on Sarah's brow. "We can't put you out like that. I mean, we just need to call someone and—"

"The lines are down," Joni said.

"Weren't you listening?" Sarah chastised.

He was given a quick recap – the telephone lines were down, and Joni's mobile was also out of juice. "It's a bit of a brick," she told them. "Doesn't last long. I tend to charge it at night but…"

She waved her hands at the candles as though to illustrate the predicament. "I couldn't even check to see if there'd been an email about the booking." It turned out Joni was well-equipped for guests, having recently converted a part of the farmhouse into an Airbnb. "Needed a fresh start," she told them, although without stating from what. In fact, she'd been expecting a young couple to arrive a few hours ago but they hadn't turned up. "No doubt for the same reason you two aren't where you're supposed to be," she said, and that grin did whatever the opposite of 'lighting up a face' was. "Still, everything's all prepared, so their loss is your gain!"

Gary looked at Sarah and she seemed almost happy. He tried to convey his thoughts with his eyes and perhaps, if they'd been dating longer, he might have succeeded, but as it was, she took his expression as acceptance.

"Lucky, eh?" she said. "Someone's looking after us. Santa, maybe? Or our guardian angel."

"That's me!" Joni announced, clapping her hands together and making Gary jump. He bit off a cry as he slopped hot cocoa over his wrist.

"I'm your Christmas Angel!" she told them, beaming with that lopsided face. There was something chilling about the statement, not to mention the childish way it was delivered and, again, Gary was struck by a strange sense of familiarity.

The words hung in his head for the rest of the evening which was, at least, blissfully short. As soon as they were warm and dry enough, Joni led them through the hallway, each of them carrying a tall candlestick with one hand cupped to protect the flame. She kept a good stash of candles, Joni explained as they went, power cuts not being unusual in this part of the country. She escorted them to a surprisingly well-appointed annexe, with a small sitting room and a double bedroom with an ensuite bathroom. There were towels laid out on the bed for them, along with two pairs of Christmas-themed long johns, both ridiculously oversized but one clearly tailored for a man and the other for a woman.

"I thought it would be a cute touch." Joni was wandering the room now, lighting more candles from her own. "Even when the heating's on, it gets very cold on this side of the house. I had to guess their sizes, of course."

Sarah bobbed her head out from the bathroom. There was a faint orange light coming from behind her where she must have left her own candlestick. Gary still held his, like a talisman.

"Look," she said, holding up two wrapped toothbrushes in one hand.

He nodded unenthusiastically while privately thinking that he might just skip cleaning his teeth for one night.

"Everything you could possibly need," Joni confirmed as Sarah disappeared back into the bathroom. There was a grubby sprig of mistletoe tacked to the headboard and Joni tickled it with her forefinger and winked, theatrically. "Honestly, I've thought of everything. You won't even have to leave this apartment."

That sounded a little too close to an instruction for Gary's liking.

"Until breakfast, of course."

"There's really no need to go to any trouble," Gary told her.

"Nonsense. No trouble at all. I've already got everything in. And we can't have you heading off on an empty stomach." She eyed the dark window and the thick flakes of snow that were still falling beyond it. "Mind you, you might be here for a lot longer if this carries on." Again, the smile cracked across her face. "Looks like I won't be having Christmas on my own after all! 'Night, then. Sleep well." She walked through the doorway but turned back with one hand on the doorknob. "May you be in Heaven a full half hour before the Devil knows you're dead!" she said.

The door closed in front of him with an audible click.

"What the hell do you think she meant by that?"

They'd hung their remaining layers on the radiator, despite the fact it was giving out no heat, and Sarah had changed eagerly into her long johns. Gary had refused at first, but after standing there shivering for ten minutes in nothing but his underpants, finally relented. He hadn't yet braved getting into bed, though, and was standing with his arms wrapped around his body protectively, watching the snow piling up outside the window.

Sarah was snuggled warmly under the covers. "Wha'd'ya mean?" she asked, her words already thick with sleep.

"That crack about the Devil?"

"I's jus' a phrase."

"But who says that?"

"'s Irish, I think."

"It's… weird, is what I think."

Sarah grunted in a manner that suggested she was done thinking for the day.

"All of this." He plucked at the baggy chest of his long johns. "And that tree with the creepy angel!"

"A pink angel," Sarah whispered.

"What?"

"I said, 'a *pink* angel'. It looked a bit tacky, I thought." The sleep had left Sarah's voice now and a good dollop of annoyance had taken its place. But that wasn't what had sent Gary's heartbeat into overdrive.

Suddenly, he realised why all of this reminded him of something. "Not a pink angel, The *Red* Angel." He stepped over to the bed and shook Sarah's shoulder. "We've got to get out of here."

She groaned but he ignored her and continued shaking. "Come on, get up! Get dressed."

Sarah pulled herself upright and then dragged the bedding up around her neck to protect herself from the cold. "You've got to be kidding me."

"It's her! It has to be."

"Who?"

"This is… I know where we are. It's the right neck of the woods, but I hadn't thought about it until…" He was trembling now, and it wasn't just the cold.

"Gary. Calm down. What are you talking about?"

"The Red Angel. I'm telling you it's her!"

Sarah shook her head, but at least she was listening now. "The what?"

"Liz—" He checked himself and lowered his voice – who knew how well sound might carry in this place? Or who might be listening at the door. "Lizzie Gordon!" he said quietly, and clutched his arms around himself again.

Sarah was still shaking her head, but Gary could see he'd reached her now. She was beginning to take him seriously.

The Red Angel. A couple of years or so ago he'd done a podcast on child killers. They'd even chatted about it briefly that first time they'd met. Lizzie Gordon was about eight or nine years old – reports varied – and she'd lived with her parents in a farmhouse in the countryside. One Christmas morning, a neighbour had called round and found Lizzie standing over the bodies of her parents, clutching a kitchen knife. She was surrounded by unwrapped presents, her white nightdress stained red with her parents' blood. She refused to talk about why she had killed them except to say that the Red Angel made her do it. Commentators had argued for twenty years or more about this, but the general consensus was that she was referring to the Christmas ornament on top of the family tree.

"But…" Sarah said now, "it can't be! Joni's older than that, isn't she?"

"She's younger than she looks. With all that weight on her, and the way she talks, it's hard to tell." Gary tiptoed across and put his ear to the door. He couldn't hear anyone on the other side but he couldn't shake the feeling she was right there, perhaps about to thrust a kitchen knife through the wood. He pulled his head back, sharply.

"But…" Sarah, too, lowered her voice. "She'd still be held somewhere. Wouldn't she?"

Gary shook his head and moved back round the bed to join her. "I–I think she was released. Given a new identity." Many of the details hadn't been released to the press at the time, given the age of the perpetrator, and he'd struggled to find much more information when he'd put together the podcast.

"But Joni… She seems so… nice. I can't believe she'd…" Sarah trailed off.

"What? Move back to her family home, set up a B&B, and lure new victims to her murder house?"

"Don't be daft!" She waved a hand in front of his face as though to physically bat away his theory. "What are the chances we'd break down here? Right outside? This can't be the same place."

"It is, though, I'm *telling* you. There was something familiar about it the minute I saw it, but I couldn't put my finger on what." He thought he could recall seeing a picture of the house once, with that gable window, and those shadowy outbuildings behind. "My God! It's probably the same angel."

"It was pink, not red."

"Well… it might have faded over time."

He saw that he'd overplayed his hand.

She grinned at him. "I don't buy it. You're just upset at missing your family Christmas and you're trying to wind me up."

"I'm not, Sarah. Really! I'm serious."

"Sure," she said, and shuffled back down under the covers, turning her back on him.

"You're not going to sleep?"

"What else am I supposed to do?" She sat back up with a sigh. "Assuming you're right – and I'm still not convinced at all – we can't go anywhere. We'd freeze to death before we got half a mile up the road."

"Better that than getting carved up in our sleep."

Sarah screwed her face up in disgust. "This is getting beyond a joke now."

"I'm *not* joking. We need to investigate. See what we can find in the house."

"You can't go searching the poor woman's house after she's gone out of her way to make us welcome. What's the matter with you?"

"Oh, I don't know. Call it, survival instinct? You can put your head down if you think you might sleep, but I won't be able to until I know for sure where she is and what she's up to." He hesitated and then put his ear to the door again. Still no sound.

When he looked back at her, Sarah was chuckling to herself, but there wasn't a lot of humour in it. "You know, I used to think this was endearing. This weird obsession of yours. Oh, I know it's how we met but, I'll be honest, Gary, I was never as into all this as you. Who could be? Now, though…" She blinked at him for a moment or two. "Now it just looks a bit sad." She sighed heavily before turning over onto her side again, ready for sleep.

"Sarah—"

"I don't want to talk about it anymore."

"But—"

"Goodnight, Gary. Blow the candles out on your way, would you?"

Gary crept through the darkness of the house, clutching his candlestick in his right hand. If he ran into Joni he had an excuse ready about needing a glass of milk, but he didn't want to meet her without some way to defend himself. Under the circumstances, the candlestick made the perfect weapon in disguise.

He couldn't believe Sarah was being like this. That last comment about her not being into the podcast was pretty hurtful. Of course she wasn't, it wasn't her baby! But still, she'd always been supportive. Why did she have to say that now?

He found himself back in the kitchen where the last embers of the fire were dying down in the grate. The flickering orange glow gave a strange hue to the room and Gary found his eyes drawn back to the macabre angel tree-topper. *Was* it the same one? It could have lost its colour over the years but it was hard to tell in this light. Joni had said she'd *found* the ornaments in the attic. Maybe she was just an innocent who'd bought the house and didn't realise its twisted history. Maybe Sarah had a point and he was letting his imagination run away with him, but how could he take the chance?

He moved on through the house; the icy chill of the tiled floor travelled up through his bare feet and legs, and lodged somewhere deep in his spine.

Most of the rooms downstairs were pretty much bare of furniture. That was strange, but Joni had implied she hadn't been here all that long; the guest suite was the first thing she'd set up in order to make some money to afford the rest of the renovations. That made sense. Perhaps Sarah was right and this was all in his head. *Was* he obsessed?

He opened a door onto a small room off the back hallway and found a desk with an old-fashioned PC, littered with correspondence and paperwork. He hesitated now. He wasn't so far gone he didn't realise what he was about to do was a flagrant abuse of hospitality. If Joni was who she said she was there was no excusing it. But if she wasn't…? Could he take that chance?

He searched carefully, trying not to disturb things too much. It was difficult though, especially by candlelight. He was on the verge of giving up when he found it, an outpatient discharge letter from a well-known psychiatric hospital down south. It was dated just over a year ago and detailed various medications the patient should be taking. The patient's name was Joni Fairweather.

Gary's hand shook as he read the letter. This was it. Proof. Joni Fairweather was Lizzie Gordon's new identity. The name even sounded a bit made up. And she was the right age, or near enough. He folded the letter and slipped it inside the buttoned chest of his long johns. He had to show this to Sarah but not until he knew for sure where Joni – where *Lizzie* – was.

Somewhat predictably, the stairs to the second floor creaked loudly. Gary did his best to stay to one side and not move too quickly. He inched up the stairs like he was in a *Scooby-Doo* cartoon and was surprised to find himself smiling. Despite everything, he was enjoying himself. What the hell was wrong with him?

He felt braver now though, vindicated by the letter, less ashamed of the actions he was taking. If he was caught, he'd just confront her. After all, she was a short, fat woman who he could easily handle in a one-to-one situation, especially with the candlestick for backup. So he began opening rooms and glancing inside. Again, he mostly found them empty but occasionally they warranted a slightly longer search. He wasn't sure what else he was looking for, but he wanted to make sure there weren't any surprises lurking anywhere. Finally, he came to Joni's room. He knew it was hers because he could hear her snoring loudly through the door. He put his hand on the doorknob and turned.

She was lying on her back in a single bed, her belly poking up in a big mound, rising and falling in rhythm with her breathing. He had to admit, seen like this, she didn't look like a serial killer. He moved into the room, the pale yellow light of the candle stretching out to illuminate the dark corners. This space, too, was devoid of furniture. There was only the single bed, dwarfed even further by the size of the room, and a small, battered chest of drawers covered with discarded clothing. He felt a swell of pity for the woman but snuffed it out when he remembered what she'd done. The candlestick trembled in his hand and he wondered if he could do what she did? Take a life. If it was necessary, of course he could. But *was* it necessary?

She couldn't have engineered the snowstorm or made the fox run out in front of them. Was she even responsible for what she'd done when she was nine years old? The law obviously didn't think so. She'd served her time and was no longer a danger to society. Who was he to say differently?

He backed his way towards the exit and walked straight into the door that had silently closed behind him. He grunted and then froze, watching Joni's sleeping form to see if he'd disturbed her, but the mound continued to snore. The door must have swung shut on its own. It happened in these old houses. He rubbed the small of his back where something had dug into him and bent down, to see it was a large, black key. This then, was his answer. He slipped it from the lock, opened the door and stepped back out into the hallway. Then he closed the door again, slotted the key back in the lock, and turned it.

He paused for a moment to make sure he could still hear the snoring and then, satisfied, backtracked along the corridor. He'd barricade their own door with something when he got back and, though he doubted he'd sleep any more soundly, at least he'd feel confident enough they'd make it to morning. There were worse things than missing a night's sleep.

He moved down the stairs a little more confidently than he'd gone up and was about to head back to the annexe when he noticed the firelight coming from the kitchen was brighter than it had been before. He couldn't help himself and glided across the hallway towards the light.

The first thing he saw was the fire, stoked high again now and giving out a bright yellow and orange glow. There were candles grouped in clusters around the room, sending shadows up across the high wooden-beamed ceiling, and together, they gave the place the feel of a religious temple.

The second thing he noticed was her. She was standing with her back to him, tying something to the Christmas tree. It was fully decorated now, baubles and shaped ornaments, silvery lametta tinsel draped across every branch in representation of the snow still falling outside. The cardboard box of decorations had been pulled forward and now lay open at her bare feet, and even from this distance, Gary could see it was almost empty.

"Sarah?" He moved towards her. "What the hell are you doing?"

She glanced back at him but carried on with her ritual. "I thought I'd finish the tree. She was getting lonely up there all on her own."

Gary reached out his arm but stopped short of touching her. "What? Who?"

"The Red Angel."

He shivered. "That's not funny. I know you think this is all some kind of prank but I've got evidence." Gary reached into his long johns and pulled out the letter. "See?" He held it out for her.

Sarah perused it in the dim light without taking it from him, a frown etched across her forehead. "Poor woman," she said. "They can be awful, those places." Then she turned back to the tree. "Especially the secure units."

"Don't worry, I've locked her in her room so we're safe enough for now."

Sarah chuckled. "Oh, Gary, she really isn't any threat, you know. A bit odd, yes, but I'm sure she's just lonely. I got a sense of that from her email when she confirmed the booking."

"What booking?"

"Like I said earlier, what are the chances we'd break down right outside?"

Gary couldn't make sense of this, but there was a rising anxiety deep inside him. His voice when he spoke came out cracked and barely recognisable, "Sa-rah?"

"You said such lovely things about them on your podcast and I knew I had to introduce you. But you were so damn stubborn, and it wasn't like I was asking for anything big. The Red Angel helped me, bringing the snow, but even if she hadn't, there would have been a fox one way or another." She bent down to pick something up from the floor under the tree. He thought he saw a glint of orange light from whatever it was. Sarah stood up and turned.

"It looks like you'll be spending Christmas with my parents after all," she said.

O MURDER NIGHT

J. T. Ellison

1.

Western Coast of Ireland
1930

When Yeats O'Malley was thirty-seven years old, he bought a
crumbling old manor house by a small inlet of the Carrowbeg River
on the western coast of Ireland. It was a crowning glory moment
for him, an achievement he'd spent a decade working toward. The
house had a long and storied but unverifiable history, as parts of the
foundation's stone walls and the dungeon, including the terrifying
oubliette, dated back to the sixteenth century and the pirate days of
the queen of the seas, Granuaile – Grace O'Malley. It was supposedly
built on the site where her castle was originally situated. The woman
who would not bow to the queen of England.

He shared the pirate's surname, though he wasn't related to her bloodline. It mattered not; what he shared with Granuaile was the mythical call of *more*… that something waited for him, something bigger than himself. The house was only the beginning.

They called it Edge House, because it sat on the edge of the inlet, perched above the water so close that a spring king tide would make the river rise high enough to kiss the first-floor windows.

Its most recent owner before Yeats was a famed mystery writer with one hundred books to her name who, rather inconveniently, had gone missing on Christmas Eve eleven years earlier, never to be seen again. There were rumors, of course, that she faked her own death because the pressure of her illustrious career was getting to her, or that her lover was a cheat and a liar and killed her outright, or that she'd drowned in the river that swept the shores of the manor's gardens after a late-night ramble.

Yeats didn't particularly care about the truth of her disappearance, only that the manor was at last available, and in disrepair, which hurt his soul. It needed millions to renovate: the roof was gone in certain spots; the walls were turning black with mold. He had just enough cash to buy the place and strip the walls back to the original stone before his accounts ran dry.

So he held a party. A Christmas Eve fundraiser. He invited everyone he knew, and the local press, and charged a thousand punt a head.

Fifteen people came.

The great ballroom was decked out and empty. He had a month's worth of food he was forced to donate to the tent people camped on the manor's grounds, those starving wastrels he hated to look upon, he with the largesse they had not, and egg on his very handsome face.

Insult to injury, fifteen thousand was only enough to patch one corner of the roof.

He knew if he could make the manor a destination, he could raise the remaining five million to renovate the old gal properly. So two weeks and seven bottles of fine Irish whiskey later, Yeats got creative. People might not be willing to give him money to renovate *his* dream home, but they would certainly come to see where the infamous Agnes Sweet was last seen.

With permission from her family, to whom he promised a substantial cut (but never delivered, the last of them having passed away before he finished, and who needs money when you're dead?), he turned the house into a shrine. He wrote an emotional script that described the history of the house, the circumstances of Agnes's disappearance, and a few suppositions of her death, and hired a couple of local boys to conduct tours, making sure they ended in the dungeons. It was a salacious tale: a century earlier, a small door had been carved into the wall to access a cat that had fallen through the angstloch and become trapped inside the oubliette, and all manner of horrors had been found. The local archaeology team had excavated skeleton after skeleton. Lord knows how many had perished after being shoved through the angstloch. Though now covered with a small wooden trapdoor that was always kept locked, it gave him the chills. He had to pass the short hallway that housed the *fear hole*, as it was sometimes called, on his way to the wine cave, and every time he felt as if the eyes of the dead were upon him.

It was cold and damp down there, perfectly spooky, and struck just the right note for an afternoon learning about a missing mystery writer. The patrons would stick their heads in, feel that ominous chill, and back away, happy to return to the surface.

Bolstered by the warm reception to his newfound profit scheme, he opened a bookshop off the grand dining room and stocked all of Agnes's titles, as well as several avant-garde biographies done on her life and career. He hired a local watercolorist to paint the house and grounds (imagining them lush and green, of course), and hung the art all over the house with discreet gold price tags dangling from the frames. The art sold as well as the books; the artist became famous and moved to Dublin. Yeats held weekly movie nights, a rare treat, showing the adaptations of Agnes's most famous novels. He commissioned a bespoke brand of tea, Irish breakfast with a hint of whiskey on the finish, which was a huge hit. He forced out the tent people and opened a section of the grounds to proper caravaners, stocked the pond with trout, and started a flora and fauna tour for the outdoorsy types.

The first year, he was able to repair the rest of the roof and plaster the walls. The second, he restored the oak and ebony parquet floors and the soaring Sicilian marble staircase. And the third, he opened the second-floor bedrooms to private groups, usually writers who wanted to soak up the glory of their hero's creative space, or the ghoulish, who came convinced the place was haunted.

It was, of course – it was too old not to be – but Yeats himself had never seen a spirit. The lore, though, grew and grew. There was a five-foot marble statue in the stairwell of an angelic woman, and some said if you stood at the base of the stairs at midnight during a full moon, she would glow red with the spirit of Agnes Sweet herself. That sort of nonsense made everyone want to visit. He'd only noticed something odd about the statue once, and he wasn't eager to repeat the experience. Yeats wasn't a superstitious man, either.

Year five, he threw the Christmas Eve party again. They capped the attendees at one thousand; the waiting list was three times that.

Yes, Yeats O'Malley had struck gold.

But all veins run dry eventually.

2.

Bunting wrapped the stairwells, and pine scented the air. Six blue spruce trees lined the foyer, so covered in tinsel and green, gold, and red baubles delivered straight from the factory that the smoky teal needles were barely visible.

They'd shot twenty turkeys, fifteen grouse, and three geese. The plum pudding was spiked with brandy, and silver trays of champagne flutes and sidecars passed through the room, glasses finding their way into nearly every hand. Tomato soup and brandy butter lined the tables. Potatoes of every ilk rode in silver chafing dishes; there were one hundred specially made Christmas cakes designed so everyone could have a slice for good luck. The pitch and tenor of the house had turned up, the happy hum of bees in an indulgent hive. Father John's nose was already red; Yeats needed to keep an eye on him to make sure he could still do the Christmas Eve service at midnight. They'd planned to do it here in the manor instead of St Mary's. The house would be full of incense from the censer, but that was all right. Yeats didn't mind the smell.

It was a merry scene. Everything he'd always dreamed of. One of his friends even showed up with a lovely gift, a recording of his favorite hymn sung by the famed German soprano Elisabeth

Schumann. The whole evening was perfect. Until his butler Dónal pulled him aside, long nose pinched.

"There is a woman in your office, sir."

Normally, this would be an intriguing, even welcome, bit of news. But tonight, with so many people wandering the house, he'd closed off a few rooms for safety, including his precious space.

"Then get her out," he whispered, jovially waving at the owner of a new sporting store in town.

"An *American* woman." The hushed horror in his voice cut through Yeats's tippling buzz.

"Who? I don't recall an American on the guest list."

"I don't know, but I heard her earlier, ordering champagne from the bar man. And I'm afraid there's no convenient way to remove her. You'll need to…"

Dónal was gripping his hands together fretfully, something rare and unexpected. He was a commanding presence. For him to be in a twist, something was truly wrong.

"All right," Yeats relented. "Lead on."

He marched with purpose so he wouldn't be waylaid, bumping into the town mayor with his hand up the dress of a local starlet made good on the London stage, but not seeing anyone else of note.

He'd set up his office in the northeast corner of the house, built it as both workspace and library. The shelves were bursting with books on a variety of topics. There was a blue velvet sofa and two leather chairs by the marble-clad fireplace, a fire chuckling merrily in the grate. His wide oak desk with a black leather blotter on top held nothing but a Montblanc fountain pen with a golden snake wrapped round its cap, supposed to have belonged to the doyenne Agnes Sweet herself, and a stack of notecards, the paper thick and creamy. The party was a dull roar here, loud enough that he knew people were in the house but removed enough for a proper conversation to be had.

This was his sacred space.

And it was defiled.

The American was draped over his desk chair, back arched and breasts exposed, a ruby necklace of wetness dripping through her blonde hair onto his precious Agra kilim dragon-themed rug. It was a one-of-a-kind piece – inherited from Sweet too, like the pen – and it was rapidly being ruined by the gentle *plish plats* of the stranger's blood hitting the soft hand-knotted silk.

That was when he noticed his prized fountain pen sticking out of the American's neck. Yeats said an exceptionally rude word in Gaelic, and Dónal, startled but unflappable, cleared his throat.

"As you can see, sir, we need a moment alone."

"Yes, quite. Who did it?"

"I don't know. No one has been allowed in this part of the house."

"Yet an American woman was able to get back here and get herself murdered. Oh, my carpet!"

He shook himself. Right. This was a disaster, but he could make it work. Now he remembered her coming in, standing in the keep staring at the gloriously decorated trees, wide-eyed as a fawn. And, if he remembered correctly, alone. If she hadn't yet been missed…

"Is there anything else that might tell us what happened here tonight?"

Dónal gestured to the fireplace. Yeats's eyes followed the butler's pointer finger to see the round heel of a boot print, rimmed in red. "She wasn't alone."

"That's not yours?"

Dónal shook his head.

A terrible idea formed in Yeats's mind, and he dismissed it immediately with a heavy sigh. This was not an Agnes Sweet novel. This was real life, and there were real consequences that must be dealt with.

"I'll call the police. Just make sure no one gets back here until they come. And keep it quiet, Dónal. I will make sure the guests are safe, and escort the constabulary here when they arrive."

Dónal went a peculiar shade of alabaster akin to the sculpture in the stairwell. "Sir, there is another option. Your party wouldn't be ruined and you could deal with—" he waved a hand toward the dead woman "—this, tomorrow."

"But there's a murderer in the house, Dónal. No, we must do what's right."

"As you wish, sir. But whoever killed her is certainly gone by now. Who would stay to risk being caught? Were she to be found tomorrow, in the oubliette…"

The logic of that statement was unassailable. Or maybe Yeats was just drunk and desperate. He couldn't envision another way out that protected both his party and his reputation.

"You're certain no one has seen?" he asked.

"I can't be completely, sir, but I feel sure the alarm would have been raised if someone had."

Now that it was Dónal who'd made the suggestion – stiff, straight-laced Dónal – Yeats was on board. He would much prefer not to let things be ruined by this interloper who'd had the audacity to be murdered during his party.

Yeats O'Malley, you're going to hell for this. "All right. To the oubliette. And get my pen out of her neck. It's an antique."

3.

Dónal cleverly managed to knot a tea towel round the woman's neck so she wouldn't drip on the way, and they rolled her in the rug. There really was no other way, Dónal argued, and Yeats relented. Walking shoulder to shoulder like two mice with a stolen baguette, they snuck through the back hall to the small door leading to the cellar. Straining under the dead weight, they made it down the stone steps and wormed their way toward the wine cave, stopping at the short hall that housed the angstloch. When opened, the vast darkness below released a scent of moss and must and wet things. With a "heave... *ho*," down the oubliette she went, landing with a *thunk* that made Dónal turn and retch into a silver crested champagne chilling bucket. It was a rare show of emotion for the lad. Then the door in the floor was closed, and Yeats was rubbing Dónal's back. "There, there. Better out than in. Now go get yourself a whiskey and take a seat by the fire in my office. You can send someone to deal with this... mess—" he gestured toward the bucket "—later. They'll just assume it was a tippler from the party who got lost below. Oh, and clean up that boot print."

With a grateful nod, Dónal departed.

Yeats took a deep breath, blew it out hard through his nose, checked himself for any untoward smudges of blood or other incriminating matter, then headed back toward the incandescent joy that was this party. He stopped by Our Lady of Perpetual Cold Palm, as he blasphemously called the marble statue, and shook her hand for luck.

Grabbing a sidecar from a passing tray, he squared his shoulders and made the rounds, again the jovial host, dropping a joke here, a well-timed comment there, watching, ever watching, for who might have committed the heinous deed. He'd done two full loops and it was nearing time for Father John to start the service, and nothing untoward was evident.

The guests gathered in the front hall and received their benediction, heard the story of Christ's birth, revelled in the familiar scent of incense from the censer and ignored the slight slurring in Father John's voice during the homily.

Yeats was five measures into 'O Holy Night,' his robust baritone ringing through the room, joining with the beatific smiles of his guests enjoying this special service, when he thought he heard knocking. He had a moment's panic – someone had come for the American, or the police were here, knowing what he'd done – but he didn't hear it again and no one else seemed perturbed. He made it through the rest of the service without another sound. Made it through seeing his guests to their various cars and bicycles, many setting off on foot for the short walk back to town, a few even sailing off, the tide having come in and allowed their keels room to go upright and slip out onto the bay. In each face, each eye, he looked for signs of terror. Of malice. The soul of a murderer, lurking in their depths. But none seemed at all perturbed or disturbed, only merry and bright, happy to be a part of this remarkable evening.

He was saved in many ways; not a soul asked after the American woman. She must have come alone.

It was a relief. He really could deal with her tomorrow. He was rather proud of himself, actually, for the discretion and fortitude with which he'd handled the situation. Tomorrow, he'd call the police to the house, show them the dungeon, explain he was missing a rug and had gone searching, and look what horror he'd found.

Someone had killed the girl; it wasn't too far-fetched to assume they'd try to hide the body. Surely, the killer had heard Dónal approaching and panicked, leaving the girl behind. No sane murderer would leave a body out in plain sight during the middle of a party. No, no, the culprit had been interrupted. Yeats was sure of it. He'd simply finished the perpetrator's devious work.

When he was finally alone, he returned to the office. Dónal was not there, though an empty whiskey glass sat on the table by the fire. It was late; he must have found his own bed. Strange, though. He acted as valet as well as butler; for him to abandon his duties was unusual.

Yeats shot back a tot of whiskey himself, enjoying the smooth burn and how it warmed him from within, and, saying a prayer of gratitude to the good man upstairs for keeping the American hidden long enough to allow him to find a plan for dealing with her, he locked the door, checked to see that the fires were banked (they were), and wearily mounted the Sicilian marble staircase. Light came from under the door in his room; he paused, curling his right hand into a fist in case someone was inside. He pushed open the door, but there was no one.

He face-planted into his bed without bothering to undress and dreamed terrible dreams all night.

4.

Yeats was startled awake by quiet singing in his ear. It was a whisper, really, so quiet that once he bolted upright, he could barely hear the words. *"O Holy Night, the stars are brightly shining…"*

There was an odd noise that accompanied the words, one reminiscent of a spade hitting dirt.

He opened his eyes, and memories of the evening's evil deeds paraded in. He was assailed by the cheery calls of the early morning birds and the lapping of water against the banks, and the homely, comforting ticking of the grandfather clock in the hall. *You dreamed it*, he thought, rolling from his bed. His head was splitting and he stopped for a moment to rest his skull in his hands before forcing himself to his feet. The sun had not yet risen; the sky's edge was the color of new milk.

He heard the carol again, so faint as to not be real. Grabbing his robe, he rushed down the staircase, tripping in his haste, missing the last few stairs. He knocked his temple against the banister and landed in a heap at the base, jarring his whole body. It took a second for his breath to return, and when it did, he thought he heard the lines from the hymn again.

"Fall on your knees. O hear, the angel voices…"

He looked up at the statue, shocked to see her limned in crimson.

"He knows our need. To our weakness, no stranger!"

He could have sworn he heard knocking, echoing through the keep, growing louder and louder, shaking his body, and under it, the note he could just about make out, a spade hitting the dirt.

The massive, cased grandfather clock struck five, and the noise was unholy in his head.

Yeats curled into a ball on the floor and moaned. His head, his head was going to burst.

"Dónal," he screamed, but it was relentless, the chorus of voices and whispers and blades hitting dirt and the knocking on the walls of his soul, his heart, his heart was pounding, shaking his body in time with the reverberations. The drumbeat of the ticking clock grew to a violent crescendo inside of him, and to escape it, he rose and stumbled forward. He moved down the stairs to the cellar slowly, afraid, hitting the switch at the base to illuminate the space. Every step echoed. He inched closer and closer to the hallway where the angstloch to the oubliette waited. He heard the spade biting into the loamy earth, again and again and again, and finally reached the door. The cacophony grew to unbearable levels, and just as he stepped into the darkened hall... stopped.

His gramophone was set up by the angstloch, the wooden door cover standing open. The record on it had finished, and the needle bumped and scratched in time. He drew closer and saw the record itself was the special gift he'd received earlier, the rich notes of the famed soprano singing his favorite hymn.

Who in the dickens would put this down here? The odd bangs and knocking had clearly come from the record, echoing in the small space. But why—

A dark shape emerged from the gloom, and before he could move out of the way, he tumbled head first down the dark, dank hole.

5.

Alone. In the pitch-black, the ancient soil seemed the same color as the night sky, making it almost impossible to tell the difference between ground and air, the oubliette hole letting in a meager light from above. He dripped sweat and the spade bit into the earth, and though his eyes were acclimated to the dark, he could sense a shine, a flickering, like a candle in the dark, illuminating a small circle to his right.

It was a bleak place, he thought, taking a break. He wiped a dirty hand across his brow, smelling the scent of death. The hole was certainly deep enough to hide the woman, was it not?

The shaft of light brightened the space, and Yeats's eyes opened, relieved. His heart was doing double time. He took a deep breath. Was the nightmare truly over?

It took him a moment to gain his bearings, and panic set in as he realized he really was in the dungeon, lying on something soft, a terrible pain in his head. His hands scrabbled and he felt the rug from his office. A moment of sanity, and memories of the night before returned. The party. The dead woman. The disposal of her body. The singing from the record. And then, the fall. He remembered nothing more. What in the hell was he doing down here?

Moving slowly, head pounding, he unwrapped the woman's body. She'd been a beauty. He hadn't killed her, had he? The night had been such a blur: Too many drinks, too many cheers. A triumph, or so he'd thought. He was painfully sober now, however, and perhaps it hadn't been such a success after all. But no, he'd certainly recall participating in such a terrible deed. Slicing into flesh with the sharp tip of the fountain pen? It was a visceral thing, killing a person with your hands. He'd remember.

Could it have been Dónal? Surely not. Mild-mannered, quiet, Dónal Barlow was the least entropic fellow one could imagine. But how well did Yeats know him, after all? They were of an age, and the man was strapping; he could have managed the physicality needed to murder the girl. But what a thought! No, Dónal was a good man.

He'd come when the house was bought, with recommendations from a local family; had served loyally.

It's a bit late to be worrying about the who, he chided himself. Whoever did it was long gone anyway, right? Who would murder a woman and stick around?

His heart, the rhythm already accelerated from the discovery of his predicament, thudded loudly. *Stop thinking. Get yourself out.*

He went to the small door, and found it blocked. He shouted and pounded on it with his fists, but the only answer was the lonely ticking of the grandfather clock, the pendulum echoing down the house vents. He'd always found it comforting when alone in the great manse, that *tick-tick-ticking* like the beat of a mother's heart.

He ran his hands along the walls of his prison, only to find the very spade he'd dreamed about leaning against the wall. As if someone had come down here in the night to bury the woman's body, but abandoned the plan. When Yeats had investigated the noise and found the gramophone, perhaps he'd chased off the killer.

Or perhaps you were drawn here to die, old boy. If you share her fate, the killer is safe.

He fought down the panic. Surely Dónal would come for him.

He'd dreamed of the spade biting into the earth, though. He took it in hand, and moved toward the woman's body. Was he meant to bury her, and then he'd be let out?

Fine. He'd play along. He'd call the police the moment he got out of here, and tell them everything. They wouldn't hold him accountable. He was an upstanding member of society, a leader in this town. He'd done nothing wrong.

He attacked the soil with vigor, and almost immediately the

spade caught on something. The *clang* reverberated through the small space, echoing in time with his heart.

He fell to his knees and edged closer, reaching a hand into the dirt. They said the house – well, this dungeon, at least, before the castle keep crumbled around it – had belonged to the pirate queen. Was there treasure buried here, in this place of pain and horror, where no one would dare enter to look?

His fingers grasped something and he pulled. The object came free easily, and he hurried over to the beam of light from the oubliette hole: a pearl bracelet. Three strands, with a thick gold and diamond clasp. It took his mind a moment to register the bracelet resided around a long, dirty white bone, which was still attached by a few shreds of ligament to the palm of a hand.

Agnes.

He screamed and scrambled backward, then found his feet and ran to the door. He pounded his fists against the rough wood and cried out, "Dónal! Dónal! Let me out of here!"

There was nothing. No one. Terror overwhelmed him and he sobbed for release. Finally, he gathered himself.

Stop. Stop and think. You're a smart fellow. You can get out of here if only you think.

He tried to ignore the fact that he was alone with the dead American and the skeletal remains of a woman who must be Agnes Sweet herself, and now he, too, was locked in this dreadful place. He needed to get out. The door was barred and there was only one other entrance, and that was through the angstloch. But without ladder or rope, there was no way to reach the hole itself. It was such an effective prison. He was done for.

Finally, curiosity outweighed his anguish, and he dug up the rest of the skeleton. It was small, disarticulated, and with the tell-tale bracelet and the large hole in the skull, he knew he'd solved part of the mystery of Agnes Sweet's disappearance. Someone had bashed her on the head and shoved her down the fear hole, then come back and buried her. Was his fate to be the same?

He sat on the moist ground and listened to his heart beating. Again. And again. And again. The grandfather clock *tick-tick-ticked* in time, and eventually, Yeats fell asleep. In his dreams, the heartbeat was joined by others, some soft, some loud. Some skittered and chirped and some thumped languorously. Many had died after being shoved down the hole. So many hearts, beating so many times, over so many centuries. They grew louder and louder, and Yeats lay down in the dirt and let his join the chorus.

6.

Three nights passed, and the clock in the hall ceased to run. The silence in the dungeon was overwhelming. To hear only his own heart beating was too much. He could feel himself slipping, the madness taking him deep in its bosom. The creatures in the dungeon seemed to come to life, and he didn't feel quite as alone. Yeats knew it wasn't real, that he was hallucinating from the bump on the head or the lack of food and water, but he welcomed the imagined company. The silence was unbearable.

Soon enough, the American began to smell, and she was embarrassed. They had conversations about her life, her childhood, and he realized he would have enjoyed knowing her, had she lived. She claimed to have come for a visit, gotten in the family way, and was in hiding at her aunt's for her confinement. She was a fallen woman, but Yeats didn't mind. She was good company.

Agnes the skeleton mocked him angrily from the corner, annoyed at his blatant tarnishing of her legacy by using her talent and fame for his own gains.

Neither could tell him who'd murdered them. Worse, no one came to look for him.

He had no voice left. His fists were raw and bloodied. He'd prayed and screamed and begged. There was no water except the moisture from the rocks, and he licked them as often as he could manage. He was growing too weak to care. Death would take him soon enough. And through it all, his heart beat, and beat, and beat.

The fourth night, there was a new noise, an eerie clomping above. He thought he heard his name, a whisper in the darkness. His mother? Come to call him home? Warmth suffused his chest, and the beating of his heart grew more frenzied.

Yeats. Yeats.

"I'm ready to see you again," he whispered back. "I've missed you. I'm sorry I was such a terrible son."

Yeats. Yeats!

The word grew louder, then louder still, and the voice closer, and closer still. He could see the body of the American in the dim light, and the form of Agnes Sweet, the horrible grin of the skull. "Farewell," he told them.

"Yeats O'Malley!"

The voice was close, and real! And he recognized it. It was not Dónal, but belonged to Father John.

There were others too, and his heart leaped for joy.

"I'm here! I'm here in the dungeon! Save me!"

"Yeats?" a voice called from above. "Is that you in there?"

"It is! Oh, you've no idea. I've been locked in for days! Please, please help."

"Dear God, what's that smell?"

"It's a woman, or I should say, two women. I didn't kill them but they're here with me. One was buried, one I was going to bury, but I didn't kill her, I swear I didn't. I found her, in my office. She was already dead, you see, and I panicked. If you'll just lower a rope, or open the door, I'll explain everything. I will!"

It took them an hour to figure out how to release him from the dungeon, and he babbled to them the whole time, detailing all the reasons why it was clear he had not killed the girl in there with him. Whoever had locked him in had clearly done it, couldn't they see? And that person had blocked the door thoroughly, so they hauled him up through the oubliette with a rope around his arms, for he was too weak to climb the ladder they put down.

As he left the dank room, he promised both women that he would solve the mystery of their deaths. He would unmask their murderers, once and for all. And after the police investigated and found no wrongdoing on his part, he tried to keep that pledge, to no avail. There was simply nothing to go on.

While Yeats eventually saw them safely buried in a proper graveyard, with Father John officiating and the whole town surrounding the site, laying them to rest was the end for him. There was no clue what had happened, and Yeats, never quite right after the incident, withdrew to his home.

Of Dónal, there was no word. He had disappeared into the fabric of the universe. Once they cleared Yeats, the police (and the townsfolk, oh, the rumors they shared!) speculated that Dónal had lured the young American to the party, killed her, and locked Yeats in the dungeon to take the fall for his crime, but there was no way to know for sure. A few strange bits and bobs were found in the butler's things: a diamond hair clasp, a pipe, three playing cards, a long piece of brown velvet ribbon. The police wondered if they could belong to more victims, wondered if Dónal was some sort of Jack the Ripper imitator.

They never would know for certain. But part of the mystery of the elusive butler was solved when what was left of Dónal Barlow was found in the spring thaw, face down in the mud of the riverbank. Escaping the house? Or searching for a way in to help his master? There was no way of telling.

7.

Yeats closed the house to the public. He puttered. He fretted. He refused all callers, having groceries and liquor delivered. He would not allow a soul to pass through the doors. He sat next to the grandfather clock, winding it every hour so it would never again run out and go silent. Silence was no longer his friend.

The week after Dónal was found, the first clock arrived.

And then another. And another.

Grand ones. Small ones. Pocket watches and grandfather clocks. Pendulums and cuckoos, water clocks, and hourglasses that chimed when the hour was up. Even an atomic clock that whirred constantly, marking the seconds as well as the minutes and hours.

Yeats chipped away at his vast fortune, searching the world for the finest timepieces money could buy, but ignored the one thing he could save, the beautiful container that housed his madness.

He spent his days making sure every one of his clocks was in lockstep time, so four times an hour, the heartbeats from the dungeon rang throughout the house to keep him company.

The roof began to leak, and the plaster peeled from the walls. Water intruded on the foundation, and the northwest corner, disappointed in the lack of maintenance, finally sank three feet into the marshy bank, cracking the walls apart. The grand home became unlivable again.

Time passed.

Yeats passed.

They found him sitting in the darkest corner of the dungeon, surrounded by pocket watches that had stopped ticking long ago.

8.

Christmas Eve
Now

"Edge House," the tour guide intoned in a disappointingly light brogue, "has over three hundred and twenty clocks, many of unknown vintage, but several that are truly invaluable, including one with provenance dating back to the early thirteenth century, claimed to be one of the first known mechanical clocks to exist. When the previous owner passed, the house went into probate and was eventually nominated to be a cultural heritage site. That nomination failed, but the house was too important to the community to let it drift into the sea. It was partially restored in the eighties, the worst of the foundation damage repaired, and has been maintained by the grace of the city since. It's taken a good deal of money, and now, the home has a private benefactor who will oversee a full renovation. The only request of the previous owner was for the clocks to be maintained, and as you can see, we've done just that. Prepare yourselves. It is nearly midnight."

This was the part of the ghost tour Julia Exeter had been looking forward to most. A famed mystery writer, she already knew the history of the place. And, she was privy to the house's deepest secrets. She was certain she knew who murdered the women who had died here. And she thought she knew why. She was going to prove her theories, then make sure everyone else knew, too. The book she was writing would expose them all. The rise and downfall of Yeats O'Malley, procurer of the clocks and finder of bodies, was a full section. But there was so much more to the story. Julia was focused on the bigger picture.

She tuned out the guide and slipped into the dining room off the central keep. She stood at the window and looked out at the water. Imagined the night her great-grandmother had done the same, almost one hundred years earlier. From what Julia had pieced together, she'd come across the sea to stay with her only living relatives when tragedy befell her own parents, and she was having an affair with someone in the great house.

What excitement it must have been for a young American visiting family nearby to be invited to the famed Edge House Christmas party by a secret lover. She couldn't have known what would happen; that this was the last place she'd be seen alive. That the distant relatives she was living with would never say a word when she didn't come home. That they would ship the baby she'd secretly had while with them off to the orphanage on the other side of town and wash their hands of the situation.

A secret baby who grew up to be Julia's handsome, rakish grandfather. This spitting image of the daguerreotype of the man called Dónal Barlow she'd found in the church archives.

Julia had discovered part of the truth in the diary of that horrible distant aunt. Or what she could make of it. It was in the last lines of the diary that she found the core of the mystery.

Elizabeth Exeter lost to the excesses and sins of Edge House, just as darling Agnes was. Someone in that house murdered them both.

The gaily decorated rooms of that Edge House no longer existed, replaced with the festooned false charm of the historical holiday, replete with wall hangings explaining the significance of the portraits and the house's history, and many stag heads mounted, glassy and staring, from the walls. Julia was going to change all of that. The sale would go through in the morning, and then she'd own her history, and the house's, forever. She would write its story and bring it back to life.

The clocks began to chime, and gong, and clong, and chirp, and whistle, and as they counted down the midnight hours, over and over, *bong, bong, bong, bong, bong,* they literally shook the walls. The tour group was appropriately awed, laughing and hooting in excitement.

When the last beat finished echoing, the guide deepened his brogue.

"The house has seen many sorrows, from its beginnings as the castle keep of Granuaile to its later purchase by the famous mystery writer, Agnes Sweet, whose body was found fifteen years after going missing in the very dungeon you will visit today. Many deaths have occurred here, and it is now one of the most haunted homes in Western Ireland. If you'll follow me, we'll go down the stairs to the dungeon now."

Julia smiled and got in line.

CHRISTMAS LIGHTS

David Bell

A MISERABLY COLD January morning.

Burke enters the kitchen just before daylight. Mercifully, he'd programmed the coffee maker the night before. The aroma of brewing coffee is a bright spot.

Outside, through the window above the sink, the world is fuzzy gray. Packed snow on the lawn. Low clouds. The sun could rise, and no one would notice.

Burke pours the first cup, lets the steam pass over his face. He moves quietly, like a burglar, hoping not to wake Anna who is lucky enough to be asleep down the hall.

Burke prefers the view of the back yard. Of the old tree, the rickety fence, the rusted swingset…

Out the front window lie all the things he doesn't want to see or think about. The Christmas lights that make him an object of curiosity, hanging from the front gutters continuously for the past nine years. And then, beyond that, four blocks south, the cemetery where they'd finally buried Morgan two days earlier.

He sips the hot coffee, tries to cut off the thoughts that inevitably come. The thoughts that keep him awake: *What was left of Morgan… What they found of Morgan… What remained of Morgan… After nine years in a remote field…*

The coffee turns bitter in his mouth. Burke retches, steps to the sink and spits the brown liquid out. His knees shake. He grips the counter with one hand, his chest heaving until he controls his breathing.

He's grown overwhelmed by it all. It might be better to move on.

He can only control one thing.

He wipes his mouth with the back of his hand and moves out to the garage.

Burke finds the ladder easily.

He pulls it out. He chooses to operate with tunnel vision, forcing his eyes not to look at the things he doesn't want to see but knows are still there. Morgan's red bike. Morgan's pink hula hoop. Morgan's soccer ball, long deflated. Things that mattered to a ten-year-old.

He hits the button, and the garage door begins its inexorable cranking open, letting in a gust of cold air. They could have moved years ago. They were about to when Morgan disappeared. They would have upgraded, found a bigger house in a better neighborhood.

But once Morgan was gone, they couldn't do it. This was the last house she lived in – the only house she knew. What if she found her way back – and discovered strangers living here?

No way. They couldn't move.

Not then anyway. And not any time in the past nine years.

They both liked the house, held tightly to the memories they had of Morgan.

But now… are they free to do whatever they want? To move? Vacation?

Fully grieve?

"What's going on?"

It's Anna. She stands in the doorway from the garage to the kitchen. She wears her soft white robe pulled tight around her body and slippers on her feet.

"I didn't mean to wake you."

"That's okay. I'm just wondering what you're doing. It's cold. And dark."

"I've been thinking. I'm going to take the Christmas lights down. Finally. They don't need to be up anymore. Do they?"

Anna's brow furrows, as if the question really deserves a thoughtful answer. "No, I guess they don't."

Burke looks out at the yard, one hand holding the ladder. "I think it would be better for us not to be known as the parents of a missing girl anymore. I don't want to be known just as the dad who kept the Christmas lights up continuously for nine years because they were up when his daughter was kidnapped. And because he wanted to leave them up until she came home."

"She's home."

"No, she's dead. And she's over there." He waves his free hand in the direction of the cemetery.

"Oh… okay…"

Burke feels like a dick. He doesn't mean to be harsh, to direct anything at Anna. She's the one person he can count on, the one person he's been through this with every step of the way…

"I'm sorry. Look, I'm—"

"It's okay." Anna rubs her hands up and down her arms, shivers slightly. "We said we'd leave them up until it was really over, when there was an arrest…"

"Do you think that's ever going to happen?" Burke asks. "The cops – after all this time, they're on to other stuff. They're overworked. Underpaid. Overwhelmed, like everybody. Morgan was only found – her body… when that farmer sold his land because it had been sitting unused for decades, and the surveyor—"

"I know what happened, Burke."

"I think I want to take them down. It's as over as it will ever be."

"Can you at least wait until it's lighter or warmer?"

"No. It's now or never."

"I didn't think so. Will you be careful—"

Headlights approach from down the street. Slowly. Cutting through the morning gloom.

Burke stops listening to Anna, leans the ladder against the wall of the garage.

"Burke? Is that…"

"I think it is. Today of all days."

"Burke, just—"

"No, I won't. I want to talk to them."

He steps into the driveway as the car gets closer.

When the media first covered the story – 'Father of Missing Girl Leaves Lights Up for Her' – plenty of cars came by and gawked. They honked in support. They left flowers and teddy bears.

Sometimes they'd stop and ring the bell – offering Burke and Anna hugs or prayers.

But it all slowed down. It all went away once Morgan had been gone for a year.

Except for one car – *one car* – that came only in the dark.

Burke would lie awake in the days and months and then years after Morgan disappeared. He'd stare at the ceiling or the walls.

Headlights would then slice through the windows, breaking through the blinds.

He'd rush to the front of the house and there – always the same car. A hulking shape in the darkness. Sometimes at the curb. Then more audaciously in the driveway.

When Burke went outside, they'd drive off. Once, Burke managed to get a bit of the license plate number, but the police ran it through their system to no avail.

Both the police and Anna told Burke not to make too much of the car. They were just another curiosity seeker, someone attracted to the story who meant no harm.

But Burke never believed it. He convinced himself they knew something. They came back to the house – over and over again – to taunt Morgan's parents. To get a sick thrill out of watching them suffer.

Why else would they keep coming back?

Even now – after Morgan had been found and buried?

"Burke, don't—"

But Burke runs. Shoes pounding against the driveway, heading right for the car.

The windows are tinted, the interior dark. Just a shape behind the wheel.

"What do you *want?*" Burke reaches the end of the driveway, waving his fists like a madman. "What on earth do you know? Just tell us."

The car sits for a long moment. Burke thinks – a flash through his mind – they're not going to leave. He can imagine the window going down, the face finally revealed.

The face that knows the truth. That knows everything.

But then the car accelerates – as it always does. Speeds off up the street and out of sight.

Burke goes into the street, slips on a patch of black ice and falls down, landing hard on his right hip.

Anna comes down the driveway. Still in her robe and slippers. "Burke, are you hurt?"

But Burke grabs at fistfuls of snow and ice, and tries to throw them at the car – which is long out of sight. An act of abject futility.

"Damn it. Damn them."

"Burke, come inside…" Anna looks past him. A light pops on in the house across the street. A face appears at the window. "Please."

"Look, everybody wants their show. Everybody wants to watch us…"

Burke pushes himself up. His hand is covered with road grit. His hip feels like it's been thumped by a baseball bat.

Burke limps up the driveway with Anna following. He doesn't bother with the ladder.

He stands at the corner of the house. The gutter – with the light strand attached – is about eight feet high. He leaps.

Once. And then twice.

"Burke. Please."

His back hurts now. His shoulders. His neck. His hip.

But he leaps again, stretching his arm as far as it can go.

He manages to grab the strand of lights.

And pulls.

They come partially down with an ugly, ripping sound. Burke keeps pulling. He moves down the length of the house, pulling and tugging. Not caring if the gutters get damaged.

Not caring if he slips and falls again.

Not caring about anything except making the lights disappear.

Burke pulls and pulls until the lights are gone for the first time in nine years. He drags the strand to the driveway and stomps on each bulb, satisfied by the popping sound as the colorful glass breaks.

When he's finished, when every bulb is smashed and he's standing on a pile of multi-colored broken glass, he looks around.

Anna is gone, back inside the house.

A couple of neighbors are out on their lawns watching. More faces stare from their windows.

The young guy across the street, Nick, cups his hands around his mouth. "You need some help, Burke?"

Burke ignores him. His hands are numb with cold, the tips of his ears and his nose stinging.

He's breathing heavily and worries he may be having a heart attack.

Nick turns away, embarrassed for him.

Burke's embarrassed too. He lost his mind. Turned into someone else for those few moments, possessed by helplessness and grief.

There's nothing for him to do but go inside, shut the garage door, and hide from everything.

Days pass. Anna and Burke eat their way through all the food their friends and family brought for Morgan's funeral.

The media stops calling. The weather remains cold and bleak. The snow in the street turns dirty and black.

The morning comes when they both have to return to work. Burke wakes before the alarm, staring at the ceiling in the dark while Anna gently snores next to him.

He's listened to – and accepted – nearly a decade's worth of well-wishes and sympathetic looks from his coworkers. He knows when a new employee starts, someone takes them aside and whispers, "You know, he's Morgan Martin's father. That ten-year-old girl who disappeared…"

And now, Morgan's recovery and burial will bring another round of comments and looks. He wishes he could pass out cards or wear a sign on his head, something that says: *Your sympathy is much appreciated. But I really hate talking about it.*

But he can't. He – and Anna – both have to endure it.

Burke swings his feet off the bed. He puts on shoes and is reaching for a red WKU sweatshirt when headlights fill the room.

"No, not again."

Burke throws his hoodie on.

"What is it?" Anna asks.

"That car, *the* damn car, they're back." He goes to the window, opens the blind a crack with his fingers. It's there. The car. The same car. The one that's always there, always fleeing. "I've about had it. The lights are gone, but that damn car is still here."

"Burke…"

"They're in the driveway, of all things. This is real harassment."

"Burke, it's—"

"Not anymore." He goes to the closet, grabs the baseball bat, and starts out of the room.

"Burke, no."

"If the cops won't take care of them, I will."

Burke charges to the front of the house, his untied sneakers clomping against the floor. He fumbles with the deadbolt, heart racing, bat bumping against his leg. He manages to undo the lock and swings the door open, letting in the rush of cold, morning air.

The dark car sits in the driveway, puffing exhaust. The driver is obscured by the tinted windows.

"Hey!"

Burke slips a little on a patch of ice, regains his balance. He knows he's cutting a ridiculous figure – a man consumed by displaced anger and helplessness.

He goes down the steps, expecting the car to slam into reverse and leave.

But it remains in place. In the driveway.

"Hey…" Burke shakes the bat in the air like a scepter. "Hey, buddy. What do you want?"

The tinted window remains closed. Burke approaches. He does something he's seen in movies many, many times. Something he isn't sure anyone ever does in real life.

He gets a good grip on the bat and swings, smashing the driver's side headlight.

"How do you like that, huh?"

For a moment, nothing happens. The car remains in place. Burke brings the bat back, ready for another blow, but he doesn't swing. He pictures himself – a depressed middle-aged man beating on a car that belongs to someone he doesn't actually know.

Someone who might have a gun or a knife or a deadly set of fists that could pound him into submission.

Beneath the hoodie, Burke wears only boxers and a t-shirt. A cold breeze hits him.

The driver's side door opens slowly, and two hands emerge, held in the air like the person is surrendering.

"Please," a voice says. "Please. I just want to talk."

Burke stands in the driveway, the bat hanging at his side.

His mouth is partially open, but he doesn't speak.

A small woman, about his age, steps out of the car, hands still raised in the air. She remains behind the open door, like she's using it as a shield. She looks tiny and frail, as if a strong wind could blow her away.

Burke already feels like a jackass. Pieces of her broken headlight litter the ground by his feet.

"You don't know me," she says. "But I know you."

"Do you… are you… do you know something about Morgan?"

The woman wears a heavy parka, and her salt-and-pepper hair blows across her face. She lowers her hands and brushes the hair away. "I know what happened to her."

Burke's grip on the bat tightens. He steps forward. "You know—"

The woman waves her hands and shakes her head. "I don't mean

I *know* know. I mean... I know. I read about her over the years... And you..." The woman moves to the side, closes her car door. She wears sweatpants and an oversized sweatshirt. She points at herself. "My son, Charlie, he disappeared twenty years ago. When he was two. See? I know. I mean – I really, really *know*."

Burke stares at the woman. One side effect of having a missing child: Burke spent hours – and hours – online, studying every other missing person's case he could find. Not just in the area but anywhere in the world. He learned the names and circumstances and outcomes of so many cases he could have written his own encyclopedia about them.

"Charlie... I don't..."

"Charles Andrew Condon. Missing since December twenty-third, 2004. *That* Charlie."

Something clicks in Burke's mind, and the sketchy details come back. Charles Andrew Condon. Kidnapped from a big box retail store while his mother Christmas shopped. She placed him in the cart while she bought last-minute gifts. The store was packed, the aisles jammed with other last-minute shoppers.

Charles's mother walked a few feet away to grab an item off the shelf. When she turned back around, her child was gone.

From a crowded store. Right before Christmas.

And he's never been seen again.

No body. No suspects. Nothing.

Burke could even summon the photo. A smiling boy in a department store portrait studio. Loosely holding a tiny football. Grinning.

Charles – *Charlie* – lived one county north of Burke. A smaller community.

"Oh," Burke says. "I remember him. I do."

The woman smiles. It looks forced and emphasizes the lines around her mouth and eyes. "Not many people do. Sometimes I think no one does. No one but me." She wipes her nose with the back of her hand. "That's why I came by here. All the time. To see the lights. When I came by and saw the lights, I felt like someone else in the world understood me. Someone else was going through the same thing I was going through."

Burke looks back at the house, at the empty gutter. His feet rest on the broken colored glass of the bulbs. "Oh. Yeah, sure..."

"But maybe that's not true anymore." She looks down at the broken headlight. She doesn't seem angry or put out. Just resigned. "Maybe I scared you."

"I'm sorry about that. I thought— Why didn't you ever stop? Ever? I wanted to talk to you, to know why you were coming by here. Why didn't you just talk to us?"

The woman— Burke realizes he doesn't know her name yet. He just knows she's the woman who turned her back in a crowded store and lost her son. She's like him in that way – she's a sketch. A quick summary of tragic details. An internet story that gets passed over more and more as the years go by.

An object of pity. Someone judged and then forgotten.

"I didn't stop or talk to you because... because I guess I was afraid you'd find your daughter and move on. And then I'd be back to being alone. I didn't want to hear your good news. I was afraid of it. I know that's horrible, but it's true, right?" She points at the house. "The lights are down. You've moved on. You're in a different place than I am. I'm back to being..." She lifts her hands and lets them fall to her sides in frustration. "I'm back to being in this place alone."

She turns, moves back to the car.

"I'm sorry," Burke says. "I mean – I'm sorry about the car. And Charlie, of course. Can I pay for the headlight? Can I do anything?"

The woman stops, her hand resting on the roof of the car. The wind blows her hair across her face again, but she doesn't brush it away this time. "You can tell me one thing. What does it feel like to be where you are? To know… something? Anything?"

Burke stares at the gray, empty sky as if an answer might appear there.

But it doesn't.

"It feels… it feels… It still just feels unsatisfying. That's all I know."

The woman nods. She doesn't say anything else but gets back in her car and drives off, leaving Burke in the driveway with more broken glass and his baseball bat.

Inside, Burke wanders through the quiet house.

The HVAC hums. The water heater ticks.

He goes down the hall, stopping at the door to Morgan's room. Untouched since the day she disappeared. He takes it all in again, as he's done a million times before.

The pink walls. The stuffed animals. The shelf of books. The soccer trophies. The academic ribbons.

Sometimes, Burke sees the room the same way he sees the Christmas lights. Not a memory but a stumbling block. An obstacle to moving ahead.

But could he ever really live without having this room – *this house and these memories* – readily available to him?

"Hey." Anna slips in beside him. Her hair stands in wild disarray. She wears her robe and slippers. She hooks her arm through his. "I woke up and you were gone. What are you thinking about?"

"Time, I guess. Memories. I don't know…"

"Burke, if you want to pack this all up, if you want to put it all away… if you want to move… I don't care. I just want us to be happy… in some way, shape, or form." Anna sighs. "You know, *she* would want us to be happy. Whatever it took."

Burke stares at all the objects in the room. His eyes settle on one thing. A strand of white lights that hang over Morgan's bed. She used to turn them on when she studied or read a book for fun.

Burke remembers those lights – the way the soft glow spilled out the door of Morgan's room and into the hallway, warming him like a campfire. Allowing him to know his daughter was home and safe inside…

A feeling that went away forever… and will never, ever return.

"Burke?"

"Yeah. No. You're right… whatever…"

Burke turns and goes down the hallway. He passes through the kitchen and into the garage. He hears Anna's soft, sliding footsteps behind him.

"Burke?"

Burke dodges the car and crosses to the metal shelves on the far wall and starts rooting around like a burrowing animal.

"Burke, what are you looking for?"

"Boxes. So many boxes here."

"We don't have to pack anything now. I was just saying…"

Burke bends over, his lower back aching. He moves boxes aside, pushing them away. The tips of his fingers getting covered by dust.

He digs down to the bottom shelf, finds the box he's looking for. It takes him a moment to work it loose. He strains and pulls, the muscles in his arms taut.

The box comes free. Burke stumbles back a little, his body leaning against the car.

He straightens, moves to the rear of the car, and plops the box onto the trunk.

"What's in there?" Anna asks.

Burke pulls the top open, sending up another cloud of dust. "I think… yes… I think it's in here…" He sticks his hand inside, fumbles around until his fingers touch the object he seeks.

"What were you doing outside this morning? It sounded like you were chasing another car. I don't think that's healthy, Burke. It could be some nut with a gun." She hesitates then, before saying again, "I just want us to be happy. Do you want to move to another town? Another state?"

"Yes," Burke says, his voice almost triumphant.

"Yes, you want to move? Is that what you mean?"

Burke tugs and tugs at the object in the box. "I know what I want to do." Burke yanks – hard. Out comes a long strand of Christmas lights. Colored bulbs on a green wire. Black clips to secure them to the gutter. "This." Burke holds the strand up like a trophy. Like a prize fish pulled from beneath black waters.

Anna tilts her head to the side. She looks confused. "Lights? Do you want to throw those away? Or smash them? I don't care if you want to smash them, but it seems a little—"

"I'm going to put them up."

"I thought you hated them. I thought you hated all of it."

"I do. Maybe. Or I did. But I guess it's not just about me, is it?"

Burke gathers the strand, wrapping it around his arm. He doesn't even know if the lights work. They've been in the box in the garage for so long.

If they don't work, he can buy more.

They're cheap, easy to find.

A small price to pay for casting some light into the darkness.

THE MIDNIGHT MASS MURDERER

Alexandra Benedict

23 December

Dusk deepened as they drove into Whitby, the sky mulled to dark magenta. Festive lights swung on the quayside. Edie O'Sullivan, self-proclaimed crosspatch crossword setter, tried not to look at the lobster pots and other cages of oncoming death. Glimpsing the red-lit ruins of Whitby Abbey on the clifftop above, she asked, "Tell me again why we're here?"

"Do we need an excuse to go away for Christmas?" Sean, her adopted son and great-nephew, replied. His tone was light, yet he gripped the steering wheel tighter.

"We could've gone to bloody Bognor in a third of the time."

"My friend Laura offered us her holiday rental here for free. No mystery behind it." The slight twitch of his left eye, though, told Edie he was hiding something.

"Still doesn't explain why we're coming up before Liam and

the girls." Sean's husband, Liam, was bringing recently adopted Juniper and her baby sister, Daisy, up by train the next day, on Christmas Eve. "You might as well tell me: I'll get it out of you in the end."

Sean sighed. "Look, you're right."

Of course she was right. Edie always was.

"You'll know as much as I do," he continued, "in under an hour. But, till then, can we drop it?"

Edie crossed her arms. "Fine. You've got fifty-nine minutes and counting." She winced as Sean drove up Church Street, the suspension bucking and juddering. "Cobbles should be made illegal."

"They look pretty, covered in snow." Sean smiled at the falling cold stuff.

"I'll soon be untethered bones in an octogenarian skin sack, but at least you'll enjoy the view."

"Luckily, we're stopping here." Sean parked outside The Last Angel Inn. "Our place is just up that path." He pointed up a slope into the dark. "But there's no parking."

"Great, so I'll just break my ankles."

Sean turned to Edie, placed his warm hand on her cold one. "We're on holiday, in a beautiful place, for Christmas. Can you just think positively for a few minutes, Mum?"

Edie swallowed an ice-cold reply. "Sorry. I'm frozen, aching and tired. Not even witnessing your unfathomable love for service stations can keep my spirits up for six hours."

"There's a log burner in our apartment, I'll get it going soon as we get in. First, I'm gonna pop you in the pub while I park."

"*Now* you're talking."

Five minutes later, Edie was in an armchair inside The Last Angel Inn with a whiskey in one hand, a pickled egg in the other. A log fire chatted to itself in the corner; in a nearby armchair, an old man slept. Shiny paper chains crisscrossed the ceiling and bar. Outside, boat masts jousted in the wind.

"You here for Christmas, too?" A young woman was perched on a bar stool, swinging her legs and smiling at Edie. She pointed to the three cases and holdall that Sean had placed around Edie in an Aspinal barricade.

"Apparently." Edie stared out of the window at the now-heavy snow, silently declaring the conversation over. Small talk made her itch like polyester Christmas jumpers.

"I'm back from university. In my last year, but none of my friends are around." She paused, then said, softly, "You look a bit like my great-grandma." Yearning was backstitched into the girl's voice, pricking holes in Edie's resolve.

"I didn't know you'd be back from Italy for the holidays, Sophie," a bald man by the bar said. He was somewhere in his fifties and therefore a whippersnapper. "Hope you've been learning the language instead of chatting up the men."

The bar stool squeaked as the girl swivelled towards him. Her eyes were bright, full of stories. "*Ho imparato a fare il pane e a fare l'amore.*"

Edie laughed out loud.

"What did she say?" the bald man asked.

"She learned life skills that will serve her, and others, well," Edie very roughly translated.

"I should hope so," he replied as a tall, broad woman came in through the back door with her arms full of logs. "Amount of taxpayers' money that goes into your education."

"What would you know about university, Bob Bertrand?" The woman dumped the logs in the basket by the fire, then opened the hatch, strode behind the bar and placed her palms on the counter. The bottle-blonde embodiment of a landlady. "You bunked off so much school that, when you eventually showed up, we thought you were a ghost."

Bob shivered. "No ghost talk, Maddie."

"Why not?" Sophie asked.

Bob and Maddie's shared look suggested shared history.

"This is the time of year for ghost stories." The old man by the fire rubbed his temples, his eyes still closed. "If we don't honour the dead, we might as well become them." Behind him, a shadow moved in the alcove leading upstairs, as if someone listening was inching closer. But no one appeared.

"Merry Christmas to you too, John." Maddie's voice was spiced with sarcasm. She turned to Sophie. "I thought I asked you to peel potatoes. You've left your brother on his own."

The young woman shrank into her shoulders. "Sorry, Mum."

"Go on, upstairs with you."

Sophie's head dipped further as she slunk off the stool.

"*Addio*," Edie called out as she left.

Sophie sparked a smile in response, but it was scowled away by Maddie.

Edie was about to reprimand the landlady, then remembered the blizzard of cool words that she'd sent Sean's way on the journey here. Maddie was staring up the stairs as Sophie ascended, chin quivering as if she were about to cry. Perhaps Maddie, too, had a difficult relationship with Christmas and took it out on loved ones.

"Funny time of year, this," Edie said. "People loop back on themselves at Christmas. Become younger, take on old roles. Everyone in a family does the same, connected in an endless festive chain."

Maddie reached over the bar to the nearest paper chain and tugged it down. "Good job chains can be broken."

The main door blew open and Sean hurried in, followed by a flurry of snow, and then a tall, angular woman in a red coat.

"Inspector Hallows!" Maddie's smile was too wide to be believed. "That's three nights in a row. This really is a thirsty time of year for police officers."

"What can I say?" Laura's tone was as abrasive as dry roasted peanuts. "Your hospitality is irresistible."

"Any news I should be aware of?" Maddie asked.

"Heavy snow is predicted," Laura replied while brushing away snow that already lay like epaulettes on her shoulders. "I'll have mulled wines, please, and some privacy." Laura was as sharp as her cheekbones. Christmas was looking up. Laura strode over to Edie. "Now *that* is an ensemble," she said, looking at Edie's black Westwood dress, tartan tights, and Gaultier boots.

"Next time we meet I'll make an effort," Edie replied. "Sean didn't mention we were seeing you."

Sean had the grace to flush as the three of them settled round the table. "I may have omitted that."

"Spit it out, then," Edie said to Laura. "Why have you brought us to North Yorkshire?"

"God, Mum," Sean whispered. "At least say 'hello' first."

Laura laughed. "No need for niceties. I prefer to get to the point, too."

"And that point is…" Edie left the sentence hanging, ready for Laura to add her own link to the chain.

Maddie brought the drinks over on a tray and Laura touched a red-tipped finger to her lips. They sat in clove-scented silence as Maddie placed warmed wine in front of them. Cinnamon sticks poked out of the glasses like fat cigars.

When Maddie was back behind the bar, Glühwein warming their hands and throats, Laura looked around, then quietly said, "I read all about your jigsaw murder last Christmas in the papers, and Sean told me about the crimes you've solved since. And now I need your help, with this." Laura shushed an envelope across the table.

Edie picked it up, took out the handwritten letter inside, and read:

> DI Hallows,
> Before this Christmas is over, unless you take steps to stop me, just under two hundred people will die by my hand. Maybe then, Whitby will remember its ghosts.

"I presume this is a credible threat?" Edie said. "Otherwise, you wouldn't have brought us here." In Edie's peripheral vision, Maddie was cleaning a nearby table, her head inclined. She swiped at the same spot over and over. Either she was obsessed with getting cheap wood to shine or she was listening to their conversation.

"It was delivered with a heart-shaped helium balloon that could barely bob. Inside the balloon, we found this." Laura swiped down her phone to show a picture.

Something grey, withered, and fist-sized sat in an evidence box.

Sean shuddered. "So small but carries so much meaning. Do you know whose it is yet? Or how it was removed?"

And then Edie realised. "It's a heart." Her head pounded as if the knowledge caused pain.

"A *human* heart," Laura added. "And an hour ago forensics told us that the DNA matches that of Brian Gardener, one-time DCI in the North Yorkshire police, and my former boss. One of my sergeants is going to Brian's house."

"Tell Mum what was pinned to the heart," Sean said.

"A little luggage tag," Laura disclosed, "with another message to me – 'Fail us this time, and yours too will be taken from your chest, still beating'."

"That's why we're here," Sean said to Edie. "Laura told me about the threat, the balloon, everything. She's one of my best friends – I couldn't let her face this alone."

Edie's own heart felt as if it were being gripped by a fist. "But that just puts *you* in harm's way." She turned to Laura. "No offence, love, but we've only just met, and you're asking my son, and his family, to be involved in something potentially deadly."

"None taken." Laura was nodding. "I underst—"

"She didn't ask me. I insisted," Sean interrupted. "Laura saved my life while we were training. It's time I repaid her."

"You never told me that!" Edie's voice raised so much that Maddie looked over.

Sean leaned forward to take Edie's hand. "You worry about me when there's no reason to, this wasn't going to help. You already thought I shouldn't join the police."

"Looks like I was right," Edie replied. "You nearly died."

"And I would never have met the Puzzling Pensioner." Laura's sardonic twinkle undercut her sycophancy.

"It's the Pensioner Puzzler," Sean said. "That's what the press calls her, anyway."

Edie yawned, the long day leaning on her. Sean caught her

yawn, rubbing his eyes. She stood and plucked her coat from the back of the armchair. "And this pensioner needs to go to bed. We'll leave tomorrow, Sean. Tell Liam he needn't get on the train with the kids."

"But we can't, I need to—"

"It's okay, Sean. Your mum's right. You two have a good rest. I'll see you off in the morning." As Laura handed Sean a set of keys, her phone rang. "It's Jin, my sergeant." She answered the call. "What's the news?" Laura nodded and closed her eyes, exhaling deeply.

"Another round?" Maddie stood next to Edie, eyes fixed on Laura.

"DI Hallows asked for privacy," Edie said. "And we wouldn't want more, anyway. The wine is too heavy on the cinnamon, too light on the booze. Now shoo."

As the landlady walked away, Sean said, "Could you try being a bit less rude? Please?"

"Rude? Me? *She's* been trying to eavesdrop. I'd call that the height of impoliteness."

Laura slipped her phone back in her pocket. "Brian was found dead in his dining room, his chest hacked open, heart missing. Looks like he was there for days." A tear skirted her cheekbone. "I'm off there now."

"If you wait ten minutes while I take Mum to the apartment, I'll come with you," Sean said, throwing on his coat.

Edie started to counter. "But—"

"Sorry, Mum, but a former fellow police officer has been murdered," Sean interrupted. "My friend is under threat, and there could be more deaths to come. I'm not leaving."

"Then I'm coming, too," Edie said.

"I thought you were insisting on leaving tomorrow?"

"If you're investigating, there's no way I'm sitting in a holiday home, waiting. I want to be by your side. After all, Christmas is a time for family."

Sean was in the back of Laura's tiny car, squished between two booster seats. His feet were in a sea of lentil crisp packets and Fruit Shoot bottles. A tree-shaped air freshener pendulumed from the driving mirror, exuding its faux-pine scent like a Lynx-happy gym-goer.

Leaning forward, he touched Edie's shoulder. "You know you can't enter the crime scene, don't you?"

"Of course I do. You've told me enough times." Edie's voice showed her tiredness. Guilt got him in the heart. He should never have let her come with them. But when had anyone stopped Edie from doing what she wanted? "I'll stay in the car," she said. "But, before we get there, I want to quiz Inspector Hallows."

"Ask away," Laura replied.

"Why did you meet us in that particular pub?" Edie asked. "And why had you been in there three nights in a row?"

"You noticed something was up."

"I notice everything."

"The letter came to me via Maddie at The Last Angel. It'd been opened, of course. Before that, I'd been in a few times at most, but no more than any other pub in Whitby, and never on official business."

"What did Maddie say?" Sean asked.

"She denied opening it, claiming not to know why it'd been sent to the inn rather than the station. Not that I believe her. But, so far, we haven't found anything that would link her, or any regulars in the pub, to a crime investigated by Brian."

Edie gazed through the windscreen at the whirling snow. "It said 'steps' in the message. Isn't Whitby known for the absurd number of steps going up to the Abbey?"

"One hundred and ninety-nine, to be precise."

Sean whistled. "In other words, 'Just under two hundred'."

"Exactly." Edie tapped her fingers on her knees. "Have any unsolved crimes taken place on those steps?"

"I've never heard of any. But I'll investigate." Laura parked behind a chain of police vehicles. They were high up on the West Cliff. Sean squeezed his way out of the car into the icy night. Edie, left in the front seat, was already writing on the notepad in her lap.

The house – tall, detached, and looming – was ribboned with crime scene tape like the most unwelcome of gifts. A wreath lay in the centre of the lawned front garden.

Laura collected crime scene overalls for them both and, after they'd struggled into them, led Sean into the hallway of the house. Purple flocked wallpaper clung to the wall. Gold tinsel snaked on the carpet. The smell of cinnamon and orange from a bowl of pot-pourri couldn't mask that of human decay.

A CSI with poinsettia-red hair bustled over. "Laura!"

"Alright, Mary," Laura replied, smiling. "Glad you're on this."

"I wish I wasn't," Mary replied with a shiver and looked to the closed door on the right. "It's not pretty in there."

Laura placed her hand on Sean's shoulder. "This is DI Sean Brand O'Sullivan, from Weymouth police."

"Mary Rank," the CSI said, rustling out a gloved hand for a fist bump. An ivy tattoo wound up her forearm and under her sleeve.

"I bet you get a lot of nicknames here." As he said that, Sean wished he hadn't. She must encounter that all the time.

Mary sighed. "Yup. It's either 'Rank by name for a rank by nature job', or variations on 'wank'."

"I may have been guilty of both of those," Laura said. "You ever thought of changing your name?"

"Changing your name should only be done for reasons that give you meaning and identity, not to dodge other people's malice." An uncomfortable silence settled between Laura and Mary. Mary shook it off, turning to Sean. "You're a long way from home."

"I'm hopefully helping on the case."

"Be good to have an objective eye." Mary beckoned them into the room on the right. "Someone who never met Brian."

The yellow smell of decay was ten times worse inside. There was a piano in one corner, a desk with all the drawers pulled and tipped out, and a Christmas tree by the curtain-covered window. The large oval dining table in the centre was set for Christmas dinner for six, complete with crackers, and a dead body.

Laura covered her mouth as she went over to the corpse of Brian Gardener. Slumped back in his chair, his neck lolled. His unhearted chest gaped at the ceiling.

"The pathologist had an initial look just before you arrived," Mary said. "He wondered if whoever did this to Brian had training in dissection. It's too clean a job."

"From the lack of blood, I'd've thought the heart removal at least took place post-mortem," Sean added.

Laura was avoiding looking at the dead DCI, and instead examining the table. "Someone must have set it up like this," Laura said. "I can't imagine Brian making Christmas dinner for himself. But then you never know what happens when we each go home at night."

"And the letter the killer left suggests we didn't know Brian at all." Laura pointed to a piece of paper on his desk.

> "Detective" Gardener,
> You didn't do nearly enough digging when it came to my loved ones, in fact you said you "didn't care", so unless you give me all your notes on the case, I'm going to excavate your body to see if you have a heart. You have till the third Sunday of Advent.

"Looks like he didn't surrender those case notes," Laura said.

"And his killer, or killers, looked for them." Sean crouched by the spilled papers and notepads next to the desk.

"It's the same upstairs, and in the attic," Mary added. "Drawers, cupboards, storage boxes, all ransacked. But we've got no idea whether they found them or not."

When Sean and Laura returned to the car half an hour later, a large cock and balls had been drawn in the snow on the bonnet. Edie was grinning at them through the window. They got in to the sound of The Pretenders' melancholic Christmas song, 'Two Thousand Miles', mourning out of Edie's phone. "I thought you might need cheering up," she shouted over the music. "For the sake of sexual equality, I also drew a vulva on the boot."

"Edie's an old punk," Sean explained to Laura.

"I know. I read that *Times* article after she captured Rest in Pieces, the jigsaw killer." Laura drove away, setting the windscreen wipers on the settled snow. "I was impressed."

"They didn't get my good side," Edie huffed.

"The photo was lovely," Laura replied.

"No, the reporter called me 'an indomitable imp of an eighty-year-old, who insults with impunity'."

"Well, you do, Mum." Sean kept his tone as gentle as possible.

"Sure, but the bastard didn't report that I also made him lavender shortbread."

"Riga made the biscuits, Mum."

"*He* didn't know that. Anyway, what have you learned?"

Sean and Laura caught Edie up on all that had taken place in Gardener's house, filling her in as they would a crossword.

"Does his level of decay match him being killed on Sunday?" Edie asked.

Laura nodded. "Nothing confirmed yet, of course. But house-to-house questioning also suggests that his neighbours haven't seen him since last weekend."

"We must go to the station," Edie said, waving her notepad. "Go through every case Gardener was assigned to."

"I'll be doing that." Laura glanced across at Edie. "Go and rest that mega brain. I'll need it tomorrow."

Edie opened her mouth, but a yawn took the place of any objection. Within five minutes of the drive, she was asleep.

As her head lolled back, Sean was gripped by the fear of her lying as Brian had, her heart discarded, wrapped up in crime scene tape for Christmas.

24 *December*

Seagulls always squawked Edie awake, but this time they were northern. She could hear it in their accents. One of them was standing on the windowsill, eyeing her through the gap in the curtains. It tapped on the glass three times, then raised its wings as if delivering a warning.

Last night's trip to the house of the heartless man came back to her. Edie sat upright. From her bed – cosy but lacking in thread count – she had a view through Whitby's lighthouses out to a satsuma-hued sea. It was already dawn – she'd slept in. The day was getting away from her.

Sean knocked on the door and came in with a laden tray. "Happy Christmas Eve!" He placed the tray on her lap, careful not to spill the tea or unsettle the Jenga of buttered toast. "I got the sourdough from a little bakery down the hill."

"Any update from Laura?"

Sean took the top tier of toast and carried it over to the armchair by the window. "She sent a message at four a.m., saying she'd made progress, and would be over this morning."

The seagull turned its yellow gaze onto Sean and jabbed its beak at the window.

Sean shook his head. "Bread isn't good for birds. Or me, but I can't resist."

"This isn't bread, it's magic." Edie held aloft a holey slice. "Riga talks to Barbara, her sourdough starter, as if it's a long-lost lover. Every time she whispers to Barbara, it bubbles."

"Are you jealous of a jar of yeast?"

"When I smell of Yves Saint Laurent? I don't think so." Edie looked down at the phone screensaver of Riga – her best friend, neighbour and love. "But I do miss her."

"I'm sorry she couldn't come with us."

"I worry about her just walking over the lawn to see me, let alone driving this far." The lack of her, though, made Edie feel like her own heart had been taken out and left with her ninety-one-year-old kitchen witch in Weymouth.

The doorbell rang throughout the apartment. Sean jumped up, as did the seagull, which flew out of sight. "That'll be Laura."

Fifteen minutes later, Edie, dressed in the grey Westwood/McLaren smock dress she'd found in Scope, sat in the little lounge. A log fire was laid, ready for flames. Wooden shelves boasted board games and, Edie was happy to see, jigsaws. Clean windows looked onto sea, white-quiffed waves headbutting the harbour walls.

Sean and Laura were on the other sofa. "I was up most of the night, going through Brian's cases," Laura said, "and three jumped out."

"Narrows things down," Sean said.

"One is from 1992, when a fight broke out at the bottom of the steps on New Year's Eve and two young men died of their injuries. Then, in 2010, two sibling teenagers were found dead on the shore below the East Cliff. Before they died, they were last seen on a bench halfway up the steps."

Edie's instincts prickled. "Who found them?"

Laura nodded as if in appreciation of Edie. "It was less who found them, than who saw them last – Maddie's son, Simon Bertrand."

"Bertrand?" Edie said. "The shiny-headed man in the bar was Bob Bertrand. What time of year did they die?"

"Christmas Eve. They were waiting for their mum to come out of Midnight Mass in St Mary's church on top of the hill. Their shoes were found on the last two steps before reaching the summit, but their bodies were discovered on the beach below."

"So that's our case," Edie said, and Sean nodded.

"Listen to this before you decide." Laura held up a final sheet of paper. "Just before I arrived at the station, in 2015, Brian was lead detective on a murder case in which a person was killed in St Mary's churchyard on Christmas Day. And the person killed was Maddie's brother, Thomas."

"At least two cases, involving Maddie," Sean said.

"Or it's the same case," Edie added. "Maybe Maddie, or a member of her family, killed Gardener as an act of retribution?"

"Perhaps." Laura reached for a chocolate biscuit and nibbled round the edge.

"But why murder him now? And why would Maddie draw attention to herself by having the note sent to The Last Angel?" Edie asked.

"I'll be asking Maddie, and her son, those very questions, as well as posing some to Bob Bertrand."

Edie thought back to the conversation she'd overheard in the inn. "Maddie mentioned that Sophie had a brother, and that she'd left him alone. I assumed that meant he was a toddler, or under ten at least."

"You never left me alone for longer than the time it took you to finish the *Times* crossword."

"Three and a half minutes," Edie said to Laura. "Quicker than a shit."

Laura raised her eyebrows, but it wasn't clear whether in an impressed salute, or shock.

"This is official business, right?" Edie said. "So, I won't be allowed to interview anyone."

Sean and Laura nodded at the same time.

"Then I'm going to the steps. See what kind of a hill we're climbing."

"You can't go up." Laura stared at Edie. "Not by yourself. You're too—"

"Too what?" Edie rose to standing, glaring down at the woman.

Sean turned to Laura, shaking his head. "Careful!"

Edie raised her eyebrows higher, challenging Laura to finish her sentence.

"It's unwise, at your age…"

Sean slumped, placing his head in his hands. "Now you've done it."

Edie slammed the front door on the way out, ignoring Sean's pleas for her to stay. The wreath attached to the door-knocker swung then settled, reminding her of the one tossed onto Gardener's front lawn. And then there were the streaks of tinsel on the floor of his home. Someone in this case disliked Christmas, maybe even more than she did.

The snow had settled into drifts that the salters had missed. Edie moved slowly down Henrietta Street, holding onto window boxes and sills till she reached the base of the famous steps. She'd popped on her trainers, and brought a cane, but the stone stairs that looked over her were even steeper than she'd anticipated.

Two bobble-hatted hikers in sturdy walking boots took deep breaths before commencing the climb. "Nice day for it," the one in the red hat said, looking up at the cloudless sky. "At least the steps have been salted, eh?!"

"I wouldn't bother talking with me," Edie replied. "I'll only snap at you."

"Like a Christmas cracker!" Red Hat quipped.

"But more explosive and containing jokes at your expense that you'll never forget."

Red Hat's smile faded, and the two hikers hurried away up the steps. When they were out of sight, Edie began her own climb.

Cane ticking off each step, she ascended, one hand gripping the cold rail.

Edie had been researching overnight, too. These steps had once been wooden, and the number of them quibbled over. They were known as The Church Stairs, as they led Christians to worship, or Jacob's Ladder, leading them to Heaven, otherwise known as death.

Heart going far too fast for someone moving so slowly, she stopped on one of the benches. Coffins had rested there, too. The dead had been carried up those steps for centuries. Imagine that being your final journey.

A gull, maybe her window gull from earlier, soared past. Edie stood and continued her climb. She rested and moved on, moved on and rested, sang The Fall songs that made her march, and Wire ones that gave her strength. The sea seemed to take up all her left-hand-side peripheral vision, closing in on the sky. Maybe she would never stop climbing. Maybe this was the Ever Road.

Then the glinting glass of St Mary's church came into view. Almost there.

At the one hundred and ninety-eighth step, Edie imagined the pairs of teen shoes that had been left on that stone and the one above. Heels together, shuffling or dancing or running no more. If those shoes had belonged to Sean, she would never forgive anyone who harmed him.

Out of the corner of her eye, she thought she saw a shape, a boy, standing next to her. Another on the last step. When she looked directly at them, they had gone.

Above, another gull swooped, dropping flowers taken from St Mary's graveyard, like a spouse swiping a cellophane bouquet from a late-night garage. A snail-topped carnation fell at her feet.

The churchyard, with its tilting, snow-sheeted gravestones, looked down to the shore where Bram Stoker shipwrecked the *Demeter* and set Dracula loose on Whitby. Famous local ghost, the Phantom Coach and Horses, reared and disappeared here at night. Edie bet the St Mary's grounds-person was forever stopping goths from gyrating against gravestones. Not that Edie blamed the youngsters – as someone more Bauhaus than boho, she knew that funereal fucks were often the best.

Something red fluttered on the church. Edie crunched across the uneven graveyard to the large wreath that had been nailed to the wooden door of St Mary's. Foliage and berries sprayed black, the only splash of colour was the scarlet bow that trailed its legs on the snow, and the green writing on the sign that hung from the wreath: '192 will be dead by midnight tonight'.

"Can you actually do that?" Sean asked Laura, standing with Edie outside the church not ten minutes after Edie had called him. "Declare St Mary's out of action on Christmas Eve?"

"You have no choice." Edie's voice carried across the graveyard, causing a gull to rise from a grave. "People's lives are in danger. All the evidence we have links the threat to the steps, this church, and Christmas Eve. We close it down and keep everyone safe." She was shivering, hugging herself. Sean wanted to get her back into the warm and away from all danger, but he knew she'd never agree. He looped his arm round Edie's bony shoulders. She felt thinner, more insubstantial, than ever.

"Stand down, Edie," Laura said. "I'm declaring it a crime scene as a death threat has been made on the premises. There'll be no more services there today." She walked off, already on the phone to her colleagues.

Edie leaned on Sean, just a little. "What did you find out?"

"Simon, her son, wasn't in the pub, and neither was Bob. Maddie said that she'd had a one-night fling with Bob – a horrid thought – and Simon was the result. She said she doesn't even know who Sophie's dad is."

"Did you believe her?"

Sean shrugged. "I think so, but then I tend to believe people. You're much more cynical than me. Maddie also insisted that she had no idea what the threat referred to, or why it had been first delivered to her. She also laughed at it having anything to do with her brother's death. And she claims she has no beef with Brian Gardener."

"She wouldn't, not now he's dead."

"You don't believe her?"

Edie frowned, her eyes sliding right as if trying to remember. "There's something going on in that pub. Her relationship with her daughter is odd, and it felt stuffed with secrets."

"You think everyone has secrets."

"Because they do."

Back at the apartment, Edie wrapped presents, choosing green instead of red ribbon, and waited the long minutes until the kids arrived with Liam. When Juniper burst through the door at four o'clock, she jumped into Sean's arms, then bundled into Edie's lap. Edie felt a candle lit inside her heart.

Night fell in on them. Juniper opened her Christmas Eve box and, once her new pyjamas were pulled on, and found to be far too long, they all snuggled by the fire, holding mugs of hot chocolate heaped with marshmallows. One-year-old Daisy smeared spoonsful of mashed banana around her mouth and giggled a gurgle when Edie did the same.

At eight, the kids asleep, Sean, Liam, and Edie sat in the lounge, picking at and drinking Santa's fireside treats, listening to winter winds laugh at the windows. Edie couldn't stop thinking of whoever had plucked out Gardener's heart. Logs shifted, restless, in the grate.

"Nothing's going to happen; no one's going to die," Sean said to her. "You made sure of that."

"Maybe." Edie took a sip of port. She knew that a killer who could uncork a heart wouldn't stop at a locked church. They were on a vigil that night, but Edie didn't know what, or who, for.

25 December

It was still dark when the call came. Not even six in the morning, and all of them were up as Juniper emptied her stocking. All it took was the look on Sean's face when he answered the phone for Edie to know what had happened.

"What's wrong, Daddy?" Juniper put her hand to Sean's face, trying to lift his lips back into a smile.

"It's a work call, Poppet, and I'm sad that I'll have to nip out for a bit." Sean kissed the top of her head and mouthed 'sorry' to Liam.

Liam's smile was thin but, Edie hoped, forgiving.

"I'll do my best to get back for Christmas pudding. Save me a sprout!"

Edie followed Sean into the corridor.

"It still happened." Sean's voice dipped into whispers. "One hundred and ninety-two people are dead."

"How did they get into St Mary's? I thought Laura put officers at the doors."

"Patrols were there all night. But the killer misdirected us. You were right that it would be by the steps, in a church, on Christmas Eve. But it was in St Agnes' church, one of the sister churches to St Mary's, built at the bottom of the hill for those who couldn't walk up the steps to the top."

Edie's heart felt squeezed, like an orange plucked from the bottom of a stocking. She told herself that she'd done everything she could, but didn't believe it.

Sean slipped on his long coat. "I'm meeting Laura at the scene."

"I'm coming with you."

Sean hesitated, then nodded.

All of Church Street was cordoned off, a growing crowd pushed back by officers. Even on Christmas Day, the rubberneckers came.

Someone grasped Edie's elbow. She turned, ready to snap or slap, but it was only Laura.

"I've got you both special dispensations to enter the scene. Not that you'll thank me." Laura bulldozed her way through the ghouls with Edie sandwiched between her and Sean. An officer lifted the cordon for them, bowing his head to Laura. "And we can only go in for five minutes, for health and safety's sake. You'll see why."

St Agnes' church had a thin, pale frontage, like it needed a good meal, maybe from The Last Angel Inn which was right next door. Edie must have walked straight past it on the day they arrived and not even noticed. Another connection between the pub and the killer.

"Take a deep breath," Laura said, her hand on the church door. In a small anteroom, a team of CSIs rustled Edie, Sean, and Laura into forensic suits and respirators. A chubby Christmas tree with a wonky angel stood in one corner.

Despite the lungs filled with December-fresh air and her mask, when Edie stepped into the church, she stopped breathing. The pews were full, but empty of life. Silent carol singers were slumped, heads on each other's shoulders, in endless sleep.

Edie walked slowly down the aisle, trying to process what she was seeing. Holly-red faces lolled on blistered necks. Mouths hung open as if trying to guppy the poisoned air. Some of them were children, up late as a treat for Christmas. Edie couldn't look at those.

They moved up the church to a votive stand of guttered candles. A vicar in a gold chasuble was prostrate before the altar, wine spilled like blood around his head. Nearby, a layperson lay on a ledgerstone. Tiny cubes of bread were scattered around him as if for the birds.

"First thoughts?" Laura was by Edie's side.

"Carbon monoxide." Edie scanned the church and the covered over windows at the far end. "Probably piped in, high concentrations; exits and windows sealed off. The congregation would have most likely fallen asleep before death."

Sean stared at her. "How did you know that?"

"I shared a house at college with a boiler almost as dodgy as my flatmate. We all got light carbon monoxide poisoning. I then looked up what could have happened. It was nasty."

"We've located, and turned off, obviously, the source of the gas." Laura pointed to each of the many portable gas fires placed around the sides of the church. "Looks like they were all tampered with."

"So, we need to find whoever supplied them to the church," Sean said.

"That's proving difficult," Laura replied. "Everyone who was at the service died. They were found by a volunteer at four-thirty, delivering fresh flowers for the Christmas Day service."

"Why one hundred and ninety-two, though?" Edie asked. "If connected with the one hundred and ninety-nine steps and the two dead kids?"

"That was the maximum number of people allowed in the church, including the clergy," Laura said. "Maybe that was enough to make the killer's point?"

Edie shook her head, unconvinced.

"Didn't any family members notice their loved ones were missing?" Sean was trembling, perhaps imagining himself trying to locate Liam and Juniper.

Laura flushed. "Quite a few did and phoned the station."

"And no one did anything?" Edie heard the judgement in her own voice.

"It's Christmas Eve," Sean explained for Laura. "The night when hundreds in every town go out on a bender and don't turn up when they say they will. Most roll in sometime Christmas morning."

"Or when the pubs shut at one o'clock," Laura added.

"These people won't roll anywhere apart from their graves." Edie did one last look round the church. "Right, that's our five minutes. I need a drink."

"Nothing will be open at this time," Sean said.

"I have a feeling Maddie will open The Last Angel for us," Laura countered.

Edie grinned. "That's what I was hoping you'd say."

⌒

Edie sat again by the window of the inn, waiting for Sean and Laura to finish talking with the pathologist. Outside, dawn was treating those awake to a Christmas show, streaking the sky with orange. Boats bobbed in the harbour, as unable to keep still as her brain.

John, the old man, was in another armchair this time, eyes closed as if they never opened. And there, again, was Bob Bertrand. Sophie, Maddie's daughter, was serving them drinks. Her eyes had dulled in the intervening days.

"Do these blokes never leave?" Edie asked Sophie. "They shouldn't be here till official opening time."

"John lives upstairs. He's my great-uncle and Mum took him on when his wife died, ages ago. He often sleeps in the chair overnight rather than risking the stairs. And Bob, well, he just turned up at the door."

"I live over the road," Bob explained. "The mob outside the church woke me up early, then I saw you come here, and got curious."

"Wanted a free pint, more like." John felt for his own glass and drained it.

Footsteps stomped across the floor upstairs. Paper chains swung from the beamed ceiling. Raised voices punched each other. Sounded like Maddie arguing with a man. And then there was a thump, like someone falling heavily.

Laura rushed towards the staircase, with Edie and Sean following behind. Edie had never felt so elderly, her legs feeling all the missed hours of sleep. As she passed John, her hearing aid caught his whispered, "This should never have happened."

Upstairs was a large flat, on two levels. The floors were slanted, the walls bulging as if they could barely contain the centuries. Strung up from a lintel was a piece of string and a bunting of Christmas cards from relatives and punters. A few cards were Blu-Tacked to the wallpaper, including one from 'the B who will dig you always'.

A youngish man was sprawled on the floor of the kitchen, staring around, eyes unfocused. Maddie was hovering over him in a grubby dressing gown, rocking towards him and away. Under her eyes, shadows pooled. "Who asked you up here?" she said, addressing Edie, Laura, and Sean. "I give you privacy, you should give me mine. Go on, fuck off into the bar."

"From what we heard, there was an assault." Sean crouched next to the young man. "Can I ask what happened, sir?"

"You can't ask him *anything*," Maddie said.

"I'm twenty-seven, Mum. You can't control everything, not anymore." He looked up at Sean. "I'm Simon, Maddie and Bob's son."

Maddie fumbled for a chair and slumped at the kitchen table, head in her hands, fingers raking through tangled hair. "I hit him, okay? Charge me with assault, or whatever. I'm too tired to resist arrest." She stifled a yawn that everyone in the room caught.

Sean and Laura sat at the table, both blinking as if trying to prise their eyes open.

A holly prick of instinct scraped at Edie's quieter-than-usual mind. "Can I use your loo?"

Maddie nodded without looking up.

Edie walked as if through setting concrete towards the sitting room. There was a large, slumping sofa with red tassels and all she wanted to do was give in to its softness, and sleep. But that was why she had to keep looking.

She opened the built-in cupboards and found, under a blanket, a storage heater. And there was another one in the large bathroom, and one in each bedroom. Opening curtains and blinds, she tried to force open windows as well, but each was locked, with no key to hand.

Fighting the unctuous pull of unconsciousness, she hurried into the kitchen. Sean, Simon, Laura and Maddie were all sitting at the table in stupored silence. "Get out." She gasped for breath that could only be poisoned. "Carbon monoxide. Everywhere."

"If you hadn't realised what was happening…" Liam said to Edie when she and Sean were driven back to the apartment late that Christmas night. They'd been given the all-clear from Scarborough Hospital after oxygen treatment but would need outpatient monitoring. "I could have lost you both."

"But we're here," Sean replied, holding his husband in his arms. Edie wished she was with Riga. "And we're fine."

"But we don't know who placed the dodgy storage heaters in the church and the pub, or why." Edie went over to the shelves by the window and chose one of the jigsaws.

"I know you want to solve the case, but I reckon it's time to leave Laura to it," Sean said. "We should all get some sleep and replay Christmas Day tomorrow."

Edie shivered at the thought of sleeping. She might never wake up. But she was also swayed by the sense of stopping. Of giving up.

Tap. Tap. Tap. The seagull was back. It never gave up.

"I'm going to stay up. Mull on things. Did Laura give you all the information she's gathered to date?"

Sean shook his head, half with exasperation, half affection, then reached for his rucksack. Rifling inside, he handed Edie a thick lever arch file and a laptop. "That's got CCTV from Gardener's neighbours."

When Liam and Sean had disappeared upstairs, hand in hand, she sat with a pot of coffee and a packet of After Eights, to look through the file. Hours of CCTV from the days leading up to Brian Gardener's murder. Accounts from neighbours. Manufacturers of the tampered-with heaters. CSI reports. The clues at the church, the sister church, the letters from the killer. Forensic results on the deaths of Maddie's brother, and brothers Ryan and Mark Robins.

Facts swirled like snowflakes, and supposition like ghosts. Everything fitted, but she couldn't see how.

Taking one of the jigsaws from the shelves, Edie added two more logs to the fire, and started recreating the scene of Whitby's steps. With every piece of Jacob's Ladder placed, things came into view. And when she got to the penultimate step, she knew.

Sean blinked at the bright phone-torch light in his eyes. "What's going on?"

Edie's cold hands pulled at his arm. "Get up, love. The night's not over yet."

Sean stumbled into his dressing gown and crept out of the bedroom, setting off a yawning floorboard.

In the hallway, Edie held both of his hands and squeezed. Her eyes flashed. "You've got to contact Laura. Get her to arrest Maddie, Bob, Simon and John. And, above all, search Mary Rank's house."

Sean ransacked his murky night brain for that name. An image of a redhead came into his mind. "The CSI?"

"That's the one. Only I think when Laura looks closer she'll find that her surname isn't really Rank, and that before she was in forensics, she trained in medicine."

Sean blinked, trying to process. "How do you know?"

"I went through the CCTV and realised that something was bugging me. It was the wreath."

"The one on the church? With the threat?"

"The one someone had ripped from Gardener's door and thrown on the lawn. The footage shows that it was in place right up until his body was found by the police."

"Which meant that someone official at the scene had removed it before we arrived."

"So, I checked the CSI reports to see who was present, and one name felt wrong to me. Mary Rank. So, I did what I do best."

"Wake me up in the middle of the night? Make me worry? Insult journalists?"

"Now who's cynical? No, I mix things up. And Mary Rank is an anagram of…" Edie stared at Sean with her usual anticipation of him getting a crossword clue, something that he never fulfilled. "'Ryan' and 'Mark'."

"Whoah."

"Quite. And she drew attention to their deaths in—"

"The sister church to the one where they died. She's their sister."

"I believe so."

Sean's head ached, though he didn't think it was the lingering effects of carbon monoxide. "But why target Maddie and her family?"

"I don't know for sure, but I think Simon either killed those young lads, or was involved in their deaths, and it was covered up by their dad."

"Bob?" Sean tried to imagine the man killing anyone, but it didn't seem to work.

"Brian, of course. Didn't you see the Christmas card from 'B', 'the one who will dig you always'?"

"Not everyone sees everything like you do, Mum. So 'B' – that could still be Bob, then?"

"No! Who digs?"

The realisation cleared his brain like salt on snow. "A gardener. He's Simon's real dad?"

"I suspect so, and Sophie's. I don't know what happened in that churchyard when the boys died, but I think that Bob, John, and Brian, the three unwise men of The Last Angel, helped push the bodies over the cliff and covered up the killing. It's the ghost story John was talking about. It haunts them all."

"And now we need proof."

"You and Laura need proof," Edie said, yawning. "I'm going to bed."

Two days later, Edie and Sean stood at the base of Whitby steps. Snow was stippling the air. A memorial was taking place at St Mary's for the victims of the midnight massacre.

"What did Laura say, then?" Edie asked as Sean pocketed his phone.

"She's got a confession from both Simon and 'Mary'. Ryan and Mark had been beating Simon up on the steps when 'Great-Uncle' John, a caretaker at St Mary's, had come to his aid, hitting the lads too hard with his spade. Simon had called Maddie, who enlisted Bob and Brian to help. They threw the bodies off the cliff."

"All DCI Brian Gardener had to do was make the case disappear, and Maddie gave John a home for life at the Angel."

"Right. It was all forgotten until Mary Rank, real name Isabelle Robins, joined the police station under a new name to avenge their deaths, and make Whitby always remember them. Killing John, Maddie, Brian, Bob, and poor Sophie would take the number of her kills to one hundred and ninety-seven. Let's face it, no one will forget any of the dead after this. She found the notes at his house and knew for sure what they had all been hiding. So she tried to poison them, too."

Edie stared up Jacob's Ladder at the procession of mourners placing wreaths on every one of Whitby's one hundred and ninety-nine steps. Less certain shapes stood on the steps, too. Spectres in the snow. As if one hundred and ninety-two ghosts had joined the other two, no longer alone.

Above, her seagull dipped and placed its own flower at Edie's feet in either thanks or warning. She raised a hand to it, and the ghosts, in salute.

THE WRONG PARTY

Claire McGowan

S HE DIDN'T even want to go to the party. But Mum had insisted. *Go on, love, you never get out. And maybe there'll be a job in it, or you might meet someone.* Jayne didn't think the place to meet someone was at the corporate Christmas party of Land of Paper UK (first drink only free), the fourth-largest stationery company in the UK, where she had been temping for the past month, but it might lead to a permanent job, she supposed. Assuming she wanted to work permanently as the admin assistant to the Head of Paperclips. Also, she'd been told the party was mandatory unless you had a broken limb or were on your deathbed. She wasn't sure if that was a joke or not. Brenda, the HR lady, had an odd sense of humour.

She'd dithered over her outfit as well, ordering and sending back several sparkly ensembles. Now, as she wobbled off the Tube in uncomfortably spindly heels, she wasn't sure she'd made the right choice. The neckline was too low, surely, for a conservative place like Land of Paper UK. At least the venue for the party was nice, one of the fancy Mayfair hotels. The outside was so Christmassy, with glowing windows and twinkling lights set into fir branches. Jayne tripped going up the stairs, and the doorman in his hat and coat caught her elbow. "Be careful, miss."

"Sorry. Um – can you tell me where the party is?"

"Of course, miss. Down the corridor to the left." As she limped through the lobby, she felt like everyone was staring at her, no doubt disapproving of her high-street dress. A pianist was playing jazzy covers of Christmas songs, and fires roared in each corner. The corridor to the left was plush and silent, and her heels left deep impressions in the thick carpet. There were so many doors! How would she know which one it was? She opened a heavy wooden one tentatively, and was hit in the face by music and Christmas lights and the roar of conversation. This must be it.

Blinking under the shifting disco ball, she couldn't see anyone she knew, but then she hardly knew anyone yet. Mr Bryant, the Head of Paperclips, wasn't coming, as his ingrown toenail was playing up and had to be put in plaster for a week. Brenda, the chipper HR lady, must be here somewhere, though. A woman Jayne didn't know, with liquorice-shiny black hair, was standing behind a table laden with name badges and glasses of fizzing champagne. Jayne spotted her name – well, it said *Jane Smith*. That had to be her. People were always writing her name without its extra Ys – and she didn't blame them. Jayne Smyth was just an annoying way to spell it. She was used to the mistake, but it felt deflating, like the balloons that were slowly coming down from the ceiling. Like no one in this room knew or cared about her at all.

The woman behind the table glanced at the name-tag Jayne had picked up. "Oh, there you are! Here's your free welcome drink." Jayne wrinkled her nose at the fizzy liquid. She wasn't a big drinker, and didn't even like the taste of champagne, if she was being honest. But people got funny if you didn't drink at a Christmas party. Maybe she could get something else? Something sweet, like a Malibu and Coke.

She moved towards the bar, carrying the glass at arm's length, smiling vaguely at people. God, she didn't know anyone! She'd hoped she might at least recognise a few people from the canteen or corridors, but not a single person so far. And the bar was queued three-deep. "Ridiculous, isn't it," complained a large red-faced man beside her. "They ought to have waiters going around. Twenty minutes I've been stood here – a man could die of thirst!"

"You're welcome to have this if you like, I haven't touched it." She offered the glass. His name badge read Herbert Duddington.

"That's very kind of you. Are you sure?"

"Very sure – I don't really like fizzy wine."

"Oh, well thank you, my dear, I'll buy you something else when I finally get through this scrum." He toasted her and took a large gulp. "So, what do you do here?"

"Just admin. I'm temping."

"Well, I'm sure we have opportunities for a lovely young lady like yourself!" His voice was very loud. In fact, everyone was so loud, shouting over the Christmas music and chatter. And it was incredibly hot. Herbert was loosening his collar too, a fine sheen of sweat over his forehead. Jayne wasn't sure why this was supposed to be fun.

"Um, I might just – it's very loud here…"

"What's that?" A drop of his sweat splashed onto her as he leaned forward.

"I said it's very loud…"

"Can't hear…" His eyes looked glazed.

"Sorry, are you OK?"

"Can't – eyes… going."

The half-drunk champagne smashed onto the floor, spilling over Jayne's new shoes, as he suddenly collapsed, out cold.

Around her, people screamed and leaped out of the way, leaving a circle about him. "Give him air!"

"Call an ambulance!"

"What's happened?"

"Too much to drink maybe, or…"

Jayne was on her knees, the floor gritty underneath them. He wasn't breathing. She had given him her drink and now he wasn't breathing. Trying desperately to remember the first aid she'd learned at school, she began to compress his chest in rhythm with the music no one had yet turned off. Urgh, she really didn't want to press her mouth onto his open, drooling one, his tongue stained black from whatever he'd been drinking. But she would have to, if no one else came—

"Stand aside, miss." A strong arm was moving her firmly but gently away. "It's OK, I've got it from here." It was a paramedic, with muscly arms and close-cropped hair. How did he get here so fast?

The paramedic worked on Mr Duddington, loosening his shirt and placing an oxygen mask over his face. "Will he be OK?" she asked.

The paramedic fixed her with intense brown eyes. "I hope so, miss." Then he lowered his voice. "You're compromised. Get out now."

"What?" She didn't understand. Did he mean she was going to be fired over this? But it hadn't been her fault – had it? "What do you…?"

"Why did you go so early? Plan was in half an hour! I was hardly ready."

"I don't know what you're talking about."

Someone else was taking Jayne aside then, pulling her to her feet and leading her away into the press of the crowd. It was the woman from the welcome desk with the shiny hair. "You've had a shock, poor thing. Why don't you come to the bathroom with me?"

"Um, I'm OK."

"No, come on, you're shaking. A bit of fresh air will do you good."

How would there be fresh air in the bathroom? Jayne felt woolly-headed, but she followed the woman along, assuming this was someone else from HR, not scatty but friendly Brenda who'd hired her for the temp role. "What do you think happened to him?" She noticed the HR woman wasn't wearing a name badge herself, which seemed odd. She had a long red dress with a slit up the side, but underneath she was wearing sturdy-looking flat black boots. That was also odd. Maybe Mum was wrong, and no one wore heels to parties anymore. Hers were already pinching, so she bent down and took them off, hobbling along the corridor after the woman. There seemed to be another party in the room opposite, the sound of 'Merry Christmas, Everyone' spilling out. "The poor man. Do you think he was ill?"

"Hmm? Oh, heart attack, most likely. Very common at that age. Nothing to worry about. Just follow me."

"It's just… it seemed to happen after he drank my drink?"

"Here we are." The woman in the red dress opened the door to the ladies, dragged Jayne inside. She stooped to see if anyone was in a cubicle, which Jayne didn't quite understand either. "Now, let's get you cleaned up, shall we?"

"I'm really OK—"

"Make-up. Here." She rummaged in a small, sparkly clutch and took out a lipstick in a gold case. "Please, allow me."

Jayne shied away as the woman wielded the lipstick at her face. "No, really, I hardly wear lipstick. I look weird in it. I'm fine, I just need a glass of water or something."

The woman looked annoyed. "All right, if you insist. Stay right here."

Jayne had no intention of staying there, but it was nice to have a moment alone to breathe. And she did look terrible, pale and trembling, her unaccustomed mascara already creeping down her face. What had happened to Herbert Duddington? Was it really a heart attack, and just a coincidence he collapsed right after drinking the champagne – her champagne? And what had the paramedic meant that she was compromised? He seemed too muscular to be a paramedic, somehow. Or maybe the uniform wasn't quite right? Something about it had just felt wrong. Weren't people always talking about the shocking state of ambulance wait times? And yet he'd been there within seconds!

Before the overbearing HR lady could come back, Jayne smoothed down her hair and crept out of the ladies, shoes in hand. She would just go home. She had tried, but there was no one at the party she knew, and she was too upset to chat and dance. If she left now, she could get into her onesie and watch a few Christmas episodes of *Friends* instead. She'd tell Mum she felt ill or something.

But as she came out, the paramedic was wheeling Herbert away on a kind of chair with straps. He looked out cold but at least breathing. That was a relief. His poor family if he'd died right before Christmas. "Is he OK?" she asked.

The paramedic – also no name badge, she noticed – looked shocked to see her. "I told you to get out! I thought you'd left!"

"I'm sorry, it wasn't my fault, or at least I didn't mean to…"

He hissed, "Juliet, what's going on? I said abort. They know. I assumed that's why you drugged him early?"

Drugged? Abort? Her head spun. "Juliet? No, my name is Jayne Smyth, but with a Y in both. They've spelled it wrong, but that happens all the time, and…"

At that moment two things happened. First, the paramedic's look of confusion cleared, and he said, "Jayne Smyth, with two Ys?" Then the door to the other party opened and Brenda staggered out, reindeer antlers on her head, large gin and tonic in hand.

"Jayne! There you are, dear. We thought you weren't coming!"

"But I thought…" She could now clearly see a little iPad on the wall by the door Brenda had come out of. Land of Paper UK Christmas Party. "Oh no – I went to the wrong party!" No wonder she hadn't known anyone.

"Well, never mind, join us now. Must tinkle." Brenda staggered towards the ladies, leaving her glass on a small table which held a large floral arrangement.

The paramedic grabbed Jayne's arm and hissed at her. "What did you say – you were at the wrong party? Your name really is Jayne, and you know nothing about TranspoCorp?"

"What's TranspoCorp? Oh, the other company? What do they do exactly?"

"Import–export," he snapped. "And on the side, arms dealing."

"What? I'm sorry, I've no idea what's going on. I just gave him my drink and he went down."

The man spoke into his wrist. "Operation compromised. Operative codename Jane Smith missing in action. Attempt on her life thwarted but cover is blown."

"What?" exclaimed Jayne. "You mean…"

"Jane Smith, no Ys, that was our undercover operative. She's been embedded in the company for six months and we were going to bust them tonight. She was supposed to slip Herbert here a little sedative so I could get him away. But you took her name badge."

"Bust them… so you're… police?"

"Special Ops."

"And I ruined it all?" Oh, she was so stupid.

"No! You saved her life. Someone is on to her, clearly. The drink was meant to kill her, and it would have killed you. Luckily, Herbert has a bigger body mass, so he should be alright. But you need to get out of here. We have to bring in the SWAT team or the company bosses will all be on private jets to non-extradition countries before we can say 'tinsel'."

Jayne was nodding slowly, backing away. This was insane. She had gone to the wrong party, the party of an arms-dealing company, and somehow got herself mixed up in a plot to kill people. She'd known it was a bad idea to leave the house. "What can I…?"

"Leave that man," came a voice from the end of the corridor. It was the HR woman, emerging from the loos, now holding a knife to Brenda's neck. "Who is that? It's not Jane Smith, clearly. You had two moles in TranspoCorp?"

The paramedic moved his body in front of Jayne and the unconscious Herbert. "It's too late. The hotel is surrounded. What have you done with Jane? I mean, the first Jane?"

"You mean *Juliet*? I was told to look out for her and give her that drink. Who's this, if it's not your operative?" She waved the knife towards Jayne. Brenda gave a small squeak of terror.

Jayne cleared her throat and stepped in front of the fake paramedic. "That's right, I'm the operative you *didn't* know about. So you'd better let that lady go or you're looking at some serious prison time. Isn't that right, eh...?"

"Matt," he whispered. Then he said, confidently: "She's right, Yolanda. I know your name too, see. There were two moles. Jane and... Jayne. With a Y."

Yolanda sounded desperate. "Look, they said I had to create a diversion, let them get away. But we need Mr Duddington – he's the only one who can access the financial paper trail. Let him go."

"He's seriously ill – thanks to whatever you put in the drink!"

"They told me to do it! Honestly, I don't get paid enough for this. I'm just a temp, you know! I've never even met the first Jane!"

Seeing her moment, Jayne didn't think twice. She launched one of her stupid impractical shoes down the corridor, as if throwing a winning strike in the bowling alley near her home, catching the red-dress woman on the hand, making the knife fly harmlessly to the ground. She yelped. "Ow, that hurt!" Brenda, showing the presence of mind that had let her stay Head of HR for twenty years, darted to grab it.

"Now, now, dear, that's enough of that. Someone's getting a written warning, I think."

And then a dozen SWAT operatives burst into the corridor, headed by a tall, muscular woman in a black silk trouser suit, wielding a gun. "Matt! They're on to me!"

He sighed. "Thanks, Juliet, I kind of got that. Hope you blocked the exits, or the top brass will soon be on their way to the Caymans."

"We got them. Just missing a Herbert Duddington, the CFO? We'll need his evidence."

At that moment, Mr Duddington let out a wet snore. "He's not going anywhere soon," said Matt. "So, where the hell were you?"

"Eh, well, you won't believe this but – there are actually two hotels with this name in London. I went to the wrong one."

"For God's sake."

"Sorry, sorry! Anyway, it's all sewn up now, no harm done." She nodded to Yolanda, who looked as if she were seriously reconsidering her career options. "You. Hands up."

"Um – can I have immunity if I tell you everything I know?"

"We'll think about it. Now – put them up!"

The red-dress woman sulkily put her hands up, as Brenda handed the knife over to one of the SWAT team, who put it into an evidence bag. "Well!" exclaimed Brenda, adjusting her antlers and retrieving her gin from the table. "What a bit of excitement! Don't be long, Jayne dear, we're about to start the conga line." And she went back to the other party, pushing her way through the crowds of bewildered TranspoCorp employees who were being herded out of their room by armed officers.

The paramedic – Matt, not actually a paramedic – turned to Jayne. "That was seriously impressive. You can cut the cover story now. Who do you really work for?"

"Um, Land of Paper UK? But I'm just a temp."

"Seriously? Where'd you learn to throw like that?"

She shrugged. "Dad used to take me bowling on his days off."

"Well, Jayne with a Y, we could use skills like yours. How would you like a permanent job?"

Jayne began to limp down the corridor to retrieve her shoe. Painful as they were, the pavements were way too dirty to go home barefoot. "That depends. There's not a mandatory office Christmas party, is there?"

UPON A MIDNIGHT CLEAR

A JOSEPH SPECTOR MYSTERY

Tom Mead

Happy, happy Christmas, that can win us back to the delusions of our childish days...

—Charles Dickens, *The Pickwick Papers*

Wednesday, 23 December 1936

Annie Edmunds entered the pub pursued by a plume of snow and a shiver of winter wind. She glanced anxiously about the place, then made for the bar.

"Half of stout, please," she said, placing a few coins on the counter.

When the barmaid set the foamy half-pint glass in front of her, Annie ventured: "Excuse me – I'm looking for someone. His name is..."

"The snug," said the barmaid, nodding toward a door at the other end of the bar. "He's in the snug."

Bemused, Annie answered simply, "Thank you," and took her drink.

Ducking through the low doorway into the adjoining snug, she was confronted immediately by a crackling fireplace and a pleasing burst of warmth. Her gaze settled on the man in black sitting in the high-backed armchair beside the fire. He was playing with a coin, rolling it back and forth with startling alacrity over gnarled-looking knuckles. When he saw her coming, he smiled. It was a pleasant smile that creased his papery face and twinkled in his pale blue eyes. He was very thin – cadaverous, she supposed. He had a mane of silvery-white hair, and wore a black suit and silk-lined cloak.

"Good evening," he said softly.

"Good evening," she answered. "Are you Joseph Spector?"

"I am," he said. "Won't you sit?"

She perched in the armchair opposite him, her discomfort palpable. "My name is Annie Edmunds," she said. "A friend told me about you."

"Yes? And what did this friend have to say?"

"She told me you had a way with… solving things. Puzzles and whatnot. Mysteries."

"And you've come to me with a mystery in need of resolution?"

Annie nodded. "I'm a housemaid. My mistress is Miss Rosamund Larch – do you know the name?"

Spector's pale eyes narrowed contemplatively. "Yes, I believe I do. She is the sister of the late Roderick Larch, is that so?"

Annie nodded vigorously. "Do you believe in ghosts, Mr Spector?"

"That is a complicated question," said Spector. "It might be better to ask whether *you* believe in ghosts, Miss Edmunds."

"I didn't used to. But now… maybe I do."

"What changed your mind?"

Annie took a sip of her stout, for Dutch courage. "As you know, the master died last winter. Took a tumble down the stairs and broke his neck. Doctor Anderson signed the death certificate and everything. It was all very sad. But then…" She took another sip. "Well, just a few days ago, in fact… he came back."

The name of Roderick Larch was not unknown to Spector. Indeed, he had followed the story in the papers at the time. It was one of those deaths that was enmeshed in mystery, and yet it had the appearance of a common-or-garden household accident. In the immediate aftermath, certain details about Larch's financial dealings came to light; he had embezzled close to a million pounds from the holdings firm he ran with his old school friend Stuart Weems. The various legal battles over the ensuing year, and efforts to claw back money Roderick Larch had squandered, provoked considerable discussion in the press. His unfortunate sister Rosamund was forced into hiding within the walls of the family home; a home which was owned by a trust, and thanks to Roderick's death was entirely safe from what his sister called 'the vultures'.

Annie Edmunds described Roderick's fall with a perfunctory absence of detail. The postman had just delivered the afternoon's letters. Annie had finished serving tea to Stuart Weems and Rosamund in the downstairs drawing room. Then, the three of them heard a horrible, cataclysmic crash, accompanied by a choked scream. They went running into the hall to investigate; Weems reached the fallen financier first.

"Get a doctor, for God's sake!" he instructed Annie. But it was too late.

Thus: Roderick Larch was dead. There was no doubt whatever about that. The register of his burial was signed by the clergyman, the clerk, the undertaker. Old Larch was as dead as a doornail; or, in suitably Dickensian mode, a coffin-nail.

"He died a year ago today," said Spector, "and now you say he is *back*?"

The housemaid nodded. "I would not say it if I had not seen him with my own eyes."

"Please go on."

"There was no mistaking that walk of his – he had a limp ever since he took some shrapnel in the thigh at Ypres. He always dragged his left leg slightly."

"Where did you see him? Please be specific."

"I was looking out of my window one night last week – I couldn't sleep. And there he was, sort of a silhouette in the moonlight, out in the garden."

"You didn't see him up close?"

"I didn't need to, Mr Spector. It was him all right."

"You could tell by his walk."

"That's it. He was out by the family mausoleum, where we laid him to rest last Christmas. I saw it sealed myself."

"And is that everything?" Spector was unconvinced.

"No," said Annie. "There is something else. Take a look at this." She produced a sheet of paper from her handbag and unfolded it carefully. It was a letter, dated 23 December 1936.

Dearest Gloria,
No doubt you are surprised to receive this –
not as surprised as I am to be writing it. But

I must see you. Come to the house tomorrow for midnight — that is, December 24th. I have invited a few others, as there is something very important I must give to you — and certain information to impart.

Yours ever,

Roderick.

Handing the letter back, Spector asked, "And who is Gloria?"

"Mrs Gloria Duggan. She and Mr Larch were married when they were very young – it didn't last long, though. They ended up with a very messy, costly divorce, and Gloria eventually married Ridley Duggan, the chess champion. But Mrs Duggan stayed on good terms with Miss Rosamund. The two were school friends, I believe, and bonds like that are tough to break. Mrs Duggan received the letter this morning and immediately brought it round to show Miss Rosamund."

"A forgery?"

Annie shook her head. "That's the real reason I'm here, Mr Spector. Both ladies swear it's *not* a forgery. Though I cannot be as positive as they, the writing on that letter is very like his."

"Do you know the names of the 'others' who have received invitations?"

"I know of two others, aside from Mrs Duggan. Mr Weems and the heiress Eleanor Valdane."

"Eleanor Valdane? Why on earth…?" Valdane was an infamous high society misfit; a mystic and erstwhile devotee of Aleister Crowley.

Annie shifted slightly in her seat, looking a little uncomfortable.

"There were certain… rumours. About Mr Larch and Miss Valdane, I mean. I've no idea if there was any truth to them."

"Did Larch share her interest in the supernatural?"

"I couldn't say, sir. But Mr Weems and Miss Valdane have been in touch with Miss Rosamund this morning, thinking perhaps that the whole thing was some kind of practical joke. Had I not *seen* Mr Larch with my own eyes," Annie said solemnly, "I'd be inclined to agree."

"You really think he's going to put in an appearance?"

"I don't know, Mr Spector. But I cannot escape the notion that he might."

"And Miss Rosamund? What has she to say on the matter?"

"She is as bemused as any of us. But she intends to let the gathering go ahead. To let things play out, as she puts it."

"She knows you've come to see me?"

"She does. Miss Larch has been a recluse since her brother died. She never leaves the house. Otherwise, she would most likely have come to meet you herself. In fact, she has asked me to invite you to the gathering. Unless, of course, you have other plans for Christmas Eve…?"

"Consider them cancelled," said Spector. "I imagine *this* will be far more interesting."

The following morning, Spector spent an hour or so making enquiries about the deceased businessman's final days. Snow had been falling throughout the night; indeed, it was falling still, and the streets of London were lined by hefty snowdrifts.

First, Spector paid a visit to the 'Doctor Anderson' Annie had described. In the intervening year since Larch's death, the doctor had set himself up in a new and illustrious Harley Street practice. Spector inveigled his way into a short-notice consultation, and promptly commenced his questioning.

"Yes," said Doctor Anderson, "I recall it well. How could I not? It was a nasty incident – the head turned almost all the way round, you know. Dead instantly."

"Was Mr Larch a fairly robust man?"

"Not especially. He was getting on in years, as are we all." The old doctor chuckled into his brandy tumbler.

"Were you able to determine what caused the fall?"

The doctor shrugged. "Particularly difficult to do, you know. Falls are funny. I often tell people it's the perfect means of murdering someone and getting away with it. Seems a little too simple, but really, simple is often the best way, don't you find?"

"Indeed," answered Joseph Spector.

The Larch family home was a mouldering old red brick construction on the outermost western edge of London. It sat in large tree-lined grounds, with sprawling snow-covered lawns on all sides. Spector traversed the long driveway on foot, taking in his surroundings. The fabled family crypt, where Roderick's mortal remains were interred, lay presumably somewhere to the rear of the house.

Spector rang the bell and was admitted to a cavernous hallway by Annie, now in her housemaid's uniform. She bobbed politely and led him through to the drawing room; the room, Spector reflected, where Stuart Weems and Rosamund Larch had heard Roderick's deadly fall. As he passed by the bottom of the wide, sweeping staircase, Spector could not resist a glance upwards, his mind haunted by the image of tumbling bodies.

In the drawing room, the party was in full swing. That is to say, the other guests were all present, though the mood was sombre. Stuart Weems already had a sherry in his hand, evidently sensing the direction the evening would soon take. He wore a pinstripe suit, and his grey hair was parted down the dead centre, giving his face, body, and gait a sense of perfect geometric alignment.

Spector recognised Eleanor Valdane from the copious photographs which graced the gutter press. She was a New Woman, perfectly unafraid to court scandal. She wore trousers and a bow tie, and twitched a quizzical eyebrow in Spector's direction.

Gloria Duggan was positively staid by comparison, with a modest chiffon evening gown. Spector found it difficult to imagine either of these women being romanced by the cipher-like Roderick Larch.

And then there was Rosamund. Bearing in mind the impromptu nature of the event, she seemed to be having a wonderful time playing hostess. She had dressed for the occasion in a belted gown of bottle-green rayon, and her face was discreetly made up. The prospect of a phantom visitation by her dead brother did not seem to trouble her.

Perhaps inevitably, Spector was the main focus of the guests' attention. He was a stranger in their midst, after all.

"So you're some sort of detective?" said Weems suspiciously.

"If you like."

"And you're here to solve the mystery of Roderick's resurrection?" Eleanor Valdane offered jocularly.

"It bears some investigation, don't you think?"

"The letters, certainly. But this little gathering? Well, it's just an excuse to get drunk in the company of old friends. Not that I'm averse to that!"

"You don't believe Roderick Larch is alive, then?"

"Whether he is or not, I don't see what he could want with all of us. What 'information' could he possibly have for us?" She drew a crumpled envelope from the pocket of her dinner jacket, and from it produced her letter. She showed it to Spector, who noted that the wording was exactly the same as the one received by Gloria Duggan.

"May I see the envelope as well, please?"

She handed it over without comment. Spector observed that the address of Eleanor Valdane's townhouse was neatly typed — she lived in Berkeley Square, not far from Roderick Larch's London office.

Weems was restless. "You'll forgive me, Rosamund, for saying I consider this to be an enormous waste of time."

"Spoilsport!" cried Eleanor Valdane in a distinctly mocking tone. Evidently the alcohol was taking effect. "You remember the letter, don't you? He won't be putting in an appearance until midnight. The stroke of midnight! Fitting for a 'phantom', no?"

"Oh, don't be fatuous, Eleanor. You weren't here when he died. You didn't see him. Roderick is dead, and he left the rest of us with a considerable mess to clear up."

She smiled. "I believe you, Weems. You misunderstand me. I don't doubt that Roderick is dead. But I am no less convinced that he wrote the letter I received."

Gloria Duggan entered the discussion. "More of your Thelemite, Golden Dawn nonsense, Eleanor? Messages from beyond?"

"More things in Heaven and Earth, Horatio…"

And the conversation continued in that increasingly tedious vein.

Eventually, at almost a quarter to midnight, Stuart Weems reached the limit of his patience. "I'm sorry," he said, "but I must be on my way. This whole foolish business has taken up too much of my time already. It was a mistake to come here."

Eleanor turned toward the clock. "Only twenty minutes to go – you can't leave now, Weems!"

"I can and will. I let my curiosity get the better of me – a mistake I shall not repeat. Some spirits are best left untroubled – your brother, Rosamund, is one of them. Good night, all. Spector, I would say it has been a pleasure, but we both know that's not the case."

And he left the room, escorted by Annie.

The last few minutes until midnight were positively torturous – not least for Spector, who was a showman himself and knew a thing or two about building suspense. The group fell silent at two minutes to midnight, and all eyes were on the clock on the mantel.

When midnight finally struck, the clock issued a melancholy chime that seemed to echo about the house. It ceased, and the assembled guests looked awkwardly from one person to another.

Just when it seemed as though the whole evening had reached a crushing anticlimax, Gloria Duggan said: "Look."

She was pointing toward the window, and beyond it, where a sudden orange light had flared in the distant darkness.

"It's a lantern," said Eleanor Valdane.

"It's coming from the crypt," offered Rosamund.

The Larch family mausoleum, a grey stone edifice, lay at the other end of a pristine white lawn, smooth with undisturbed snow. Approaching the window, Spector saw that Rosamund was correct: the lamplight was issuing from the open doorway.

He darted out into the hall and made for the front door, but Annie Edmunds called him back. "The kitchen door is quicker. This way, Mr Spector." She led him through the kitchen and out the side door. He followed her round and onto the rear lawn, where the light still blazed inside the mausoleum.

Spector took long, loping steps, his feet crunching ankle-deep into the snow. He kept pace with Annie, and they soon reached the building. Just as they did so, the lamplight flared briefly and then died, leaving the building in darkness once more.

"Annie," said Spector, "do you have a torch?"

"There's one in the kitchen."

"Go and fetch it, please."

She went.

Spector drew a book of matches from his trouser pocket and lit one before stepping into the mausoleum. The small, flickering light cast long, eerie shadows. He paused briefly to examine the open door – there were scratch marks around the keyhole.

Then he turned his attention to the mausoleum proper; like any other, it was a simple square stone building, with no windows to speak of. At its far end, six coffins (one for each guest, plus the housemaid into the bargain, Spector reflected morbidly) stood on simple, unadorned catafalques.

Spector crept forward, cupping his hand around the lit match to protect the flame. He read the name on each brass plaque, and paused when he reached RODERICK LARCH. Unlike the other five coffins, this one bore the fresh marks of gloved hands on its dusty surface.

Cautiously, Spector reached out and gripped the handle at its side. To his surprise, the lid lifted easily. Holding the match high, he peered inside. The coffin was empty.

"Mr Spector!" hissed a voice, making him jump. When he spun round, the match went out.

"Who's that?" he said into the darkness.

Suddenly a battery-powered torch cast a strong white light to all corners of the mausoleum. It was Rosamund Larch. "What's happened?"

There was no use in trying to keep it from her. "I'm afraid your brother's coffin is empty."

"*What?*" There was pure horror in her voice. "What are you talking about? Not a soul has set foot in here since we laid my brother to rest. I wouldn't allow such a desecration!"

Ignoring her remark, he asked, "Where are the others?"

"I left Gloria and Eleanor in the drawing room. I haven't seen Annie."

"Come," said Spector decisively, "I think I have an idea of what is going on."

"You do?" She followed him out into the snow once more, the lone torchlight casting bright swathes in the dark.

"There," said Spector, pointing. "The footprints."

He was not looking at the overlapping trails which led to the kitchen door. No; his attention was focused on a separate, lone trail, which led away from the mausoleum and around to the *other* side of the house, toward a set of French windows which now hung eerily open. The footprints were distinctive; the left foot having dragged noticeably.

"It's Roderick's study," Rosamund explained.

"And where is the key kept?"

"It hangs on a hook in the kitchen. Anyone could have grabbed it – anyone. But I swear, no one has been in there since Roderick died."

Spector nodded. "Go back inside, Miss Larch. And telephone for the police. If possible, ask for Inspector George Flint of Scotland Yard. Tell him it's Joseph Spector. And then, return to the drawing room."

Next, Spector followed the lone trail of limping footprints toward the open French windows. He entered the room, fumbling in the darkness until he reached a light switch on the far wall.

And that's when he saw he was not alone in the study.

Stuart Weems was sitting in an armchair by the unlit fireplace. He had a faintly smug, satisfied smirk on his face, as though he held the winning hand in a high-stakes poker game. His gloved fingers were gently interlaced over his belly. He might simply have been enjoying the fire, were the carefully curated symmetry of his appearance not ruined by a kitchen knife protruding from his right eye socket.

Aside from the windows, the only means of accessing the room was the oak-panelled door. With a crimson silk handkerchief over his hand, Spector tried the handle. The door did not budge. A key was protruding from the lock, as though Weems himself had locked it before the fatal blow was struck.

Spector gave the key a twist and stepped out into the hall. There stood Annie Edmunds, looking stricken. "I couldn't find the torch," she said. "Has something happened?"

"I'm afraid so. Go back into the drawing room with the others. I'll join you shortly."

He closed the study door once again and had a look around the room. Several other unusual details presented themselves to him immediately. First, the corpse of Stuart Weems was shoeless. The shiny dress shoes he had worn earlier in the evening were down by the side of the chair. He was in stockinged feet. Second, the nearby desk drawers were all open, and the papers therein ransacked. This, coupled with the leather gloves Weems wore, seemed to indicate he had broken in. After incriminating papers, Spector supposed. Evidently Stuart Weems was not as blameless as he had claimed.

"Ladies," said Spector, "I regret to inform you that Stuart Weems is dead."

They exchanged worried glances, but no one said a word.

"In order to resolve this strange case, I should like to ascertain *where* exactly you all were during those few confused minutes after midnight."

"We were in here," said Gloria Duggan. "That is, Eleanor and I. Rosamund went out to the kitchen, looking for a torch to bring to you out at the mausoleum. She thought perhaps you might need it."

"Yes," said Rosamund, "I went to the kitchen to fetch the torch."

"And you didn't enter the study?"

"No. I didn't even go near it. As I said earlier, nobody's been in there since Roderick died."

"What about you, Annie?"

"Well, I just went back to the kitchen for the torch like you said, but it was already gone. Presumably because Miss Rosamund had taken it. We must have just missed each other in the darkness."

"I found you in the hall outside the study. Why was that?"

"Because I saw a light under the door. So I went and tried the handle, but it was locked."

"You knew where the key was kept?"

"Yes – on a hook in the kitchen. I returned to look for it, but it was missing. Then I headed *back* to the study, and that's when you came out and found me, Mr Spector."

"I see," said Spector thoughtfully.

"But what does all this *mean*?" demanded Eleanor Valdane. "The footprints, the empty coffin... is Roderick alive? Is *he* the one behind this?"

Spector removed a thin black cigarillo from a silver case he kept in his jacket. As he lit up, he said, "The police will be here soon."

While they waited, Spector sat in a chair pointing toward the window and the now darkened mausoleum. But before the authorities could arrive, he suddenly stood and said, "I have it."

The four women stared.

"At least, I think I do. But I must ask – Mrs Duggan, you and Roderick Larch were divorced, isn't that so?"

"Correct."

"But you remain on good terms with his sister."

She shrugged. "Of course."

"Did you have any further contact with Roderick Larch before he died?"

"None. But the divorce wasn't particularly acrimonious, in spite of what you may have heard."

"Did he trust you? Would he have shared his secrets with you?"

"Perhaps... if he had nowhere else to turn. We were estranged, Mr Spector."

"I see... That appears to explain certain terminology in the letter you received. I believe I understand what has taken place here this evening. Tell me, did Stuart Weems leave the drawing room unaccompanied at all before I arrived?"

"Well, yes," answered Rosamund. "To use the facilities and such."

Spector nodded. "And, we may assume, to unlatch the kitchen door, so that he could sneak back in before midnight after a noisy departure."

"But why?"

"The wild goose chase about the garden was all orchestrated. It was all *his* doing, with no connivance from Roderick Larch – phantom or otherwise. He did it to attract our attention to the mausoleum. Or rather, to *distract* our attention from the house. He knew that even if we did not *all* venture outside, that those who remained would nonetheless be focused entirely on the mausoleum. Therefore, he would be able to ransack the study, and remove the papers he was so desperate to obtain."

"So you're saying *he* was involved in Roderick's shenanigans?"

"More than that. I'm saying he was the prime mover, and that Roderick Larch's death last year was wonderfully convenient for his purposes, since it enabled him to neatly shift the blame onto a man who could not defend himself. The fact that Weems was actually in the house when it occurred made the whole thing even better.

"Let us examine the details of Roderick's fall last year. It occurred in the afternoon, just as Annie was serving tea in this very drawing room. And what was the other detail you pointed out to me, Annie? Ah yes, the postman had just stopped by. I think you knew, perhaps unconsciously, that this was significant. Because it explains the fall, does it not? Roderick fell because he was descending the stairs in haste. Why? Because he was endeavouring to catch the postman. Why? Because there was something he wished to give to him. And what could that be? What else but a letter – or letters?"

"But," said Rosamund, "he didn't have any letters."

"None that you saw. But you will recall that it was Weems who reached your brother's body before you did. He wouldn't let you look. And he immediately sent Annie to fetch Doctor Anderson. Why was he so keen to keep others away from the body? Because he saw the letters clutched in Roderick's dead hand, of course. Those were the letters that you, Mrs Duggan, and you, Miss Valdane, would receive precisely one year later. I found it interesting to note that the letters were handwritten but the envelopes were typed. To me, this suggested that they had been opened, and the original envelopes damaged or destroyed. You see, Roderick Larch had evidence that *Weems* was an embezzler, and he wished to share the knowledge with the few people in the world he trusted.

"Finding Larch dead on the ground, with the letters still clutched in his hand, Weems felt his troubles were over. Whatever evidence Larch had, it would remain untouched in the drawer of his desk. Out of curiosity, though, Weems opened the envelopes and examined their contents. This gave him another idea – but it was one he could not put into practice until exactly a year later. The only amendment he needed to make was to change the '5' of '1935' into a '6', and he could create the illusion that Larch was *not* dead – that he had faked his death. He went about it meticulously, and it might even have worked. Indeed, certain facts beyond Weems's control seemed to support the theory – Doctor Anderson's move to a prestigious Harley Street practice might indicate bribery, for instance. But it was pure coincidence."

Eleanor Valdane cut in: "None of this explains how Weems ended up dead."

"No? I rather think it does. His scheme was quite convincing – if only in its fatal ambiguity. After all, pinning his crimes on a dead man had given him a clean slate, but a man of Weems's proclivities could not simply abandon his life of crime. And if he continued, he might attract the attention of the authorities once more. It would be handy, therefore, to have a 'straw man', a person on whom he could lay the blame. Hence his decision to resurrect Roderick Larch. To paint *him* as the career criminal, living in hiding.

"But he had bargained without Roderick's sister.

"The Larch home was part of a trust in the name of both Roderick and Rosamund. With Roderick dead, it became the sole property of Rosamund. However, if Roderick was *not* dead, then the house would be fair game for the various financial concerns seeking to claw back money Roderick had apparently squandered.

"You would never have permitted that to happen though, would you, Rosamund?" He looked at Miss Larch, who now sat upright and attentive, but otherwise perfectly serene.

"No," she said calmly, "I wouldn't."

"You fell for Weems's duplicity and became convinced Roderick had faked his death. You were curiously sanguine when I informed you that his coffin was empty. Perhaps you had already discovered that for yourself, in spite of your words about desecration? Regardless, you were as bemused as the rest of us when you saw that lantern burning in the mausoleum, but for different reasons. It was a simple enough trick, by the way. I imagine Weems set it up earlier in the day – while the snow was still falling, thus covering any trail he might have left behind him. The lantern was placed in the open doorway to the mausoleum and loaded with flash paper soaked in white phosphorus and carbon disulphide. When that solution evaporates, it is prone to spontaneous combustion – and that is exactly what happened. The flash paper burned brightly but briefly. I'll bet it took some careful experimentation, but he was able to control the timing of the ignition by altering the volume of the solution, and thus the rate of evaporation. Schoolboy stuff.

"And you, Rosamund, knew this was a mere distraction, but you were unsure precisely *who* was doing the distracting. You headed for the kitchen: the torch was already missing, but so was the study key. Grabbing the kitchen knife was an instinctive reaction, I'm sure. And with the blade in hand, you headed for the study. There you found the door unlocked, and a man sitting in the dark, going through certain documents by torchlight. You struck out with the knife. You were quite prepared to kill for the sake of your home, weren't you? Even if the victim had turned out to be your own brother. Because, as far as you were concerned, he was already dead – you were perfectly happy for him to remain that way if it enabled you to keep your precious home. And of course, given his supposed wrongdoings… You could always say afterwards it was an accident; it was dark, all you saw was an intruder.

"But I imagine you didn't know for certain the identity of your actual victim until you grabbed the torch from his dead hand. On seeing that it was Weems, you realised *he* was the one who had deceived you, not Roderick. So you decided to appropriate his scheme for your own ends. You noticed something unusual about him – he had removed his shoes. Why? Because he had swapped them for a *different* pair; a pair which you placed on your own feet before heading out via the French windows.

"As part of his scheme, Weems planned to leave via those very windows, and to head off into the woods; that's why he had the torch. But he also intended to use his escape as a further means of framing the late Roderick Larch. One of Larch's most distinctive features was his gait, thanks to a wound he received at Ypres. Weems had the brilliant idea of creating a pair of dummy shoes with the soles nailed on *backward*. This meant that by walking *forward*, the wearer left a trail of heavy footprints apparently heading in the opposite direction. And by dragging his *right* foot, he could create the illusion of a man dragging his left; the snow would just make it that much easier to leave those incriminating tracks. He had brought these doctored shoes with him, possibly left outside when he arrived or perhaps concealed in his coat, and was wearing them when you killed him, Rosamund. With the torch, I've no doubt you saw them and perceived their purpose.

"This gave you an idea to save your home *and* deflect suspicion at a single stroke. You had to go through with Weems's plan, before subsequently destroying any evidence of the shoes' existence. That way, it would appear that *he* was responsible for the footprints between the mausoleum and the study, and therefore prove he was responsible for the burning lantern, and the various other tricks designed to make it seem that Roderick was alive. You might even be able to salvage your brother's posthumous reputation into the bargain. By playing a bold psychological game, you could also eliminate yourself as a suspect in the killing of Weems – if it was generally accepted that you had left the house via the kitchen, you would have a perfect alibi for the time of his death; your footprints on the way back would muddy the water there, plus the snow was already well trodden by myself and Annie. So, you took the doctored shoes from the dead man and put them on, tucking your own into your belt, out of sight behind your back. You should by rights have replaced his regular shoes on his feet, but you were painfully conscious of time, and so you left him conspicuously barefoot. Then you left via the French windows and headed for the mausoleum. Of course, you had to extinguish the torch, otherwise everyone would see you approaching from the wrong side of the house – and notice you limping, of course. I thought it a little odd that you entered the mausoleum without turning on the torch; there is the explanation. And you only ventured inside very briefly; you could not risk my noticing the strange shoes you were wearing, so you kept the torchlight focused on your face, or on the empty coffin."

"The coffin," said Gloria Duggan suddenly. "What happened to Roderick's body?"

"Ah," said Spector, "this was perhaps the most gruesome element of Weems's plan. He had removed the body from its coffin some nights previously. That was when he'd forced open the door, leaving it closed but unlocked. Indeed, Annie saw him, but mistook the image of a man dragging a body along the ground for the limping gait of Roderick Larch. In silhouette, they would look similar, I admit. I presume Weems loaded the remains into a waiting car and took them elsewhere to be incinerated."

He returned his attention to Rosamund. "When we ventured outside again, you were safe because the thick snow covered your shoes. I immediately noticed the footprints leading toward – but actually *from* – the study. Even if I had not, I'm sure you would have directed my attention toward them. While *I* was investigating the footprints, you quickly swapped the gimmicked shoes for your regular ones and returned to the kitchen. The altered footwear was presumably abandoned somewhere between the mausoleum and the house. But you had made a mistake – as it turns out, a fatal one. You were so concerned with the shoes that you neglected to consider the door. That is, the door from the study to the hall. Instinctively, you had turned the key in the lock so that none of the house guests might wander in and find Weems before I had the opportunity to do so. But you failed to unlock it again before leaving via the French windows. You did not consider that this would create an 'impossible crime'; that with the key on the inside, not to mention the single set of footprints in the snow, it would seem that the killer entered the study and then vanished into thin air. In fact, there was nothing ingenious or otherworldly about it. Just a crime committed in haste, with enough loose ends for an old man to unpick.

"And," he gave an embarrassed little smile and spread his fingers, as though he had just performed an underwhelming magic trick, "there it is."

"I won't deny it," said Rosamund Larch. "But I couldn't let them take this place away from me. It's all I have. You do understand that, don't you?"

The doorbell rang.

"Ah," said Spector, "the police. Better let them in, don't you think? It's a chilly night out there."

LAST CHRISTMAS

Fiona Cummins

THE HOTEL was closing due to heavy snowfall.

Veda Shaw and her family had spent every Christmas at this remote Highland setting for as long as she could remember, and she'd be damned if the weather was going to prevent them from getting there, especially this year.

She glanced at her granddaughter Bea in the rearview mirror. The ten-month-old was sleeping peacefully, and although her snowsuit was unzipped, her cheeks were flushed. She hoped Alys was making sure she wasn't overheating because accidents could happen so easily. She chastised herself. *Stop catastrophising, Vee.* As a nurse, she'd witnessed some awful tragedies, and just because they'd experienced one of their own this time last year, it didn't mean it was going to happen again.

The windscreen wipers were barely able to clear the snow that fell in thick flakes and settled as soon as it hit the frozen ground. Not for the first time, Veda was glad that Malcolm had insisted on a car that could handle such wintry conditions.

"Dad would have loved this, wouldn't he?" she said to Alys, who was gazing out of the rear passenger window, watching the blizzard transform the Cairngorms into a scene from a Christmas card.

Alys laughed, a soft sound. "He'd have packed the snow shovel, blankets and emergency rations in September." She deepened her voice in a facsimile of her father's. *"Have you filled the flasks, Vee?"* Her face crumpled. "It's not going to be the same without him."

"No, love." Veda touched the brake gently and kept her eyes fixed on the road ahead. "But the three of us will have fun. Especially as it's Bea's first Christmas."

"I wish he could have met her."

"Me too. He would have been tickled pink."

The light was fading fast, snow-heavy clouds casting a smoky pall over everything. Veda tried to ignore the stirrings of anxiety inside her. The road to the hotel was steep, prone to drifts, and they risked getting stuck if the weather didn't ease soon. Forecasters had warned of the occasional flurry, but they'd been taken by surprise by the violence of this weather system. No one had predicted a storm like this.

The baby cried out, a solitary note that told mother and grandmother she'd be waking soon. Veda estimated they were about ten minutes from the hotel, provided the roads remained passable. Management had warned it was planning to close for the safety of its staff and had sent out emails, urging guests not to travel, but Veda and Alys had left hours earlier. By the time they picked the warnings up on their phones it was too late for them to turn back, and even if they could have done, they had nowhere else to go. Their festive getaway had been booked almost a year ago and there were no other hotels for miles. A skeleton team, made up of staff already in situ, would care for existing guests and any travellers who made it through the snowstorm.

Veda hit a patch of ice and felt the wheels spin beneath them. She drove into the skid, as Malcolm had taught her to, and managed to correct the car's course, yet it still scared her. She was a confident driver, but it was impossible to see even the markings on the road. This was rural Scotland. The snow plough would pass this way at some point, but it might not be until later in the week. Locals relied on their 4x4s and the goodwill of tractor-owning farmers, but if they ran into difficulty here, on this remote stretch of the journey, they would be in trouble.

As luck would have it, Veda kept both her nerve and the wheel steady, and she didn't need to use the shovel until they were in sight of the hotel. It was too dark to clear the sweeping drive that bisected the impressive grounds, home to its own herd of elk, and when she swerved to avoid one of these majestic animals, their car became lodged in a bank of snow with a soft crump.

Bea was awake now, wide-eyed and watchful, but Alys was asleep, her head resting against her daughter's car seat. She was an artist with her own business, and the festive season was her busiest time of the year. Thanks to the wonders of social media, her fine art prints, hand-painted Christmas cards and private commissions were in fevered demand.

Watching her daughter sleep, Veda was surprised by a pang of maternal wistfulness. She'd hardly seen her for months. The young woman had been thoughtful enough to send her a coveted *Alys Shaw* advent calendar in the post and what had she, Veda, done? Nothing. Alys was juggling her job with the responsibilities of new motherhood, and she ought to have done more to lighten her load.

Her poor girl. All those late nights must be catching up with her. She wouldn't wake her, but manage alone.

Through the intense snowfall, Veda glimpsed the warm lights of the hotel and felt her heart lift. Not far to go. The shovel was heavy in her hand and its weight gave her pause. This was usually Malcolm's job, and she felt a stab of grief at his absence. With determination, she began to dig.

Mulled wine and warm mince pies were waiting for them as soon as they stepped inside the hotel, snow in their hair and eyelashes. A fire roared in the grate and Veda inhaled the fresh pine scent of the tree which dominated the lobby. Carols played softly in the background. For Veda, this was the moment that Christmas began.

Mr Duncan, the hotel's manager, strode across the carpet to greet them, a warm smile on his face. "Mrs Shaw, such a pleasure to see you again, especially in this inclement weather. And who do we have here?" He beamed at Bea, who buried her face in her mother's shoulder. "We have lots of activities planned for tomorrow. There's a snowman-building competition or, if you prefer, a chance to make mince pies in the kitchen with one of the chefs. Santa Claus was supposed to be arriving by sleigh in the afternoon, but we've had a message to say the snow's too deep for his reindeer to make it through, unfortunately." Veda wanted to tell him that he didn't need to maintain this charade for her granddaughter's benefit, but decided that would be uncharitable. "Then we'll have carol singing in the chapel before dinner. Will you be joining us for our annual Christmas Eve tree ceremony and gift opening?" He froze mid-patter, as if he'd committed a terrible faux pas.

Veda placed a hand on his arm and squeezed it. "We don't blame the hotel." She smiled to show that she meant it. "It was a terrible accident, nothing more than that. We have so many happy memories of our Christmases here, so please don't worry."

He gave a stiff nod. "Thank you. We didn't know if we would see you again this year, but we're delighted you're here with us, of course." His smooth mask of professionalism returned. "Do let us know if there is anything we can do for you. As you're aware, we're a little short-staffed, but that should not affect the quality of our service. Now, let me show you to your suite."

Everything was exactly as it had been last year. A vase of festive greenery, its holly berries, plump and vivid, stood on the bureau, and a garland of fresh ivy lined the mantelpiece above the empty grate. A Christmas tree in a scarlet pot twinkled in the corner. She didn't need to stick her head around the corner to know that a tray of bone china teacups and a plate of expensive petit fours would be laid out in the sitting area.

The ghosts of Christmases past came rushing at her, and here, in the silence, Veda sat on the edge of the bed, consumed by memories of years gone by.

They had first come here when Alys was five, and Malcolm had received an unexpected but sizeable bonus. Her parents were dead and Malcolm's lived abroad, and neither of them had siblings, so they'd decided to spend Christmas in a fancy hotel to see what it was like.

Malcolm had found this one in the *Good Hotel Guide* and liked the name of it. A wealthy family had cancelled their booking at the last moment, and they'd been upgraded to this particular suite of rooms. Veda could still remember Alys's shining eyes at the sight of the talking doll with golden ringlets, a velvet dress and leather patent shoes that had been waiting for her on the bed. Alys was now twenty-seven and they'd come back here every year since, scrimping during leaner times for those four nights of Christmas wonder.

Malcolm had loved it here. He talked of nothing else for weeks before and afterwards. It was the highlight of his year, even more so than their two-week summer holiday to a caravan in Wales. She was certain that if he'd known he was going to die – and he'd been able to choose the place of his demise – he'd have chosen this very spot.

Alys peeped her head around the door, Bea on her hip, chewing a breadstick. "You okay, Mum?"

Veda swallowed down the lump in her throat, lost in happier times. "Yes, love. Just being daft."

"It's not daft to miss someone." She sat down on the bed next to her mother. Bea reached out a sticky finger and stroked Veda's cheek. Veda reached for Alys's hand, but her daughter moved it away and busied herself with the baby, smoothing her hair off her face. "I miss him too. Especially here."

Veda relished this moment of intimacy between them, although she was hurt that Alys had pulled away. Her daughter had become distant over the last year, and Veda had allowed that gulf to widen. She'd put it down to the chaos of grief and motherhood, either one of those enough to fell the most mentally robust of women. Her own status as new widow had meant that she'd been too preoccupied to focus on Alys at a time when her daughter had needed her most.

She hoped this festive break would help to repair some of that damage.

It snowed all night, and, in the morning, the road to the hotel was impassable.

"No one's coming in or out," said the waitress on breakfast duty. "We're stuck here all Christmas." It was clear from her expression that she was far from happy about that, but then she remembered she was talking to a guest and forced herself into jollity. "And I can't think of a lovelier place to be." But Veda understood. The girl wanted to be with her own family.

After breakfasting alone – Alys and Bea were sleeping in – she returned to their room. Outside, through the window, the world was quiet and white. Her gaze fell on the hand-painted advent calendar that Alys had made for her. When she had opened the first window at the start of December, it had touched her deeply to discover Veda, Malcolm and Alys in miniature, smiling and wearing woolly hats and scarves. Every window since had revealed a memory of the three of them, recreated in meticulous detail, from ice-skating to decorating a Christmas tree to singing carols. Veda's grey curls. Malcolm's reading glasses. It must have taken her hours.

And now it was Christmas Eve. She opened the penultimate window.

Her heart clenched, as if a fist had closed around it. Unsurprisingly, Alys had painted a picture of her father. He was standing outside the hotel, holding a star, dressed in the same jumper he wore every Christmas Eve. The one he'd worn *last* Christmas Eve.

She pressed a fingertip to his face.

"Do you like it?" Alys's voice made her jump. Her daughter was standing behind her in pyjamas. Mascara smudges from yesterday's make-up hollowed out her eyes.

"It's wonderful," said Veda. "You've captured his likeness perfectly."

A ghost of a smile crossed Alys's lips.

"Do you think you'll be up to going to the tree ceremony later?" It was a sensitive question, but Veda had always enjoyed this part of Christmas and she still wanted to go, despite what had happened to her husband last year.

Alys offered a watery smile. "Yes, I–I think so."

The crowd was much thinner than last year's, but that was not surprising, given the weather. Some of the guests, and a few locals from a nearby village, had trudged through heavy snow to the tallest Scots pine on the hotel's estate for this traditional start to Christmas.

Hotel staff were handing out mugs of hot chocolate and glasses of mulled wine, and the mood was festive. Veda and Alys hung back, content to watch from a distance. Bea was already asleep in her cot under the watchful eye of the hotel's babysitting service.

"I thought they might have been forced to cancel it," said Veda, stamping her feet to stay warm. Alys gave a slight nod but did not speak. In silence, they watched as one of the guests – a woman this year – climbed a ladder to fix a huge star to the top of the tree.

An expectant hush descended over the clearing. A minute passed. It stretched into another. Then a bright glow illuminated everyone's faces as, finally, the star was lit.

Despite everything, Veda clasped her hands together, a ray of hope surging through her. The light cast shadows on the trees, stirring memories from last year. Everyone cheered except Alys.

"I can't watch any more of this," she said, and tears were streaming down her face. "I'm going back to the hotel." She turned away from her mother, away from the pain of loss.

Veda hurried to catch up with her, stumbling through the deep snow. "I'll come with you, love. This was a mistake, I agree. I'm so sorry. It's too soon."

Several guests in evening dress were milling around the hotel lobby, preparing to take their seats at the lavish six-course banquet. Veda recognised a couple of them from previous years, smiled and nodded. A woman in a fitted red dress and matching lipstick opened her mouth to say something, but then thought better of it. Veda stared at her, daring her to. Let her try.

Alys refused to join her mother for the meal. "I'm not hungry, Mum. I just want to go to bed."

"But it's all paid for, love. We go every year." She reached for her daughter, gently tugging on the sleeve of her coat. Alys pushed her off.

"Not this year."

She hated waste, and so Veda went alone, but for the first time in twenty-two years, the food was tasteless and dry in her mouth, and the empty seat next to her felt like a rebuke.

As was tradition, she joined the rest of the guests in the tiny hotel chapel for Midnight Mass, and as she walked back across the grounds, past the tree and the ornamental lake, the stars bright and cold, she swore she could hear Malcolm's annual greeting echo around the estate. *Merry Christmas, Vee. It's going to be a good one.*

She slipped into their suite, trying to be as quiet as possible.

"Did you enjoy your evening?"

Veda jumped, surprised to find Alys sitting in the dark on one of the sofas. She was holding a stocking for Bea on her lap, stuffed with presents.

"It was nice. But it would have been much better with you and Dad."

Alys laughed, a sound striated with bitterness. "If you say so."

Veda sat down next to her on the sofa. "I'm sorry this is so hard for you, love. We can do something else next year, if you prefer. Start some new traditions of our own with Bea."

Alys looked at her coolly. "It's Christmas Day," she said. "Aren't you going to open the last window?"

"That's a lovely idea," said Veda, and reached for the advent calendar.

For twenty-one years, Malcolm Shaw had wanted to be the one to place the star on top of the Christmas tree, and this year, finally, he'd got his wish.

Puffed up with pride, he strutted into the hotel bar and ordered himself a pint. Louisa Pryor, one of the regulars like him and Vee, was sitting on a bar stool, sipping a cocktail with an olive in it.

"Merry Christmas, Malc," she said, crossing her legs. He couldn't help noticing they were slim and shapely, and she was wearing high heels. Vee never wore high heels, and she never called him Malc.

"Lou," he said, and raised his pint, toasting her. "Where's Dave, then?"

"Who knows?" she replied. "Who cares?"

Two hours later, they were still there. Malcolm was several pints down, and Louisa was working her way through the cocktail menu.

She'd moved her barstool closer to him so their knees were touching, and Malcolm's hand rested on her thigh. She was attractive, good fun and smelled nice. When she pointed to the sprig of mistletoe above their heads, and moved in to kiss him, Malcolm didn't protest.

It was unfortunate that Veda chose that moment to enter the bar.

Malcolm had often wondered what would happen if Veda caught him playing around, mostly when he was in bed with some woman or another, and now was his chance to find out.

He pushed Louisa away and waved his wife over to join them.

"What do you think you're doing?" Her tone was hard, unyielding.

"Lighten up, Vee," said Louisa, offering Veda a sip of her cocktail. "It's just a bit of festive fun."

Veda took the cocktail and poured it over the woman's head. She gave Malcolm a pointed look. "When you've finished here, Mr Duncan is looking for you. It's time to light the star."

Malcolm didn't realise how drunk he was until he was standing at the top of the ladder, swaying in the night air. The star was heavier than he'd anticipated, it was windy, and before he knew what was happening, he'd toppled from the ladder and hit the ground with a sickening thump.

Someone in the crowd screamed. Nobody spoke. Until Malcolm groaned and sat up.

The paramedic who attended to him said he was lucky to be alive and the alcohol must have relaxed him, cushioning his fall.

Veda stared at the painting that Alys had done. It was a picture of the hotel's ornamental lake and she was crouching by the water, peering intently into it.

"I know what you did, Mum."

Veda looked at her steadily. "I know you loved him, but he was not a good husband."

"Tell me what happened that night."

So she did. She told Alys what she had seen in the bar, and how her father had fallen from the tree, and how they had walked back to the hotel together, she burning with rage and shame at his drunken antics, and he mocking her for being boring and dull. As they'd walked past the pond, he'd told her that every woman he'd been with during the course of their thirty-year marriage had been better in bed than she was, including Louisa Pryor, who he'd had sex with last Christmas and for several Christmases before that, and in her fury, she had pushed him into the water.

She would never forget the expression of surprise on his face. *Merry Christmas, Malcolm. Love Vee.*

He had cried out to her for help, splashing and panicking in the murky depths, but she had hardened her heart and watched him drown while their pregnant daughter, who had hurried after them, concerned by their raised voices, had witnessed her mother letting him die. Veda had no idea that Alys had been hiding in the undergrowth, watching her father's murder unfold.

Veda told the police he had wandered off. She didn't know what had happened, but when he hadn't come to bed that night, she'd searched the grounds for him before discovering his body floating face-down in the lake. The post-mortem concluded that he'd been concussed in the fall, lost his balance and died from cold water shock.

She had waited all year for guilt to overwhelm her, but all she had felt was grief for the marriage she'd thought she'd had – and a sense of liberation.

Traumatised, Alys could not face the loss of both her parents, and so had convinced herself that her mother's version of events was true, that he was already dead when Veda found him, pulling away from her so that she did not have to confront the knowledge she'd buried inside. But now, here at this hotel at Christmas, the memories were surfacing, and they were raw.

"Why did you drag us back here?" Alys was crying now. "It's too painful."

And Veda told her.

The Christmas luncheon was in full swing. Bea tasted her first Brussels sprout, and her nose wrinkled comically, which made them both laugh, and Alys let her try a spoonful of ice cream. They pulled crackers, wore silly hats and drank too much champagne. Veda was replete with seasonal joy.

Her daughter's attitude had softened too, and, in a moment of candour, she had admitted that she'd often thought about how poorly her father had treated her mother. Veda had squeezed her hand then and Alys had let her. She was determined to repair their relationship, and intended to focus all her energies on that. But there was something else she needed to do first.

"Are you sure about this?" A worried expression crossed Alys's face. "I don't want her to upset you."

Her mother smiled. "Remember what I've always taught you? The joy of Christmas is in the giving, not the receiving, love. Goodwill to all mankind."

Louisa Pryor was standing at the bar, playing footsie with a man whose wife and grandchildren were oblivious in the dining room.

She stopped as soon as she saw Veda, eyeing her warily, and the man hurried away, a flush to his cheeks that wasn't entirely down to his post-lunch brandy.

"In the spirit of the season, I just wanted to say there are no hard feelings," Veda informed her, leaning against the bar. "It wasn't a very nice thing for me to see, but it takes two to tango, right?"

Louisa visibly relaxed. "Thank you for being so understanding. I'm sorry for your loss and everything. But he was a bit of a pig to you, wasn't he?"

Veda inclined her head in acceptance of the observation. She had been on the receiving end of many platitudes over the last twelve months, but Louisa's astute acknowledgement of her husband's behaviour was the most honest. "Can I buy you a drink?"

Louisa's eyes gleamed. A cocktail. The most expensive one on the menu. And while the barman was mixing it, she was going to pop to the ladies' room.

Veda carried their drinks over to the fireplace and set them down on the table. The fire blazed merrily and outside, the snow was thick and deep, no thaw expected for days, and no chance of the police or ambulance making their way through.

She felt a pulse of regret for the hotel and its staff, unsure if their reputation would sustain another Christmas tragedy, but she found she didn't care. Alys had shown her some hotels online. Next year, the three of them would try some winter sun.

As Louisa took her seat opposite, Veda passed over her cocktail, the last gift of Christmas, and raised a toast. "To the future."

THE NAUGHTY LIST

Sam Carrington

JOSEPH GLANCED up, the bellowed demand for silence coming from the man seated to his right jolting him from his inbox. The 8.20 a.m. train from Newton often carried college students and usually without issue, but today their banter appeared to have triggered a fellow passenger.

"At least have the decency to bugger off to another carriage. This is the quiet coach," the man, his face a map of disgruntled wrinkles, said to the group while stabbing his finger at the sign. The teenagers exchanged questioning frowns for a few seconds before erupting into laughter. Joseph raised his eyebrows and, not wishing to make eye contact with the irate man, quickly returned his attention to the unread emails.

"Jesus, they have no respect," the fellow muttered, getting up from his seat. Joseph hoped *he* was moving to a different carriage – it was too early in the morning for a scene. But instead of backing away from the situation, the man stepped towards the students.

Joseph blew out his breath. He knew how quickly a confrontation could escalate.

"Hey," Joseph said, reaching out and grasping the man's elbow. "It's almost Christmas. Season of—"

The man yanked his arm away. "Goodwill? Yeah, so where's theirs?" He shook his head.

"They're teenagers. Don't you remember what you were like? Come on – it's not worth getting stressed over, eh?" Joseph sensed a shift in atmosphere; the students were rapt, probably hoping for an entertaining showdown, their mobiles poised ready to record the unfolding drama and upload it to TikTok, or whatever their favoured platform was right now. Perhaps they were already livestreaming. Back when Joseph was at college, the most he'd had to worry about was MSN. For kids now, social media was on another level. "One more stop and they'll be off," Joseph added quickly. The man sighed, his jaw slackening a little. Just as it seemed his peacekeeping was working, Joseph's mobile rang. His eyes widened as the shrill tone ripped through the carriage. Joseph grabbed it. "I'd better…" he indicated to the *Quiet* sign, "take this elsewhere." He got up, smiling as he squeezed past the man, the phone pressed to his ear.

"Sorry, Eve." He leaned against the toilet door. "Was in the midst of a storm in a teacup." He laughed.

"Sounds intriguing, you'll have to tell me later. But look, wanted to give you the heads-up…"

Joseph groaned. "What is it? Your jilted friend is coming around again tonight to slate every man in existence?"

"No, no. Nothing like that." Joseph swore he caught an edge of concern in her voice. "Some bloke turned up just after you left this morning, asking for you. Never seen him before. Stern-looking, in a suit, said your name was on his *list* and that he'd be back. And not in a nice way, if his tone was anything to go by…"

"Oh, right." Joseph absently stroked the stubble on his chin. "Probably something to do with the charity auction, love. I wouldn't worry. I likely just forgot to respond to his email."

After putting Eve's mind at rest, Joseph returned to the carriage. The college kids were still chatting loudly, but the angry passenger was nowhere to be seen. Relaxing back into his seat, Joseph ran his fingertip over the laptop mousepad and the screen illuminated again.

He had a new email notification. Joseph blinked several times while reading the bold lettering in the subject line:

JOSEPH SNOW – Your name is on THE NAUGHTY LIST!

He tutted. More junk mail his system had failed to filter. He was about to hit 'delete', but a niggling feeling left over from the call with Eve made him click on it.

An invitation to meet SANTA that you cannot decline! it stated. Joseph gave a little laugh, his tension lifting. It was a joke – some annoying chain mail challenge. There'd been something on social media about such games doing the rounds; he felt sure he'd heard some of his colleagues talking about it at the office.

As long as he didn't click on any links, there was no harm in reading it before he deleted it. He could do with a spot of light relief. But as he read, his smile slowly slipped. The train's brakes squealed. Joseph lifted his head, scanning the carriage. No one's attention was on him. The students were huddled in the gangway about to disembark, and the angry passenger was nowhere in sight. Joseph shuffled in his seat, his sense of unease growing again as he read the second paragraph.

There are four rules you MUST follow:

1 – Do NOT attempt to contact any other person named
   on The Naughty List.

2 – You cannot decline the invitation to meet Santa.

3 – No one else can go in your place.

4 – Do NOT disclose the content of this email to *anyone.*

This was stupid. Why was he giving the time of day to a scammer? He exited the message, slumped back in his seat, and stared out the carriage window. The people on the platform at St David's scurried like beetles, each seemingly lost in their own thoughts. All bar the students who moved together in a group, like a swarm of bees heading noisily towards the exit. He'd had that kind of friendship group once. These days his social circle consisted of a few work colleagues and his wife's family and friends. Probably for the better, he thought.

As the train juddered into motion and the station fell away from sight, Joseph's eyes were drawn back to his inbox. He ran his hands roughly through his hair, fighting between his instinct to simply delete the message and his curiosity to read on.

"Dammit." He tapped on the email and skipped to the final paragraph.

When it's your turn to visit Santa in his Grotto, you'd better be prepared. You will be given a choice. Will you do what is needed to earn a spot on The Nice List? Or will you refuse Santa's offer and remain on The Naughty List?

There will be consequences.

"Oh, for God's sake," he said, slamming the laptop shut. Joseph closed his eyes, weary already, and it wasn't even nine a.m.

The huge tinsel tree dominated the foyer of the For All Seasons insulation company – its silver branches sending sparkling fragments of light in every direction. Today, a group of people in red and gold costumes gathered in front of it, readying themselves to burst into joyous Christmas songs. While waiting for the lift, Joseph rolled his shoulders, tilted his head to the left and right, like a boxer preparing for a fight.

"Snowy, my man. What's up?" Paul, a data analyst in Joseph's department, joined him, slapping Joseph on the shoulder. "Rough night?"

Joseph turned, giving Paul a shrug. "No. Does it *look* like I have?"

"Let's just say you don't look your cheery self. Mind you, all this shit…" he said, turning to the sudden burst of song coming from the foyer. "Can't say I blame you. *Why?*"

"Well, my train journey kinda put me in a—"

"Why the singers, I meant." The lift pinged and Paul stepped in. "What next? Dancing elves? It's an office, not Santa's fucking Grotto."

Joseph gave a laugh as fake as the Christmas tree. He got into the lift and rode it to their floor, vaguely aware of Paul talking as his mind wandered to Eve's call. He'd been confident of what he'd told her – that it was likely something to do with the upcoming auction he arranged every year for the children's charity. Because, what else *could* it be? Joseph was careful with his finances, so it wouldn't be a debt collector.

The lift doors whooshed open. Paul was first out.

"See you later, Snowy," he said, turning and strutting into the large open-plan office.

"Yeah. Have a good one, mate." Joseph walked in the opposite direction towards the break room. He needed caffeine and to gather his thoughts before the morning briefing.

Multiple coffees, two meetings and seven hours later, Joseph was sitting at his desk overlooking the city centre, taking in the bird's eye view. Something he made sure to do at least once each day, while giving gratitude for being in this enviable position. Not just the plush, modern office block he worked in, but his position in life. The grafting and the grovelling had paid dividends, enabling him to move on from his shaky start. He was proud that he provided for himself and Eve and gained huge satisfaction from his work with the children's charities, especially over the Christmas period.

That was what he told himself almost every day.

Joseph took the award plaque from beside his computer and buffed it with the cuff of his shirt. *In recognition of extraordinary fundraising – Joseph Snow.* He smiled, a warm sensation filling him.

"You'll rub off that inscription if you polish it every five minutes."

Joseph snapped his head up, surprised to hear his brother-in-law's voice. "Charles! What are you doing here?" He leapt from his chair, jutting an arm out to shake Charles's hand. Then froze. "Oh, God. Is everything okay? Is Eve—"

"Of course. I was just seeing a client on another floor. Thought I'd say hello."

"I was about to pack up for the day, actually," Joseph said, pulling his jacket from the back of the chair. "You driving? Could I grab a lift home?"

"Yeah. It would kill two birds anyway."

Joseph raised his eyebrows. "Oh?"

"Eve messaged. Something about me coming over tonight. I haven't had a chance to reply, but I'm sure she won't have revoked the invitation."

Joseph hesitated, one arm still dangling out of his jacket. Eve must want her brother there as back-up in case that bloke returned. A tingling sensation crept down his spine. Didn't she think that Joseph could handle the situation alone?

"Let me just shut everything down," Joseph said. "I'll meet you in the foyer."

"Okay. Don't be too long – they gave out a snow warning. Don't want to get stuck on Haldon Hill."

Joseph wondered who the stranger could possibly be that'd unsettled Eve so much. He went to his desktop computer to close the multiple windows he had open. The Naughty List email was way down in the inbox now, but Eve's words to him that morning repeated loudly in his mind: *...said your name was on his* list *and that he'd be back. And not in a nice way...* Joseph narrowed his eyes and his fingers trembled slightly as he opened the email again. Had to be a coincidence. He skim-read the words until he got to the list of names. There were ten, with *Joseph Snow* last. At first glance, he hadn't recognised any of the others. But now he saw it.

He knew the name in the number three position.

"Oh, you sneaky shit," Joseph said, smashing his hand down on the desk. He rushed out of the office, along the corridor, knocking into the office tree and sending a few baubles scattering. "Hey, Paul!" He strode around the partitions. *It's an office, not Santa's fucking Grotto.* Isn't that what he'd said? "Very good, mate." But Paul wasn't there.

"Oh, he's gone already," a co-worker, Monica, said, without taking her eyes from her screen. "Had an appointment."

"Yeah, right." Joseph shook his head. "Well, joke's on me, I guess." He turned, annoyance and relief battling for top place. It was Christmas, not April Fool's. Where did he get off playing a prank like that this time of year?

In the car, Joseph debated whether to share the content of the email and who was behind it with Charles, but his brother-in-law rattled on and on about his Christmas plans for the entirety of the journey and Joseph barely got a word in. The first flutters of sleet began as they reached home.

Eve poured herself and Charles another glass of wine, but Joseph placed a hand over the top of his own.

"I'm good, thanks," he said. "And Charles is driving, so…"

"And you wonder why your nickname's Snowy." Charles laughed, knocking back his second glass of red.

Joseph sighed. He'd long given up trying to persuade his colleagues and mates to drop the moniker. "Pure as the driven snow," Charles had declared during his speech at his and Eve's wedding. There was nothing wrong with being thought of as a good person, someone who'd never do anything wrong, but the ridiculing wore really thin sometimes and he'd had to bite his lip on more than a few occasions.

Despite the odd glance towards the front door when a car's headlights seeped through the curtains, Joseph managed to relax. Having Charles there clearly gave Eve confidence, and she didn't mention the caller once. More importantly, the stranger didn't return. Obviously just another storm in a teacup.

With continued flurries overnight, a thin white layer of snow covered the ground. Joseph stepped gingerly along the pavement, thankful it was a light scattering and not deep enough to cause disruption to the train service. The air was crisp, his breath clouding as he made his way to the station.

Taking the first seats in the carriage, Joseph shifted up to the window and immediately opened his laptop to check his emails. No spam today.

"Morning."

Joseph looked up to see the man from yesterday smiling down at him. "Oh, hi." He returned the gesture thinking that would be the end of the interaction. But the bloke sat down heavily right next to him.

"Name's Alistair. Sorry about… you know. Had a few things on my mind. The kids riled me a bit."

"Sure," Joseph said absently. He heard the man – Alistair – suck in a shuddering breath, and a twinge of guilt tugged at his gut. Joseph finally turned to meet the man's gaze. "It happens. This time of year can be a little, well, stressful."

"It certainly can." Alistair gave a curt nod. "Thank you." Then without saying anything further, he got up and carried on through the carriage, leaving Joseph frowning at the curious exchange.

The foyer was minus the singers today, but festive music filled the space. With only ten days left until Christmas, and a week until the firm closed up for the holidays, Joseph had a spring in his step as he headed for the lifts, casting his gaze around for Paul. He was keen to tell him he'd figured out his stupid email prank and to ask who else he'd suckered in. *Never trust a tech geek.* But there was no sign of him. He'd catch him in the break room, no doubt.

"He's not here," Monica said, when Joseph enquired after him.

"As in, he's off sick?"

"No. As in he hasn't shown up, not called in." Monica furrowed her brow. "Typical of him. Would rather others take his share of the workload so he can have an easy run-up to Christmas."

Joseph stared at her for a moment, in two minds whether to stick up for his colleague or leave it. That was a fight he feared he'd lose, seeing as Paul did usually take the easy way out of things. Instead, he turned on his heel and marched to his office. The same niggling feeling he'd felt yesterday squirmed in his stomach. The Naughty List contained ten names. Paul's was third. And he'd apparently left for an appointment last night and now hadn't shown up for work.

Joseph trawled social media searching with the hashtag #TheNaughtyList. It was trending. No surprise given the time of year, he guessed. But one post in particular caught his attention. Made his legs weaken. Had he been too quick to assume Paul was behind the prank, and not simply a victim of it?

"Shit." He leaned forwards, his eyes so close to the screen he could make out the pixels. The post read: *Festive scam or scare? Has*

Devon man who was reported missing two days ago become psycho Santa's latest victim?

Joseph backed away, his hand covering his mouth. No, it *had* to be a scam. If this were real, the police would be involved. Joseph paced the office, thoughts of why anyone would think this was funny beyond him. He was up for a laugh, naturally, but it seemed someone was taking the theme of ghosts of Christmas past, present and future a bit too far.

"This is absurd," Joseph mumbled, storming out into the main office. "Anyone else heard about this?" he shouted. A few heads turned and Monica made her way to him.

"About what?" she said, folding her arms.

"You lot were talking about some game – or challenge or something – the other day? On social media. Was it this Naughty List thing?"

Monica wrinkled her nose. "Naughty List? No, but there've been some wild things doing the rounds about a psycho Santa – weird stuff on YouTube. I mean, not that that's new."

"Right. Okay." It was a start. "Thanks."

"Why? Have you been targeted?" Monica raised one eyebrow, her face set in a serious expression. Joseph stuttered his denial and she burst out laughing.

"What's so funny?" Joseph smarted. "Was it you?" A rush of heat burned his cheeks. It made sense to him now, thinking about it. The names on the list all appeared to be male. Was this a feminist thing?

"Like I'd have time for that. Ah, Joseph, sometimes you make it too easy." She chuckled to herself. "You don't believe everything you see on the internet, do you?"

Joseph clenched his teeth as he gave a tight smile. Usually he'd take this stuff with a liberal pinch of salt, join in with the office banter, even laugh at himself if he had to. Maybe it was the stress of Christmas, like he'd told the guy – what was his name? Alistair – from the train.

Alistair.

Joseph's breath caught in his chest. Couldn't be… could it? He retreated to his office, closed the door, ignoring the questioning look from Monica. He checked The Naughty List. There, at number four, was the name Ali Holden. Joseph's heart crashed against his ribcage. Sitting down, he did an online search of the names in position one and two. Other than multiple Facebook profiles with the same or similar names, there was nothing. He searched 'psycho Santa' on YouTube, swallowed hard as multiple videos came up. Mostly they were podcasters discussing their theories, one saying he believed psycho Santa was 'taking out society's garbage' and that it was a 'new and novel way for criminals to pay for their crimes'. Joseph shivered at the video mentioning 'death was too good for some of them'.

What the hell was this?

Whatever Monica said, Joseph couldn't help but worry that this was real. That people were being targeted and possibly… what? Tortured? *Murdered?* The email stated that there would be consequences. *Jesus Christ!* Joseph swept the back of his hand across his forehead, wiping the moisture on his trousers. The rules in the email were explicit. But how would the sender know if he were to speak with another person on the list? They couldn't be keeping tabs on all ten names, surely? Besides, if other people on the list were known to him, worked in the same place, then it was inevitable they'd have contact. He would see Alistair in the morning, on the train. He'd subtly ask if he knew anything about The Naughty List. Joke or not, the whole thing had started to really piss Joseph off, and he had to get to the bottom of who was behind it before it was his turn to visit Santa's Grotto.

There was no sign of Alistair on the 8.20 a.m. train. Joseph had quickly checked the other carriages before taking a seat, and now his eyes frantically scanned the platform for the man who'd been a total stranger just a few days ago. Alistair's absence from the train didn't mean something untoward had happened, but it increased the uneasy feeling sitting like a stone in the pit of Joseph's stomach. If Alistair was missing, that made two people he knew from the list that had seemingly disappeared into thin air. That, together with the reports and online chatter surrounding a psycho Santa, added weight to the email's authenticity. And weight on Joseph's mind.

Paul's voicemail kicked in for the third time, but Joseph didn't leave a message. He went around the office asking, "Heard from Paul?" like a stuck record. With each 'no' he received, his panic rose. Not even the boss knew the reason for Paul's absence yet brushed off Joseph's concerns, convinced that if there was an issue, Paul's partner would've reported it.

Not able to concentrate on work, Joseph scrolled the news stories, checked social media for mentions of missing persons, psycho Santa, or anything that might link to The Naughty List. Joseph stopped scrolling at a post containing a paused still from a video recording.

He clapped a hand across his mouth, but it didn't stop the bile rising. The image was of a man tied to a chair, his t-shirt covered in blood, with someone in red standing behind him. No caption. Just lots of comments and shares.

Joseph shook his head as he read some of them.

One way to rid the country of the lowlife.

WTF is this?

Is the dude dead?

Guess he's on Santa's Naughty List.

Joseph drummed his fingers on the desk. Was the man in the seat Paul? Alistair? It wasn't clear enough to be sure.

But it was the last comment that caused Joseph's chest to tighten.

You reap what you sow. Is it your turn next?

Joseph opened The Naughty List email. He studied it. There was no mention of 'psycho Santa' – did that mean these were two unrelated things? Someone had caught on to the awful internet craze and thought it amusing to copy it. He collapsed back in the chair, massaging his rigid neck muscles. Then he grabbed his mobile and texted Eve:

That guy show up again?

Her response was almost instantaneous: *No. You must've been right about it being to do with the charity auction.*

There, Joseph thought, mentally giving himself a shake. Nothing for him to worry about. He'd allowed this idiotic prank to unnerve him. Paul had likely taken it upon himself to break early for Christmas, and Alistair, well he could've simply caught a different train.

The ping of a new email took Joseph's attention and his heart jolted when he read the subject line: *Christmas is coming early for you, JOSEPH SNOW!*

"Oh, great," Joseph said, opening it.

You've moved up the list. You will see Santa next.
The Grotto awaits your presence…

Joseph groaned and laid his head on his arms, a sense of inevitability sucking his energy.

"You win," he told his empty office. He'd just have to face this, get it over with. Let Paul have his laugh. Hope it wasn't his last.

"Yeah, okay. Get on with it," Joseph said, not bothering to resist the man who accosted him as he walked to the train station. Paul would laugh hard enough: Joseph didn't fancy giving him total satisfaction by showing his panic. Dressed in a cheap grey suit, his abductor was around six feet tall and looked like he'd had a few too many mince pies. "Are *you* Santa?" Joseph scoffed. The man grunted, gripping him a little tighter. He bundled Joseph into a black van, then shoved something over his head, tying his hands behind his back. Paul was going all out, he had to admit.

Joseph's stomach churned with each corner the vehicle swung around. The moment the van stopped he was hauled out, his head covering tugged off. Joseph stumbled forwards and retched like a teenager following an all-night rave. Once his stomach had done ejecting its contents, Joseph spat several times, trying to clear the sour taste of vomit. Before he was able to get a good look at where he was, the child's fluffy Christmas stocking was rammed back over his head and he was dragged forwards, downwards, through what felt like a series of tunnels. An icy chill whipped Joseph's body, and his mind started down a dark path.

What if this wasn't Paul? Wasn't a prank at all?

One way to rid the country of the lowlife. Wasn't that what the people on social media were saying?

Despite anxiety gripping his guts and twisting them, Joseph still held out for the sounds of laughter – of Paul's voice saying, "Got you good, Snowy!" And then, stocking removed, seeing his colleague doubled over, revelling in how hilarious he was. But minutes passed and when Joseph was pushed down to his knees, his pulse racing, his breaths rapid and hot within the thick stocking – the only sound he could hear was the tinkling of bells. Like those on Santa's sleigh.

Joseph tried to swallow his rising dread, but his tongue filled his mouth like a large, dry sponge and he lurched forwards, choking.

"Don't think you're getting out of it that easily." The voice boomed above Joseph, as though it were being played through a loudspeaker. "You know why you're here, Joseph Snow."

Joseph regained some composure. "For your entertainment," he mumbled.

"In a moment, you'll be given a choice," Santa said. "Do what is needed to earn a spot on The Nice List… or refuse my offer and remain on The Naughty List. Is that clear?"

The voice was distorted; Joseph didn't recognise it. A pain shot through his knees, his wrists were sore from the binding; he wanted whatever this was to be over so he could go back home to Eve and snuggle up in front of the fire, maybe drink a sherry and watch a naff Christmas film.

"Yeah. Let's do this," Joseph said.

"Keen, eh? The last man on The Naughty List didn't share your enthusiasm – took six hours to get his confession."

Confession?

Joseph's mouth twitched beneath the material of the stocking and he shuffled, redistributing his weight.

"Feeling a little uncomfortable, Joseph?" Santa mocked. "Dark secrets will have that effect." He gave out a loud *Ho Ho Ho*, making Joseph jump.

"You taking this thing off me so I can see you?" Joseph said.

"Not yet, Joseph. All will become clear soon enough."

The air left Joseph's lungs as he was hoisted up. A harsh grating sound echoed in the room and his legs pressed against something solid. A chair? His bound hands were wrenched up and over the back of the seat and Joseph winced with the searing pain shooting through his shoulder sockets. Then he was pushed down into a sitting position and secured by a rope tied around his waist.

Shit. Like in the video he'd watched. The one with the man who looked as though he'd been tortured. Killed, even, if those commenting were right. Joseph shook his head to clear the image from his mind. Why hadn't he fought against this?

"Are you ready?"

"I don't know," Joseph said. "You haven't informed me of my choices yet!" Despite the chill in the air, a trickle of sweat ran down the centre of Joseph's back and he shivered.

There was a round of clapping, coupled with another burst of Ho Ho Ho. Joseph winced.

"The stage is set, Joseph. All you have to do is confess your deepest, darkest secret for the world to hear. Simple."

"Or?" Joseph asked. He wriggled, hoping to find the ties and rope were slack, his mind on escape.

"Or Eve gets a Christmas present like no other," Santa said, his voice low. Menacing. "And as is fitting, it will be delivered to her on Christmas Eve."

The mention of Eve's name rendered Joseph mute… until he realised. "Look, mate," Joseph said. "Well done. Good job and all that. But the jig is up. Almost had me going until you said Eve's name."

"My elves did their homework, Joseph. One had a lovely chat with your wife. She was very concerned about you. Shouldn't you think about her now? Or are you too selfish?"

"Your elves didn't do that good a job, or they'd have known I'm the least selfish person you could ever meet," Joseph retorted.

"Ah, yes. Your charity work for the little children. Very noble of you. Now, confess, or suffer the consequences."

Joseph groaned. "I got a parking fine a month ago," he said. "Left it a full week before paying it."

"Ho Ho Ho! Very funny. Last guy thought he could get away with that, too. He broke in the end. Literally."

Joseph heaved a sigh. "Seriously, I don't have anything to confess. You're wasting your time."

"Everyone's got something, Joseph. Even you."

What seemed like several hours passed. It was difficult to tell in the darkness. The inside of the stocking was wet with the moisture of Joseph's breath; his legs were cramped, his hands numb.

"Come now, Joseph, you must be getting tired."

Joseph laughed. "Tired of your games. Let's call it a night now, shall we? You've had your fun. We could grab a pint—"

"Enough!" The noise of an electric saw cut through the air. Joseph's heart tumbled in his chest.

He'd messed up. Not taken this seriously enough. Paul wouldn't have organised anything this elaborate. A chainsaw? Horrific thoughts clouded Joseph's mind until the pressure in his skull threatened to explode it.

Who the fuck *was* this Santa? What did he think he knew?

"Okay, okay," Joseph said, squirming in the chair. "You have my attention."

"It's just you and me here now." The voice was so close to Joseph his muscles froze. He held his breath. "Your secret will be safe with me."

"I really don't have anything worth sharing," Joseph argued, his voice cracking.

"Poor Eve. Her husband's severed head wrapped up with a bow wasn't on *her* Christmas list."

"Oh, come on! This is fucking ridiculous." Joseph pushed against the ground with both feet, and he moved a short distance. Adrenaline surged with the idea of propelling himself forwards, angling the chair in the hope of crashing into a wall. There was a chance of the wood breaking upon impact, potentially freeing him from the rope. He could then use the friction of the wall to remove the stocking from his head and put an end to this ordeal.

The sound of the chainsaw stopped him carrying out his plan. Something cold touched his neck.

He swallowed hard.

"I wouldn't," Santa said.

"Fine!" Joseph shouted. "If I tell you then you let me go?"

"That's the deal. I'm not a monster."

Joseph scoffed.

"But don't think you can pull the wool over my eyes by making something up. If I smell deceit, you won't get a second chance."

"Why are you even doing this?" Joseph asked, his energy depleted.

"It's Christmas, the season—"

"Of goodwill?" Joseph finished, the memory of the train journey coming back to him. How he'd stood up for the college students against the irate passenger, Alistair. Somewhere in the depths of his brain that moment had stirred up a memory. One he'd tried to bury.

"Was going to say season of forgiveness," Santa offered. "But whatever. Now, be a good man and spare your wife the horror of opening a gift that she'll never recover from."

Joseph's shoulders slumped. "Yeah, it's about time anyway," he said.

"Oh? Go on."

"Here's your confession, Santa…" Joseph took a deep breath. "When I was seventeen, on a college trip over the moors—" Joseph's mouth was so dry he wasn't sure if the words would come. He didn't want to hear himself say them. But he was done. Enough was enough and every muscle, every bone in his body ached for release.

"I murdered my best friend."

Joseph hung his head, the five words absorbing the air that remained inside the stocking.

The stocking was whipped from his head, and light assaulted his eyes. Joseph gulped in lungfuls of air, glad he could breathe freely again. He turned his head to finally see where he was. Santa's Grotto wasn't what he'd imagined.

Santa wasn't who he'd imagined either. Joseph's heartbeat stuttered, threatening to stop.

"*Charlie?* What the hell?" Joseph said, his eyes wide with a mix of bewilderment and dismay.

"I could say the same, mate."

"Of all the dumb pranks." Joseph's face flushed. He shook his arms, pulling against the rope. "Eve will be fucking furious with you. Untie me."

"But Joseph…" Charlie yanked his red Santa hat off and his arms fell limply to his sides. "I'm not sure I can do that." He began pacing the room.

"What do you mean? Of course you can."

"You just confessed to a *murder*."

"Yeah, I did," Joseph said, his eyes imploring. "What else would've worked? Jesus, Charlie. The parking fine was all I had. And you were going to keep me here indefinitely unless I gave you something meaty! Now, you've had your laugh – Ho Ho Ho – can we get out of here, please?"

Charlie's face was pale, pinched – his eyes narrowed. "All this time," he said, continuing to pace. "Everyone believed you were this… this perfect *do-gooder* and you were hiding a murderous secret?"

"Don't be stupid, Charlie. It's a lie, mate. You know me. Thought you were going to harm Eve for Christ's sake! I'd have spouted any bullshit to stop your absurd game. Now come on, this has gone far enough. Untie me."

Charlie seemed to think about it, then gave a nervous laugh. "Yeah, you're right. That makes more sense than my brother-in-law being a killer." His expression softened, and he took a few steps towards Joseph. Charlie removed the ties binding Joseph's wrists and released the rope. Joseph rubbed his wrists, then stood up, unsteadily at first, until the feeling returned to his limbs.

Joseph shook his head. The room was in a basement, no windows, just a couple of chairs and a table with a camcorder, its lens directed at where Joseph had been. A red light blinked like a steady pulse. Charlie's eyes followed Joseph's gaze.

"Good job I *wasn't* streaming it live, eh?" he said. "That would've made for an awkward conversation with the police."

"Not really," Joseph said, moving towards the table. "Not like I gave a name, is it? And I think they'd be more interested in you. I mean, kidnap and false imprisonment? That's a hefty sentence."

Charlie let the rope fall. "Fair point. Guess you're off the hook, then." There was an edge to his voice. Joseph lifted the camcorder, flicked a switch and started to replay what had recorded. He saw himself bound to the chair, his demeanour shifting from nonchalant to panicked, and his gut twisted. He looked weak. Pathetic. His chest tightened, his heart beating hard. Joseph dropped the camcorder to the ground and stamped on it, crushing the black plastic casing. Shards flew in all directions as he continued to drive his heel into it again and again.

Charlie glanced anxiously from Joseph to the door, and he began to take steps towards the exit.

"Can't believe you roped Paul into this," Joseph panted, out of breath from the effort of destroying the camcorder. "Is that why you were at the offices the other day?"

Charlie paused, inches from the door. "Paul let it slip that he was going to disappear early for Christmas, so I added his name to the list to lend it some authenticity."

"I see. You're not the psycho Santa people are talking about?"

"'Course not. Got the idea from that to prank you, though. Didn't think it'd work out as well as it did." He laughed. "I honestly thought you'd rumble me way before it got to this point."

"Well, clever you. And the guy you got to bring me here?" Joseph's jaw clenched.

"A mate from the pub. Told him it was a team-building exercise. Look, I only meant to make you sweat a bit. Your holier-than-thou routine can get a little wearing, you know?"

"Yeah. I know exactly what you mean." Joseph's eyes sparkled. "Trust me, it's a lot tougher than it looks. But I was doing pretty well. Even convinced myself."

"What do you mean?" Charlie's voice wavered, then it was like the curtains were pulled back and realisation hit. He darted for the door, but Joseph was quicker – grabbing the rope from the ground, he lunged at Charlie. With a swift movement, Joseph looped the rope around Charlie's neck and dragged him backwards. Charlie's feet scrabbled to make purchase on the stone floor; his hands pulled at the noose around his neck.

"What... the fuck?" Charlie's strangled voice was a whisper.

Joseph sighed as he bent to pick up Santa's hat. "My turn," he said, placing it on his head. "Now, Charlie. I'm sorry to say you're on Santa's Naughty List. And there's just one consequence."

Joseph tightened the rope.

INDIAN WINTER

Vaseem Khan

1.

Bombay, 1950

If you're going to die in Bombay, Christmas is as good a time as any.

Certainly, it was better than dying during the monsoon when the local cemeteries invariably flooded, to the extent that coffins floated up out of the ground, releasing from their eternal rest, amongst others, foreigners who had had the misfortune to perish in the city.

Inspector Persis Wadia arrived at the home of Harriet McCann on Boxing Day morning. The call had come through to the Malabar House station just thirty minutes earlier. The shift had been threadbare with only sub-Inspector Birla on duty alongside her, snoring gently on his seat, twitching in dreams like one of Bombay's army of pie dogs.

She decided to leave the man to his rest. Birla was a dish best served in small doses, or, better yet, not at all.

She was let into the mansion by a pair of statuesque Sikhs standing sentry at the gate, the kind who wore turbans and uniforms and looked as if they would willingly charge a tank – or a rank of elephants – if commanded to do so.

She parked the jeep beside a flotilla of expensive cars, including a gleaming white Rolls-Royce that looked as if it had only just been unpacked from its crate.

Crunching across the gravelled forecourt, she craned her neck to look up at the vastness of the estate before her. The McCann pile had the air of a Gothic castle about it, complete with pointed turrets and flying buttresses. She knew that Oliver McCann had been an industrialist of some sort, a man who had made a fortune during the latter decades of the Raj. She knew, too, that he had passed away just a year earlier, hogging the headlines for several days, before the exigencies of newly Independent India elbowed their way back onto the front pages.

She was met at the door by a liveried houseboy, who led her through the house to a drawing room the size of an aerodrome, where a white man in an immaculately tailored suit was sitting behind a mahogany desk.

A wariness came into his eyes as she approached. She was used to it.

As the country's first female police detective, she was still something of a novelty. The fact that she had been involved in several high-profile cases since joining the force had given her a notoriety that she found uncomfortable at the best of times.

The man stood, walked around his desk, held out a hand.

"Thank you for coming so quickly. My name is Clyde Barker. I am the CEO of McCann Industries." His accent was American.

Persis introduced herself.

"I know who you are, Inspector. I've seen you in the *Times of India*." His gaze lingered on her khaki uniform, the revolver at her hip.

She saw that he had hazel eyes, flashing behind gold-rimmed spectacles. His hair was cut short and flecked with grey. She estimated him to be in his early-to-mid fifties, well preserved and austerely handsome.

"Please follow me. I'd like to show you the body."

2.

She trailed him as he led her up a winding double-staircase, and along a maze of carpeted corridors.

His voice floated over his shoulder. "Yesterday, the McCann family gathered for their annual Christmas dinner. At around eleven, Harriet – that's Harriet McCann, the head of the family – retired to her bedroom. This morning, she failed to come down for breakfast. When a servant knocked on the door, she didn't answer. I ordered the door to be broken down. We found Harriet in her bed. It seemed obvious that she had died during the night." He paused, then continued: "I called her doctor in. He certified death, and then told us that it looked as if Harriet had been poisoned."

"Poisoned?"

"That's what the man said. The only problem is that the door was locked from the inside, and the windows were latched. So if it was poisoning, it had to be suicide."

"But you think that isn't possible?"

"There's not a chance in hell that Harriet killed herself."

"What makes you so sure?"

"Harriet was sixty years old. She came out to India with her husband, Oliver, when she was nineteen. She'd spent her whole life in his shadow. But when Oliver died, she was left in charge of the company. It was as if she had been given a new lease of life. She was having more fun than she'd ever had."

They arrived at a white-painted door. Persis saw that the lock had been broken.

Barker led her into the bedroom.

Inside, she found Sengupta, the pathologist, conferring with another very elderly native man that Barker informed her was the family doctor.

Stretched out on the bed was the corpse of the dead woman.

In death Harriet McCann resembled a doll. Not the sort of doll any young girl would have wanted to play with, but, nevertheless, a neat and slender presence, limbs set tidily by her side, dressed in a pink nightgown with thick grey hair in a tidy braid, and high waxy cheeks bloomed with rouge. Her fingernails were painted, as were her toenails.

The neatness of her appearance contrasted with the disorder of her bed, which looked like the scene of a recent wrestling match, possibly involving crocodiles.

Beside the bed, on a polished wooden unit, was a collection of photographs of Harriet with a small dog, a white Pomeranian. Persis looked around and saw that several large blow-ups of Harriet with the dog adorned the walls, and another cluster of photos sat on the dresser. The woman had clearly adored her canine friend.

A fuss at the door forced her to glance back over her shoulder.

A tall white man, bespectacled and darkly handsome, entered the room, trailed by a young Indian dragging a wheeled case large enough to contain several corpses.

Archie Blackfinch dipped his head in greeting. "Persis."

"Archie."

Blackfinch had worked with her on several cases over the past year. A forensic scientist from the Metropolitan Police in London, he had been called to India to help the Bombay Police Service set up its first forensic science lab, an endeavour that had been so successful he had now been prevailed upon to replicate his efforts in other Indian cities. The youth by his side was his protégé, Mohammed Akram, one of his students – and now chief assistant – at the lab. Akram, a tall, skinny specimen, sporting a haystack of Brylcreemed hair, gulped as she walked up. He was somewhat in awe of her, she knew.

Persis explained the situation, then left them to photograph the scene and gather forensic evidence.

Blackfinch's presence unsettled her. They had been engaged in a sometimes on–sometimes off liaison that invariably left her feeling as if she were trapped on a small boat in a heavy gale. Blackfinch failed to see the problem. The man had all the sensibilities of a brick wall. She was an Indian woman in post-Independence India. Any public relationship with a white man – an Englishman, at that – would be akin to clambering onto a keg of dynamite and lighting the fuse with her own hands.

She walked over to speak with Sengupta and the McCann family doctor, a man who looked one violent sneeze away from his own deathbed.

"What made you think Harriet had been poisoned?" she asked.

"There was dried foam around her mouth," replied the old man. "That wouldn't be enough on its own, of course. But she also displayed dilated pupils, her body was rigid, and she looked as if she had thrashed around ante-mortem, judging from the dishevelled bed linen. I've seen strychnine poisoning before – it causes severe agitation and involuntary skeletal muscle contractions."

"I've called for an ambulance," added Sengupta in his patented monotone. "The autopsy will be conducted immediately and will, no doubt, confirm the diagnosis."

"Is strychnine a fast-acting poison?"

"Yes," said Sengupta. "Symptoms usually appear within fifteen minutes. Death within an hour, two, at the outside. I'd suggest less for someone of our victim's age."

"Thank you," said Persis, a little taken aback. Sengupta was usually about as helpful as a tax inspector with a grudge.

She turned to Clyde Barker. "Who else was here last evening?"

3.

Leo McCann was a slender man in his forties, with thinning blond hair, a weak chin, and a nervous manner. His cheeks were hollow and scarred with acne. A faint moustache sat on his upper lip, looking as if it wanted nothing more than to flee the scene.

He wore absurdly tight golfing trousers, and a thin yellow sweater. A cigarette jittered in his hand.

"I understand that you are an only child?" said Persis.

"Yes." McCann was sitting on a couch. Light fell in from tall bay windows. He seemed to shrink from it, like a vampire.

"Are you the sole beneficiary of your mother's will?"

"What's that supposed to mean?"

"It means: are you the sole beneficiary of your mother's will?"

He glared at her, then sucked violently on his cigarette. "I haven't the faintest idea. We never spoke about that sort of thing."

"Did you work for the corporation?"

"No."

"Why not?"

He cracked his jaw. "Because my mother deemed it so."

"Is it fair to say that you and your mother did not get along?"

"Do you get along with *your* mother?"

"My mother died when I was seven."

"Your father then?"

"My father is the world's most cantankerous man. He sits in a wheelchair all day running a bookshop. He once threw a woman out of the store simply because she told him that she didn't think much of Dostoevsky."

McCann sneered. "Sounds like he and my father would have made great pals."

"What did your father do?"

"You mean you don't know?"

"I'd like to hear it from you."

He sniffed. "My father was the legendary Oliver McCann. He came to this country with nothing save a handful of coins rattling around in his pockets and a head full of dreams. Through sheer grit, he fashioned a business that became a multi-million-dollar conglomerate. Mining, metalworks, chemical plants. My father fancied himself an old-fashioned robber baron, the sort of industrialist who printed money, and had his picture taken with a cigar in his mouth. Not bad for an Iowa farm boy, huh?" His voice held more than a trace of sarcasm.

"He was American?"

"Yes."

"Do you consider yourself American?"

"I don't consider myself to be anything, Inspector. I was born in India, to American parents, and educated in England. Frankly, I'm a fish out of water no matter where I go."

She allowed a beat, then: "Tell me what happened yesterday. At the dinner."

"Nothing happened. I mean, we ate Christmas dinner, then we all went to bed. This morning, I found out that my mother was dead, possibly poisoned."

"Do you think your mother was suicidal?"

He gave a non-committal shrug. "No. I mean, I don't know. She didn't seem suicidal, but who can tell? Human beings are good at keeping their feelings bottled up inside. I know she was pretty broken up when my father passed away. This was her first Christmas in forty years without him. Maybe it was the straw that broke the camel's back."

"Clyde Barker thinks your mother was enjoying life a little too much to want to end it."

McCann's expression changed. "He *would* think that."

"What do you mean?"

"Clyde is a snake. He had his fangs in my father's heel for years. And as soon as *he* was out of the picture he started on my mother. Unfortunately, she fell for his dubious charms."

"But not you?"

"The man thought he could control the company through my

mother. A regular Svengali." He flicked ash from the cigarette onto the marble floor.

"Are you suggesting he may have had something to do with her death?"

"It wouldn't surprise me."

"But how would he benefit?"

McCann grimaced. "I'm betting that my mother's will might leave him in command of the company."

4.

She next interviewed Leo McCann's wife, Ida.

Ida was much younger than her husband, in her mid-twenties, overdressed – in Persis' opinion – in an expensive-looking dress and pearls, with a stylish bob haircut and enough lipstick to put a chorus girl to shame.

Her manner was frosty. "I really don't see why I should sit here and answer your questions. Anyone would think you suspected us of having something to do with Harriet's death."

"Did you?"

"Did I what?"

"Have something to do with her death?"

She flashed a cold look, then poured a whisky from a bottle on the tray beside the couch.

"How long have you and Leo been married?"

"About nine months. I came out here from England with my fiancé. He works for the civil service. But then I bumped into Leo at a jazz party at the Ambassador. It was love at first sight.

We were married within the fortnight. Sometimes you just have to listen to your heart." She said this with about as much passion as a woman explaining her selection of a turbot at the fish market.

"And what did Harriet think about this marriage?"

A hesitation. "Not that it was any of her – or your – business, but she didn't approve."

"And yet you were here at the Christmas dinner yesterday."

"Well, she didn't really have a choice. It's a McCann family tradition, don't you know? A simple Christmas get together, just immediate family. And Leo is her only child. He refused to come along without me, of course, the dear."

"You and your husband don't live here?"

"No. We moved out. Or rather, she kicked us out."

"Harriet?"

"Yes. She wasn't happy that Leo had eloped with me."

Persis considered this. "What did you live on?"

"She didn't cut him off completely. Once she'd calmed down, she agreed to give him an allowance. Frankly, it's humiliating. A grown man having to beg his mother for what is rightfully his."

"You think Leo should be running the company?"

"Well, of course he should. It's not as if Harriet built the firm. I'm certain Leo's father would have wanted his son to follow in his footsteps."

"Then why didn't he specify that in his will?"

"You'd have to ask Clyde. Not that I'd trust that man further than I can throw him."

"Why do you say that?"

Ida hacked out a laugh that failed to reach her eyes. "Clyde Barker has had designs on this family's fortunes for years. With Oliver out of the way, he made his move."

"What do you mean by that?"

"Leo didn't tell you?" She sipped at her whisky. "Clyde and Harriet had a thing. Last night she announced that they were to be married. Now, what do you think of *that*, Inspector?"

Persis allowed a moment. "If that's true then Mr Barker would have every reason to wish Harriet *good* health. On the other hand, everything *you* have told me suggests you had every reason to want your mother-in-law out of the way."

"Hah!" Her scorn could have peeled the paintwork. "The whole point of last night's dinner was so that Harriet could hold out an olive branch. She invited us along so that she could make amends for treating me like some gold-digging harlot who'd ensnared her son."

5.

The final participant of the previous night's Christmas dinner was an older woman, Gertrude Harrison, Harriet's oldest friend.

Gertrude had a slightly Bohemian air about her, but seemed genuinely upset, dabbing at her eyes with a silk handkerchief. "We'd known each other for almost four decades. I used to be her piano tutor, when she first came out here. Oliver felt that she needed to learn a few 'graces', as he called it. Harriet hated the piano, but she would have done anything for Oliver. Not that she had much choice. The man was a tyrant. Flew into a rage whenever he couldn't get his own way." She grimaced. "Harriet confided in me. I guess you could say a friendship developed between us. Frankly, I still can't believe she's gone."

"Did Harriet have any reason to take her own life?"

She blinked. "No. None. After Oliver's death it was as if she'd been given a second wind. She was enjoying herself far too much to end it."

"In that case, it would seem that she was murdered. It's highly unlikely that she ingested a lethal dose of strychnine by accident."

"Murdered!" The woman's eyes rounded with shock. "Who in the world would want to kill Harriet?"

"There were only four of you at dinner with her. And a handful of servants. I've interviewed the servants and discounted them."

"You think one of *us* poisoned Harriet?"

"Yes."

"But that's ridiculous. We were all there together, in full view of each other throughout the meal. The food – and drink – was served at the table. And afterwards, we sat around for a couple of hours, drinking and talking. She was fine when she went up to bed. She *must* have been poisoned in her room."

Persis hesitated. Therein lay the puzzle.

Even if motive could be established for Harriet McCann's killing, it was going to be nigh on impossible to explain just how the killer could have gotten into her room to poison her. Which meant that the poison had to have been placed in the room beforehand. She knew that Archie Blackfinch was busy examining the contents of Harriet's bedroom to determine precisely that.

But she couldn't imagine the killer would have left incriminating fingerprints behind.

"Tell me about her."

Gertrude considered the question. "She was a resourceful woman. While Oliver was alive she played the perfect hostess. But the truth was she hated it, hated the life he'd forced her into. All that noblesse oblige."

"How did she get on with her son?"

"She couldn't stand him. I know that's a terrible thing to say about a mother, but the feeling was mutual. Leo was a sore disappointment to Harriet. They actively disliked each other. As for that woman he married, Ida…" She grimaced. "Heaven knows, I'm not one to judge. But the pair of them were like vultures at the feast last night."

Persis changed direction. "What about Clyde Barker? Why was the company's CEO at a family gathering?"

"He was there for the same reason I was. Harriet considered him part of the family, as she did me."

"And the fact that the pair of them were getting married had nothing to do with it?"

She paused. "Leo told you about that?"

"Ida did."

"Well, I guess it wouldn't have been a secret for much longer." She sighed. "I feel devastated for Clyde. He's an honourable man. After Oliver died, Harriet naturally turned to him for guidance. One thing led to another. I was tremendously happy for her. Finally, she was free to be with a man who loved and respected her, who allowed her to be herself… And now, to see it all taken away…" Gertrude shook her head. "The gods really can be cruel, can't they?"

6.

Before leaving, she tracked down Clyde Barker.

He was sitting behind the desk she had found him at earlier, a glass of Scotch in hand, tie at half-mast. A photo album was spreadeagled in front of him, more pictures of Harriet.

The day's events appeared to have rattled the urbane CEO's composure.

"Why didn't you tell me that you and Harriet were to be married?"

"It didn't seem relevant." His eyes held a faraway look. "Besides, it doesn't matter now, does it?"

"Did you really love her?"

"What kind of question is that?"

"An honest one. She was sixty years old. An heiress to millions."

"I'm no spring chicken myself, Inspector. I was married for a while, when I was younger, but it didn't stick. A messy divorce. My ex-wife took our only child and vanished halfway around the world. Frankly speaking, the affair with Harriet took me by surprise." He drew air in through his nostrils. "Yes, Harriet was a few years older than me. But she was a lively and attractive woman. Kept herself in great shape. And since Oliver's death I saw a whole new side to her. I watched her take over the company and apply herself in a way that Oliver could never have imagined her capable of."

"Why did he leave the company to her and not to his son?"

"Because Oliver despised his son. Considered him a weakling and a fool. He thought that if he left the company in Leo's hands, the boy would run it aground."

"Is that what *you* think?"

"As a matter of fact, yes. Leo is a first-class wastrel. I wouldn't trust him with a child's bicycle, let alone an enormous corporation."

"And Harriet felt the same way?"

"She did."

"So Leo had every reason to want her out of the picture. Presumably, he inherits?"

"In theory, yes. Though Harriet was about to change her will."

"In favour of who?"

"In favour of me, Inspector."

She allowed a beat. "When you broke into the room, what did you see? I'd like your immediate impressions."

"I saw Harriet stretched out on the bed. I knew instantly that something was wrong. But in a million years I couldn't have guessed that she had been poisoned."

He hauled in a deep breath, fell silent. The Scotch remained in his hand, the glass still full.

She looked down at the album open before him. "May I?"

Without waiting for an answer, she picked up the binder and flicked through the pages. The photographs were entirely of Harriet with her dog. In almost every picture she was hugging the animal to her chest, nuzzling its neck, kissing it.

"She loved that damned dog," mumbled Barker. "I honestly think the animal meant more to her than her own child. Possibly even more than me."

Persis couldn't imagine developing such an attachment for one of Bombay's flea-bitten pie dogs. But white people *were* different.

Mad dogs and Englishmen, as the saying went.

Perhaps it applied to Americans, too, and every foreigner insane enough to venture onto the subcontinent.

7.

She arrived back at Malabar House with evening on the way.

Bombay's smallest police station was housed in the basement of a four-storey Edwardian building with gargoyles on the roof and dogs in the lobby. Its chief claim to fame – among those on the force, at any rate – was that it served as a punishment posting for those who had soiled the police bed. Persis had been sent there because her seniors had no idea what to do with a woman. She might as well have been a mythical creature, a fire-breathing dragon threatening to burn down all that they held so dear.

She made her way through to her commanding officer Roshan Seth's office, where she discovered Archie Blackfinch also waiting for her.

A ceiling fan turned above them, doing little more than shuffling the turgid heat around the room like a geriatric usher. She knew that in other countries Christmas came with the promise of snow. In Bombay, Christmas came with the prospect of heatstroke and the redolent scent of dung on the breeze.

Seth sat red-eyed behind his desk.

Malabar House's commanding officer had once been a man that others on the force had talked about in admiring terms, an officer going places in a hurry. But Independence had put paid to all that. Rumours that he had toadied up to the British during their time in charge had poisoned the well of Seth's career. He had been summarily decanted to Malabar House and put in charge of a team of misfits and rejects, effectively given a life sentence for a crime he wasn't even sure he had committed.

She took a seat, then waited for Blackfinch to report.

"The autopsy confirms that it was strychnine poisoning. Not a heavy dose, but for a sixty-year-old woman a small dose was more than enough."

"How was it administered?"

"Ingestion. Though, strangely, a little residue was left on her nose."

Persis considered this, then, "Did you find the container?"

He hesitated. "That's where it gets odd. We tested everything in her bedroom. There wasn't a single container that held a trace of the poison."

She frowned. "That's impossible. The room was locked from the inside and we've established that she wasn't poisoned at dinner. Strychnine is a fast-acting poison and Harriet was perfectly fine for hours after the meal, and fine when she went up to bed. So the poisoning had to have happened in the bedroom."

Seth chimed in. "Could the killer have removed the poison container when they broke into the room the next morning?"

"Unlikely. There were three of them who broke the door down. Two servants and Clyde Barker. One of them would have seen something if either of the other two tried anything. Besides, Clyde Barker had no motive to want her dead. They were due to be married. Regardless of what we think of the relationship, he would have stood to inherit. If anything, he needed her alive."

They sat in gloomy silence, turning the problem over in their minds.

Harriet McCann had died on the night of December twenty-fifth – more accurately, the early hours of December twenty-sixth – of that there was no doubt. She had been poisoned – or had poisoned herself – with strychnine. The mystery lay in exactly *how* the death had occurred. A death that, on the face of it, simply could not have happened, at least not in the way it appeared.

A locked room mystery. With no motive for Harriet to take her own life and no sign of the container within which the poison had been delivered to the room.

Persis realised that something was knocking on the door of her subconscious. A nagging feeling that had been with her since she'd met with Clyde Barker just before leaving the house. She allowed the encounter to tick over in her mind... something she'd seen... and then she had it.

She turned to Blackfinch. "You said that you found some of the poison residue on her nose?"

"Yes. It is a bit odd... Perhaps the killer forced the poison into her mouth and spilled some onto her nose as he – or she – did so?"

She hesitated. "There's another way it could have ended up on her nose."

8.

Persis arrived back at the McCann house with night having fallen.

In short order, she assembled the key players in the drawing room: Leo and Ida McCann, Clyde Barker, and Gertrude Harrison.

"Tell me about Harriet's dog," she said.

They stared at her as if she had lost her mind.

"Did Harriet take the dog into her bedroom last night?" she continued.

"Yes," said Barker. "She slept with the dog. Every night since she bought it."

"In which case the dog was in the room with her when she died. Was it there in the morning when you broke in?"

He frowned. "Now that you mention it, yes. It scooted out when we kicked the door in."

"And where is it now?"

They all looked at each other.

"Why is this of any consequence?" said Ida testily.

Persis held up a photograph. She had taken it from the album Clyde Barker had been looking at earlier. It showed Harriet with her face buried in the dog's muzzle.

"I believe that the poison was administered via Harriet's dog. I believe the poison was sprayed onto the dog's collar and possibly onto the fluff of hair around its face. When Harriet climbed into bed, having locked her bedroom door, she kissed and nuzzled the dog, as was her nightly custom. That's when she ingested the poison. We found traces of it on her nose."

They stared at her in astonishment.

"But who would do such a thing?" Leo looked genuinely astonished.

"I spoke with the servants. It seems that Harriet bought the dog after her husband's death. Prior to that he refused to allow her to keep a dog – he was allergic to them. By the time she bought the animal, Leo had moved out of the house. He rarely spoke to his mother. Of the people at dinner last night, only two knew how much Harriet adored the dog, and of her habit of taking it into bed with her each night." She turned to Gertrude Harrison and Clyde Barker. "Of those two, Clyde Barker had no reason to wish Harriet dead. The opposite, in fact. Harriet was about to marry him and write him into her will. Which leaves you." She looked at Gertrude.

The woman blinked rapidly. "You're saying that *I* killed Harriet?"

"Yes. And I will soon be able to prove it. We'll find the dog, confirm the presence of poison. After that it won't be too difficult to find out where you purchased the strychnine – it's not readily available. Within a day or so we will have someone able to identify you."

A final moment of resistance, and then the woman's shoulders caved inwards. Her face trembled; tears began to flow down her cheeks. "She knew. She knew and she did it anyway." Her voice was a whisper.

Persis waited.

"Gertrude," said Barker gently. "Did you kill Harriet? For God's sake, why? You were best friends."

"That's what I thought too. That's why I confided in her." She looked at him with unbridled misery. "I told her that I'd been in love with you for ever. I asked her to talk to you, to see if you might be interested in me. Instead of helping me, she seduced you. Oh, she apologised, of course, threw herself on my mercy, shed crocodile tears. Said it was an affair of the heart, she couldn't help it. Promised to make it up to me, to help me find a man just right for *me*. Someone every bit as good as you. But there isn't, is there? There isn't anyone as good as you, Clyde."

Persis walked over to the woman, thinking how strange was the human heart, capable of divine acts of love, but, in the same instant, able to compel the greatest evil.

"Gertrude Harrison, I am arresting you for the murder of Harriet McCann."

Note: This short story features characters from the Malabar House novels by Vaseem Khan, beginning with the CWA Historical Dagger-winning Midnight at Malabar House *(2020). Characters used with permission of Hodder & Stoughton.*

POSTMARKED MURDER

Susi Holliday

TILLY HAD decided over a month ago that she was no longer sending Christmas cards. Never mind saving the trees, a first-class stamp was one pound twenty-five! Daylight robbery, that was. They should be ashamed of themselves, what with the cost of *just existing* being unmanageable for half the population these days. That didn't apply to her, of course.

But still.

Her recipient list had been carefully pared back, year on year, based on who actually sent cards to her… even so, with over thirty people that she might get a card from – assuming they had not decided to stop sending them too – then that was going to be nearly forty pounds, plus the cost of the cards themselves – which to be fair, were becoming cheaper every year – she was barely going to get change from a hundred quid. Think what she could buy with that instead! She would, of course, tell everyone on social media that she was donating the money to charity. Something worthy, like the homeless, or rescued puppies. But of course, she had no intention of doing anything of the sort.

By mid-December, despite the incessant pushy marketing of all things festive, Tilly was steadfastly sticking to her decision not to send any cards. But she did, most unexpectedly, suffer from a small, but intensely irritating itch of guilt every time a card plopped onto the mat.

She had considered throwing them away unopened. But what if one contained a cheque? Or an invitation? Or just some salacious gossip that she would regretfully miss? Plus, it was an awful waste. If the sender had taken the time to buy the card and the stamp, to write a personal message to her, and to go to the effort of sending it – it was only fair that she at least opened them up and read them and displayed them on her mantelpiece or her bookshelf for a couple of weeks.

The latest delivery had brought three cards. All approximately the same size. All rectangular rather than square. All with neatly written addresses. Well, actually, no. Two like that, and then another with a printed sticker instead. She peered at the one with the sticker. It was unusual for any of her friends to address an envelope like this. Most of her schoolfriends, in particular, were almost ferally competitive about their perfect cursive. She inspected both handwritten envelopes, both with the same festive robin redbreast stamp, and she knew who both were from. Marion Grayson and Lauren Keating. Their handwriting was as recognisable as their cut-glass vowels (Marion) and irritating tinkle of a laugh (Lauren).

The third envelope, she realised with some alarm, contained no stamp at all.

She flung open the door just in time to see the postman disappearing around the corner on his bicycle. Other than that, the street was empty. Everyone who worked had gone to work. It was long past dog-walking hour. For a moment she thought she saw someone lurking under the old oak by the junction with the main road, but when she blinked, there was no one there. A cold wind whipped around her bare ankles, and she stepped back inside, closing the door tightly behind her.

She kept the letter opener on the bureau in the hallway. Ostensibly for opening letters and parcels, but also a small security measure near the front door, should she ever need it. She slid it along the back of the typed-address, un-stamped envelope and pulled out the card from inside, turning it over to see the design on the front.

It was a woodland scene. Thick trunks and bare branches huddled together to form a dark, twisted canopy blocking out any hope of sun on the damp, mossy floor. In the background, standing stiffly apart, were three shadowy figures. The heads were bowed towards something on the ground. Well, two of them were. The third one was turned towards the camera, providing a clear shot of a pale, startled, flash-blind face.

It was not a very good photograph, but she recognised the place all the same. She recognised the face too.

It was hers.

She bit her lip to avoid a swear word leaking out. *Bloody* was her limit, usually. But this needed something stronger and she closed her eyes tight and bit harder, shearing a shred of skin away from her bottom lip in the process. When she opened her eyes and caught a glimpse of herself in the hall mirror, all she could see was that pale, startled, flash-blind face staring back. This time with a smear of crimson on her lip that she slowly wiped away with the back of her hand.

Charles Winnersby. It had to be him. She'd never known for *sure*, but she was able to bring that day back with a frame-by-frame recall as if it had happened last week, instead of almost thirty years ago, and every time she did, she was almost certain that it was his threadbare blue chinos and scuffed plimsolls that she had spotted running out of the clearing, camera rattling on a leather strap around his scrawny neck.

It had been the last day of term. The four of them: her (Tilly), Gloria Saxby, Rupert Hogg and Mallie Kitteridge had agreed to skip the last lesson (double maths with Goatface Grantly) and go into the woods. Mallie was showing off, as he always did, saying he had a bottle of Dubonnet that he'd stolen from his father's drinks cabinet, and a packet of Benson & Hedges that he'd lifted from his mother's secret stash in the garden shed that no one was supposed to know about. Tilly disliked alcohol and cigarettes, but she disliked maths more, and she wasn't sure if he knew or not, but she found Rupert extremely appealing. Gloria was pretty annoying, but her and Mallie had been together all term and spent most of it entwined in the corner of the common room, firing insults at anyone in earshot, then snogging one another's faces off when anyone dared confront them.

They were incredibly embarrassing: Tilly was glad that she was moving on to the Ladies College next term and wouldn't have to put up with their insufferable nonsense any longer. As she'd hoped, Gloria and Mallie had sloped off to find a comfortable bush somewhere, leaving her and Rupert and the bottle of Dubonnet, which didn't taste all that bad after the first few swigs, and infinitely better when dribbled out of someone else's mouth into your own. If the others hadn't returned when they did, pink-faced and grinning, arms wrapped around one another like vines, she had no doubt that Rupert would have pushed her to the ground and lain on top of her... and she had no doubt that she would have let him.

Unfortunately, the jovial, sexually charged mood soured quickly when Mallie picked up the bottle of Dubonnet to find a mere dribble left at the bottom; fired up on post-coital testosterone, he decided to take a swing at Rupert's head. Even more unfortunately, Mallie did not take account of Rupert's nimble moves, and as Rupert ducked and bobbed out of the way, Mallie's momentum took him to the point of no return. He fell forward at some speed, although the whole thing seemed to occur in slow motion, and in place of the hard crunch they all expected as he hit the ground face first, there was instead the frantic rustling of a wild animal forcing itself through a thicket, followed by a dull *whump* as Mallie disappeared into a monstrously large hole and hit the bottom at full pelt.

Rupert and Gloria had their heads cast downwards.

"What the hell is this? An animal trap?" Rupert said. "Mate, are you OK down there?"

"Is he... dead?" Gloria let out a shocked sob.

Tilly whirled around at the sound of the shutter, catching the flash face-on. Stars swirled and spun in front of her eyes, and she blinked hard, regaining her vision just in time to see the retreating back. The bouncing camera. Recognising the trousers and the shoes but just never being completely sure of who it was, and what they might do with the photograph they just took.

It was an accident though, wasn't it? None of them could have known the hole was there. That Mallie would be enraged enough to attack Rupert and find himself falling down it.

"Mate?" Rupert tried again, but there was no answer from the hole.

Gloria burst into tears. "We're going to be in so much trouble."

Rupert caught Tilly's eye, giving her a sharp look. "Did anyone see us together?"

Tilly shook her head. "I came on my own. Gloria arrived a few minutes later."

Gloria forced words through her mucus. "Mallie was already here. He told me he was setting up a surprise for us." She sniffed hard. "You got here last, didn't you?"

Rupert nodded. "That's right. Good."

Tilly realised then that the others hadn't noticed the cameraman. She decided it was best not to bring it up. Years later, she would wonder why she made this choice, but at the time it had seemed like a complication that none of them needed.

Rupert snapped a dead branch off one of the smaller trees and crouched down at the hole. He leant forward just enough, poking the branch down into the space. In the darkness of the wood, it was hard to even make Mallie out. If you didn't know he was in there, you wouldn't see him at all. Rupert stood back up, throwing the branch into the hole. "He's unconscious or he's dead. Either way, we're not getting him out of there."

"Let's run back to the school. Call an ambulance?" Tilly was starting to feel a bit sick, adrenaline kicking in. The bottle of Dubonnet lay on the ground near the hole, the last dregs of crimson liquid like a small pool of blood.

Rupert turned away from them, while Gloria looked on helplessly.

Then he started to grab at clumps of bracken, at dead roots and dried up shrubs. He began tossing them into the hole.

The pit.

Tilly gasped. "What are you…?"

"Don't you see?" Rupert said, snapping branches and tossing them in. "He made this. He knew about this hole, or he made this hole, but either way, he concealed it, and he brought us here, and he had a plan… one of us was going in there." He shrugged. "Probably me. I did think it was odd when he invited me here. It's not like we were friends or anything." He picked up a stick and pointed it at Gloria. "Did you actually like him, or did you just enjoy a bit of rough and tumble now and then?"

Gloria flushed pink, turned away.

"Thought so." Rupert directed the stick at Tilly. "You and he were *definitely* not friends. Am I right?"

Tilly nodded slowly. She had wondered, too, why she'd been invited. If it hadn't been the last day of term. If she hadn't already known she had a future elsewhere – away from this place, away from these people. Would she have come? No. She had hoped for a last-day-of-term memory. She'd hoped for a first kiss. Maybe more.

She had got more.

"He was sleeping with my friend, too," Gloria said quietly. "Sandrine LaVey." She sniffed hard again. "Actually, I think Mallie is a bit of a shit."

"He's bullied me constantly since we started school together," Rupert said with a shrug. "In the last few years, I've fought back. I could see the rage building in him. I should have predicted something like this."

"But what… Was he going to try and kill us all?" Tilly asked.

It all seemed too far-fetched. But then, Mallie had definitely changed towards her after his father lost his job at *Tilly's* father's factory. He'd barely paid her any attention until then, but since that day – a scandalous drinking-at-work incident that could not be brushed over – Mallie had definitely eyed her with a look of pure, measured hatred.

Rupert shrugged. He didn't need to ask why Mallie hated Tilly. Everyone knew the story. "Scare us, maybe? Make sure we had an awful summer break?" He picked up another clump of dead twigs and leaves and dumped it into the hole. "If he's still alive, he'll get out of there somehow. If he's not? Well… I haven't seen him today. Have you?"

Gloria shook her head firmly. "Not me."

"Nor me," Tilly said, feeling her heart rate start to return to normal. "I think I'm going to head home now. My parents will be wondering where I've got to."

Rupert wiped his hands on his trousers and took a step towards her. Then he lifted a hand to her mouth, gently wiping her lip with his finger. "Have a nice life, Tilly Whitmore." He turned away, disappearing into the woods.

Tilly licked her lips. They tasted of dirt, and salt, and just a hint of Dubonnet.

"He likes you." Gloria gave Tilly a weak smile, and with a final glance towards the hole, she spun round and jogged off towards the playing fields. Tilly hurried off in the other direction, heading for the river, craving the noise of the rushing water to calm her racing mind.

She never saw any of them again.

They found Mallie's body a week later. Rumour had it, he was slumped in place over the edge of the pit, arms reaching for something to help pull himself out. He didn't make it. They'd have found him sooner if they'd been looking – but one of the teachers discovered a note sticking out of his locker saying he'd gone off for a summer adventure. Tilly had managed to look shocked when the news broke that someone from her school had died in a tragic accident, falling down a collapsed badger set and finding himself with no way out. He'd been intoxicated. Poor lad. Tragic and shamed, like his father before him.

Tilly had never touched a drop of alcohol since.

She took a deep breath, blew it out slowly. She hadn't even looked inside. She wasn't even sure how long she'd been standing there in the hallway, remembering. She opened the card, and found that it contained seven words, written in neat capital letters.

TEN GRAND. I WILL COME FOR IT.

Tilly sat down on the long padded bench that lined one side of the hallway, and read the words again. She had the money, no question. But why should she give it away for something like this? The accident was years ago. There was no suggestion of foul play. The players had never laid eyes on one another again. There was nothing but this grainy photograph, that no one other than those who were there could possibly understand.

Why now? Charles Winnersby had fallen on hard times, she supposed. Blackmail always came down to money. He thought he'd try his luck. And why not?

Of course he would choose *her*.

The others were not easily identifiable in the photograph, but more than that, she was sure that they didn't have a spare ten grand to hand over either. While she had struck gold by taking over her father's business, the other two had not fared so well. She might not have seen them, but she had kept track of their whereabouts via social media.

Gloria Saxby had emigrated to Australia a year after the accident, and had never returned. She was married now, to a surf instructor, and they lived in a shared housing community near Byron Bay with their two cutely feral children. The surf instructor liked to beat her sometimes, but she was good at covering it up and carrying on. She was all smiles and sunshine, but those filters she used couldn't hide the fear in her eyes, and the deep-seated rage in his. Tilly knew the type.

Rupert Hogg died from a heroin overdose ten years ago. He was found behind the bins in a sink estate on the outskirts of Hull. The scars of a life being bullied run deep.

Mallie Kitteridge was not a nice boy, and he would not have become a nice man. They had done the world a favour, leaving him to die in that hole. That's what she told herself, when she sat alone in the dark of an evening, pushing away all thoughts of any normal life she might have had, if she'd made a different choice that day. She had her money, and her house with her nice things. But she had nothing else. No one else.

You can't take a life and expect to have one yourself.

She was just so very tired now. The two other cards that came through the letterbox lay on the bureau unopened. Tilly had no interest in Christmas cards, or who might have sent them to her. She propped up the card that she had opened, making sure the photograph faced away. She didn't need to see it again. The words inside were clearly visible.

TEN GRAND. I WILL COME FOR IT.

She picked up the letter opener, turned it over in her hands.

Touched the tip against the soft bulb of her pinkie. A bloom of blood. A smear of Dubonnet on lips bruised from kissing. She leaned back against the wall and closed her eyes; smiled.

Waited for the knock on the door.

FROSTBITE

Samantha Hayes

THE TRAIL of blood leading to the barn is stark against the fresh snow. Globules of berry-red festivity in the moonlight at first glance, followed by a run of frantic heartbeats, a gaping mouth. Fear.

"What the *hell*..." Ellen gasps, her eyes flicking about the silent, snow-blanketed yard. She holds the empty log basket in her left hand, the Maglite gripped firmly in her right. A useful weapon if it comes to it.

For a fleeting moment, she thinks the blood almost seems beautiful in the pink-hued twilight of the December evening – the sun having barely made it above the scrub-covered hill looming over the remote Derbyshire cottage that was supposed to be a getaway-hideaway-country-retreat-lock-up-and-leave or some other estate agent bullshit for her and Dan. An easy weekend bolthole away from the city. They deserved it, didn't they, with their six-figure salaries and hectic schedules?

But now Dan is dead.

"Only a couple of hours from London by car," they'd been told on the first viewing, their jaded London eyes lapping up the rural idyll on a sunny spring day nine months before that fateful winter's night. Though in reality, the journey to the cottage had averaged four hours after work on a Friday, and they'd arrive pissed off, tired and hungry, already resenting the drive back.

Ellen gasps as she stares at the fresh blood in the snow, covers her mouth, her heart racing when she realises what it means.

Someone else is here.

She pulls her jacket around her, hugging her body. Her eyes search around the yard again, behind the cottage, the cone of torchlight revealing shadows in the darkness, then she flashes it back to the barn where she's heading to fetch more logs for the fire – her only source of heat since the power went down this morning. The tang of woodsmoke from the cottage chimney catches in her nostrils, and the silence after the earlier snowfall is almost deafening with the countryside blanketed in blue-white powder.

She presses on cautiously, her booted feet crunching and creaking in a strangely comforting way. But there's more blood at the entrance to the barn, as if whatever was dripping dripped harder in this spot. She stares down at it, her breath coming out in fast puffs.

"It'll just be an animal," she tells herself, nodding. "A badger searching for cover after being hit by a car on the lane." Hearing a human voice, even if it is her own, makes her feel a little better. Grounded. Not quite so scared at being out here all by herself. But then she spots the footprints in the snow.

Ellen pulls open the barn door, giving it a couple of hard yanks.

It creaks on its hinges – *part of its rural, shabby-chic charm…* or whatever crap the estate agent had spouted.

"Hello?" she calls out, shooting her torch beam around the dusty interior.

When it's clear there's no one there, and she confirms that the trail of blood ends at the door, Ellen heads over to the wood pile in the corner, dropping the log basket down. She holds the torch under her chin and sets to work filling the basket. Once done, she drags it across the courtyard back to the grey stone cottage, one window dimly lit by a couple of candles flickering inside. She'd have checked the electricity provider's website to see if there was news of the power coming back on if she had 4G or Wi-Fi. More of that rural idyll right there.

Ellen shoves the back door open with her boot and pulls the log basket inside the tiny kitchen. She pauses, listening out, still rattled by seeing that blood in the snow. She tries to convince herself that the footprints she saw are hers from earlier, but she can't be sure. To distract herself, she considers heating a can of soup on the log burner given that the cooker is electric (of course it is), or if she should just resign herself to having it cold from the tin. Then she remembers the cheese.

"*Haappy* fucking Christmas," she chants, but there's no one to hear that her voice is wavering on the edge of despair as she lugs the basket through to the living room. She bends down to open the door of the wood burner, log in hand ready to chuck it into the remains of the fire.

But something makes her stop.

Something makes her turn her head slowly towards the armchair beside the fireplace in the small, flagstoned living room with its sweet damp patches and its cute woodworm in the beams. The overpriced Christmas tree that she'd brought up from Borough Market two days ago stands undecorated and lopsided.

Ellen screams.

A blood-freezing, throat-lacerating shriek that propels her upright and reeling backwards until she stumbles into the bookcase, lined with all the books she and Dan were going to read during their weekend getaways.

"*Fuck…*" she yells. "What the hell!" She brandishes the Maglite for all she's worth, her thumb fumbling to flick it on, as if the light beam is a death ray that will instantly zap and kill the man sitting in the armchair.

"Sorry, sorry." He stands up from the shadows, holding out his hands – palms facing her. "Don't… don't shoot." He glances at the torch. Smiles a bit.

Ellen jabs the Maglite at him again, scowling at the dishevelled, blood-stained man. "What the actual *fuck*?" She's shaking – bone-juddering fear spewing out. "Why are you in my house?"

"I didn't mean to scare you," he says, frowning and dropping down into the chair again. He lowers his head between his knees, like someone about to pass out would do. Then he briefly looks up. "I saw the light through the window." A glance at the candles over on the coffee table. "I knocked on the back door but there was no reply. It was open so I came inside." Head down between his knees again.

That's when Ellen notices the gash on the side of his skull. A matted patch of congealed reddy-brown in his unkempt sandy hair. And his nostrils are caked in blood, too – the left one still wet, as though it's recently been dripping.

"I... I hit my head..." he says, his eyes narrowing. "There was an accident... my car. Everything's fuzzy. My name is... I think it's... it's Baker," he says, his voice muffled and slow. "My first name, that is." He rubs his hand through his beard as if it will help him remember. "My mother must have been having an off day when she named me."

Ellen pauses, thinking, looking at him intently, before scowling and lowering the torch. Then she ventures closer, assessing the threat of him, creeping around the edge of the room as if he's a wild animal. "Maybe you have concussion," she says. Not that she cares about his memory or head injury. She just wants him gone.

He looks up, and Ellen sees something dark and lost and confused in his eyes. Something unpredictable.

"What do you want?" She edges closer to the fire, flashing a look at the iron poker lying on the hearth. Way better than her Maglite.

"That's the thing. I... I'm not sure." Baker taps the side of his head, wincing. "It's in there, but I can't quite reach it."

Ellen's brow creases. "You don't know why you're in the middle of nowhere? There's three feet of snow out there. It's minus five degrees. It's virtually dark. Yet here you are, bleeding in my living room." She flaps a hand in the air.

"It's stopped, I think," Baker says, inspecting his fingers. "The bleeding. Merry Christmas, by the way."

"What are you, the ghost of Christmas fucking past?" Ellen squeaks. "Anyway, it's still three days away yet."

Baker smiles, just one side of his mouth. "Are you suggesting I'm an accurate representation of all your prior festive seasons?"

Ellen stares at him, wondering if it's *her* who's hit her head,

266

perhaps slipping in the snow when she went to fetch the logs. She pinches the skin on the back of her hand to see if she can feel it, to see if she's real. Then she pauses, her mind flashing back.

Last year, Christmas was spent in bed at her parents' place, dosed up on painkillers and alcohol. Dan had barely been dead a week. The year before, they'd gone to Dan's family home in the South Downs for the festive season. Sixteenth-century barn conversion, three black Labradors, a hundred cousins and elderly relatives, a twelve-foot Christmas tree with red velvet bows. A massive goose. That kind of thing.

"I like Christmas," she tells Baker, scowling at the undecorated Nordmann fir that she'd managed to squeeze in the back of her Mini. *Liked*, she corrects in her head. "No ghosts." She swallows down the lie.

The year before that, she and Dan were in Lanzarote staying with friends and it was a barbecue by the pool on Christmas Day. They had Christmas at home a few times, just the two of them with the pattering of tiny feet that never happened echoing through their Islington townhouse, the mortgage paid with the money they'd have otherwise used for school fees. But on the whole, they preferred being with other people. The company seemed to dilute the tightness that she and Dan harboured – as though the secret misery hanging between them had become their family, something to be nurtured, grown, cared for.

What it meant was that Dan went out for more and more business dinners, getting home well after midnight on weeknights. And Ellen volunteered for work trips that took her to Europe – bagging the jobs that none of the reps with families wanted to take.

After a time, weekends here at the cottage had become solo affairs for Dan, with Ellen preferring to stay in London. In the months before he'd died, they'd barely spent an evening together. It was just the way things had become, even though the perfunctory *I love yous* were still offered up once a week. Usually in reciprocal texts, or when they crossed paths at the front door.

Ellen drops the torch and lunges at the poker, grabbing it with both hands and brandishing it at Baker. He recoils in the tartan armchair, sticking up his palms again.

"Get out!" she yells, hating that her solitary Christmas plans have been interrupted.

"Don't hit me. Please. I've a lousy headache already." Baker sounds weary, she thinks. Someone who's had enough. "My car…" He trails off, his eyes narrowing as he stares at the fire. "I remember now. It's in a ditch."

"I said *get out!*" Ellen shrieks again. "Or I'll call the police."

"Good luck with that. There's no reception." That crooked half-smile again.

Ellen fishes her phone from her back pocket, tapping the screen. No reception isn't her main problem – but it would be if she wasn't out of charge. She doesn't tell Baker that. More brandishing. "Look, just leave."

"Put that down. I'm not going to hurt you."

She makes a *pah* sound, and then Dan is on her mind again. He'd promised that, too.

"I'm here because of my wife." Baker's face lights up, the darkness behind his eyes illuminating. "Yes… yes, that's it. My wife."

Ellen stares at him, her mind racing.

"I found an address in an old coat pocket when I was searching through her things." He squints, faltering, as though he's wringing out a memory. "Suspicion will do that to you." Baker snorts. Winces. Wipes his big hands down his face.

"'Suspicion haunts the guilty mind', or whatever the expression is," Ellen tells him, scowling. "Anyway, what's it got to do with me?"

"Because the address I found is *here*." Baker half stands up and takes something from his jeans pocket, showing Ellen a small piece of paper. "Look, Pear Tree Cottage, Abbot Lane, Tyedale."

Ellen glances at it from a distance, confused, feeling the heat of the fire on her legs. That address, *Pear Tree Cottage*… They'd really been sucked in by it, her and Dan. Truth is, there's not a pear tree in sight. Just endless scrubby grass, dry brick walls and sheep.

"Look, I was about to decorate my tree," she says with a shake in her voice. She really wants to put down the poker as her arms are beginning to ache, but there's a menacing look in his eyes she doesn't like. "I've got… I've got people coming for festive drinks. I need you to leave." Her heart is thumping so hard that she's worried he'll hear it.

Baker snorts, glancing around the cottage, sizing up the miserable scene made only vaguely festive by the bare fir tree, the orange flames in the stove and the two candles. "Where are your decorations then?" He sits back in the armchair, groaning and holding his ribs.

"In there." Ellen gestures to the wooden dresser.

"How about I get them for you?" He touches his head, inspecting his bloodied fingers again. "Do you have a wet cloth? And I could really use something to eat."

"I'm not a bloody hotel," she says, riled by his nerve. "There's a pub in the next village. You can walk there and get help."

"Or you could give me a lift."

"You're kidding me, right?" Ellen so wants to hit him with the poker – even draws it back over her shoulder. But she stops when

Baker flinches. He suddenly seems lost and pathetic. Then he surprises her by going over to the dresser and opening the cupboard.

"What the hell are you doing?" Ellen strides over. He's an easy target as he crouches down, peering in at the virtually empty shelves, looking for Christmas decorations that aren't there. One swift blow with the poker on his already split head and she reckons he'd be down. It would serve him right.

Baker takes out a single cracker and is about to say something but stops, turning it around and around in his hands as he examines it, his eyes narrowing in thought. Then he swivels round and waves it at her. "Is this it?" He has a twisted grin on his face. "The sum of your decorations? Anyway, no one's getting through the snow for festive drinks." He stands up again. "Are you lying to me?"

"The cracker is to go on the tree," Ellen says, making a swipe for it, but he's too quick and holds it up high. "It's... it's all I've got right now." *That much is true*, she thinks – the single cracker that she brought up from London. The cracker she's kept for a year. It's the potential contained inside it that's made her cling onto it – a wretched motif of all she's lost.

"Pull it with me," Baker says, thrusting it towards her.

Ellen freezes, her mouth hanging open, her eyes fixed on the gold ribbon curls, the annoying glitter, the company logo glued on the front of the shiny red tube – the logo representing her and Dan's demise.

That fucking cracker.

Baker shakes it, holding it up to his ear. "Wonder what's inside?"

"It'll just be crap. A crap toy, a crap riddle, a crap hat. Give it to me." Ellen reaches out for it again, but Baker whips it away.

"Tell you what – I'll leave when you pull it with me." He walks back to the armchair and drops down into it, making a face that tells Ellen he's in pain.

"You're blackmailing me with a cracker?" She perches on the arm of the sofa the other side of the fireplace, watching him. "Where is your car?" She prays it's not far, that maybe a tow truck would get through the snow. She just wants him gone.

Baker huffs out a sigh. "On its roof in the snow two miles away. I walked here. Good job I screenshotted the location."

"Yeah. Good job." Ellen wraps her arms around herself, still holding the poker and trying to ignore the cracker on his lap.

"Sit," he says. Against her better judgement, Ellen does. Then he leans forward, holding out his arm, the cracker in his hand. "Now... pull it with me."

"I... I really don't want to," Ellen says, half-turning away from him. She's not sure she's ready for that. Probably never will be.

"Oh, come on now," he says in a voice an adult might use to coax a child. "It'll be fun. Pull the cracker with me, Ellie..."

"Don't call me that!" She feels repulsed and scared at the same time, knowing she can't afford to rile him, yet the thought of appeasing him makes her nauseous.

Suddenly, Baker is kneeling in front of her, his hands resting on her thighs – the cracker in one of them. She stiffens, remembering that night a year ago when it all began. Dan's work Christmas party – when he went missing for most of the evening. Ellen had only realised that her husband wasn't sitting beside her at the dinner table when they served dessert. She'd been chatted at endlessly by the boring guy from Accounts – Andy or Angus or whoever – sitting the other side of her and, when she turned round, Dan's seat was empty, most of his cutlery unused.

Baker grips Ellen's wrist, yanking it hard. She yelps.

"I said, pull the fucking cracker. It's almost Christmas. We're celebrating."

Ellen gets a whiff of his breath, realising instantly why his car is upside down in the snow.

Rum, she thinks, turning her head slowly and looking him in the eye. *And lots of it.*

The first time she'd met Baker, that's what he'd been drinking – the same Christmas party where she'd mislaid her husband. That's what she'd joked to everyone as she walked around the ground floor of the hotel after the meal, awkwardly asking Dan's colleagues if they'd seen him. His whereabouts was a mystery, and it was fucking embarrassing – being left alone, fighting back the tears.

If the hotel hadn't been in the middle of nowhere and she hadn't drunk half a bottle of wine already, she'd have got in her car and left. Dan could make his own way home in the morning (they'd arrived separately from work and were planning on making a weekend of it; golf, swimming, Sunday lunch).

Ready to give up her hunt, thinking about the dressing down she'd give Dan when she found him, Ellen needed a drink. A man was standing at the bar. Then she was standing at the bar beside him, one foot on the brass rail, each of them trying to get the server's attention.

"You an employee?" the man had asked her.

She'd laughed, shaken her head. "Not likely. You?"

"Nope, not likely either. Drink?" He finally got the bartender's attention.

"Sure, thanks. Whatever you're having," Ellen had replied, grateful to have someone to talk to, though her eyes were still scanning around the large ballroom in the hope she'd spot Dan.

"I'm Baker," Baker had said, sliding the rum towards her.

"I'm Ellen," Ellen replied. "Dan, my husband, is in Production."

"My wife, Sue, is in Design. Tall, blonde. You can't miss her." He casually looked around the bar area. Missing her.

They'd both shared a look of understanding, with Baker giving her an eye roll, perhaps indicating that he also knew what this company did to marriages. Ellen had liked his neatly clipped beard. It kind of glistened in the festive lighting. Looked inviting and safe when he spoke. He was a few inches taller than Dan, self-possessed and in control, wearing his dinner suit with ease – bow-tie undone and hanging loose around his neck. A smattering of salt-and-pepper chest hair creeping up between his shirt collar wings.

"I'm not sure where Dan is, or I'd introduce you." Ellen had smiled awkwardly, glancing around, feeling even more like a work widow than usual in her glittery black evening dress. She was upset with Dan for leaving her to talk to people she didn't know.

"Likewise, my wife," Baker had said, raising his glass in a lazy kind of cheers. He'd tipped his head then, gesturing towards one of the many large round tables – the table where Ellen and Dan had been seated earlier. Employees and their spouses were now either dancing or had swapped tables to chat to their colleagues over coffee, or they'd snuck outside onto the terrace for a smoke. Dan was doing none of these things – she'd checked. She'd tried phoning him, of course, but it went straight to voicemail. "Let's go and sit."

Alone at the table – apart from a drunk guy who had his back to them as he watched the live band, singing to himself and occasionally swigging his pint – Baker and Ellen sat next to each other in an uncomfortable silence. There was a corporate cracker on the table between them, left over from dinner. *Dan's* unused cracker.

"Want to pull this?" she said for some reason, instantly feeling stupid. She picked it up and held it out to him, but he'd sort of smiled and looked away. Perhaps he hadn't heard her, or thought it was a clumsy attempt at a chat-up line. She put it down, embarrassed.

And that's when the guy who'd sat next to her at dinner sidled past – Andy or Angus or whoever from Accounts. She knew it was him because of his crooked nose and tartan bow-tie. To her horror, he stopped beside her, giving Baker a glance before he bent down, positioning his mouth close to Ellen's ear. She also knew it was Andy or Angus or whoever because of his sour breath.

"Dan is up to no good with a woman," he whispered. "He does it all the time. I just thought you should know." As he drew back from her, he looked nervous. Reluctant. Apologetic.

Then Andy or Angus or whoever walked swiftly away, leaving Ellen with nothing but the tang of sour breath in her nostrils and a sick feeling in her belly.

She stared at the cracker lying on the table.

"You OK?" Baker asked, fiddling with his empty glass. "Fancy another?" He pushed it towards her.

It took her a moment, but she nodded and stood, knocking back her drink before taking the empty glasses to the bar. She returned with two doubles and drank hers in one glug. And then, because Baker was too slow, she drank his as well.

"Whoa," he said, peering across at her.

Ellen stared at him, wondering who the hell he was and why she was sitting with him, but suddenly, behind him, she caught sight of Dan hurrying across the other side of the ballroom.

Was it Dan?

She stood, feeling lightheaded and sick, before chasing after him. As she pushed through the partygoers, she could have sworn he'd had a tall blonde woman in tow, their hands joined as he led her on. Ellen wondered if they were going outside because they'd been heading to the foyer.

But despite searching, she lost sight of him. And the woman. Maybe she'd imagined them both. Maybe Andy or Angus or whoever had been a figment of her imagination, too. Maybe this whole night was just a bad dream.

She went back to the table, where Baker had bought two more drinks. "You look like you need it," he said, and Ellen thought he was the only thing that seemed real at that precise moment. Something to hang on to, at least.

"I do." She knocked hers back again, her eyes constantly flicking all around, searching for Dan and that blonde woman. The sickness inside her grew.

"Fancy a smoke?" Baker asked. "A *smoke* smoke?"

Ellen hadn't had one of those since university and, since she was now feeling in a self-destructive mood, she nodded and followed him out onto the terrace. It was freezing cold, so Baker took off his jacket and draped it around Ellen's bare shoulders, removing the ready-rolled spliff from the inside pocket first.

"Thanks," she said as they walked further along the terrace, away from the hotel and other people.

Baker handed Ellen the joint and she drew in deeply, trying not to cough as the smoke flooded her lungs. She held it there, waiting for the hit before blowing it out into the night, wanting to blunt her worst fears. That was when Baker roughly pulled her into an embrace, forcing his mouth onto hers, pressing himself against her.

Shocked at first, but also angry as hell with her husband, Ellen fought the urge to punch him and scream, kissing him back instead. Truly and deeply, as though she meant it. Even though she really, really didn't.

When she pulled away, gasping for breath, she saw Dan standing about six feet away from her, the expression on his face telling her that he'd seen everything, freezing those few seconds forever in her mind.

"Dan!" she called out when the world started moving again, when he turned on his heels and strode across the terrace and back through the hotel. "Wait!" Ellen flew after him, shoving past people in the ballroom, screaming out as she ran through reception. "It's not what you think!" she cried, following him out of the main entrance as he headed for the car park.

But he was too fast – him running, her wobbling in her heels. There was nothing she could do to stop him getting in his car and roaring off down the long driveway to God-knows-where with a bellyful of alcohol and a headful of rage.

"I said pull the bloody cracker," Baker says now, hitting her round the face with it. The fire crackles and spits in the log burner. "God knows, the damn thing caused enough drama with my wife."

Ellen is snapped back to the present – to the idyllic cottage in the middle of nowhere that she and Dan bought in the hope it might stick them back together.

She puts the poker on the floor and lifts her hand, noticing it shake as she takes one end of the cracker. She hardly has the strength to keep hold of it as Baker tugs against her. "You... you have no idea, do you?" Ellen whispers under her breath, hating that he got away with nothing more than slapped wrists for ruining her life.

"Grip harder," he barks, making her flinch. Tears sting her eyes as she remembers walking back through the ballroom after Dan had sped off, catching sight of Baker gesticulating at his wife, the pair clearly having words with each other. But then Baker had led her onto the dancefloor, wrapping his arms around her for a slow dance, their faces close. That's when Ellen found Andy or Angus or whoever sitting alone at their dinner table drinking the dregs in all the glasses. Dan's dinner jacket was draped over his chair and his cracker, unpulled, was sitting between his unused cutlery.

Ellen had picked up the cracker and tucked it inside her clutch bag. Perhaps she and Dan could pull it together another time. Make things right again somehow. They usually worked it out.

"Sorry to have been the bearer of bad news," Andy or Angus or whoever said, looking up at her. "About your husband. Everyone in the company knows what he's like." He smirked. "He's a bit of a joke, to be honest."

"And that's coming from *you*," Ellen said with a sneer that wasn't at all like her. Then she walked off, wondering why she was still protecting Dan, even though she knew what Andy or Angus or whoever had said was true. She'd known for a long time, if she was honest. When she next saw Dan, she'd give him a piece of her mind.

Except she didn't get a chance because, six hours later, the police had tracked her down and told her that her husband had driven into a tree and was dead. A horrible accident. "No one else injured, thank God," they'd said.

Ellen, still wearing her evening dress, still drunk from the night before, muttered vaguely in reply, "Yes, thank God." She didn't feel real.

She grips the cracker harder and Baker yanks, triggering the snap with an anticlimactic pop.

"You win!" he says, and Ellen sees she's left holding the larger part. She chucks it at him and gets up, going to the kitchen to fetch some bread and cheese and the can of tomato soup.

"You got a plastic magnifying glass," he calls out.

"Oh, good. I can examine the remains of my life in minute detail," she says, returning with a tray – food, cutlery, plates. She chucks a wet cloth at him.

"Here, put your paper hat on." He hands it over and Ellen does as she is told, sitting down. "Want to hear the riddle?"

Ellen shrugs, picking up the sharpest knife she could find in the kitchen drawer, cutting a wedge of cheese.

"What do you get when you cross a vampire with a snowman?" Baker looks at her, beaming, chuckling, shaking his head.

His *wife is still alive*, Ellen thinks, remembering the tall, blonde woman being led across the ballroom by Dan. Andy or Angus or whoever had confirmed it was her, enjoying the scandalous exposé at her husband's expense. *He's still got his life.*

"Go on," Baker demands. "What do you get?"

"I don't know," Ellen whispers, feeling dead inside. How she misses the cold stares that she and Dan shared, their frosty *I love yous*, their tense, unbearable Christmases with false smiles and gifts bought without sentiment or care.

And more than anything, she hates this man for still having that with his wife. Even with blood oozing from his nose and his car in the ditch, he still has that to go home to. Sue from Design will no doubt grill her husband about where he's been, and in return, Baker might confront her about that time she was late home from the gym, and she'll pout and cry and then they'll have sex, then counselling, but really, she's biding her time as she hunts for another Dan.

Meanwhile, Baker will still get his kicks from going through her pockets and emails, desperate for the holy grail of a suspicious spouse – the address of a secret liaison, a hotel receipt, a lover's memento.

"I said, what do you fucking *get*?" Baker looms above her, spit flying from his mouth as he waves the paper riddle in her face.

Ellen stands up, the knife still in her hand, and does what he did to her that night. She forces her mouth onto his in a kiss neither of them wants, mumbling the answer between his lips as the knife slips easily under his ribs.

When it's over, when Baker's knees have buckled and he's on the floor, blood not just dripping but spilling from him now, Ellen wonders when the thaw will begin. Wonders when she'll unfreeze from the frostbite deep inside.

A DEADLY GIFT

Angela Clarke

IRIAM PYE wasn't particularly keen on her cousin Edward, but she still didn't wish to find him lying dead under the Christmas tree. He was sprawled out, a shiny gold bauble hanging above his head in a macabre approximation of a halo. Several wrapped presents, which had been ostentatiously piled up for this morning's festivities, had been kicked and strewn. One gift, intended for a younger member of the family, squirted bright Play-Doh from its split Rudolph paper. The large spruce Edward had ordered be cut from the estate and decorated for the holidays had been knocked to a concerning angle. It was obvious, even to the untrained eye of Miriam; there'd been a struggle. A string of decorative pearls from the tree had been looped round Edward's neck, over his clip-on velvet bow-tie, and presumably his airway. She doubted even Edward – a veteran mansplainer who claimed to be an expert at whatever task he encountered – could strangle himself from behind.

The advice of an anti-anxiety podcast a friend had sent her after her marriage collapsed popped into Miriam's head: list five things you could see. It helped reassure your mind it was safe. Miriam was in the drawing room of Critchley Court. Under the (faux) lavish Rococo ceiling her great-great grandfather had installed in 1932. There were the two large golden-yellow fleur-de-lis sofas, and matching wingback chairs in the familiar central horseshoe shape. The personalised advent calendars that had doubled as Edward's showy invitations to Christmas at Critchley Court were lined along the ornate marble-topped console table that ran down the side of the room, leading the eye to the Christmas tree and what was underneath. Miriam jumped at the tick of the domed carriage clock on the mantelpiece. Had it always matched her heartbeat? *Five things, Miriam. Focus. One.* There are the booted feet of her dead cousin. *Two.* There's the large picture window overlooking the driveway – locked from the inside. *Three.* There is no one else in this room. *Four.* There's Edward's distinctive nineteenth-century wrought-iron key, hanging from the string looped over the internal door handle. *Five.* There's the only other key in existence, cold and rough in her palm, which she has just used to unlock the door from the outside. The key she's had since housekeeper Ms Laverwick entrusted it to her last night. Miriam acknowledged her calming mental health exercise had fought a brave tussle, but ultimately met its match in the face of discovering a murdered body, in a locked room, when she had the sole other key.

Yesterday, Miriam's Christmas Eve train had been predictably packed and late, meaning she'd arrived only minutes before dinner, and the rigmarole of Edward's Christmas traditions had been well underway. She'd joined the other nine adult members of her extended family at the table, just in time to endure the fireworks.

Edward, whose frustration that, as the current heir of Critchley Court's fifty-five-acre estate, he was beholden to host all the Morgan-Wests annually for Christmas was only matched by his sadistic zeal in punishing everyone else for not having the good fortune of being the eldest male, was on peak awful form. Before the amuse-bouche had been bouched, he'd outed old-school, stuffy Great Uncle Roddy as having a secret gay paramour (which actually made most of the family more disposed to like Roddy). Then he'd accused a dignified and silent Ms Laverwick – who had been with the family for decades without reproach – of stealing from him. And finally revealed he, Edward, had been dating the lost love of cousin Andrew's life; the girl who had brutally dumped him at the altar five years ago. Over the entrées, Edward had a pop at Miriam's own failed marriage. After the initial stab of panic and prick of hot tears – this was the first Christmas since they'd separated – Miriam consoled herself that her ex had had the sense to decline Edward's twisted invitation to join them at Critchley Court. She was only here because at forty-three, with no children, all her friends were busy with their own families, and she'd promised her mother she'd sneak in the Greggs mince pies she liked.

Today, Miriam was all set to nip in after her morning power walk and add her own small but tastefully wrapped gifts to those under the tree, well before the rest of the family had departed the breakfast room. She was still in her sixteen-hour fast window. But all thoughts of the number of Ms Laverwick's roast potatoes she would delightfully consume at lunch were now gone. Her reusable tote from the village bookshop bumped forlornly against the hip of her size twelve bum-sculpting leggings. She supposed she was shaking – probably the shock. It was understandably exciting to have so many presents for the younger members in the party, but she knew already Edward would have had the majority wrapped for himself. He liked to say: "Another for the host with the most!", a rather self-serving statement if ever there was one. But then Edward was the great-great-grandson of a man so aggressively aspirational the family still euphemistically referred to the 1930s family fortune as being built on 'hygiene products'. The inherited distaste about the foundations of the Staffordshire country pile being built on toilet rolls also explained why their snobby ancestor had hyphenated his middle name to double-barrel their now-surname. Mum always said the Morgan-West men were all as bad as each other, and it was a shame Miriam's silly great-great-grandfather hadn't had the sense to let the women inherit.

It was the thought of her mum, and the sound of breakfast chatter and clatter overspilling from the dining room behind, that spurred Miriam into action. Swiftly stepping back, she pulled the double doors to the drawing room closed, and turned the key in the lock again. With a big smile and open arms, she intercepted the toddling twins of her cousin Emma, and the questioning faces of their mother and father, resplendent in matching M&S Christmas robin jumpers. Miriam halted the frontal quartet that led the rest of the assorted three Morgan-Wests (and guests), and Ms Laverwick in their approach.

"You will never guess?" Miriam was proud her voice only shook a little, and she thought she covered the quaver as excitement. "Tom – the gardener…" she added as she saw the fluffy eyebrow rise of Geoffrey, her Mum's latest beau (a tanned former town planner from Reading she'd met at a U3A table tennis meeting). Her cousin Andrew, a fresh clip of holly and berries adding the seasonal touch to the well-loved three-piece tweed suit he wore to run his antiques store, wavered next to Geoffrey, looking more perplexed than usual. He pushed his glasses up his nose in a move that always reminded her of Badger in *The Wind in the Willows*. Miriam pushed on. "Tom said he saw Santa flying over in his sleigh outside." Whereas in reality, Tom would've left for his holidays the day before.

"Santa!" squealed one of the three-year-old twins – the red bobbles in her hair jiggling in unsuppressed glee.

"Santa!" the sibling with gold bobbles replied, as two sets of identical dimples released a gush of cuteness into the room. It was a valiant effort by Emma to delineate the pair, but to Miriam they remained interchangeably adorable. And both capable of ear-splitting pitch.

"And," Miriam added, trying to signal the severity of the situation to the adults gathering, as her Uncle Roddy appeared, her own mother, making this year's festive sequinned minidress and candy cane striped tights look chic, clutching his arm in solidarity. "Tom, said several parcels – from Santa – fell, but can be found in the garden!" Miriam's mum caught her eye, her whippet-thin frame, shrouded in an excess of colour and texture, almost imperceptibly shifting to attention, and Miriam was once more grateful for the steel at the core of the woman who was often misjudged as purely decorative.

"Outside!" Miriam gave a final flourish with her hand, to try to propel them away from the drawing room. And from the point of view of the twins it was a resounding success. Their little legs, deliciously podgy, and still somehow at that age before they seem to fully point forwards at the same time, started the canter for the large black doors out to the back terrace of Critchley Court.

"Come on, dears." Ms Laverwick, her eyes always kind under her uncompromising grey bob, and in her best tweed skirt, helped herd the youngsters – not to mention Emma and her husband – out. Geoffrey altered direction toward the door, Andrew bobbing amiably in his wake.

"How about some warm mince pies and mulled wine outside?" Ms Laverwick added, shooting a quick look back at Miriam. Could Ms Laverwick tell something was wrong? Was this the finely attuned antenna of a housekeeper used to managing the whims, vagaries, and sometimes cruelties in Edward's case, of this family? Or did Ms Laverwick already know what had happened to her employer because she'd played a part? Only Ms Laverwick knew Miriam had the one other key last night, and she knew her way round this house better than anyone. Was it possible she'd snuck into Miriam's room, took the key, strangled Edward, locked him in, and then put the key back before anyone realised? As one of the twins tripped in their exuberance, and Ms Laverwick swiftly grabbed their hand, pulling them steady with barely a wobble and no grazed knees on the cold stone floor, Miriam knew she was strong enough physically to do it. But she couldn't possibly, could she? It was Ms Laverwick for goodness' sake! What was Miriam even doing thinking this? It was shock.

"Mince pies on the terrace! Cracking day for it, hey?" said Geoffrey, all posture and trying a bit too hard as he clapped Andrew on the back winningly.

"I've just had breakfast," Andrew said, near tripping as they reached the exit. He ran a finger round the waistband of his trousers and hitched the sagging back up so his hems cleared the floor.

"It's Christmas," Geoffrey replied with a laugh as they disappeared outside, presumably assuming this was all part and parcel of the

Morgan-West traditional experience. What was he going to think of them when he found out? Miriam quelled the fizzing in her stomach. The edge of her mother's mouth turned down at one corner. She knew something was up.

Uncle Roddy remained oblivious. "Nonsense – I'm going to sit by the fire. That's what we always do." He expertly flicked and tapped his walking stick down onto the stone floor, stepping toward Miriam with the practised air of a man used to others moving aside.

Miriam tugged at the tight fabric round her thighs; she felt hot, when she usually felt cold in Critchley Court. She really hoped the increased blood flow was due to the stress of finding a dead body, and not a sign of perimenopause. She could do without her oestrogen buggering off in the same year as her ex-husband.

Tripping over in her dainty birdlike manner, Miriam's mother's sequinned arm snaked through Roddy's, and gave an unarguable tug. "Come on, Roddy darling. The fresh air will do us all good."

As a squeal that teetered on the edge of a shout punched through the open door to the Capability Brown-designed terrace, Miriam thrust her tote bag at her mum's free hand. "You'd better hide these in the flowerpots and statues outside."

"But it's snowed!" Uncle Roddy blustered, yet still allowed himself to be led toward the door, not quite able to bring himself to argue with a lady.

Miriam reconsidered her austere relative; he carried himself like a posh Tory from a bygone age, and no one had known about his secret love life until Edward outed him. Hadn't her mum said Uncle Roddy worked with logistics in the army during the Cold War – that was a euphemism for a spy, right? Was he faking his doddery ignorance? Or was he involved in Edward's demise? Was it in revenge for revealing a part of his life he'd prefer to keep private?

Her mum paused to yank open the huge cupboard that housed everyone's outdoor clothes, almost disappearing inside. "I've got your coat, Roddy dear," her muffled voice called, before she reappeared, and she soon had Uncle Roddy helping her carry scarves and fleeces to the others outside. Her voice drifted back up and in on the frosty air. "I wanted to talk to you about chair yoga. It really is quite extraordinary for your flexibility, you know?"

Uncle Roddy was right – Miriam had disturbed the fresh snow with her morning power walk. There had been no other footprints or tracks outside. Indeed, she had initially felt guilty walking on the flawless dusting, and then rather childishly began to enjoy herself. With any offspring Edward managed to create, and her cousin Andrew to go, this would be her only chance to leave her mark on the Critchley estate. The damp kisses from her boots were still visible across the entrance hall's stone floor. And her footprints were the only ones. Her morning exercise proved whoever had done this had already been inside the house.

With decision, Miriam strode across the hallway and shoved her own arms into the large cupboard, then scissored them between the remaining forest of coats and ancient wellies. She hadn't really thought there'd be anyone hiding in here – but she had to make sure. Empty. Which meant no one had entered or left Critchley Court since the snow fell after her arrival last night. Whoever had killed Edward was definitely part of the Morgan-West Christmas party. Extraordinary to think that, but it helped her remain calm if she focused on the facts. Emotion would have to come later.

And with that, Miriam dialled 999. Would the hold music be Christmas carols? She watched cousin Andrew next to the Venus statue, blowing warm air onto his fingers before wiping the fog from his glasses, as Ms Laverwick reappeared with a tray of steaming red glasses and mince pies from the kitchen side of the house. Everyone had to stay outside. She heard herself talk to the call handler as if she were hearing someone on one of her favourite crime shows. Her hand was shaking as she hung up and slid her phone back into her pocket. Hopefully the police wouldn't be too long – Miriam had no idea how busy Christmas Day was. Was it like *Casualty* on the telly? The odd turkey-related incident in the morning, before the full force of the Baileys really started to hit numbers? Would the police wear reindeer antlers atop their shiny uniforms and boots?

Something tugged at Miriam's mind – something about footwear? Like a faulty fairy light on the string, it winked suggestively at her in the dark recesses of her memory. A quick headcount confirmed everyone was still safely on the terrace. Checking no one could see, Miriam crossed to the door of the drawing room, sliding the key back in, and unlocking the crime scene once more. Being careful not to touch anything – she took a few steps toward the body. Yes, there it was: the one winking fairy light, something out of place; there was a small piece of silver foil half-pressed into the tread of Edward's shoe. Now where had that come from? There was no tinsel nor shiny ribbons on the tree. Besides, it looked more like kitchen foil. Where had he picked that up?

As she heard the distant sound of police sirens, Miriam retraced her steps and once more locked the door. This was a conundrum. Her odious cousin had last night bullied, humiliated and goaded four members of the family   including herself. Now his murdered body had shown up locked inside an empty room. A room to which she had the only other key. Miriam had led enough book group discussions on crime thrillers to know her DNA would be in there. And the police would quite reasonably want to take her in for questioning. If she didn't want to spend Christmas Day – and worse, longer – in a police cell, Miriam knew she had to work out who had killed Edward. And just how they had done it.

Detective Inspector Adam Rushton did not arrive at Critchley Court wearing reindeer antlers, nor was he full of the Christmas spirit. With the roads quiet, and everyone mostly at home, he'd been hoping to ride today's shift out at the station with a hot chocolate and a sausage meat sandwich. Instead, as he pulled up to the imposing Critchley Court, he appeared to have found himself in an ITV Sunday night murder mystery. Who lived like this anymore? The rich pricks you encountered nowadays tended to be found in glass architect-designed 'spaces', which had sprung up in the Gloucestershire countryside like herpes. Even the organised crime bosses were all electric cars, Waitrose deliveries with additional food bank donations, and responsible planting – though Adam suspected a lot of that was driven by their wives trying to navigate the competitive private school system. It was easier to get an AK-47 in West Gloucestershire than it was to get your kid into certain nurseries. Adam knew this from his sister's constant stress over his five-year-old niece's social standing, and the fact he'd recovered a box of machine guns from the back of an abandoned Land Rover just two days ago. Christmas was good for one thing – a low-stress shift. Investigating a murder was not part of his plan.

He'd thought all the old estates like Critchley Court had long since been turned into boutique hotels with whimsical Lego stag heads, and the kind of cocktails his last girlfriend had loved but he couldn't pronounce. He should have known it wouldn't last when she'd asked for a strawberry pomerita, and he'd got excited because he thought she'd meant a dog. But this place, with its columns and big gaping windows, was just a straight-up slap in the face to the cost-of-living crisis. As the smooth sole of his office shoe slid on the snow-covered gravel, Adam just caught himself from doing the splits. He already knew he was going to hate every member of what the young lanky PC – flapping around like a damn garage forecourt inflatable next to him – was referring to, with reverence, as 'The Family'. Merry bloody Christmas indeed!

He tuned back in to the PC's download, just in time to catch him say: "…so she seems to be the place to start."

DI Rushton glanced at the sallow lad, his beat duty helmet pulled down extra low, trying to protect his ears from the cold. His long fingers were turning pink clutching his notebook in the wind. He was clearly fired up at being involved in a murder case. And Adam begrudgingly accepted he'd put in a sizeable amount of effort sticking all the family into one room in the house, sealing off the crime scene while they waited for the CSIs, and ascertaining an impressive amount of information. "PC… Klein, isn't it?"

"Yes, sir." He beamed at Adam naively. Of course this was the only other cop on duty. Adam daren't call up any more experienced colleagues today – not worth the hassle.

"Are those socks regulation?" Adam pointed at the lad's bony ankles.

PC Klein looked confused, pulling up the leg of his uniform trousers and looking at the garish pattern. "They're sprouts, sir."

"I can see that." Adam took the PC's pad from him and began flicking through his neatly written notes.

"For Christmas," PC Klein added. Unnecessarily.

Adam was beginning to feel a little too aware of what could be deemed his middle-age spread standing next to this twig of a boy. Perhaps it was good he'd missed his lunch. Adam stopped on the third page of the lad's intel. He'd done a bang-up job – he might be of use. If he could get this Labrador puppy behaviour in check.

"I could... I could go home and change them?" PC Klein's eyebrows had drooped, as he still stared at his socks.

"Forget the sprouts," Adam said. "What's your first name?"

Klein glanced toward the big house, and back at him, his watery eyes unsure. "Levi. The guys call me Jeans. Sir."

"'Course they do." Adam tried to force his face into something approaching reassuring. The lad blinked at him. "Righto, Skinny Jeans..." He abandoned what was beginning to feel like a grimace. Grinning like a fool wasn't his style, he prided himself on being a straightforward man. "Run this past me again? But this time – remember to take some breaths. We don't all have the attention span of TikTok teens. I won't swipe you away."

Jeans blushed but straightened his hunched frame a touch. It was a good sign to have a nickname. And Adam had a flash of memory, picturing the senior officer who had first listened to him all those years ago.

"'Course, sir. So, one of 'The Family' found the body when she came down this morning. Locked inside a room, the key still on the inside—" Jeans lowered his voice as they started climbing the large stone steps to the front of the house.

"Did she break the door down?" Adam interrupted, taking in the large glass window behind which he could see the back of a lone boiler suit-clad CSI dusting for prints. They would've been the ones on call, and he hoped they didn't have young kids left at home.

"Er no," Jeans said, momentarily knocked off his game, then he caught hold of the tail again. "And she reckons there are four possible suspects."

"Great. Some nosy housewife with opinions," Adam said with a sigh.

"She did seem quite astute, sir." Jeans's line-free face was once more bobbing animatedly next to him. Adam was yet to recover from his sister recently describing him as craggy. "She offered me a mince pie. And I *was* hungry."

A bit of melting snow slid from the portico and slopped onto Adam's shoulder. He batted away the incoming hand of Jeans. "I don't need help, Constable," he snapped.

"Yes, sir." Skinny Jeans looked like Adam had just stolen his only Christmas gift.

"Look, you don't have to call me sir," Adam told him, rubbing his eyes with his hand and trying to keep the strain from his voice. "Just tell me how this family member got into the crime scene if the door was locked?"

"Oh, Miriam had a key – the only other one. The victim's copy was inside the room with him." Jeans beamed as if this explained everything. They stepped out of the bitter wind, and into a large, cavernous stone hallway; a wide ornate staircase curved up and away from them. If it wasn't for the pile of messy opened post on the side table, this room, with its formidable oil portraits, and what were probably Ming vases on antique tables, looked like a National Trust property. It smelled of musty antique fabrics, cinnamon, and money. There was even a bloody suit of armour.

"Miriam?" Adam shook his head in disbelief at Jeans. "You're kidding me? That's all we need, some little old lady who's watched one too many Agatha Christies on the box!"

"I prefer to read, actually," a female voice interrupted him from the left. Skinny Jeans coughed and looked at his shoes, and Adam turned to see not a little old lady, but rather a good-looking woman his age standing in the hallway to his left. Her shiny red hair bounced around the shoulders of the purple hoodie she was wearing over black leggings, and her eyes seemed to be amused at his expense.

Adam held out a hand. "I'm Detective Inspector Adam Rushton. DI Rushton. Mrs – err," he looked at Skinny Jeans's notes, "Morgan-West?"

"Pye," Miriam corrected. "My mother was a Morgan-West, but she took my dad's name when they married. And I prefer Ms. Or Miriam," she said with a smile. Her teeth were a lovely shade of white; Adam clamped his own mouth shut.

He looked down the corniced corridor Miriam – the witness – had emerged from. There was an open door, and the sound of voices, accompanied by the scent of bacon, wafting toward him. "If you could return to the rest of your family—"

"In the dining room," Jeans interjected a touch too keenly.

"Yeah, thank you, Skinny Jeans," Adam said, exhaling.

A giggle now sprang from Miriam – *the witness.* "Oh, how lovely – because of Levi's." Her face was illuminated with glee. "Detective

Adam, right? I'm saying it wrong, aren't I? But Detective Inspector Rushton feels weirdly formal – given how we've met." He pursed his lips, which she seemed to take as encouragement to keep talking. "Is it all right if I just show you something?" She strode toward the door on their right, through which he could see the crime scene. The CSI was photographing the body of a large Caucasian male, mid-forties, brown hair, probably six feet or over when he was alive and not bent backwards on the floor where he'd fallen. Little yellow markers were scattered around denoting evidence. Before he realised what was happening, Jeans had happily bounded after her – passing her two shoe covers from his own pockets.

"Thank you, Levi." Her fine pale hands took them and slipped them over her white and pink trainers with practice. He'd clearly let her in already. The title, this house, his readiness to help had obviously got the best of the lad.

"Now hang on a second," Adam said. "This is an active crime scene, you can't just—"

"Oh, I know." Miriam waved a hand at him. "But my DNA will already be all over the shop, so I thought it wouldn't make any difference—"

"That's not how this works!" The DI felt his jaw clench. This was preposterous. This woman couldn't just waltz into his life and do anything she liked.

"It won't take a second," Miriam said, looping her red hair into a bun as she stepped into the room.

Adam scrabbled to pull shoe covers and plastic gloves from his own pocket, grabbing for the pen that was making a break for freedom. "You can't just…" He hopped on one foot to try and get his wet shoe inside the damn plastic.

Skinny Jeans made a rangy grab for him, and Adam shot him a warning look. He was responsible for this breach of protocol.

"I knew Edward," Miriam was saying as she passed one of the large settees in the room. "And it's – well, it's wrong."

This was *his* crime scene, he was a seasoned – hard-bitten, one could argue – CID member, he was the one in charge. "Even allowing for you being a key witness, it's against procedure to let you enter the crime scene." He glared again at Jeans.

Miriam neared the body – and he saw a brief look of horror flicker over her, before she seemed to steel herself, keeping her gaze resolutely away from the victim's face. That was interesting.

Adam took in the scene of destruction. Who knew when they'd get a pathologist out to look this one over. He gave a brief nod to the female CSI who'd stood aside for them. Now he could see her face under the white boiler suit hood, he recognised her as one of the young ones, what was her name? Ngozi? Something like that. She'd obviously drawn the short straw covering the holidays.

He passed Miriam to bend down next to the victim, keeping his hands out of the way.

"Strangled," said Skinny Jeans, noticeably hanging back, his bony fingers plucking at the sleeve of his uniform jacket. It wasn't just Miriam who'd not spent much time with dead bodies. "With pearls from the Christmas tree," he quickly added, still not looking at the body beneath it.

"I wouldn't be so sure about that, lad," Adam said, peering at the body. "No bruising. If he'd been strangled, we'd see marks."

"So how did he die?" Skinny Jeans's voice and eyebrows raised in a question.

Adam leant forward, placing his face over that of the victim.

The man was grimacing. Adam took a sniff. Nothing. "Can't tell for sure till we get the pathology report. And I wouldn't like to promise when that'd be." He offered an apologetic look to Miriam. "Christmas."

She nodded thoughtfully. And he saw a little wrinkle had appeared between her eyebrows. "Then there's this." She pointed one red painted fingernail at the bottom of the victim's shoe.

Adam pushed up from his heels, keeping his hands in his pockets – no point needlessly contaminating the scene further. This was already going to be tricky to explain if anyone asked. He stepped across to join her at the poor guy's feet, to see what she was pointing at.

"The silver foil?" He shrugged. "Probably just from last night's dinner." All this for that? Civilians. You couldn't rely on them. Adam never laughed on principle, but he allowed his lip to curl.

"Out of the question, I'm afraid," Miriam said, interrupting his reverie. "Edward was the kind of man who insisted on food – even sweets – being arranged and carried up on the family silver salvers."

"Salvers?" Adam shook his head again in case he had dozed off in the station. No, this was real. "'Course. Can't have the likes of common silver foil up here. And you think that suggests what?"

Miriam grinned at him. "Apart from the fact Edward was a terrible snob, who also never set foot in what he called 'below stairs'? I don't know," she said, the crease appearing on her forehead again. "But I feel it must mean something."

This was a waste of time. But Adam crouched down again. "There's a mark," he said, and pointed. A perfect circle, barely a millimetre in diameter, was visible on the silver foil. "Like whatever it was wrapping was sharp, and poked through? A cocktail stick? I reckon it was just from food."

"We didn't have anything like that last night." Miriam shook her head. "French onion soup with Ms Laverwick's cheesy croutons – she uses two types. A side of smoked salmon caught fresh from the lake. And apple strudel." Adam's stomach audibly rumbled, and he straightened again to try to cover it.

Miriam twinkled at him. "There'll be kippers from breakfast, or some truffles on the side in the dining room. Edward has – had – a sweet tooth."

"I'm fine. Thank you," he added a touch too late. It was disturbing having civilians in his workspace. "I do need you to rejoin the others now, though."

The crease appeared on Miriam's forehead again, but if she had been about to question him, she thought better of it. Adam knew he'd sounded a little gruff. He tended to do that when he was nervous.

He called Skinny Jeans over as she left, but by the time he'd run through the record the lad had taken from speaking to the family, and Adam had walked repeatedly through the room, locked the door, tried it, failed to get in and out any other way, it had grown dark outside. The white smudges of snow that hadn't melted were glowing eerily in the lights from the house.

"It sounds like a right doozy of a night." Jeans shook his head as they watched the body being zipped up and carried out to the waiting ambulance. No need for blue lights now. "Talk about family rows. I want to kill him and I wasn't even there."

Adam gave the lad a stern look over the mug of tea he'd fetched from the dining room. The Family had thankfully now stayed put, dutifully, pale-faced, sitting, eating cheese and biscuits instead of the turkey they presumably originally had planned. Or maybe you had your turkey at dinnertime in posh houses? Who knew?

"Sorry. Sir." Skinny Jeans looked contrite.

"It's all right, lad." Adam sighed. This was not how anyone wanted to spend their Christmas. A two-man skeleton team, no lab work, and he had yet to call the guv. He didn't relish ringing him at home on Christmas Day, and wanted to wait till he had something concrete to tell him. And that was the crux of the issue. Adam looked back at where the body had lain, the clear signs of struggle, and thought of the shapely yet capable woman who'd pointed out the silver foil on the victim's shoe. The woman, who by her own admission, disliked the victim, and had the only other key to the locked crime scene. He was going to have to face it, Miriam, with her little forehead crinkle, was looking like the prime suspect.

Miriam felt the shock ripple over her body as Detective Adam stepped closer. He was really doing this? The solid stone hallway seemed to shift under her feet. The watching faces of her family blurred as she blinked. She'd never understood the phrase clutching at her pearls, till she saw Ms Laverwick's fingers grasp at her neckline. *Pearls...* Cousin Andrew's mouth gaped like a fish. Even lovely PC Klein looked shaken, as if the detective's words were still echoing through him. *Questioning. Caution.* Emma clung to her husband's arm, as he whispered back: "They're safe." Presumably about the twins who were watching kids' shows in the other room. No one wanted to see this. No one took their eyes off her.

Geoffrey cleared his throat, and looked like he was about to unleash another jaunty colloquialism, but her mum got there first. "You've made a mistake, officer," she said, her voice quavering. She broke free from her clustered relatives, as if she might insert her sequinned self between her daughter and Detective Adam. Miriam was surprised she noticed the scent of citrus from the detective's cologne. A burst of joyful cartoon beeps from whatever the twins were immersed in filled the space.

"It's okay, Mum." She tried to muster some positivity. "Call Falk & Maine."

"Who?" Her mother's voice rose in pitch. Miriam's heart broke at the fear on her face.

"The family lawyers – what's his name?" Miriam remembered the smiling white-haired man who smelled of peppermint when her cousin had inherited fifteen years ago.

Geoffrey gently folded two tanned hands onto her mum's shoulders. "We'll look on Google," he said. And the mundanity of it made Miriam's eyes prick with tears.

"Chin up, girl." Uncle Roddy's stoic tone provided a moment of real comfort. Miriam had thought this Christmas would be one to be endured, but not like this.

"I won't have to wear handcuffs, will I?" The words were out before she could help it. Detective Adam looked pained, and gave a slight shake of his head.

"Sir, there must be…" PC Klein's voice petered out.

Detective Adam laid a hand so gently on her arm – as if he were guiding a child, not a suspect toward the front door, toward the police car. *Oh God.*

Miriam wondered if this was how Edward had felt when his

killer stepped toward him in those last moments? Someone up close, in his space. As if it was the end of the world? But that didn't feel right. She blinked. PC Klein ran round them to open the door, the dark cold air pouring in from outside. The door. The strewn and trampled presents. The knocked tree. The pearls round Edward's neck. The piece of silver foil… the piece of silver foil. "Wait!"

There was a ripple of reaction among those watching. Had Ms Laverwick gasped? Detective Adam looked surprised. "Miriam," he said softly. "This will be easier if…"

But thoughts were speed-walking through Miriam's mind. She laughed. It was so awful in its simplicity. So horrid. Oh, he'd been very clever. "I need to see the advent calendar," she stated, and stepped toward the drawing room, pushing both doors open wide.

Adam raced after her. But he couldn't bring himself to put a restraining hand on her arm. He still couldn't believe a woman like this had it in her to kill someone. Her ex-husband sounded like a jerk, but she just didn't seem that cut up over losing him, to react to such goading from the victim. Yet everything pointed to her. He caught hold of himself – he wasn't acting like the experienced cop he was. It was Christmas, but that was no excuse. "Ma'am, you can't just walk away."

"Please, I just need a minute," Miriam said. The crinkle in her forehead was practically dancing now. Her hazel eyes seemed alight. Now they'd both crossed the threshold and were back in the drawing room, back at the crime scene.

The CSI, finished and packing up her kit, looked up in surprise, and Jeans lolloped in behind. The Family crowded through the door behind them to see.

"Just stay there," Adam barked. He didn't want them coming further into the crime scene, even though the CSI had given the nod.

"Sir, do you want me too?" Klein looked terrified as he signalled at Miriam, who was striding across the room – but she wasn't headed for where the body had been. Instead, she went behind the large sofa, and toward the sideboard.

"Give her a second," Adam said, sliding his hands in his pockets, and clicking the pen he found there open and closed. The CSI pulled her hood down. All eyes were on Miriam as she approached the row of advent calendars displayed on the sideboard; she bent to look at one, just to the left.

"I knew it!" she exclaimed, as those manicured fingers fluttered in front of one calendar. "Someone's eaten today's chocolate – the big one you get on Christmas Day!"

"Well, it *is* Christmas Day," Jeans said. "Doesn't seem that unusual…" He glanced at Adam.

He knew his junior was looking to him for guidance. It was certainly not protocol to allow persons of interest in a murder case to stroll off after you'd just invited them to accompany you to the station for questioning.

"It's the only one." Miriam looked from the calendar to Jeans, a delighted expression on her face.

That did it. Adam glanced back at the tree. The squashed present. Oh my God. It was as if the pinball had just rung all the bells. "But no one had been in here yet?" he said, as all feelings of hunger were replaced with the familiar fizzing of anticipation in his stomach.

Miriam locked eyes with him, her face seeming to glow even more in recognition. Did it feel the same to her?

"So?" Jeans interjected. Adam remembered there were other people there. The Family. Klein shrugged his shoulders uncertainly. "Someone opened their last window early?"

"But they didn't," Miriam argued. "Or at least I don't think they did. I mean, if I'm right, then one of your team…" She smiled at the technician. "They could confirm it, right?"

Adam stepped closer to the door, so he was now behind The Family that were gathered in a semi-circle, as if they were watching a theatre show. And it was a show. Miriam had everyone's attention. He signalled with his head for Jeans to join him. Adam's mind was scrabbling to keep up. He should have said yes to a mince pie; he should have kept his blood sugar up. The truth was so close, the pieces of the puzzle all there, he knew now. Had she really worked it out before him? Protocol be damned, he gave her a nod.

Miriam took a deep breath, as if rooting herself, and Adam could just see her doing the same in the gym, before she started to lift weights. Or maybe she had a set at home, in some pretty colour that coordinated with her flat.

"Edward, we all know, was a bit of a shit," she started. There was a punch of nervous laughter from cousin Emma. The Family shifted. Murmured. No one liked to speak ill of the dead. Adam watched them: would they run?

Miriam was still talking. "He loved to say that he had been born early precisely because he wanted to take Critchley Court as his own. But it didn't stop there, did it?" She took a step toward them. "Edward derived real pleasure in taking things from people. He was always competitive, ever since we were little. I remember him snatching my favourite present when I was younger – right here."

At this, Miriam's mother gave a huff, and she offered her a reassuring look. "It's okay – it's just how he was. It's also why he was lonely and miserable and bitter." Her purple-hoodied shoulders raised and dropped. "Life was a game to him, and he always played to win. To destroy. Uncle Roddy, he went after your privacy. Ms Laverwick, your spotless reputation. And Andrew and I, he went after our hearts."

Miriam's mum sniffled and Geoffrey pulled a white handkerchief from his pocket for her. But everyone's attention remained on the woman in exercise gear stood in front of the advent calendars.

"I think it was this impulse – to take someone else's joy – that got Edward killed," Miriam said, the crinkle in her forehead pointing down. "Last night, when everyone else had retired after the dinner from hell, Edward let himself in here and locked the door. I can't say if it was for the express purpose of what he did next, or some other reason. But at some point, he helped himself to someone else's Christmas Day chocolate. A petty little act of greed that was ultimately his downfall."

Miriam took a step toward the Christmas tree, and the disrupted presents underneath. "It looked like there was a fight, pearls had been strung and pulled round Edward's neck, and he was grimacing. Sorry, Ms Laverwick," Miriam added as the older woman made a noise between a gulp and a sob.

"Fetch some chairs in, PC," Adam barked. He didn't want any of them leaving.

Geoffrey disentangled himself from Miriam's mum and made a move to help. Adam spoke again before the silver fox could disappear through the doorway after the PC. "If I could ask everyone else to stay here, please." There was a flurry of consternation among The Family. Uncle Roddy audibly tutted. Ms Laverwick's violet eyes flitted to him and held his gaze a second too long before looking away as Jeans lumbered back.

Klein had two ornate, heavy-looking wooden dining chairs, carrying one under each arm in an alarmingly ungainly way. Adam hoped they weren't fragile, as they looked like walking paperwork. The lad squatted so the two chairs reached the wooden floor at the edge of the room with an expensive, uneven thud, and a grunt from him.

"Thank you," Ms Laverwick murmured as Adam positioned one for her. But he'd seen the nerves in her eyes. Was it her?

There was a momentary impasse, as Miriam's mum and Roddy both offered and declined the other chair to each other, before Roddy acquiesced, straight-backed, his hands folded on the top of his walking stick.

"Can we please get on with this?" Emma asked. Was she trying to distract them? "It's the twins' nap time soon – and all hell will break loose if that goes awry," she added sheepishly.

Miriam's mum glared at her.

"Sorry," Emma looked at her feet, muttering, "but it's true."

Miriam gave a nod and cleared her throat. "As I was saying, we all assumed Edward had been strangled to death, but as you said, Detective, there was no bruising around his neck?"

"Yes, that's correct." Adam was aware his voice sounded loud in the space. If his bosses could see him now they'd have some serious questions.

"But you suspect he could've been poisoned?" Miriam's questioning eyes turned on him.

You didn't see many poisonings. Murders were usually much more mundane: a brief bit of brutal violence. That's why he'd known this wasn't a struggle: it didn't look like other crime scenes for deaths or punch-ups. And Miriam was right, poison *had* crossed his mind. He'd sniffed the victim to see if there was a scent of something to indicate that. But he wasn't a pathologist. "I can't say for sure, until after the post-mortem."

Miriam beamed, as if he'd affirmed it out loud. "Thank you, Detective Adam. As I thought."

Ms Laverwick spluttered. Uncle Roddy's chair creaked.

"But we all ate the same food last night," Andrew pointed out, fastidiously pushing his glasses up his nose.

"Oh, yes, but the poison wasn't in our dinner," Miriam explained, "it was in the advent calendar chocolate Edward helped himself to."

They all stared at her. Jeans pulled his notebook from his pocket and started scribbling furiously.

Call himself a good cop? Adam couldn't believe he hadn't spotted it himself. "That's what the silver foil on his shoe was from?"

"Exactly," Miriam said. "It was from the advent calendar, covering the chocolate."

Adam felt the familiar buzz as elements started to click into place. "That's what the little circle was – not from a sharp piece of food?"

"No." Miriam's voice took a more sombre turn. She clasped her hands loosely in front of her, rotating her head to take in the group as she spoke to her family, to Ms Laverwick, to people she had known and loved her whole life. "I thought that as well to begin with. But I think the killer pierced the foil cover, injecting the chocolate with a poison – without removing it from the calendar."

"Miriam, darling," her mum's voice shook, "are you suggesting someone else was… was the target?"

Geoffrey looped his arm round her, his mouth set in a grim line. Uncle Roddy twisted to look swiftly between the assembled family, with a move nimbler than his age may have suggested.

Adam felt like the pieces, like snow in a globe, had all shaken up again. Was that what he'd been missing? Had he been considering the wrong motive all along?

"You think someone else was the intended victim?" He looked at Miriam seriously. They had to move fast if that was the case. He couldn't have another body on Christmas: one was bad enough for the guv's PR. It would be all over the papers tomorrow; far juicier than how many WI-knitted postbox toppers had been pilfered.

Miriam shook her head, a lock of red hair escaping her bun and settling round her face. "That's what was so clever of the killer: I think they knew there was a strong chance Edward would steal their chocolate. It was such a petty 'Edward thing' to do. To take someone else's simple pleasure. To take their joy. Perhaps he'd done it to them before."

Click! Everything fell into place. Adam gave an involuntary harrumph. Police procedure wouldn't have got here, or it wouldn't for some time. Not until it was too late. He was going to get an arrest. Miriam had just knocked several days off his paperwork. He tilted his chin at her in approval, then stepped closer to Jeans: blocking the exit. They knew no one was getting out through those windows.

"Do you want to…?" Miriam waved her hand at The Family grouped between them.

"Oh no," he said. "You've worked it out, you take it home, my girl." Adam realised what that funny feeling was – he was enjoying himself.

"I don't understand," Emma said. "Why would anyone poison their own chocolate? What if they ate it?"

Her husband murmured in support.

"I love you, darling, but don't you think it's best to leave this to the police now?" Miriam's mum glanced back at the DI and Jeans, unsure. Adam resisted the urge to give a little wave.

"I suspect the killer never had any intention of eating the chocolate," Miriam went on. "They would probably have disposed of it had the bait not been taken. I don't think they wanted anyone else to get hurt. They just left it there – almost like a booby trap for Edward."

"Like Russian Roulette." Uncle Roddy squeezed his walking stick.

"Exactly!" Miriam pointed at him, and for one surreal moment Adam could imagine them playing charades.

"But Edward did bite the bullet," Adam said grimly.

Miriam nodded, looking thoughtful. "Yes, I don't think we'll ever know for sure what happened next, but I assume whatever the poison was, it was fast-acting, and maybe induced hallucinations?"

Jeans's eyes widened; his Biro paused mid-word in his notes.

"Possibly a neurotoxin," Adam posed. That would be less good. He'd have to get in environmental control. He hoped Miriam's hunch the killer hadn't meant to hurt anyone else was correct, or else they could all be looking at a very nasty post-Christmas illness. Perhaps they shouldn't have stayed in this room?

Miriam nodded. "I'm assuming your – err – pathologist will be able to work it out?" Her gaze tracked from the CSI to Jeans.

The lad made a sort of squeak, and Adam suppressed the urge to tell him to man up. He would have done biohazard contamination training too. "Yes," his PC managed.

Miriam didn't seem perplexed. She turned away and held her hands up, as if to frame the scene she was picturing from the night before. "Perhaps Edward was delusional, and he thought someone was attacking him? Or he was dancing?" She squinted slightly, toward the advent calendars, before bringing her attention back to in front of the tree. "It would account for the mess in here. We mistakenly thought Edward was attacked by someone physically. But maybe he was out of his mind?"

Adam looked afresh at the kicked and trampled presents, the concentration in where the victim fell. If it was just one man doing this damage… "Strychnine," he said.

"Sorry?" Ms Laverwick yelped.

"It's a poison. It can make the victim spasm, tense up…" He looked back to Miriam. He could picture Edward, who'd clearly been a big man in life, greedily plucking the chocolate from behind the cardboard window, dropping the bit of silver foil from his fat fingers. Popping the stolen treat into his mouth with a satisfied grin. Strychnine didn't take long. Fifteen minutes, in which Edward could have stoked the fire up, placed the calendar back for the disappointment of the morning, inspected the gifts. Checked the balance of presents were in his favour. And did it start then? That he began to tense, spasm, his arms and legs jerking around, crushing the presents, barrelling into the tree. Flailing for his life. "He got caught in the pearls – not strangled by them."

"Well I never!" Jeans shook his head in bemusement. "She's cracked it. The poor sod." The fairy lights pinned round the large windows clicked on, their timers clearly set to coincide with early evening. Adam suppressed a shudder – as if any remaining warmth from the day had also seeped out.

"Oh God," whispered Ms Laverwick, her eyes on the remaining strings of pearls on the tree. Presumably she had decorated this room with much happier thoughts in mind. Uncle Roddy's chair creaked again. The air seemed to shift from the cinnamon sweetness into something quite bitter, as if they were watching it all unfold in front of them.

"How awful." Miriam's mum buried her face into her partner's Christmas jumper. Emma was wide-eyed. "Edward was… well, he wasn't the greatest." Her blonde blow-dried helmet quivered. "But who would do this? Whose chocolate did he eat?"

Adam dropped his arms down, transferred his weight equally between his feet: he was ready if they bolted. All eyes were turned to Miriam again, as the lights glittered behind her, a sparkling drumroll to her words.

Miriam's thoughts seemed to be chasing themselves round her body. Her fingers felt hot, her heart racing, but it wasn't anxiety now. She hadn't liked Edward, but no one deserved this. But what if she'd got it wrong? The entire Morgan-West clan were gazing at her, expectant, ready. Saliva pooled in her mouth; her stomach felt like it was trying to invert itself. Now was not the time for an IBS episode. She looked at the open door, caught the eye of Detective Adam, and the almost imperceptible nod he gave her. He believed in her. She could do this.

"Strychnine's quite an old-fashioned poison, isn't it? I only know it from Golden Age crime novels – I've always loved those." *The ridiculousness of this situation.* "In those books it was always fairly easy to come by – prescribed in small doses as a medicine. Or bought as a rat or mole poison." She knew she was sounding like the Wiki-page she was reciting. She took a shaking breath in. You build confidence by doing, and Miriam had always been a doer. She just had to get on with it. She dug her nails into the palms of her hands.

"And I guess that availability, that usage, was taken from real life. It was the kind of household product that was just lying around, the kind of thing that was kept in a cupboard and forgotten about. An antique cupboard, for example."

Miriam looked directly at cousin Andrew, and he gave one of his amused smirks.

"It was your advent calendar, Andrew. You found strychnine – I'm guessing through something that came your way at the shop?" Miriam swallowed. "You injected the chocolate, primed the trap for Edward, and waited, didn't you?"

There was an intake of breath, the wooden floor creaked as The Family shifted away from the killer in their midst. Uncle Roddy was staring, his eyes wide at his great-great-nephew, as if seeing him for the first time. The grandfather clock in the hallway started its melancholic chime for seven o'clock.

"No," breathed Emma.

"Oh, Andy," said Ms Laverwick softly, her eyes glistening. "How could you?"

"Oh, come on." Andrew's voice was incredulous. Miriam had always thought he'd been different, softer, kind. But she saw in that moment, as her cousin rocked back on his heels and smirked at his horrified family, he too had the male Morgan-West entitlement. "Edward deserved it."

And Miriam closed her eyes as Detective Adam stepped forward to read him his rights.

Adam watched the tail lights of Jeans's squad car disappear down the drive, bearing Andrew Morgan-West to the station. He'd alleged Edward had stolen his chocolate, so he wasn't to blame for his resultant death. Adam didn't like to think what the CPS would make of that. The whole case had been surreal. Behind him, in another room in the mansion, the fire had been lit, music started up, as – no doubt giddy from shock – The Family tried to salvage their Christmas evening. He'd been due to knock off work two hours ago; this was going to be one hell of an overtime bill to get past the guv. Time to go home.

The thought of his cold, empty terraced house was not appealing. Maybe next year he would get that dog, rehome some poor mutt from the local shelter, find someone to walk it while he was at work. That could be his Christmas present to himself – the only one he'd get this year, he thought ruefully. Then tried to shake it off. *Stick a pie in the microwave, get a can of beer on the go, and you'll feel better, man.*

The snow had melted now, and crunchy patches of gravel squelched underfoot as he trudged toward his Astra. He heard the excitable vibrato of the young twins, followed by laughter coming from inside Critchley Court. The circle of life. The Family would recover from this, and he'd be back arresting car thieves by Monday. Life moved on.

He blew on his cold fingers and took the fob from his pocket, pausing by the car. The memory of Miriam smiling at him, framed by glimmering fairy lights, blinked in front of his eyes. She really was quite an extraordinary woman. The way she'd assessed, deduced, and delivered her theory was something to behold. He had her number – Jeans had taken everyone's contact details – but you didn't ask out witnesses from murder investigations. Not the done thing. Besides, he was being daft, he likely would never see her again in his life, and that was fine. He was too rational to believe in love at first sight. He unlocked the car with a *thunk*. The handle was wet and cold as he pulled it open, then tipped the newspaper he'd left on his seat across, as a beam of warm yellow light fell onto him.

He looked up to see one of the large doors into Critchley Court had been opened, and Miriam stood at the top of the stone steps, framed by the glow from inside. She'd changed into what had presumably been her party outfit: red glittery shoes and a pretty green dress. It suited her.

"Oh, Detective Adam – you're not going already, are you?" she asked. Was he imagining it, or did she look genuinely disappointed at the prospect?

He swallowed as she ran down the steps to catch up with him. "Careful, it's slippy underfoot," he cautioned, as she gave a little cry when her right foot kept going.

Instinctively Adam reached out to steady her, holding her right in front of him, his hands on her arms. He could feel the warmth of her skin through the soft, silky fabric.

She looked up at him with a grin, and those radiant big brown clever eyes. "Oops."

His mouth suddenly felt dry. He swallowed. "What can I help you with?"

Miriam raised an eyebrow. "I don't think I've seen you eat all day. Would you like to stay for Christmas pudding?"

Adam blinked. He still hadn't let go of her, and she hadn't moved away. In fact, she'd stepped closer still. "Can I ask you something?" he said.

"Of course," she said quietly, tilting her face up toward him.

"How do you feel about dogs?" *Smooth, man, smooth.*

"Oh!" Surprise and delight danced across Miriam's face. "I love them – that's my job. I work at the rescue shelter."

And the hard-bitten, Christmas-hating grinch of a cop Adam laughed.

SECRET SANTA

Liz Mistry

I N THE wake of the afternoon's rain, clouds hung heavy outside. It was dark, the twinkling lights from the small tree by the window casting multi-coloured shadows over the shape that lay, head resting on a plumped-up pillow. The scent of cinnamon hung in the air and 'Last Christmas' played quietly from the radio. If it hadn't been for the whimpering figure in handcuffs being led away by the detective and the flock of crime scene investigators flooding the room, one might have thought the person on the bed by the door was merely sleeping…

Three weeks earlier
1 December

It was the dreaded Secret Santa draw in the office; after last year's debacle, Gary Evans was well aware that everyone's eyes were on him as he stood up to choose his recipient. Once more cowed into submission by the instructions of his personal assistant – and self-appointed office social manager – Nila to make an effort for the occasion, he was dressed, rather against his better judgement, in a turkey hat left over from last year's festivities. After all, nothing said Christmas more than turkey, did it? With his heart hammering against his chest as he stepped into the centre of the circle, like a turkey to the slaughter, he prayed, *Please not him again. Please not Mr Grimes, not after last year.*

Nila, eyebrows raised, thrust the receptacle towards him. Not even the jovial tinkle of the bell on her elf's hat could disguise the silent warning in her brusque actions. *Why did she have to always be such a bitch?* "You couldn't just have worn a Santa hat, could you? Trust you to mess it up."

Why did he always get things so wrong? He thought he'd nailed it this time, but apparently not and, with the memory of Christmas Past hovering in his mind's eye, Gary wanted nothing more than to escape back to the safety of his office. If he could have, he'd have spun on his heel and left the canteen, but then they'd laugh at him even more than they usually did.

Already flustered by the situation and with all eyes on him, Gary lowered his gaze. Over the years they'd worked together, he'd allowed Nila to gradually become more and more dominant in their working relationship. It was his fault: if he'd only been more assertive and put her in her place when she first started at the company, she wouldn't think it was all right to act like she was the boss rather than the other way round. Even when he managed to summon a modicum of grit and started to reprimand her, he always seemed to flounder at the last moment, allowing her to ride roughshod over him. He wasn't the only one either. The office juniors and even some of the clients allowed Nila's abrasive manner to go unchallenged. And now she'd made sure all eyes were on him. Everyone in the office would be on her side – they wouldn't dare not side with her.

Trying to ignore Nila's laser gaze, he slipped his trembling hand into the long, fur-trimmed hat. Eyes lowered, his fingers grappling inside the fluffy interior, he grabbed the first piece of paper he touched. Pulling his hand out he spun round, tripping over his feet, before rejoining the circle and sinking into his plastic chair. After the last name had been pulled from the Santa hat, Nila plonked her skinny backside down next to him and nudged him in the ribs. "Gonna read it then, Mr Evans?"

Gary inched away from her bony elbow, aware that his entire staff waited expectantly. A flush bright enough to match the circulating Santa hat warmed his face and he silently cursed his annoying PA. The last thing he wanted was to find out the identity of his Secret Santa recipient in front of all those eager eyes, each of them no doubt dreading that the boss had pulled their name from the hat. Of course, in previous years he'd begged Nila to do his Secret Santa shopping for him, but she'd drawn the line at that. "I already buy the individual gifts for staff members, Gary. The least you can do is show willing and buy your own Secret Santa gift. I mean, how hard can it be?" Her scathing look told him exactly how low her regard for him was, yet he was well used to being looked down on. Teachers, his foster parents, the other kids at school and later university had made the geeky introverted kid's life hell: he'd learned to keep his head bowed and internalise his hurt.

Resigned to his fate, he nodded enthusiastically, feeling like the silly dog he'd seen sat in the rear window of Nila's car, only, to make things worse, wearing a stupid turkey hat. "Y-Y-Yes, of course."

As he began to unfold the small square of paper, he tried to purge the memory of Mr Grimes's angry face when he'd opened his gift last year. He'd been so upset that he'd snatched his party hat off his head and stormed out of the room, stuffing both wrapping paper and gift into the bin as he passed. Not one to miss out on anything, Nila had immediately scurried over and grabbed the scrunched-up parcel. "For God's sake!"

Shaking her head, she'd held up a box of socks, each pair depicting a caricature of one of the seven dwarves. Lips pursed, she glared round the room. A few people sniggered but were quickly silenced. Her eyes then rested on her 'superior', who had flushed brighter than Sneezy's nose, and the truth was out. "How *could* you, Mr Evans? You know he's very touchy about being only five feet two."

Despite Gary's explanation of an unexpected and quite complicated business issue raising its head at the last minute, stopping him from browsing for Mr Grimes's gift in one of the brightly lit department stores, Nila had remained unimpressed. Up to his ears in work, he'd had the choice of showing up at the Christmas party empty-handed or dashing last minute to the petrol station. Unfortunately, the petrol station didn't have much of a choice, hence the socks. The repercussions from his ill-thought-out purchase stayed with him all year. Even after numerous attempts at an apology, Mr Grimes had refused to be mollified. His eyes darted now to the man, whose glower was enough to force Gary's gaze down to the piece of paper clutched in his sweaty hands. The memory of the incident still appeared to be the source of great anger for Mr Grimes, but Gary was just upset by it. He hadn't meant to insult the older man, and yet, somehow, as usual, that's exactly what he'd done. Even now, a full year later, he avoided Mr Grimes at all costs.

This year, Nila, her arms folded under her breasts and her lips pinched tight together, had sighed. The elongated sound emphasised, as loudly as a death knell, her expectation that he would fail again as she issued her warning, "You better not mess this up… or else!"

In trepidation – with flashbacks of everyone's faces, Mr Grimes's flushed angry exit and Nila's condemnation flying before his eyes – he held his breath and, still reluctant to read the name of his Secret Santa recipient, he shut his eyes for a second, before finally flipping the final fold open. For a moment he couldn't quite believe it as he read the name on the chit. He risked a glance at Mr Grimes, who glared at him with a frostiness that showed no signs of thawing, and his heart sank. *Would he* ever *forgive him?* Gary double-checked the name then, grinning, he refolded the paper and placed it neatly in his pocket.

Nila leaned over, a frown troubling her brow. "You look pleased."

He nodded. "Indeed I am, Nila. Indeed I am."

"Hmmm." She studied his face, scepticism curling her mouth into an ugly moue. "Good! No silly mistakes this year then. You've got plenty of time to find the perfect gift. Show us what you're made of, Mr Evans, for a change. Lead by example and show them who's boss, eh?" Nila hesitated, then lowered her voice. "Whose name did you pull?"

With the heavy weight of her expectation on his shoulders,

Gary's early enthusiasm dimmed. He'd thought he'd be able to find a suitable gift for his Secret Santa, but now those kernels of doubt began to niggle again. He frowned and, pulling his shoulders back, looked at his PA. "It's a *Secret* Santa, Nila. I'm not telling you. Besides, nobody will know which gift I've given."

Nila snorted. "Yeah right. With the way your cheeks light up like Rudolph's nose, everyone will know which present you bought. Better make it a good one." She stood up and began to walk away, then turned back to him. "Or, at the very least, a thoughtful one. Maybe something personal. Something you know they will enjoy, *not* something from a petrol station."

And therein lay the problem, for Gary Evans wasn't the most sociable of men and had never spoken to the person on his chit, thus buying a personal gift seemed well out of his grasp. Still, this year he was determined to try, so after a few hours locked up in his office with the blinds down and his thinking cap on, and with Nila's advice ringing in his ears, Gary came up with a strategy of sorts. One that he hoped would provide him with the inspiration he so desperately needed. After all, it seemed that all eyes would be on him at the Christmas party, and this year he was determined not to mess it up. Bring on Operation Secret Santa.

Of course, Gary had seen Miranda before, maybe even spent a few self-indulgent moments watching her. But, now, with phase one of Operation Secret Santa underway, he *studied* her. At break time he scrutinised her, unobserved through the small window that looked out from his office into the staff kitchen. With one finger pulling the closed blinds slightly apart, he stood close to the pane, rolling back and forth on the balls of his feet as he waited for her to enter the kitchen and flick on the kettle, before taking her neatly labelled packet of fresh Arabian coffee from the fridge.

Since he'd pulled her name from the hat, he'd enjoyed watching her small ritual. It had become a highlight of his day. One that sent his heart aflutter and one he could almost set his watch by. Holding his breath, he watched as, with eyes closed, Miranda held the open packet to her nose and savoured the scent before inserting an unbleached paper cone into the plastic dripper and placing it above her stained, glass coffee jug. When the kettle came to the boil, she poured a precise amount of water onto the filter, moving the kettle in a slow circular movement as she did so. Once satisfied, she discarded the water from the bottom of the jug and replaced the filter and damp paper on top. After another long inhalation of the coffee, she took her plastic coffee measure and scooped the grains up, levelling them off with the back of a knife. Her eyes narrowed as she assessed the spoon's contents. With a small 'tut' she repeated the flattening movement of the knife to dislodge a few excess granules, then smiled, before tipping the earthy grains into the waiting filter.

Again, she lifted the kettle and repeated her circular motions bit by bit with the hot, not boiling, water. It was mesmerising. Gary, on tiptoe now, licked his lips as the dark brown liquid began to drip slowly into the glass jug. It was an agonising wait until finally the jug was filled. As her lips curled up, her eyes flickering lazily, Gary wished he too could inhale the coffee aphrodisiac. With bated breath, he peered through the window as she took her first caffeine-filled sip, then at last he exhaled as her shoulders relaxed and she smiled.

Then, her lips scrunched up and the tip of her tongue emerged from her painted lips. With matching red nails, she picked a few stray coffee grains from her tongue before leaning over to flick the offending grit into the bin, inadvertently revealing a glimpse of smooth, stockinged thigh. A soft growling noise left Gary's throat and, breathing heavily, he returned to his desk. For once, Nila had been right. The key to Secret Santa success was getting to know the recipient of your gift and because he'd taken his PA's advice so seriously, he now knew what he would buy for Miranda. All he had to do was some online research.

18 December
Secret Santa Day

Gary had positioned himself at the back of the room and, resisting Nila's persistent instruction to wear a flashing Rudolph nose, he focused on the flutter of anxiety that had taken up residence in his chest. As he'd wrapped his Secret Santa gift that morning, he'd been certain that his choice was perfect and that, after today, last year's Secret Santa debacle would be a forgotten memory. Now, however, with Wham!'s 'Last Christmas' playing in the background and the swathe of brightly wrapped gifts in all shapes and sizes huddled under the Christmas tree, his habitual self-doubt invaded him. The flutter moved to his gut and sweat gathered under his armpits. *What if I've made another dreadful choice? What if, as Nila fully expects, I've messed up again?*

As Nila handed out gift after gift, the desire to run from the room accompanied by the taunting words of the famous track was overwhelming. Nila moved closer and closer to his gift – the one with the ice blue shimmering paper and matching bow. His heart clattered against his sternum as George Michael morphed into an enthusiastic if somewhat tinny rendition of 'Jingle Bells'. At last, his present was in Nila's hands and she announced in a loud voice that echoed tauntingly round the room, "Miranda."

Miranda jumped up, clapping her hands and grinning as she hurried over to accept her gift. Gary hoped that her enthusiasm wouldn't fade when she unwrapped it.

As she took it from Nila, her smile deepened. "Wow, so beautifully wrapped. Can't wait to see what's inside."

Nila glanced across at Gary, her eyes lasering him with a *you better not have messed up* look. How did she know that he'd pulled Miranda's name from the hat, anyway? He met her accusing stare with more confidence than the globules of perspiration dotting his brow would indicate.

As she peeled the paper from her Secret Santa gift, Miranda's eyes widened. "My goodness! This is brilliant! Just what I needed. Whoever got me this clearly knows me so well. Has one of you been stalking me?"

With gentle hands she rotated the coffee pot, marvelling at the clear glass jug with the inbuilt coffee dripper. When she noticed her name engraved on the silver handle, her lips stretched wide and she scanned the room. "This is the *best* gift ever! Thank you, Secret Santa."

Gary's heart rate slowed and a huge grin covered his face as Miranda's eyes swept the room, her smile radiant. Had her gaze rested just a tad longer on him? He thought so. His lips twitched, realising that she sensed *he* was her Secret Santa. He was sure of it:

the thought sent a warm glow through his entire body, distracting him so he almost missed his name being called to fetch his own gift. Even after the disappointment of receiving from his Secret Santa seven pairs of novelty socks with insults on them – *Grumpy Old Git* being the least offensive of the lot – the toasty feeling remained… although he couldn't help wondering who had sent him that somewhat uncharitable gift. Never mind, though. Miranda loved her present and, more importantly she, he was convinced, knew that he was the sensitive, intuitive thoughtful giver.

19 December

The following day, Gary bounced lightly on his toes as he waited by the window, his warm breath leaving bubbles of steam on the glass through the gap in the blinds. Finally, he heard Miranda clipping along the corridor and strained to see her carry her new coffee pot into the kitchen. He watched her repeat the motions he'd seen her doing for weeks now, but this time there was a lighter spring to her step – a more intense feel to her coffee ritual. Her scarlet nails rested momentarily on the silver handle and her finger traced her engraved name before she removed the filter paper. Humming to herself, she poured the rich coffee into her mug – unaware that behind her, in the quiet sanctuary of his office, Gary observed her as she drank, a new plan formulating in his head as he imagined joining her in the kitchen and declaring his love for her. After all, surely, he knew her better than anyone else now. Hadn't he been the one to buy her the perfect gift? Wasn't it *he* who knew everything there was to know about her; from where she lived to what she ate, to where she parked her car and the route she took from home to the office? They were compatible in every way. The Secret Santa gift had proved that. Still, Gary wasn't prone to impulsive acts, so he decided to leave it a few days before confiding his feelings for her. Let her enjoy her new coffee ritual for the time being, then he'd introduce his matching pot to the kitchen and they'd take it from there. He suspected that she hadn't worked out yet that the handle with her name on made up one half of a love heart.

21 December

Persistent rain had soaked Gary on the quick walk from the car park to the office; nevertheless, he hummed as he shrugged his raincoat off and hung it on the hook by the window. A sudden crash of thunder rattled the pane and Gary turned to watch as the deluge outside worsened. Drenched pedestrians danced round puddles and huddled in shop doorways. Cars, their wipers barely fast enough to scrape their screens dry, slowed in unusual deference to the elements. Then, through the waves of water obscuring his vision, a car pulled right up to the kerb outside the office. The passenger door swung open and, holding a briefcase above her head, Miranda stepped out, skirted the large vehicle and approached the driver's side. Immediately, a frown formed on Gary's forehead. *What is she doing in someone else's car?* He squashed his nose against the window and his eyes screwed up, peering down at the street below. No, not just anyone else's car. It was Mr Grimes's car. What was she doing in *his* car? Had hers broken down or something? Was he giving her a lift because hers was out of commission? An uncomfortable lump settled in Gary's throat as he tried to make sense of the strange situation.

Oblivious to the rain, Miranda dropped her briefcase to the floor and, as she leaned down, the car window purred open. Gary scraped his nose further up the glass for a better view. Then, unmoving, he released a long hissing sound. She was *kissing* the driver. *His* Miranda was kissing the driver! No, not just the driver. His Miranda was kissing Mr Grimes! Out there, in front of the office. Right under his nose. With both hands splayed against the glass, his enraged hiss faded to a whimper and then died to nothing as he slid downwards until he was huddled against the wall beneath. Like a monkey rocking senselessly in a tree, Gary remained where he was until activity in the outer office roused him.

With a deep breath, he dragged himself to his feet – the last thing he needed was Nila finding him like this – and adjusted his suit, rubbed his wet face with his hands, and sat down at his desk just as his PA entered, full of pointless chatter about the weather. Despite being dazed, Gary responded as normal and eventually, armed with a list of tasks, Nila left him alone to contemplate Miranda's betrayal.

He should never have listened to Nila's instructions to get to know his Secret Santa giftee. He should never have taken advice from that interfering know-it-all. As for Miranda herself, how dare she? How dare she build his hopes up like that? Making him believe his feelings were reciprocated. His turbulent mind rested on Mr Grimes. Was this payback? Was this the other man's way of getting back at him for last year's mistake? He wouldn't put it past the mean-minded git.

As it neared morning break time, Gary, an empty weight dragging in his gut, left his office for only a moment and returned with his lips creased into a humourless line. Just before eleven, he hefted on his half-dry raincoat and left the office, ignoring Nila's calls and expressions of concern. "Leave me alone. You've done enough damage. Just do your work and mind your own business."

Later, after he'd slipped indoors, out of the rain, Gary stripped off his wet clothes, pulled the plump duvet back from the bed and lay down in a foetal position, naked, the soft fabric covering him. The overpowering stench of coffee that had irritated his nostrils on the journey from the office dissipated, replaced by the soothing Christmas cinnamon scent that rose from the satin-covered pillow. He pulled the duvet tighter around him and, cocooned in its fragrance, breathed slowly and deeply, until finally he slept.

Back at the office, Miranda gasped when she entered the kitchen on her break. Her slender fingers covered her mouth as she tried to make sense of the mess on the floor. A strong coffee aroma hung heavily in the air and in the middle of the floor in a small mound, was a pile of pungent coffee granules with a moat of sludgy foam around it. Sitting on top of the heap, like a turret, was her beautiful coffee pot, smashed into shards, the handle with her nameplate scratched and disfigured at the side. Wordlessly, she bent and picked it up. Then, with tears rolling down her cheeks, she collected a dustpan and cleared the mess away.

When Gary finally woke, the rain had nearly stopped. He lay, his stomach knotted with a rage he'd never experienced before, listening to the infrequent melodic drops on the skylight. And as each slight, each nasty word, each impatient gesture flashed into his mind, he devised a strategy. When he was happy with his plans, he stretched, rolled to the side of the bed and hopped onto the rug. *Time for payback*. Finally, after rummaging through drawer after drawer, he found some clean clothes, got dressed, and walked through to the darkened kitchen to prepare. When he heard the car pull up outside, a strange calmness settled over him. Cold as ice, he picked up the house phone and dialled 999. When it connected, he stammered as he recited the address, then in a panicked, breathless rush that was a key component of his plot, he added, "She lured me here. She's going to kill me. Please help. She's got a knife. Come quick…"

By the time the key turned in the lock, he'd hung up. Eager to see her reaction, he faced the door, wearing *her* oversized hoodie and joggers and gripping *her* carving knife. With his lips pulled into a sneer he savoured her confusion that was soon replaced by fear as the homeowner faced him.

"What the hell…?" She stepped forward, her brows gathered together in a dark frown, her voice trembling just a little. "What are you…?"

But Gary stepped forward as well, grabbed her, and dragged her through to the cinnamon-scented bedroom. "You set this all up, didn't you? All the 'get to know your Secret Santa giftee, find out their interests, make it something personal'. You did this. *You*."

She struggled, but his rage made him strong and she was skinny. Ignoring her strangled protestations, he flung her onto the bed.

"You and your interfering caused this. You've only got yourself to blame. You *knew* she was seeing him. You wanted to *humiliate* me. That's what you do, Nila. That's what *you* get joy from, humiliating people! But your time has come. Secret Santa's got a gift for you now."

All trace of his PA's usual irritation was replaced by a flicker of fear as she backed away from him, edging closer to the headboard. A pulse thrummed at her temple and, as her shaking fingers gripped the neck of her blouse, she said, "I don't—"

But Gary was having none of it. With the sound of sirens growing ever louder, he had to act quickly if his plan was to work. He'd showed willing, made an effort… He was determined not to mess *this* up.

Gary lunged forward and pushed her over the edge of the bed onto the floor by the window, with the duvet trailing after her. Before she could stand up, he rolled onto his back, rested his head on the pillow and, using both hands, thrust the knife into his own heart. As the detectives burst through the front door, his dying words for her ears alone were, "You got what you deserved in the end, you interfering cow. Tell Miranda that coffee break's over."

MARLEY'S GHOST

Sarah Hilary

A T ANY other time of year they would not have looked remarkable: an old woman and a young boy travelling together. But it was Christmas Eve, their arms were full of packages, and Ninna was insisting on sitting where she shouldn't.

"I'm afraid this is a first-class carriage." The ticket inspector may well have been afraid, had he known what was coming.

"First class…?" Ninna made a point of looking at the stains on the plastic table. "I wouldn't go that far."

"The tickets, ma'am. Are the wrong ones for this part of the train."

"Not at all," Ninna said with the air of someone graciously accepting an apology. "I know what I paid for."

By now the inspector had processed the fact of Ninna's extremely tweedy coat and stout shoes and, moreover, her manner, which was stolidly self-assured. Her tickets might say otherwise but she was clearly built for first-class travel. His gaze flickered to her young companion. Kim kept his hands in his lap, sitting upright, his expression solemn.

"I'm afraid I am going to have to ask you to move down the train."

"Nonsense." Ninna settled herself more emphatically in the seat. "I paid for first-class tickets. If the imbecilic machine at the station saw fit to furnish me with second-class stubs that is hardly my concern. A human being wouldn't have made that mistake. But it's all machines now, isn't it? Kim, open the lunchbox. This is my grandson," she lied, before adding in the tone of a bomb disposal expert clearing a crowd, "and we're about to eat egg sandwiches."

The inspector, admitting defeat, moved on.

Kim shared out the sandwiches. He was wearing his best clothes – a blue jumper with an itchy neck and brown corduroy trousers that rasped when he walked – a gift from Ninna, like everything he possessed. He'd only lived with her for eight weeks but was already up to his neck in debt to her. This did not occur to him at the time, of course; he was only eight years old. Had it occurred to him, he'd have rationalised it like this: she was the one who'd asked for him, he'd certainly never asked for her. Two months ago, he'd been taken to an unfamiliar part of London that looked like the set from a 1950s film about the future. It was 2024. The future, as dreamt of by those bold imagineers, had failed to materialise. Cable cars swooped across the Thames, it was true, and a train ran on elevated tracks. But, overridingly, there was pollution, never-ending building works, rats and tourists (Ninna made no distinction between the last two). From the windows of her large house in this unfamiliar part of London, she surveyed this world as an iceberg might the maiden voyage of an egotistical ocean liner.

Kim picked a stray crumb from his jumper. "What will Salisbury be like?"

"Deadly." Ninna wiped her chin with a handkerchief. "We'll be lucky if we survive it."

Kim digested this as he'd learnt to digest much of what she said, as if it were a tricky bit of bacon, stringy all the way down. "And what will Douglas and Lionel and the others be like?"

She tucked the handkerchief up her sleeve. "Even luckier."

To survive it, she meant, this deadly family get-together called Christmas. As far as Kim could tell, spending Christmas in Salisbury with her son and grandchildren was the last thing Veronica Marley wanted to do. It surprised him, therefore, that she was doing it. Ninna, who never did anything she didn't want to, who didn't return library books on time or pay bills until they changed colour from black to red, or buy the right train tickets for those rare occasions when she had to travel from the comfort of her own home.

"Christmas is for families," she said ominously, taking a large hardback from her overnight bag. Kim recognised it as one of the overdue library books: a Western with an angry man on the cover, trying to ride a horse that didn't want to be ridden.

Kim took out a book of his own: *The RSPB British Handbook of Birds*. The book had been waiting for him in the attic bedroom of the big house with views across the Thames to cable cars and cranes strung with Christmas lights "for some godforsaken reason," Ninna had said. The attic, like the rest of the house, was cold and spartan. Ninna didn't believe in home comforts, she said. The social worker who'd brought Kim looked shocked at this but after referring to the paperwork seemed happy to leave him in her care.

The RSPB British Handbook of Birds was a very good book. As soon as he'd seen it on the bedside table, he'd been happy to stay. There were no books in the children's home, let alone ones about birds. It must have been the children's home that told Ninna how much Kim loved birds. He wished the train would move more slowly so he could watch from its windows for whichever species were living in the trees planted alongside the tracks. Crows, of course, and jackdaws. Magpies. When they passed a flooded field, he saw seagulls sitting on the water, looking confused. The floods confused everyone. Kim would've thought they'd be used to rivers bursting their banks by now; they'd been doing it every winter since he could remember.

"Peel me an orange," Ninna said, "there's a good boy."

Kim put down his book and peeled one of the oranges from the paper bag in his rucksack, trimming the pith neatly before handing it to her. "What's in the big box?"

"A nasty surprise for a nosey parker."

"There's a lot of presents."

"I have a lot of family." Ninna fixed him with a stare above the spine of the library book. "An excess, you might say."

This made him wonder, again, why she'd agreed to foster him when she had more than enough family already. But the children's home was flooded like the fields, only with children not water; Kim had been encouraged to count himself lucky he had somewhere safe to stay for a while. "Call me Ninna," she'd said, so he did, even after the social worker said "Mrs Marley" was more appropriate.

"What're they like?" he asked. "Your family?"

"That's what you're going to find out." She finished the orange and tucked her chin into her scarf, like a sandpiper settling into its ruff.

When the ticket inspector made his way back down the train, he caught Kim's eye and smiled. The boy seemed nice enough; not his fault his grandmother was a dragon. Besides, they weren't the only odd people on the train. At Basingstoke a hen party staggered aboard in spiked heels, shedding red feathers from their boas, followed by a troupe of actors still in costume, one smoking an elaborate pipe shaped like a trumpet. The inspector was relieved to discover the pipe was a prop. Dealing with Kim's grandmother had used up his quota of insouciance for the day.

The house in Salisbury was small and boxy, built of pale stone and flint, its windows full of fussy little leaded panes of glass that caught what light was in the sky and shone it into Kim's eyes. Ninna, finding the door locked, rapped on it with her fist. The afternoon smelt of dead leaves, rotten. The spire of Salisbury Cathedral poked up behind the chimneys. The garden had a lot of knotty bushes like knuckled fists. Halfway up the lawn a blackened arbour stood like a gallows.

"Never say I don't take you anywhere nice." Ninna thumped on the door again. Then she rubbed her gloved hand at her chest, pulling her face into a strange shape.

"Are you all right?" Kim asked.

"I'm in the arse-end of Wiltshire about to spend Christmas with my least favourite crowd of sycophants. What d'you think?"

"What are sycophants?"

"Trucklers, toadies, lickspittles…" She looked down at him. "Oxpeckers. You know what those are?"

"The red-billed oxpecker is a native of the savanna of sub-Saharan Africa."

"The boy is a book…" Ninna moved to peer through the nearest window into the unlit house. "And what do these red-billed birds get up to?"

"They eat ticks off zebras and impalas and giraffes."

"And what do ticks eat?"

"Blood…?" Kim followed her around the side of the house. "They suck blood from mammals."

"So an oxpecker is a lazy bloodsucker. Speaking of…" She pitched her voice at whoever was standing behind Kim. "Where the hell've you been? We're freezing half to death out here!"

"We were at choral evensong, of course. Happy Christmas, Mother!"

Four of them all together, in dark coats that made Kim think of crows; a murder of crows. The middle-aged man with a long face like a guttering candle must have been her son Douglas, the others her grandchildren: a man in his early twenties with thinning hair, another who looked like a drunk teenager, and a girl of about Kim's age in a velvet-collared coat. Ninna batted away her son's attempt at an embrace. "Get me inside and near a fire, with a stiff drink."

In the years between then and now, Kim often thought of that Christmas spent with the family Ninna described as lazy bloodsuckers. There was nothing overtly lazy about Douglas or his eldest son Lionel, whose hair was thinning in his twenties. Both exerted themselves to please Ninna, dancing around her like a pair of mating albatrosses. Lionel's younger brother Jonas wasn't lazy so much as dormant.

And eight-year-old Lena was far too watchful to be described as lazy. Her bright eyes followed Kim everywhere. Ninna had warned him about Lena: "A born actress and a bottomless pit of cunning, trustworthy as an adder," which made Kim wonder how she'd described him to her family. None of them looked pleased to see him, a cuckoo in their nest. Ninna had told him, "Just be yourself, boy. And keep your eyes open."

Discovering he was to sleep on a camp bed in her room, Kim braced himself for a battle similar to the one on the train with the ticket inspector, but Ninna just smiled and said, "Excellent."

"I'm afraid at such short notice it was the best we could manage."

"Noted. Kim, take your bag upstairs. Lena will help. I'd like a glass of port and a mince pie. Warmed, with lots of cream."

No one, Kim was quick to notice, said no to Ninna. Douglas looked pained whenever she issued orders but he complied every time. There was something a bit squeamish about Douglas. Ninna had said he'd found his wife Kathleen dead in bed one morning two years ago: "Wouldn't go near her, not to check her pulse or cover her face. Won't sleep in the same room even now."

This was the bedroom assigned to Ninna and Kim, the one where Lena's mother had died. Standing in the room, Lena said, "You're not my real cousin. She's not your real grandmother. She's only fostering you to annoy us."

"Why would that annoy you?" Kim asked.

"Dad and Lionel are counting the days until the reading of her will." Lena pushed the shiny toe of her shoe at the carpet. "You know what a will is, don't you?"

"Oh yes."

"Gran's been teasing them about it for ages. Dad says it makes no difference since she's getting older every year." She dipped her head at him. "You won't be in it, anyway."

"Of course not." Kim put *The RSPB British Handbook of Birds* onto the pillow of the camp bed. Lena watched him with the eyes of a parakeet. "It's nice of you all to let me stay."

She wrinkled her nose. "That won't get you anywhere."

Downstairs, Ninna had fallen asleep in an armchair by the fire. A plate with a demolished mince pie was in danger of slipping off her lap, but no one seemed to think it a good idea to rescue it. Douglas and Lionel looked aghast when Kim walked across the room to do exactly that, setting the plate on a low table. Lena tucked herself into the window seat with a book. Jonas was nowhere to be seen. Since there wasn't anywhere else to sit, Kim settled on the rug at Ninna's feet. This appeared to render him invisible to the rest of the room, who began to talk about her first in whispers, then more loudly when she didn't wake.

"She doesn't look well, do you think?" Douglas said.

"She hasn't looked well in a while," Lionel agreed.

Neither man sounded sad about this. The opposite, if anything.

"The way she shovelled that cream up… Her cholesterol must be monstrous."

"And the port. Mind you, she always liked her booze." Lionel used the past tense, as if Ninna might've died in her sleep.

Kim looked up at her. From his vantage point on the floor, he could've sworn her right eyelid twitched in a wink. Afterwards, he'd feel awful about this, reminded of the time he saw a magpie bowing in a tree and bowed back, only to watch as the bird toppled through the branches to land dead at his feet.

Christmas Day started early with church, then became peeling potatoes and stepping around Jonas's outstretched feet to lay the table. Kim was worn out by the time they were all sitting down to an enormous lunch of duck, watercress and cranberries that stuck in his teeth like the pudding that followed. Ninna ate hugely, far more than she managed at home, almost as if she were making a point – although Kim couldn't think what it might be. She was in a good mood, laughing along with her son's attempts at humour, in contrast to which the jokes inside the crackers appeared Aristotelian.

"I'm going for a nap," Ninna said after lunch. "Kim, give me a hand up the stairs."

In the bedroom, she set her handbag aside and kicked off her shoes to lie on the bed, breathing noisily through her teeth.

"Are you all right?" Kim asked.

She snorted. "Go back downstairs, there's a good boy. Play with your little cousin."

Downstairs, Douglas, Lionel and Lena were setting up a game of Monopoly. Kim settled with his book in the armchair where Ninna had slept, half-listening to Douglas and Lionel debating London property prices and the wisdom or otherwise of erecting hotels in boroughs where gentrification had proved an expensive experiment. Lionel had a lot to say about the latter, beginning and ending with a history lesson that involved, for some dark reason, Jack the Ripper. Before long, the talk turned to Ninna's house in Docklands.

"Must be worth well over three million by now," Lionel said.

"The way she's run it into the ground?" Douglas shook his head. "It'll need to be torn down and rebuilt. How she affords to heat it in that condition, I've no idea."

"Well, there's money. Of course there is. We've always known that."

"If Gran is rich," Lena rolled the dice, "why doesn't she give us better Christmas presents? That nasty old recorder didn't even look new…"

It wasn't a recorder but a pungi, used for charming snakes. Ninna had put a lot of thought into her gifts. An elaborate set of brushes for Lionel's thinning hair. For Jonas, who was barely awake during lunch and who'd snored loudly in church, an alarm clock. Douglas was presented with a very large and ornate silver spoon which on closer examination proved to be silver-plated. Kim's gift, which Ninna had insisted he unwrap in the camp bed before they went down to breakfast, was a pair of field binoculars. "Keep those to yourself, kiddo."

The game of Monopoly ended in a bad-tempered property crash north of Mayfair. Lena was left to pick up the pieces knocked to the floor by Lionel, while their father stood blinking down at Kim in the armchair as if he couldn't remember who he was or why he'd been let into the house.

"Having a nice Christmas, are you?" he enquired sourly.

"Yes thank you."

"I'll bet you are." Lionel gave the carpet a savage kick.

Shortly after that, Kim took himself upstairs to check on Ninna. When he returned, he was pale enough to make all three of them look at him in surprise.

"She's not breathing. I think she's dead."

Lionel's mouth hung open. Douglas climbed to his feet, snapping at his son, "Call an ambulance, will you?"

Kim followed him up the stairs. From the landing he stood watching as Douglas hovered in the doorway, peering in at Ninna lying stiffly on the bed.

Kim thought of the magpie bowing in the tree and he gave a little bow of his own, in honour of the fierce old lady who'd taken him into her home.

The paramedics came very quickly in response to Lionel's phone call. Two of them climbed the stairs to the doorway where Douglas was standing with a nauseated look on his face. A third took his arm and led him back downstairs to the kitchen, where she asked questions and offered to make a cup of tea.

"I'll make it," Kim said.

In due course, the paramedics came down to break the sad news that Ninna had suffered a fatal heart attack. "In her sleep, by the look of it. She won't have suffered."

As the house was so small and since Douglas was a funny colour, the kindest of the paramedics suggested they stepped outside while the police came to take Ninna's body on behalf of the coroner. When Kim pulled on his coat the others did the same, even Jonas who'd been shaken awake by his father. They walked in a group to the cathedral, where Douglas told them to light candles and where they sat in prayer for a time. Back at the house, Douglas spoke to the police, answering any questions they had before leaving the family alone.

Kim climbed the stairs to look at the empty bed where Ninna had slept for the last time.

"You'll need to change the bedding," Lena said. "If you're thinking of sleeping there." She reached for Ninna's handbag, smoothing the leather. "Is this crocodile…?" She opened the bag, stirring at the contents before snapping it shut. She must've caught her fingers in the clasp because she gave a strange little cry of pain and sucked at her injured hand. "I guess you're an orphan again now. Back to the children's home for you. What's the number for your social worker? Dad will want to know."

"I don't have it here. It's in London. In Ninna's house."

"Our house," Lena said. "Don't you mean?"

Kim had expected the evening to be sombre. He was surprised when Lionel brought out a bottle of champagne, popping the cork violently into the fireplace. "Let's toast her…!"

Kim stayed in the background, thinking about red-billed oxpeckers. When it was time for him and Lena to go to bed, he climbed the stairs to the room where two people, Lena reminded him, had now died. "Aren't you afraid to sleep in there?"

"Where else would I sleep?" Kim asked.

Lena didn't have an answer to that.

He brushed his teeth, washed his face and changed into his pyjamas. Then he sat for a while cross-legged on the camp bed, learning how his new binoculars worked and reading *The RSPB British Handbook of Birds*.

Out of nowhere, he heard Ninna's voice ask, "Seen any vultures lately?" and imagined he heard a hissing grunt from downstairs.

"That's a turkey vulture," Ninna's voice continued. "More than one, by the sound of it. What do we call that, a group of vultures?"

"A volt," he replied promptly, "or a committee. If they're feeding, we call it a wake."

The boy is a book.

"And what do they like to feed on?"

"Roadkill. White-tailed deer or carrion. They can digest toxins that would kill most scavengers. You can dissolve a shovel in their stomach acid."

"A volt of vultures…"

"Or a kettle, if they're in flight."

"I should like to see that." Ninna's voice was sly in his head. "A kettle of vultures."

Kim closed his book and uncurled himself from the bed. He padded to the top of the stairs in his pyjamas, standing a moment before he started to scream.

Lionel was the first to come, elbows working like wings. "What…? What's happened?"

Douglas was behind him, wearing the red paper crown from a cracker, a glass of champagne in one hand. Kim stopped screaming to stare at him. Douglas scraped the crown from his head and hid the glass behind his back. "What's the matter?"

"It's Ninna." Kim pointed towards the bedroom. "She's in there."

"She's not," Lionel said. "They took her away. She's with the coroner."

Kim pointed mutely in the direction of the room where two people had died. He stood back when Lionel marched past to peer inside. Douglas stayed back. From the foot of the stairs, Kim saw Jonas blinking owlishly.

"There's no one in there." Lionel fixed Kim with a stare. "You're imagining things."

"Seeing things," Lena said. "Ghosts."

"She spoke to me," Kim insisted.

"What did she say?"

"She asked me if I'd seen any vultures lately."

Douglas made a strangled sound of outrage.

Lionel thinned his lips. "*What* did you say?"

"Vultures. She knows I like birds."

"Are you trying to be funny?"

"What's funny about that?" Kim asked, perplexed.

"Go to bed. We'll be calling your social worker in the morning."

"She won't be working on Boxing Day, but thank you."

Kim went into the bedroom, closing the door behind him.

He waited until midnight before stepping onto the landing to scream a second time. Lionel and Douglas were a lot more inebriated by midnight, and a great deal jollier, at least until Kim disturbed their celebrations.

"He's seen her again," Lena said from the other end of the landing. "Gran. He's going to be seeing her all night."

She was right. In the end, Kim was told to sleep on the sofa in the sitting room. Lionel had to clear two empty bottles of champagne out of the way to make room for him. *Everyone*, Kim thought sadly, *seemed a lot happier now Ninna was gone.*

The next morning, he made himself a breakfast from the leftovers in the fridge before going upstairs to wash and dress. He packed

Ninna's things into her overnight bag, and his own into the rucksack. Christmas was over. He hung the binoculars around his neck and left the house, walking until he found a park where he spotted a woodpecker, two pigeons and a murder of crows.

Back at the house, Douglas snapped at him for going off without telling anyone, but he was hungover so Kim didn't take much notice. He considered saying there was a train to London later that day which he wanted to be on, but decided it was probably best just to get on the train without waiting for permission. This plan was thwarted by Lionel's decision that he and Douglas take Kim to London in their car. Kim suspected they wanted to value Ninna's house and its contents, but he kept his peace. Whatever happened next was none of his business.

The car journey passed smoothly since the roads were clear. Lena sat beside Kim in the back while Lionel navigated from the passenger seat for Douglas, who drove. Jonas had stayed in bed in Salisbury. In Docklands, parking proved tricky but eventually a space was secured and the four of them proceeded on foot to the front door of Ninna's big house.

"Who has a key?" Douglas eyed Kim. "Presumably you, since you packed her things."

Kim unpocketed the key and passed it across, standing back as Ninna's son and grandson entered the house. Lena followed Kim, her head cocked to one side.

The hallway looked the same. As did the sitting room with the sash windows Douglas said he deplored due to the draughts they let in. Back in Salisbury, he'd said he was prepared for the place to be in a terrible condition. He was not, however, prepared for the house party settled on the sofa. Or in the fireside armchair, whose occupant demanded to know what the hell Douglas thought he was playing at.

"Mother…!" Douglas crossed himself.

"Grandmother!" Lionel was an echo, aghast.

Only Lena said, "Hello, Gran, we missed you," and walked to where Ninna was sitting to plant a dutiful kiss on her cheek.

Ninna's gaze was on Kim. "You brought the kettle here, then. Good boy."

"What on earth is going on?" Douglas demanded of the policeman seated on the sofa whom he'd last seen taking Ninna's corpse away to the coroner.

The policeman took out his pipe, shaped like a trumpet, and sucked on it pensively. Of the two paramedics who'd confirmed Ninna's death in Salisbury, one rose to her feet and offered to make tea while the other stayed on the sofa.

"But I phoned for the ambulance myself!" Lionel insisted.

"You did," Ninna agreed. "Immediately after which my friends here, who were keeping a close eye on things, called 999 to cancel it, explaining you'd made a mistake and no ambulance was needed."

Kim thought of the poor ticket inspector on the train who, having dealt with Ninna's first-class fraud, was confronted by this acting troupe who'd fallen in with them on the last leg of the journey and who, it turned out, were very keen to be hired for special occasions such as the unmasking of sycophants at Christmas. Then he thought of the way in which Ninna had hired him from the children's home to act as her eyes and ears in Salisbury. He thought of floods, and overcrowded rooms, and books on birds that were left by his bedside.

"What a foul trick to play!" Douglas paced the room.

"Disgusting," Lionel added.

"So neither of you has a tape measure in his pocket?" Ninna popped a chocolate in her mouth. "Or the phone number for a local estate agent?"

Lionel, red-faced, put a hand over his jacket pocket defensively.

Douglas repeated, "What a foul trick! And on Christmas Day!"

"When else do we all gather together?"

"Pretending to be dead...!"

"I imagine it gave you an excuse to break open the champagne. Or were you too busy searching for my last will and testament? Which I'll be changing, incidentally, just as soon as my solicitor's office opens next week." Ninna patted the arm of her chair. "Kim, dear, come and tell me exactly what these vultures had to say about my tragic demise."

Kim, ever-obedient, did as she asked. It wasn't until later, when it was just the two of them in the house, that he said, "The Egyptian plover bird has a very special relationship with the crocodile. He eats the bits of food that get stuck in the crocodile's teeth."

"Does he now?" Ninna's expression was opaque.

"Because of this, they live together very happily." He began to peel an orange. "Not just at Christmas."

"Is that for me?"

"Of course." He handed her the orange.

"Kim Marley," she said. "Has a ring to it."

"Like a bellbird. Or a dark-eyed junco. They sound like a telephone ringing."

"Save it for Salisbury, child."

"Will we be going back there?"

"I expect so," Ninna said. "Where would the fun be in staying away?"

ICARUS

Belinda Bauer

THE OLD man thinks I'm better than this, and sometimes I think he's right.

I'm watching Eddie riding a pink Barbie bike in the falling snow, with his knees around his ears, laughing that stupid laugh.

"Stop arsing about."

That's Frank. He's the brains. He keeps the records. Eddie tosses the Barbie bike in the back of the van with the others, and we get in the cab and watch Frank write in the big book. *87 Capstan Road, 1X Barbie, 2X 13" BMX.*

It's a full load. All kids' bikes – BMXs, mountain bikes, tricycles. You name it. More than thirty just today. We drive the lot to a farm near the railway and dump them in a pit. Frank gives the farmer £20 to cover them with slurry.

It's a week before Christmas and my fingers are numb. All through November and December we're on the bikes. After Christmas we'll be back for the brand-new replacements. *That's* where the money is.

I never had a new bike. None of us did. The old man spent his whole life guarding treasure and never had two pennies to rub together. Forty years of standing by a door, staring at people staring at Picassos and Rembrandts. In all that time he only stirred once – and then never tired of telling anyone who would listen how he stopped a woman pushing a bronze of Icarus out of the museum in a pushchair. "I knew something was up," he always said when he told the story, "because the baby looked nothing like her!"

When I was little I laughed. Not now. Now it makes me angry to think of him saving a million-quid statue – then he gets the Big C, and no one from the museum even sends a card.

Nick and Charlie are playing Snap on the old man's legs. Nick works at a timber yard and Charlie makes small metal things in a factory. The old man's proud of both of them. Tells people about them. Not me. He doesn't tell anyone about me.

He's asleep and I sit down.

"Want to play?" says Charlie, but I shake my head and look at the old man, all wasted and papery and with his teeth beside him on the bedside cabinet. He opens his watery eyes and I lean in to hear him whisper:

"Been thieving?"

I get up and knock the cards to the floor. The old bastard knows how to push my buttons, even on his deathbed.

The snow is falling harder, and the lights are on in the museum. The skating rink is strung with stars and filled with rosy children.

"Hello Mikey," says the ancient blazer at the gallery door. He knows me. They all do. Been in plenty when I was a nipper. We'd come in after school and wait for the old man to get off work. He'd lead us home through Impressionism, pointing out beauty while we whined.

Icarus is hidden in a little alcove all his own. He's shiny as treacle, and the wings strapped to his arms are metal perfection. He hasn't taken off yet; hasn't flown too close to the sun in his quest for one moment of glory.

Hasn't fallen.

I tip him over and take off the tag. The old man told me how these things work; they transmit a signal to the security office, to show the exact location of each piece of art. As soon as it's moved, a buzzer goes off and the blazers are alerted. I open the door at the back of the gallery and throw the tag down the stairwell. Then I pick up the statue, put it in my backpack, and together we walk past the old grey guardians, who shout into walkie-talkies as they hobble in confusion towards the basement.

Outside, the Christmas crowd quickly swallows me.

A million quid feels good on my back. That's a lot of bikes.

Nick and Charlie have gone home, so I play Patience in the dark. The nine of clubs is missing.

Something in the old man's eyes changes when he wakes to find Icarus at his bedside, watching over him.

"The museum sent it," I say. "They want you to know they appreciate what you did. What you've always done."

The old man stares at the boy with the wings and smiles.

He dies on Christmas Eve.

On Christmas morning I call the police from a phone box and leave Icarus there for them to find.

On Boxing Day, Frank calls from the van and asks why I'm not at work, so I tell him I don't feel well.

But that's not true...

I feel just fine.

ABOUT THE AUTHORS

C. L. TAYLOR is an award-winning *Sunday Times* bestselling author of ten gripping psychological thrillers including *The Guilty Couple* and *Sleep* – both Richard and Judy Book Club picks. Her most recent book is *Every Move You Make*. Her books have sold over two million copies in the UK alone, hit number one on Amazon Kindle, Audible, Kobo and Apple Books, and have been translated into over thirty languages and optioned for TV.

HELEN FIELDS is the author of thirteen novels that have sold more than a million copies. Her books have been translated into twenty-three languages. Her Scottish-set crime series featuring DI Luc Callanach has captivated audiences globally. Her books have been longlisted for the McIlvanney Prize and the Ian Fleming Steel Dagger award. Helen is a former criminal and family law barrister. She splits her time between California, West Sussex and Edinburgh. For more information, visit Helen's website helenfields.com or find her on X (formerly Twitter) @Helen_Fields.

TINA BAKER worked as a journalist and broadcaster for thirty years and is probably best known as a television critic for the BBC and GMTV, and for winning *Celebrity Fit Club*. Her debut novel *Call Me Mummy* was a number one Kindle bestseller. This was followed by *Nasty Little Cuts* in 2022, *Make Me Clean* in 2023 and *What We Did in the Storm* in 2024. She lives in London with her husband and too many cats. Find her on social media @TinaBakerBooks.

RUSS THOMAS lives in Sheffield, UK. He grew up in the eighties reading anything he could get from the library and largely avoiding the great outdoors. After a few 'proper' jobs (among them: pot-washer, optician's receptionist, supermarket warehouse operative, call centre telephonist and storage salesman) he discovered the joys of bookselling, where he could talk to people about books all day. His critically acclaimed bestselling crime series set in Sheffield featuring DS Adam Tyler consists of *Firewatching* (*The Times* bestseller; Waterstones Thriller of the Month), *Nighthawking* (*The Times* Book of the Month), *Cold Reckoning* and *Sleeping Dogs* (published October 2024).

J. T. ELLISON is the *New York Times* and *USA Today* bestselling author of more than thirty novels and twenty short stories, and the Emmy award-winning co-host of the literary TV show *A Word On Words*. She also writes urban fantasy under the pen name Joss Walker. With millions of books in print, her work has won critical acclaim and prestigious awards. Her titles have been optioned for television and published in twenty-eight countries. J. T. lives with her husband and twin kittens in Nashville, where she is hard at work on her next novel.

DAVID BELL is the *New York Times* bestselling author of sixteen novels, including his most recent books *Try Not to Breathe* and *She's Gone*. He is a professor of creative writing at Western Kentucky University in Bowling Green, KY where he lives with his wife, YA author M. Hendrix. David can be reached through his website davidbellnovels.com.

ALEXANDRA (AK) BENEDICT is an award-winning writer of bestselling novels, short stories and scripts. As Alexandra Benedict, she writes Golden Age-inspired mysteries with a darker, contemporary edge. *The Christmas Murder Game* (Bonnier Zaffre, 2021), an Amazon fiction bestseller, has been published in twelve languages and was longlisted for the CWA Gold Dagger Award. *Murder on the Christmas Express* (Simon & Schuster) is an international bestseller and reached Top 12 in the UK paperbacks chart. *The Christmas Jigsaw Murders* (Simon & Schuster) was also a bestseller in hardback and is now out in paperback. *The Christmas Cracker Killer* (Simon & Schuster) will be out in autumn 2025.

As AK Benedict, Alexandra writes high-concept speculative fiction, short stories and award-winning audio drama. She has been shortlisted for the BBC Audio Drama Award for *Children of the Stones* (BBC Sounds/Radio 4) and won the Scribe Award for her *Doctor Who* audio drama *The Calendar Man* (Big Finish). Her debut novel, *The Beauty of Murder* (Orion), was nominated for the eDunnit Award, and her next novel, metafictional thriller *Little Red Death* (Simon & Schuster) is out in February 2025.

Alexandra lives in Eastbourne on the south coast of England, with writer Guy Adams, their daughter Verity and dog Dame Margaret Rutherford.

CLAIRE MCGOWAN is the author of over twenty books, mostly in crime fiction but also literary and romcom. She's been a *Washington Post* bestseller with her crime novels, had two number one Kindle bestsellers, and sold almost two million copies of over twenty novels, publishing in over twenty countries. She grew up in Northern Ireland and now lives in London. As well as books she also writes TV and radio scripts.

TOM MEAD is a Derbyshire mystery writer and aficionado of Golden Age crime fiction. His debut novel, *Death and the Conjuror*, was an international bestseller, and named one of the best mysteries of the year by *The Guardian* and *Publishers Weekly*. Its sequel, *The Murder Wheel*, was described as 'pure nostalgic pleasure' by the *Wall Street Journal* and 'a delight' by the *Daily Mail*. It was also named one of the Best Traditional Mysteries of 2023 by CrimeReads. His new novel, the third in his Joseph Spector mystery series, is *Cabaret Macabre*.

FIONA CUMMINS is an award-winning former journalist and a graduate of the Faber Academy, where she now teaches her own Writing Crime course. She is the internationally bestselling author of six crime thriller novels, all of which have received widespread critical acclaim from household names including Val McDermid, Lee Child, David Baldacci, Martina Cole and Ian Rankin. Her books, which include *Rattle* and *When I Was Ten*, have been translated into several languages and three have been optioned for television. Her fifth novel, *Into The Dark*, the first in a series featuring DC Saul Anguish, was described by the *Daily Mail* as 'breathtakingly good' and was shortlisted for the Theakston Old Peculier Crime Novel of the Year 2023. Her sixth book, *All Of Us Are Broken*, was published in July 2023. When Fiona is not writing, she can be found on Twitter, eating biscuits or walking her dogs. She lives in Essex with her family.

SAM CARRINGTON worked for the NHS for fifteen years, during which time she qualified as a nurse. After gaining a psychology degree she changed career path, taking up a role as an Offending Behaviour Programme Facilitator in a male prison. Her experiences within this field inspired her writing and she left the service to follow her dream of being a novelist. In 2016, her debut psychological thriller *Saving Sophie* became a Kindle eBook bestseller, reaching the top 100 in the UK and US and hitting number one in Canada. Sam was recognised as an Amazon Rising Star that year. Her eighth novel, *The Girl in the Photo,* was published in 2023. Sam also writes crime fiction under the pseudonym Alice Hunter. For upcoming events and book news you can follow Sam on Instagram and Facebook @samcarringtonauthor.

VASEEM KHAN is the author of two award-winning crime series set in India: the *Baby Ganesh Agency* series set in modern Mumbai, and the *Malabar House* historical crime novels set in 1950s Bombay. His first book, *The Unexpected Inheritance of Inspector Chopra,* was selected by the *Sunday Times* as one of the 40 best crime novels published 2015–2020, and is translated into seventeen languages. In 2021, *Midnight at Malabar House* won the Crime Writers' Association Historical Dagger. Vaseem was born in England but spent a decade working in India. In 2023, Vaseem was elected the first non-white Chair of the seventy-year-old UK Crime Writers' Association.

SUSI HOLLIDAY's short stories have featured in publications such as *Alfred Hitchcock's Mystery Magazine* and in multiple anthologies. She has written eleven novels and a novella, and a film adaptation of her Trans-Siberian-set thriller, *Violet*, is currently in development.

SAMANTHA HAYES is the author of over twenty novels, most of which are psychological thrillers published by Bookouture, Penguin Random House and Headline. She can't remember a time when she didn't write, and her career took off when she won a short story competition in 2003 (with a ghost story!). Her books are family-based 'domestic noir' thrillers and are published in many languages.

Sam grew up in Warwickshire, left school at sixteen, avoided university and took jobs ranging from private detective to barmaid to fruit picker, factory worker, and car cleaner. She's also lived in Australia and the USA, and has three adult children. When she's not writing, she loves cooking, hiking, swimming and painting.

ANGELA CLARKE is a bestselling novelist and a screenwriter. She is the author of the crime thrillers *On My Life* (Hachette, 2019), *Trust Me* (HarperCollins, 2017), *Watch Me* (HarperCollins, 2016) and *Follow Me* (HarperCollins, 2015). She also wrote the humorous memoir *Confessions of a Fashionista* (Penguin Random House, 2013). A sufferer of Hypermobility Ehlers Danlos Syndrome (hEDS), Angela is passionate about bringing marginalised voices into the industry.

LIZ MISTRY moved to West Yorkshire in the late 1980s. Her gritty crime fiction police procedural novels set in Bradford embrace the city she describes as 'warm, rich and fearless' whilst exploring the darkness that lurks beneath. Yet, her heart remains in Scotland, where childhood tales of bogey men, Bible John and grey lady ghosts fed her imagination. Her latest work, The Solanki and McQueen crime series, is set around West Lothian, where she uses the distinctive landscape, historic heritage and Scottish culture as a backdrop to her gritty yet often humorous stories. Struggling with clinical depression and anxiety for many years, Liz often includes mental health themes in her writing. She credits her MA in Creative Writing from Leeds Trinity University with helping her find a way of using her writing to navigate her ongoing mental health struggles. The synergy between creative and academic writing led Liz to complete a doctorate in creative writing researching the importance of representation of marginalised groups within the genre she loves. You can connect with Liz at lizmistry.com, @LizMistryAuthor on X (formerly Twitter) and www.facebook.com/LizMistrybooks.

SARAH HILARY's debut, *Someone Else's Skin*, won the 2015 Theakston Old Peculier Crime Novel of the Year and was a World Book Night selection, as well as a Silver Falchion and Macavity Award finalist in the US. Her standalone novel *Black Thorn* was one of *The Guardian*'s Best Crime and Thrillers of 2023. *Sharp Glass* came out in July 2024. As well as writing, Sarah is Programme Director for St Hilda's Crime Fiction Weekend, and co-founder of Ledburied, a crime fiction festival in her hometown. Her short stories have won the Fish Criminally Short Histories Prize, the Cheshire Prize for Literature and the SENSE Prize.

BELINDA BAUER failed as a screenwriter and so wrote a book instead to appease her nagging mother. *Blacklands* won the CWA

Gold Dagger and launched her career. She writes dark, wry books about crime and its effects on victims, their families and their communities. In 2018 her book *Snap* became the first crime novel to be longlisted for the Booker Prize.

ABOUT THE EDITORS

MARIE O'REGAN is a British Fantasy Award and Shirley Jackson Award-nominated author and editor based in Derbyshire. She was awarded the British Fantasy Society Legends of FantasyCon award in 2022. Her first collection, *Mirror Mere*, was published in 2006 by Rainfall Books; her second, *In Times of Want*, came out in September 2016 from Hersham Horror Books. Her third, *The Last Ghost and Other Stories*, was published by Luna Press early in 2019. Her short fiction has appeared in a number of genre magazines and anthologies in the UK, US, Canada, Italy and Germany, including *Best British Horror 2014*, *Great British Horror: Dark Satanic Mills* (2017), and *The Mammoth Book of Halloween Stories*. Her novella, *Bury Them Deep*, was published by Hersham Horror Books in September 2017. She was shortlisted for the British Fantasy Society Award for Best Short Story in 2006, Best Anthology in 2010 (*Hellbound Hearts*) and 2012 (*The Mammoth Book of Ghost Stories by Women*). She was also shortlisted for the Shirley Jackson Award for Best Anthology in 2020 (*Wonderland*). Her genre journalism has appeared in magazines like *The Dark Side, Rue Morgue* and *Fortean Times*, and her interview book with prominent figures from the horror genre, *Voices in the Dark*, was released in 2011. Her essay on *The Changeling* was published in PS Publishing's *Cinema Macabre*, edited by Mark Morris. She is co-editor of the bestselling *Hellbound Hearts, The Mammoth Book of Body Horror, A Carnivàle of Horror – Dark Tales from the Fairground, Exit Wounds, Wonderland, Cursed, Twice Cursed, The Other Side of Never* and *In These Hallowed Halls* (the first ever Dark Academia anthology) as well as the charity anthology *Trickster's Treats #3*, plus editor of the bestselling anthologies *The Mammoth Book of Ghost Stories by Women* and *Phantoms*. Her first novel, the internationally bestselling *Celeste*, was published in February 2022. Marie is also the Managing Editor of PS Publishing's award-winning novella imprint, Absinthe Books. Marie was Chair of the British Fantasy Society from 2004 to 2008, and Co-Chair of the UK Chapter of the Horror Writers' Association from 2015 to 2022. She was also Co-Chair of ChillerCon UK in 2022. Visit her website at marieoregan.net. She can be found on X (formerly Twitter) @Marie_O_Regan, and Instagram @marieoregan8101.

PAUL KANE is the award-winning (including the British Fantasy Society's Legends of FantasyCon Award 2022), bestselling author and editor of over a hundred books – such as the *Arrowhead* trilogy (gathered together in the sellout *Hooded Man* omnibus, revolving around a post-apocalyptic version of Robin Hood), *The Gemini Factor, Hellbound Hearts, Wonderland* (a Shirley Jackson Award finalist), *Exit Wounds* and *Pain Cages* (an Amazon #1 bestseller). His non-fiction books include *The Hellraiser Films and Their Legacy* and *Voices in the Dark*, and his genre journalism has appeared in the likes of *SFX*,

Rue Morgue and *DeathRay*. He has been a Guest at Alt.Fiction five times, was a Guest at the first SFX Weekender, at Thought Bubble in 2011, Derbyshire Literary Festival and Off the Shelf in 2012, Monster Mash and Event Horizon in 2013, Edge-Lit in 2014 and 2018, HorrorCon, HorrorFest and Grimm Up North in 2015, The Dublin Ghost Story Festival and Sledge-Lit in 2016, IMATS Olympia and Celluloid Screams in 2017, Black Library Live in 2019, and the UK Ghost Story Festival in 2019 and 2023, plus the WordCrafter virtual event 2021 – where he delivered the keynote speech – as well as being a panellist at FantasyCon and the World Fantasy Convention, and a fiction judge at the Sci-Fi London festival. A former British Fantasy Society Special Publications Editor, he has also served as Co-Chair for the UK chapter of The Horror Writers Association and co-chaired ChillerCon UK in May 2022.

His work has been optioned and adapted for the big and small screen, including for US network primetime television, and his novelette 'Men of the Cloth' was turned into a feature by Loose Canon/Hydra Films, starring Barbara Crampton (*Re-Animator*, *You're Next*): *Sacrifice*, released by Epic Pictures/101 Films. His audio work includes the full cast drama adaptation of *The Hellbound Heart* for Bafflegab, starring Tom Meeten (*The Ghoul*), Neve McIntosh (*Doctor Who*) and Alice Lowe (*Prevenge*), and the *Robin of Sherwood* adventure *The Red Lord* for Spiteful Puppet/ITV narrated by Ian Ogilvy (*Return of the Saint*). He has also contributed to the Warhammer 40k universe for Games Workshop. Paul's latest novels are *Lunar* (set to be turned into a feature film), the YA story *The Rainbow Man* (as P. B. Kane), the sequels to *RED* – *Blood RED & Deep RED*, all collected in an omnibus edition by Hellbound – the award-winning hit *Sherlock Holmes & the Servants of Hell*, *Before* (an Amazon Top 5 dark fantasy bestseller), *Arcana* and *The Storm*. In addition, he writes thrillers for HQ/HarperCollins as P. L. Kane (plkane.com), the first of which, *Her Last Secret* and *Her Husband's Grave* (a sellout on both Amazon and Waterstones.com), came out in 2020, with *The Family Lie* released the following year and described as 'Agatha Christie meets *The Wicker Man*'. Paul lives in Derbyshire, UK, with his wife **Marie O'Regan.**

Find out more at his site shadow-writer.co.uk, which has featured guest writers such as Dean Koontz, Martina Cole, Thomas Harris, Abigail Dean, Stuart MacBride, Cara Hunter, M. W. Craven, Sarah Pearse, John Connolly, Catriona Ward and Stephen King. He can also be found @PaulKaneShadow on X (formerly Twitter), and @paul.kane.376 on Instagram.

ACKNOWLEDGEMENTS

And now for the important bit – our opportunity to say thank you. Firstly to all the authors for their superb contributions, to Sophie Robinson for starting the ball rolling, and Daniel Carpenter for keeping it rolling. And to all of the team at Titan Books for their tireless support and efforts on our behalf, as always. Finally, thanks to our respective families, without whom etc.

For more fantastic fiction, author events,
exclusive excerpts, competitions, limited editions and more

VISIT OUR WEBSITE
titanbooks.com

LIKE US ON FACEBOOK
facebook.com/titanbooks

FOLLOW US ON TWITTER AND INSTAGRAM
@TitanBooks

EMAIL US
readerfeedback@titanemail.com